ALFA ROMEO 1300
AND OTHER MIRACLES

Fabio Bartolomei

ALFA ROMEO 1300 AND OTHER MIRACLES

*Translated from the Italian
by Anthony Shugaar*

Europa
editions

Europa Editions
214 West 29th Street
New York, N.Y. 10001
www.europaeditions.com
info@europaeditions.com

Translation by Anthony Shugaar
Original title: *Giulia 1300 e altri miracoli*
Translation copyright © 2012 by Europa Editions

Library of Congress Cataloging in Publication Data is available
ISBN 978-1-60945-083-0

Bartolomei, Fabio
Alfa Romeo 1300 and Other Miracles

Book design and cover illustration by Emanuele Ragnisco
www.mekkanografici.com

Prepress by Grafica Punto Print – Rome

Printed in the USA

To my father, the only creator
to whose existence and minor miracles
I can testify

ALFA ROMEO 1300
AND OTHER MIRACLES

THE LIGHTS OF CLAUDIO

L ast job was five years ago . . . "

"That's right, five."

"In charge of sales, fashion sector . . . and, specifically?"

"I was a shopgirl. At Cherì, you know the place? It's that big store at the corner of Viale Marconi . . . "

I give a wry smile and a nod when she says "shopgirl." I hate resumes, I hate it when they try to pull the wool over my eyes, I hate the way they always think that they need to fill up at least two pages, I hate how I inevitably have to read the phrase "team player, works well with others," I hate "good spoken English," but, above all else, I hate the section "Personal Interests." If you love movies and cooking and you took a course in Ayurvedic massage, just guess how little I give a damn.

"In this particular sector, though, you have no experience," I say as I rapidly skim her resume.

"Supermarkets, no."

"We're looking for experienced self-starters." This is when it gets difficult. I have to forget about the sheet of paper and look her in the eyes.

"But that's what I am: a self-starter. I really want this job."

"That's what they all say, the first week all the girls are sweet and smiley, but then . . . "

"I smile all the time, I wake up smiling every morning."

"But they get over it the minute they clock in . . . You see, we're not fooling around, here. There are cashiers in other supermarkets, but not here. You people are this supermarket's calling card, you are its public face. If you're down in the dumps, the supermarket has an image of depression. You know what our electric bill is here?"

"No . . . I have no idea."

"Thirty thousand euros a year. And you know why?"

"No."

"Because we want the interior to be sunny, bright. We want our customers to come to the cash register in a good mood, be greeted by your winning smile, and pay without giving us a hard time. Are you quarrelsome? One out of every three customers will bust your chops."

Damn it. At the end, my voice went up into a falsetto.

"Of course."

She looked at my hair. She must have been doing it the whole time I read through her resume and just now she happened to glance at my alopecia again.

"Do you think you can live up to that commitment? I'm not spending thirty thousand euros a year to have pissed-off cashiers."

"I think I can."

"You think? Well, then, you think it over and when you're certain then come back and see me."

"No, no, I meant to say certainly, I think I certainly can, that is, I'm certain of it."

"Ah, one last item. You're thirty-two years old and you still don't have any children . . . "

"No."

"Children are fundamental . . . "

"They certainly are."

She took the bait. If I had asked her whether she planned to have children, she would have answered with the most reassuring no.

"But they're fundamental for you, not for me. Children cause trouble and, really, I have plenty of trouble of my own,

and so does everyone who works here. And if we all start bur-
dening each other with our problems . . . Do I make myself
clear?"

"Certainly, no problem."

"Let's hope not."

I think that went pretty well. Toward the end my voice was
quavering slightly, but I don't think she noticed. They have to
understand one thing from day one: this is not one big happy
family. This is a company, and everyone has a job to do. I'm
their boss, and they're my employees. The line about children
is one of the most challenging moments—my lip always quiv-
ers a little. If they get annoyed and tell you that, by law, that's
not a question you can ask, then you can count on it: they're
going to be ballbusters, and I don't want any more people who
come in the door as employees but, before the week is out, are
acting like they're the boss.

Take Marino, a guy in his sixties. He rarely if ever took his
eyes off the floor during the interview, but now he looks me
straight in the eye and challenges me every chance he gets. A
lifetime of working behind the deli counter without so much as
a raise or a surge of self-confidence, never thinking he could
try something new. So I figured: great, he's perfect, what you
need to sell cold cuts, cheese, and salami is an experienced,
reassuring face. Because customers are a strange breed, they'll
buy canned goods without a second glance, but for fresh
foods, things that they can see for themselves just what and
how they are, no, there they need to be reassured over and over
again. Is it fresh? Is it good? Is it tender? It takes someone like
Marino, I thought, someone who's been repeating for forty-
five years: so fresh, so good, so tender.

If you act like a human being, they take you for a weakling
and a patsy, they talk behind your back, they make fun of you
because you're losing your hair or, even worse, they smart-talk

you in front of the customers. They're all so full of themselves. So full of personality, damn them.

It's not easy to be punctual if your mother was anything like mine. I'm not sure what the exact word would be, but what pops into my mind is 'catastrophist.' It's crucial to be on the lookout because everything can collapse, everything can explode, everything can catch fire. In other words: everything can go wrong.

A slave to her phobias, my mother spent an entire lifetime confined at home. She never took a plane because planes crash, never took a train because trains derail, ferryboats sink, buses flip over on mountain curves, cars catch fire, cars that run on liquid propane blow up. She wasn't so much a housewife as she was an inmate, forced into indefinite incarceration by the martial law of her fears. Fears that were instilled in me, year by year, drop by drop. Fear of pressure cookers, cracks in the wall, thunderstorms, electric appliances.

For someone like me, someone who lives in a perennial state of alarm, even a five-mile trip is a demanding undertaking. If you're walking down the sidewalk, take care not to walk under the balconies; a flowerpot, or even a dog, could fall on your head. Take care not to walk on manhole covers; they could fall in or deliver a fatal electric shock. If you're driving, beware of tree-lined roads; a branch could fall. Avoid putting the car in reverse; you could run over a child who's wriggled out of his parents' grip. When you're driving by a park, slow down—a ball could always roll into the street, or a dog, or a dog *and* a ball. Unfortunately, I only realized how bad things had gotten when it was already too late, and my mother's illness had become all mine.

Antonia is already outside waiting for me. But she's not mad. She doesn't get mad at me anymore. Now that we're divorced, she loves all my little shortcomings. She's learned to love them now that they're only ruining my life, not hers.

"Sorry I'm late," I say to her.

"The usual fifteen minutes, don't think twice about it."

It feels good to give her a hug. Now I can hug her. After a few months of quarantine, when every display of affection was abolished, now we can go back to hugging and smiling at each other without any fear that it'll be taken the wrong way.

"How are you? You look a little worried," she tells me.

I shouldn't be so happy to hear her say it. That phrase contains the explanation of our failure as a couple. I'm Claudio the helpless one, the one who makes her apprehensive, the one who needs taking care of. And she preferred Gaetano, who's got balls and knows how to take care of her. Still, I'm happy just the same, because I need to feel loved, because I could never stand it if she had it in for me. What an outstanding woman she is, to keep a space just for me in her heart. And I'm a good guy, too—for avoiding any scenes or tantrums, for understanding that it was all over and that I'd have to do whatever it took to maintain some shred of a relationship.

"Listen, Claudio, a couple of nights ago I talked Gaetano into buying a few bottles of spumante."

"Thanks, Antonia, but really it's not like I need . . . "

"No that's not why, don't be silly. He needed to give gifts to a few people and it struck me as a good idea. But . . . what I'm trying to say is . . . we opened a couple ourselves and they were old, the corks were rotten."

"Are you joking? What do you mean, rotten? Which bottles did you buy?" I ask. "Those bottles cost me an arm and a leg, I select them personally in a wine cellar in Piedmont. Let me take them back and give you replacements. Are you kidding? That's first class stuff."

"Claudio, it's not like you have to convince me."

"It must have been the delivery people, they must have left the crates out in the hot sun," I say.

"Of course it was, the delivery people . . . " she echoes, with a hint of sadness in her voice.

"Tell Gaetano how sorry I am. No, wait, give me his number. I want to apologize to him personally."

"Look, it's not a problem, he didn't even want me to tell you."

Oh, no, of course not, it's much better for him this way. It gives him a chance to confirm that I'm a failure and he's a gentleman. But she's wonderful, the reason she told me is that she knows that's not the way I am. That I'd never try to cheat her.

"You look really good, you know that?"

I say it with conviction and it doesn't hurt me as much as it ought to. "She's reborn," that's what her girlfriends must be saying. "She's reborn since she broke up with him."

"Tomorrow or the day after I'll bring you the replacement bottles, okay?"

"Whenever it's convenient for you. Don't worry about it."

But I do worry. I don't know how to do my job. I'm a catalyst of loss and fraud. The thriving family business, founded by my grandfather in 1910, is wilting and dying under my leadership.

THE LIGHTS OF FAUSTO

You need to get that shadow off my hand!"

"I can't, that would take more lights," a tall gangly kid replies as he positions a 100-watt spotlight.

"I'm not going on the air like this, damn it to hell! We're not doing home shopping for steak knives here! What am I supposed to do, talk about the sheen of the scratch-proof crystal with the shadow of my hand covering it up?"

"You'll just have to hold your hand behind the watches," says the beanpole. Not satisfied with the disasters he's brought about as a lighting assistant, he's now decided to try his hand at directing, too.

"Sergio! Could I speak to Sergio, please?"

"Now what is it?" asks Sergio's voice, emerging from the loudspeaker on the director's booth after a long piercing whistle.

"Is there anyone who knows how to do their job in here? Send me someone who understands something about lights and get this shadow off me, please?"

"You can't get the shadow off, you'll just have to hold your hands behind the watches," Sergio replies.

"No, there must be some mistake. You're not giving me the space for free. I'm paying top euro here, and I expect everything to be perfect. Do you know what perfect means? It means just like the crisp new euro bills fresh from the bank that you're pocketing!"

"Now you watch me, I'm going to kick this asshole down the street!" the loudspeaker rasps out.

"I heard that! You forgot the microphone was still turned on, I heard you!"

"I didn't forget the microphone was on. I said it loud and clear in front of witnesses because we're taping in five minutes and if you don't cut it out what we'll be showing is the video of me kicking your ass!"

"Oh, yeah?"

"Yeah."

"Aha!"

"Hmph."

We could go on like this for who knows how long, but an array of considerations persuades me to desist. First of all: the lights aren't really all that bad and, on local TV, perfectionists are never particularly welcome. Second: they haven't seen the crisp new euro bills fresh from the bank mentioned above nor will they ever see them unless this broadcast sells through. Third: Sergio is a former steelworker who scuffed up his fists and his personality by trading punches with cops in riot gear. I sort of doubt my Armani suit is going to throw too much of a scare into him.

So I restrict myself to one last "ah" with a note of challenge in my voice, with a tacit, "oh, I'll show you later," even though we both know perfectly well that there won't be any later. I live in a spoiled, oafish era, a time when men face off through their car windows, through television cameras, or through lawsuits. Every so often there's a brawl, but the utter absence of any code of chivalry makes me shudder in horror. Riding boots, fluttering white shirt, a dueling sword in hand: those were the days! Those were the challenges of honor! Try and explain *that* to Sergio. My blade of Toledo steel against the vanadium of your oversized crescent wrench, ye varlet!

The makeup artist comes over. From the way she's biting her lip, I can guess that she's trying not to laugh.

"Your forehead's all shiny," she tells me.

"With this fucked-up lighting . . . "

"One minute and we're rolling," says Sergio.

A minute from now I'm going to pretend I'm being broad-cast live, I'm going to pretend I have some incredible watches on my hands, I'm going to pretend that this is a once-in-a-life-time price, and who cares that I've been saying the same thing for months? I'm going to pretend that this is a limited offer, even though I have two hundred of these contraptions and I have to move every last one of them if I don't want to wake up with Sergio's knuckles tattooed on my jaw.

"And three, and two, and one . . . " says Sergio.

"Good evening, friends, good evening, timepiece connois-seurs! You all know me by now, I don't have a lot to say, but I do have a lot to sell . . . And here's what we have to sell tonight: four chronographs incorporating Swiss technology, and I said Swiss, as in Switzerland, not Taiwan! With the finest steel available and a crystal face manufactured to NASA standards. Now listen, friends, before you overload the switchboard with calls, let me say a few more words about these jewels of the watchmaker's craft . . . Do you know the first thing a woman looks at? Of course you do: your hands. So let your hands speak for you. With a Gold series chronograph on your wrist, your hand will speak of style, class, power, and, between you and me, money!"

What do you do for a living? I'm in television. Really? Doing what exactly? Just now I'm doing televised home shop-ping. I've been offered a couple of host positions, but I'm not looking to burn my options with formats I don't really think would work for me. At this point, I can't really imagine the expression of the person I'm talking to but, yeah, it could work. This year I'm turning forty-two—I know what people are like, and I know that if I just said, "I sell watches on local TV stations," it wouldn't do justice to the work I do. Most people

would assume that I'm one of those losers who shout themselves hoarse, standing next to a pyramid of saucepans. What
do they know about what it takes to project yourself into the
homes of disgruntled housewives and insomniac retirees, than
persuade them to pick up the phone and order things they just
don't need? It might seem like I'm boasting, but what I do is I
sway the masses. I'm a televised swayer of the masses, is what
I am. Not bad, eh?

I know I can count on Alvaro. He told me that there would
be plenty of pussy at this party. And knowing him the way I do,
I assume he doesn't mean stuck-up babes, babes that are only
impressed by journalists, radio DJs, or television actors. Babes
who have always worked for a living know that, in the work I
do, I'm a sort of Rambo. One man against the world.

This is the third time that I've driven around the building
and there's not a shadow of a parking place for my SUV. With
the money I spent on this thing, I ought to have a reserved
parking spot in front of every apartment building in the city. I
give civic consideration one more spin around the building,
and then I'm going to do some creative parking.

Reinforced bumpers with a bull bar to shove dumpsters out
of the way, off-road tires and suspension to take on the challenge of the steepest curbs and sidewalks, and before you
know it, I'm parked. I get out and, I have to say, my SUV is a
spectacular sight. Tilted at a rakish angle off the sidewalk like
that, it looks like a steel predator. I stop to light a cigarette and
lean on the hood in an understated, natural pose, just making
it clear that I am the lord and master of this animal. Two girls
come walking up the street arm-in-arm. Miniskirts and stiletto
heels: they're definitely going to Alvaro's party. I start monkey-
ing around with my cell phone to justify my impromptu
bivouac. Out of the corner of my eye, I scrutinize their gazes.
It's a textbook scenario: their eyes stray first to the car and then

come to rest on me. And to think that there are still people who say that money spent on cars is money wasted. The two girls stop at the street door, push the buzzer, and then take turns looking at me.

"Is that yours?" the brunette asks me, a firecracker standing five foot two.

Absorbed in my imaginary phone call, I respond with a smile and an almost imperceptible wink, by no means vulgar.

"You're parked on the handicapped ramp," she tells me.

I look down at the asphalt, pretending I didn't hear her, then I cover the mouthpiece of my cell phone with one hand and reply.

"Thanks, I'll move it right away."

Before I can finish the sentence my phone starts ringing. The two girls exchange a puzzled glance and then they slip through the front door laughing. What kind of woman pays no attention to a 40,000-euro SUV but can't seem to miss a wheelchair ramp that no one's ever going to use? Well, what the hell, they're not likely to be the only women there tonight. I answer the cell phone that's still ringing. It's Piero: he tells me that we received twenty orders and ninety-seven phone calls from people berating us and threatening to report us to the police. Those were the furious customers from last month's home shopping. As if it were somehow my fault, as if the supplier hadn't defrauded me as well as them with those defective chronographs. Twenty orders is pathetic, but tonight and tomorrow morning the show will be rerun twice. I can still catch up.

Up in Alvaro's apartment the scene is dispiriting. A dozen men surround the two girls, the only girls at the party, where they sit side by side on the sofa. It's a good thing I showed up. Gives them a chance to catch their breath. Alvaro throws his arms around me like a long-lost brother, after opening his arms wide, theatrically. He smacks me hard on the back. I greet all the others like long-lost brothers, even the ones I think I might have met only once before, or maybe not even. These boisterous displays of camaraderie and familiarity, for whatever reason, make a big impression on women. Not these two women, particularly, but women in general, for sure.

"The other guys?" I ask Alvaro, by which I obviously mean, "the other girls?"

"Soon, soon," he replies with a wink. The buzzer sounds and everyone's eyes swivel toward the door.

The two girls' eyes swivel with the rest. Before it's too late I take the opportunity to introduce myself. I stretch out my hand.

"Fausto Maria," I say.

"Giovanna Maria and Serena Maria" the brunette replies. It's such a dumb joke that I fall for it and ask: "Really?" While I try to read their expressions, Michelone and Sandrino come in.

"Excuse me for a second," I say. And I run to embrace them like long-lost brothers.

The girls drain their glasses in a hurry. Then they get to their feet and take advantage of everyone's distraction to grab purse and overcoat.

"But . . . you're not already leaving?" says Alvaro.

"Sorry . . . we just dropped by to say hello . . . we've got a long day tomorrow."

"There's lots of people who just haven't showed up yet; they'll be here soon!"

Unfortunately, I got there too late; these idiots have suffocated the two girls and now, of course, they're about to leave. We're left alone, a roomful of long-lost brothers who barely know each other. We drink, we talk about this and that, pretending that we're having a great evening anyway. Now and then Alvaro's phone rings and we all fall silent.

"Come on, not even for five minutes?" says Alvaro.

It's midnight. The doorbell has been silent for hours now,

and the pauses in the conversation grow longer and increasingly awkward. Even Alvaro, who's worn himself out keeping the evening alive, is starting to show signs of exhaustion. Then he pulls a PlayStation CD down from the shelf next to the television set.

"Lookie here," he says to us.

"What is it, the latest?" shouts Michelone.

"Come on guys, we'll take turns playing, round-robin tournament!"

"You could have gotten it out earlier, couldn't you?" I say.

"Thirty-six inch flat screen, it'll be spectacular, better than being at the stadium!"

We gather in a circle to draw straws for the matches. Just when the referee's whistle marks the beginning of the first match, the doorbell buzzes.

"Guys, turn it off," says Alvaro.

He heads for the door and, as he walks past the stereo, he turns up the music. Then he picks up the receiver and yells:

"Fourth floor!"

Silence . . . We look at him, trying to decipher his expression.

"Ah . . . of course, right away," he says.

"Who was that?" I ask.

Alvaro shows the first sign of exasperation and glares at me.

"It's some guy who's going to kick your ass black and blue unless you go down and move your car."

THE LIGHTS OF DIEGO

Here they are, my favorite couple. He's thirty-five or so, an elegant clotheshorse carefully dressing down in fake casual; she can't have hit thirty yet, putting on the sloppy chic of the radical community center, though her hippie drab is blatantly betrayed by a good 800 euros' worth of accessories. The young man is circling the most useless SUV yet manufactured. Fifteen feet of steel and aluminum that you wouldn't dream of driving in the city, 4000 cc of engine displacement, 300 horsepower, every single horse of which serves no purpose other than to guzzle gas, three low-ratio gears to effortlessly take on the challenge of even the most heroic sidewalk parking spots. All credit to the lighting. I designed a new configuration for the halogen spotlights and I artfully calibrated their brightness and intensity. This way, cars going by in the street are reflected along the side panels of the SUV, making it look dynamic. An elementary optical illusion, a soap-slick funfair slide that inevitably brings people into the dealership.

He's fascinated like a little boy looking at a Christmas manger. She's standing off to one side with a critical scowl, and seems to be wondering how many polar bear cubs will pay the price for this latest whim, though she's not asking any hard questions about the shreds of tender young calfskin that fit snugly around her feet.

I walk over, open the car door for the young man, and take a reassuring step backward.

"If you need anything, just give me a call," I say.

"Thank you," he says after watching the door swing open as if it were the thighs of a fashion model.

It's the same for every kind of car: ninety percent of success in sales depends on how skillful you are in getting the customer to sit inside. That new-car smell, that undefinable synthetic aroma of silicon and benzene, it's an authentic drug. It's the smell of triumph. An odor that will soon be gone, but here and now it's impossible to resist. SUV's have another booby trap: they're tall. Once you get aboard, you look down upon the world, you dominate everything you can see and you feel like a giant hard-on. There he is, a smile on his face, feeling like a giant hard-on. He grips the wheel with both hands, sniffs the air, looks around envisioning his friends' faces when he pulls up to the café where they all hang out downtown. Now that I've got the little boy safely strapped in, it's time to go to work on the girl. She's the source of all sales resistance. I walk in her direction discreetly, as if I had to straighten up a pile of brochures.

"Nice, isn't it?" I say.

"Nice enough . . . but I don't see what it's good for."

I put on a courteously surprised expression.

"What need is there for these enormous cars that guzzle so much gas? It just seems like a colossal insult to the environment," she goes on.

This is where you see the difference between me and Oscar. Oscar is the other salesman, age fifty-five, twenty-five of those years having given him a meaningless body of experience in the business. He knows all the catalogues forward and backwards, never misses a presentation, reads every article in the trade publications. I have less than half his experience, but I know people. Oscar would tell the girl that the high-tech engineering of the six-cylinder engine reduces fuel consumption to a minimum, and with the turning radius tightened by a full degree, the vehicle handles surprisingly well in city traffic. Not me.

"You're right," I say.

She stares at me in surprise. And waits for the rest. She waits because she knows I'm a salesman and that the next sentence out of my mouth is probably going to begin with a "but." Instead, I just say: "You're right," full stop. I don't add another word.

"Then why do you sell them?" she asks, unable to stand my silence any longer.

Her husband has just discovered the lighting of the instrument panel and, encouraged by my conspiratorial smile, he starts playing with all the different buttons and switches.

"You see, *all* cars pollute. But this SUV could pollute less than a smart car. It's up to us. I would buy it for its absolute security and safety, the confidence when I'm saying goodbye to my husband in the morning that I'll see him come home safe and sound that evening. You can imagine, the roads are dangerous, but with a car like this one . . . "

"True," she says.

"Really, that's why I'd buy it, and then I'd force myself to use it only when absolutely necessary. How often do we use our cars when we don't really need to?"

"Almost always," she replies.

"Believe me, this car gives the gift of confidence and it helps you to change your lifestyle. A new lifestyle is the finest technology available to help safeguard the environment."

The woman is impressed. An environmentalist car salesman is really something she wasn't expecting.

"Now it's a question of whether I can get him to understand that," she says to me.

Together, we turn our gazes on this dispiriting specimen of a modern adult male, completely lobotomized by his discovery of the variable-intensity dashboard lighting.

"He seems like an intelligent young man . . . and you seem like a very persuasive young woman," I observe.

I give her a smile and my intense gaze for a perfectly cali-brated second. Then, to keep from letting it spill over into the realm of the creepy, I move away.

"I'll leave you two alone to make up your minds," I say.

I take a seat at my desk under Oscar's horrified gaze. I pre-tend not to notice and force him to stand up and take a seat across the desk from me, so he can rerun his expression for me, exactly the same as before.

"What are you doing here? Your customer should never be left alone. You need to push them, you need to make them dream. Did you get a look at her face? Now she's going to start stinking up the air with her doubts and that's when you need to be there, by God!" he tells me.

"The car is as good as sold," I tell him.

"What kind of gas mileage does it get?" the young woman asks me from the far end of the display floor, clearly and openly challenging her husband.

"As much as forty MPG!" Oscar replies while I shout: "About fifteen."

The couple exchanges a puzzled glance. Oscar looks dag-gers at me.

"My colleague is referring to out-of-town driving under optimal conditions, that is, on level roads at a constant speed of 55 mph. My mileage figure refers to in-town driving, which I'd imagine is what you'd mostly be using this car for."

I say "mostly" and not "exclusively" because I don't want to crush the young man's dreams—he's probably already envi-sioning himself barreling down a dirt track in Patagonia.

Oscar gets up, indignantly.

"It's your business," he hisses at me. And resuming his seat, he adds: "Arrogant bastard."

I start reading a catalogue while the couple comes over to my desk.

"Welcome, take a seat," I say, looking up unhurriedly as I

lay the brochure down on the desk. He's beaming, while she has the expression of a mother who has just given in, but not before making her overgrown puppy promise that in exchange he'll try to be a good boy.

Other questions will follow, but I could just as easily give answers at random while thinking happily about other things. Like the tartar sauce, for example, that I need to remember to buy tonight. The movie starts at 9:10 P.M. I have to run by the dry cleaners, too. And tomorrow, I have to go visit my father.

I give myself a quick neatening up outside of the sliding front door of the hospital. A summer thunderstorm has cooled the air and now a steady breeze has sprung up, making my sweat-soaked shirt icy cold. I shouldn't still be in the city in July, I should be on holiday. I tell myself the same thing every year, but not until late July, obviously.

You're going to wind up just like your father, everyone used to bet. Maybe so. Average height, average build, incipient gut like an average forty-year-old, brown hair, brown eyes; if you ask me, I don't resemble him in the slightest. I've got the classic face that makes me look like the slightly homely kid brother of plenty of American actors, most of them TV stars. You vaguely remind me of this guy, you sort of look like that guy, people tell me—resemblances, however, that don't do a thing in terms of people remembering my face. The point is that I'm not much of a talker, I always do my best to pass unobserved and I conceal my face behind four days of accumulated stubble. And the main problem is that I don't give a damn. I'm perfectly happy to be by myself. Every so often, I fantasize imaginary friends who are up to my level and a girlfriend who can amaze me, but I'm not the kind of guy who's going to tear myself away from the television to go chasing after fantasies.

Here I am, ready to act like the dutiful son to a man who never gave a second thought to performing his paternal duties.

The man that I'm supposed to resemble is an outsized motor-mouth, a friend to everyone he meets, a coiner of mala-propisms and misnomers of biblical proportions. A mysterious object to me. He's never shown the slightest sense of duty or spirit of sacrifice. The minute I came of age, he started disappearing for days and then weeks at a time, weeks that occasionally turned into months. He wrongfooted all my adolescent yearnings for independence. It was as if he'd just turned eighteen and couldn't wait to get rid of me. My mother died when I was twelve. Too young to fully understand, but old enough to understand that "It won't be easy to replace her" isn't the kind of thing a father ought to say to his son at the conclusion of an emotional conversation during the drive home from the cemetery, between an aw-go-fuck-yourself to a driver who seemed to have fallen asleep at the stoplight and an excessively lingering glance at a young female pedestrian in a miniskirt.

Hospitals are irritating from the minute you walk in the front door. I look for Building C, but there's no sign. There's Building A, Building B, and then a series of unmarked doors. I come to a halt facing a wall covered with sheets of paper with scrawled notes in sharpie and magic marker or printed with inkjet printers from at least twenty years ago. Camouflaged among the posters for labor union excursions—"Summer with us . . . or summer not!"—and a cloud of signs, including a prominent and mysterious "Please don't kick down the doors," I find a sign that says "Building C." I follow the arrow that points in the direction of the "Men's Ward" and when I come to the door I find a sign that says "Women's Ward." Just as I'm trying to remember which way the arrow pointed and the direction to follow now, I spot a nurse. She's about fifty years old and compactly built, without any of those useless frills such as a neck or anything like a waist separating upper body and pelvis. When she notices that I'm looking at her, she looks down and speeds up her pace in the hope of discouraging me.

"Excuse me, the Men's Ward?" I ask as she whips past me.

"If it's not this door it must be the other one," she replies without even slowing down.

Lucky for her that I hate arguments. I have an extremely acute form of cowardice that masquerades as an innate sense of superiority, and it prevents me from wasting time arguing with individuals of the kind. I head for the "other" door that was pointed out to me by the human parallelepiped and, when I reach the end of the short hallway, I discover a rapid-fire series of doors. So, before I can reach the Men's Ward I wind up, first, in the administrative offices, then in the pharmaceuticals dispensary—unguarded of course—and then in Radiology.

When I finally happen to stumble upon the Men's Ward, I'm greeted by a gust of wind. It's coming in through the big casement windows thrown open by the two cleaning women who are washing the floors with no regard for the patients, many of whom are well into their eighties, in sad shape, and worst of all, not even covered by their sheets and blankets. One of them even has his legs exposed to the blast and for a moment I have the impulse to enter the room, cover them all warmly, and then throw a fit.

While I wait my turn to talk to the doctor on the ward, I muse about the reasons I'm unable to pitch a tantrum. I think it's because I hate being the center of attention. After all, when you fly off the handle good and proper, you inevitably find people looking at you.

The chief ward physician would be more convincing as a grocery store clerk; he's a font of serial courtesy, a little too hasty to be fully convincing. When I ask about my father, he flips through the pages of his chart, wetting his index finger with saliva. My business suit, which is my uniform as a car salesman, makes me look mature, well-informed, educated. Three qualities I do not actually possess and which force me to swallow five minutes of a very technical and absolutely incomprehensible diagnosis. Acting the part, I nod with my lips clamped tight and prominent.

"We'll do all we can, but as you can imagine . . . " says the doctor, bestowing one of his paternal looks on me.

I shake his hand, deeply grateful for the list of new words he's given me to Google later this evening, and head for Room 21 at the end of the hallway.

It's been more than a year since the last time I saw him. I wonder whether I'll even recognize him and, especially, whether he'll recognize me. I'm not particularly nervous about it. I took a full week to prepare myself for this and now I'm ready for anything: to see him emaciated, in a coma, enraged, delirious.

I stride briskly into the room and recognize him immediately. He's so thin. But he seems wide awake and untroubled. When he sees me, he raises a hand and smiles. He's doing better than I feared, after all.

"I thought you'd never get here," he says. "I was about to leave . . . "

Okay, maybe he's not completely lucid.

"And just where you would have gone?" I ask, forcing myself to give him a smile.

I kiss him on the cheek. His cheek is cold. The two cleaning bitches must have come through here too. I sit down and take his hand.

"Shall we order?" he asks me.

I stand there a little uncertainly and I ask him if he wants a glass of water. He looks around, eyes wide open, smiling intermittently. It doesn't take a genius to see he's delirious.

"The food's not bad here," he says.

He thinks he's at a restaurant. That strikes me as absurd, considering that he's stretched out in a bed with an IV stuck in his arm and all around him are beds with other patients attached to other IV stands.

"So what's new?" he asks.

After all this time it's strange to hear him address me as if we'd talked the day before. I had imagined anything and everything in my head, but not this. I had prepared hundreds of useless answers and above all a superior attitude that's of absolutely no use to me now, because he's not being aggressive in the slightest. He's not even sorry, he's not mortified, he's not sad, he's not anything at all. He's lost in a world all his own and I'm there in that world too. Maybe the me of many years ago.

"So? You don't have anything new to tell me?" he says, after gazing around the room in search of a waiter.

My life is nothing much to speak of, so I do what comes most naturally to me, I lie. I invent a job that's full of responsibilities, a job that absorbs me heart and soul, I invent the decision to try to rein in my ambition and devote a little more time to myself, I tell him about bosses and bosses' bosses who are envious and worried about my irresistible rise through the ranks, I lay out the details of a trip to Mexico that I never took, and I season the whole tossed salad with my plans for marriage.

I had expected an hour-long visit, the minimum acceptable that would allow me to go home without feeling guilty. But now it's been almost three hours and I can't tear myself away. The thing is that at a certain point, without warning, my father has started talking about pussy. It's pretty upsetting if you consider that in forty years I never once heard him say a dirty word, unless you count those that were crucial to the successful completion of a joke, and never a word about sex.

"There are naked women wandering all over this hospital. Somebody ought to tell the doctor. And they come around and touch you. I even told them: 'What do you want from me? Why don't you just leave me alone?' But they won't listen to a word I say!"

There are four other patients in the room, and two of them are conscious, so I do my best to show a little dignity. I reply in a soft undertone, hoping to persuade him to lower his voice.

"And then there was your mother, who acted like such a little saint all the time . . . one night I caught her watching a porn film! At first I made fun of her, then I sat down and watched with her for a while. It's incredible how well made it was, what an elegant treatment it afforded, with an intricate interplay of chiaroscuro in the lighting and camera work."

I hear a sob from the bed behind me, or maybe it's a hiccup, though more likely it's someone stifling their laughter before it gets out of hand. I'd budgeted for a certain level of discomfort, but I was expecting to cringe at something a little more tragic, I'd imagined him asking me: "I'm about to die, aren't I?"

"Your mother was quite the slut, don't you find?" he says.

"Hmm, she was always a woman with an active mind," I reply, hoping to salvage something of the dearly departed's reputation.

Still raving, he eagerly recommends that I check out Channel 61, which has the best porn films. Within seconds, however, he starts yawning, mutters something, and then dozes off. While one of the other patients in the room hurries out into the corridor, incapable of stifling his laughter anymore, I tuck his blankets in and carefully extend the arm with the IV tubes. I'm proud to have a father who can focus on the camera work of a porn film.

1

I'm toying with Alice. We've been living together for more than a year now, but after just the first month of cohabitation we were on closer terms than a government bureaucrat and the automatic espresso dispenser. If I want love, understanding, tenderness, passion, or even if I just want to piss her off, all I have to do is push the corresponding button. She's twenty-eight years old, with a nice sinuous body and two white streaks in her mass of raven black hair that she never thought for a second of dyeing to match. She's a smart one. And so mature that, if she were my age, she'd avoid me like the plague.

It's raining again today. The bronzed Air Force colonel who delivers the weather report on Italian state television tells us that what's behind this weather is a stream of cold air pouring west out of the Balkans and temporarily fucking up the Azores anticyclone completely. I'm dealing with two opposing wind systems: one is a gust of conscience that's forcefully driving me to tell Alice that I'm not in love with her anymore and another powerful current, testicular in origin, that is generating instability and the distinct thought that you should never kick a good-looking girl like her out of your bed, if not your life.

I'm in the mood for a little passion; leaning against the kitchen door jamb, I watch my automatic espresso dispenser as it washes the dishes. My gaze is glued to her derriere as it sways in solidarity with her arm, which is furiously scrubbing a food encrusted saucepan.

"What is it, Diego?" she asks me brusquely, barely turning her head in my direction.

"Hey, what's up?" she asks a little more sweetly after taking the time to notice my gaze focused on her ass cheeks.

"Nothing," I reply.

"What do you mean nothing?" she says, smiling at my trance.

"No, it's just that . . . " a technical pause, "you just manage to be sensual even when you're washing the dishes."

"What an idiot you are!"

Fifteen seconds later, the idiot in question, thrown savagely down onto the bed, has obtained exactly what he wanted. And no, he wouldn't have obtained it just as easily by sneaking up behind her and kissing her on the nape of the neck. That works with new espresso dispensers. After a year, the gears get all encrusted and you have to operate with cunning and patience.

It's always the woman who demands the first lie, no two ways about it. First, she drills it into your head how important honesty is in a relationship, then not two months into that same relationship she's pressuring you to tell her that she's the only woman you've ever loved and that you'll never betray her. In other words, before you've even gotten started you've already told the biggest lie of all, so how big a deal are all the other lies that follow going to be?

I see the sarcastic smirks playing on the faces of women my age when I go out with one of my girlfriends in her mid-twenties. You don't have the balls to go out with a woman your age, they say. You keep chasing after worshipful schoolgirls because you couldn't take a relationship with a woman your age, a woman your equal, they think. Bullshit. Here's how it works: You're a male, you're sixteen years old, and you're desperately looking for a girl your age to go out with. Unfortunately, you have acne, you're fighting a losing battle against dandruff, and if you want to go somewhere, you have to drive your second-hand motorscooter; the girls your age, in contrast, already know how to dress and apply makeup like grown-up women, they know where the shower is and how it works, and they're dating guys in their twenties, guys who pick them up in their father's car. And so, eight out of every ten sixteen-year-old boys are forced to turn to fourteen-year-old girls for their dating needs. Now you're still a male, but this time you're twenty years old, you're a little confused about life, you're in college majoring in a subject you picked at random, and you don't know what you want to do when you grow up; the girls your age don't know either, but they like a little stability so they're going to bed with guys in their thirties, forcing you to avail yourself of sixteen-year-old girls for company. You're still the same old male, now you're twenty-seven, you have a distinctly unexciting degree and a blank resume, and you're struggling along in your first few underpaid and depressing jobs, but still you hope against hope to make a big impression on at least one of the girls your age. Unfortunately, they *all* have at least ten years of failed relationships behind them and now they're looking for safety with guys in their forties. So now you're forced to fall back on freshman college girls. In other words, an average male makes it to age thirty with only the slimmest of chances that he'll be noticed by a woman his age. For years, they've been telling you that girls mature earlier and they grow up faster, so then, by the time you're in your forties, when finally, thanks to their vastly superior maturity they've burned their love lives to the ground, instead of calling themselves pathetic idiots, they call you a miserable coward. Have they lost their minds?

Through no fault of my own, then, here I am with yet another girl in her twenties who obviously feels sufficiently mature to take on a love affair with a guy in his forties. She's a cornucopia of silly fondness, little gifts, hugs and kisses, giddy surprises. She's all over me like a shawl on an old man's knees. The problem with twenty-somethings is that when something serious happens and you really need them, or even when you just need them to know enough not to bust your balls, they tend to go a little haywire.

"So what are we doing tonight?" she asks me.

"Tonight I have to go see my father."

"Oh, again?"

"What do you mean by 'again'?"

"No, no, it's nothing, but you already went over there yesterday and the day before, and since we said we were going out tonight with Susanna and Marco . . . "

"Oh, I'm sorry, do you mind if we do it tomorrow night?"

"Tomorrow night I have to go to the gym."

"The day after tomorrow?"

"I have theater."

"Couldn't you just miss one class?"

"Listen to you! You won't give up your things, but I'm supposed to . . . "

"My things? My father's tumor isn't just one of my things, it's a tragedy! A nightmare!"

After I finish going haywire, I see the lights come back on in the windows in her head.

"Hey, don't get all worked up! Look, I understand perfectly, I'm happy that you're going to visit your father . . . Don't you remember last week? Wasn't I the one who told you to go see him?"

Wasn't she the one? I don't know, I don't really think so. I think I said to her: "I'm going to see my father," and she was the one who was going out with her girlfriends anyway, and she said: "Oh, all right, you go ahead."

She goes on talking but it's pointless, she's twenty-eight years old and her parents are in their fifties and go hiking in the mountains and run city marathons. What does she know about it. The idea of death and disease is light years away. And right now so am I.

I find a parking spot after driving around the hospital three times. I walk through a dreary little park at a pace that falls well short of brisk. In the past few days, the visits with my father have become agonizing. Every time I cross the threshold of the hospital room, I hope to see a smile on his face but every time his gloom has just deepened. He's in pain. He's frequently delirious. Watching him going through his death throes without a chance to do anything even remotely helpful is killing me. I walk straight toward the main entrance of the hospital, while a part of me is shitting his pants and loiters, wandering to and fro in the park. I climb up dark stairwells while at the same time I sit on a bench and take the sun. I head down the right hallway without allowing myself to be misled by the thousands of contradictory signs, and I simultaneously pet a little stray dog that sniffs the grass, sneezes, and forces me to smile. I take the smile to my father. I walk over to the bed with the imperturbable serenity of a Buddhist monk. The old man is thrashing in the bed, he's hallucinating. I lay a hand on his forehead and look him in the eye.

"How are you?" I ask him.

He swivels his eyes in my direction. My brain registers that blank gaze and catalogues it among the images I'll never be able to forget.

"Yesterday I was all right, but today just look at me . . . what are they doing to me in here?" he says.

I cover him with the blanket, I say something reassuring, and I leave the room in search of a doctor. Instead, I find the grocery store clerk. He talks to me about critical condition, test results that are all over the chart, home care assistants, and palliative treatments. Nothing really makes sense right now. The only reason I'm standing here listening him is to avoid my father's gaze. We agree on a short course of rehabilitation that will allow me to take him back home, and I head back down the hospital corridor. The stray dog follows me and licks my hand, a strand of spiderweb glitters for an instant in the filtering sunlight and then I find the strength to enter the room, sit down, and perform a myriad of tasks that are completely useless in terms of alleviating my father's suffering and my own frustration. I straighten his covers, I check his IV, I take a look at his urine drainage bag—it's so full it's just short of popping. So I call the nurse who shows up all irritated and changes his bag, muttering angrily about the attendant who should have checked it but never bothered. My father tells me that his feet are itching. I pull the blanket back and look at them: they're covered with cracks, and I tell him to wait just a minute, I leave the hospital, I walk to the nearest pharmacy, I buy a moisture cream and, without any conscious awareness of all the things I did from when I left the room until when I returned, I start massaging his feet, I think I see a hint of a smile and I tell myself, there, now I can't stop, if I stop he'll be in pain and so I'll keep doing this for the rest of my life, and as these thoughts go through my mind, my eye wanders to the IV tube which is starting to fill with blood, I stop massaging his feet just long enough to call the nurse who bustles in all pissed off asking me what is it this time, I point to the blood in the IV tube, she picks up a syringe without a needle and shoots some liquid into the nozzle to clear it of blood, and my father jerks and barely manages to repress a cry of pain. Deep inside, from the bottom of my heart, I curse.

2

I took my father home to his apartment and arranged for a modicum of home care. Then, drawing on my last remaining reserves of energy, I set about taking care of the outstanding issues with my automatic dispensers.

When I moved in with Alice, we exorcised the idea that our

relationship might go sour by applying little stickers to all my things, labels that said "This belongs to me." "Come on, let's do it, that way when things come to an end, we won't be like other people who are ready to cut each other's throats over a cookbook," we told each other. And that's exactly how it was. Maybe, along with the stickers, we should have drawn up a list of hackneyed phrases not to use, but we forgot, so I found myself telling her that it wasn't about her, true enough, that I was going through a bad stretch and I just needed to have some time to myself, the absolute truth, and that I still loved her, which was a bald-faced lie.

And I circulated a rumor among the extended family that my father was looking for a lawyer who could help him draw up a will, which instantly convinced an elderly aunt and a cousin to volunteer a few hours of patient care every other day.

After moving my things over to my father's house, I take advantage of a morning with nothing to do and drive in the country, just to catch my breath. It's a beautiful day, bright and sunny, and as I drive the SUV I've borrowed from the dealership, I manage to leave behind me all of my scary thoughts. Every time I pull onto the highway and see a strip of asphalt stretching out in front of me, clear and unobstructed, I'm seized with a powerful impulse to take off, to go somewhere far, far away and forget about everything. While waiting for this lurking impulse to develop into an unbridled migratory instinct, I settle for a jaunt southward for an hour and forty minutes, my destination a "renovated farmhouse, three stories, five acres of farmland, immersed in the magnificent countryside," in the wording of the classified ad I'd read while watching over the old man as he slept. I'm curious to see what's wrong with this piece of heaven on earth that costs only about as much as a 900-square-foot apartment on the outskirts of town. I mentally run down the list of possible answers to the riddle. For instance, the renovated farmhouse is actually a tumbledown hovel that's recently been repainted. Or the five acres of farmland is actually a sheer, rubble-strewn hillside where not even a mountain goat would venture. Maybe "immersed in the magnificent countryside" is a description that applies to one of the four sides, while the other three over-look, reading from left to right, an industrial oil refinery, a drainage canal, and a luxuriant gypsy trailer park.

They're excellent thoughts, and they manage to distract me from the crux of the matter: why am I going to look at this farmhouse?

We are a Plan B generation. Working in this country is such a disaster zone that, even if a miracle happens and you manage to get a job in the field you studied, after two years you're sick and tired and you start working on your Plan B. Almost invari-ably, that involves a bed-and-breakfast in the countryside, at least when you're as disgusted with life in the city as you are with your job. It's the mirage of a better, healthier life, with more free time on your hands. More time to think, more time for it to slowly dawn on you that you're still unhappy, that work had nothing to do with it and neither did the city. You moved to a new place and the first thing you put in your suit-case when you left were your problems. And now here you are, on your lovely hilltop, immersed in the unspoiled countryside. You dreamt of a village where everyone's friendly and sweet but you're surrounded by the same assholes as ever, with the one difference that you can't leave home without always find-ing them underfoot.

A highway sign announces that from this point forward, the word "Lazio" should be considered a typo that's been crossed out with a red diagonal slash. The correct term from now on will be "Campania."

3

The GPS navigator, which I've learned to mistrust implicitly, guides me onto a dirt road that cuts through the middle of a vast field of tomato plants. The SUV bounces and jerks indecorously over the potholes. On page six of the brochure, at the bottom right corner under the photograph of the suspension, the copy reads: "Raised suspension to easily face up to the challenge of even the most grueling off-road environments." That's bullshit, right there. I slow down to avoid cracking my raised suspension and, certain that I must have made a wrong turn, I start looking around for a stretch of road wide enough to make a three-point turn and retrace my route. But right after a curve in the road the farmhouse comes into view. From a distance it looks good, at first glance. There are no oil refineries or gypsy trailer parks in sight. The land is on a slight slope and it's run to seed, but it wouldn't take a lot of work to make this place beautiful. Standing in front of the farmhouse, next to a parked SUV and a Swedish station wagon, are two guys looking at me. The taller of the two must be the real estate agent. Six feet tall, about 185 pounds, a bodybuilder, expensive-looking suit, wraparound sunglasses, a goatee long out of fashion, a little bit of a redneck. The other guy is short and skinny, with bald spots and a suit his mother must have bought him. So he has to be the owner.

I park next to the station wagon, get out, and before walking over to the agent I click on the car alarm with the remote control. I only realize how idiotic that appears when I hear the double beep echo away into the silence of the deserted countryside. I pretend nothing happened and reach out to grip the hand that the bodybuilder extends to me.

"Are you from the real estate agency?" he asks me.

"No, actually I thought . . . Are you both here for the ad?" I ask, with a smile.

"Yeah, and I got here first," says the skinny short guy, and already I don't like him.

"Have you seen anything? What do you think of it?" I ask.

"Just took a little walk right around here. It looks pretty. It's perfect if you want to bury yourself in the countryside," the bodybuilder responds.

Now that we've exhausted all conversational gambits, I decide to escape the ensuing silence by taking a stroll around the building.

Stone walls and a pitch roof covered with terracotta tiles. It's the farmhouse of my dreams. It's exactly like the pictures in the ad. It looks as if it's made up of three houses built side to side, with a larger, taller central structure and two smaller additions on either side, like an Olympic medal podium. Ivy has taken over an entire façade, sparing only the windows. On the right is a nice veranda covered by a wisteria plant that seems to be withering. To my mind, a farmhouse is a good place if the first thing it makes you think of is a long groaning table in the open air decked out with flasks of wine and serving trays heaped high with smoking grilled meat. That makes my mouth water, and then some.

I think about my father, stuck in his hospital room, and I feel a wave of guilt. I push the thought out of my mind by focusing on a small vineyard. There are about a hundred grapevines, nothing much but enough to conjure up the fantasy of making my own wine. The courtyard in front of the farmhouse is unpaved, with patches of gravel here and there, and in the middle is a patch of grass and a tree. On the left side of the house, in the middle of the field and with a panoramic view over the valley below, I notice an excavation, about eight feet deep and at least sixteen feet wide. On the scuffed up dirt the track marks of a bulldozer are still visible. No doubt about it, somebody started work on a swimming pool here. Not a bad idea. Fifty yards further on is a little shed, two brick walls with a tin roof. According to the ad, the farmhouse comes with five acres of farmland. There are no enclosure walls, but here and there wooden stakes seem to mark the boundaries of the property. The road that leads to the farmhouse is bisected at right angles by a larger dirt road that to the left runs toward a grove of trees and to the right vanishes behind a hill. At a glance, I'd say that it marks the end of the farmhouse property and the beginning of the tomato field. All around the farmhouse are a dozen or so trees. Certainly not many, but at least they don't block the splendid panoramic view that the house enjoys on three sides. On the fourth side, behind the farmhouse, a line of industrial sheds, albeit in the distance, blights the countryside.

I hear the sound of a car coming closer and retrace my steps.

"Okay, here he comes now," decrees the tall thug.

"If it's not him I'm leaving," says the other guy with a resolute glare, betrayed however by a tremble in his lower lip.

A man in his mid-forties steps out of the car, hair nicely highlighted, an impressive physique, dressed in the latest fashion. He shakes hands with the bodybuilder and the physical proximity instantly suggests the two men could be brothers. Or at least that they go to the same gym.

"Well, well, you're all here already!" says the man as he flashes an obtuse smile that immediately convinces us that there would be no point in starting an argument about how late he is.

"I got here first," the skinny guy points out again, winningly. If you've ever had dealings with a real estate agent, you know what comes next. The location is unrivalled, the town is just a ten-minute drive away, you have all the necessary conveniences and services, and the farmland stretching out in all directions guarantees that the view will remain intact and unspoiled. The house has thick walls, the way they don't build them anymore, and not even an earthquake would put a dent in them. The interiors have been completely brought up to date, the plumbing was just redone, and the electrical system is up to code. You can knock down any or all of the interior walls and redesign the rooms however you like. Hell, you can dynamite the place if you feel like it and use the crater to build a nice Olympic swimming pool.

If I wasn't a salesman myself, I might be able to swallow half the things he's telling us. Instead, I recognize him as a member of the Oscar school of salesmanship and I don't fall for a single one of them. The interior renovation is restricted to the bathrooms alone, the electrical system is up to the same code as my testicles, and even though shafts of daylight are filtering through the roof, I have to admit that he does have a point; they do make the interior quite luminous. From the way the rooms have been subdivided and the few projects that were started, it seems that someone else had the intention of turning the farmhouse into an agritourism bed and breakfast. The attic loft could be used as a rec room, the second floor has five bedrooms, three full bathrooms, and brand new parquet floors, and the ground floor has an oversized living room, a big kitchen, and a sort of separate suite with a bedroom, an office, and a full bathroom.

I know what they teach these guys: you have to study the customer and show him his dream house. Incredibly, the agent with streaked hair has guessed that my dream is to have a wine cellar that is the envy of all my friends. I take that nasty surprise philosophically and let him lead me downstairs to see the *taverna*. This is a classic cold cellar used to store wine or salamis, carved out of rock, and usually clean and quite livable. A long tunnel carved out of the living tufa stone leads from the kitchen and emerges into a large room lined with wooden wine racks. On one side there's a broad stone counter with an unfinished wooden counter top and a small door that conceals a half-bath. No question about it, it may not be my dream but it's beautiful.

When we get back to the living room it's time to guess the big oaf's hidden dream.

"Such a nice big space could easily accommodate a regulation pool table," says the agent. A smile comes to my lips, but I'm wrong: the big oaf leans forward, turns his head to make sure that the butt of his imaginary pool cue is not about to encounter obstacles, and mimes a short, sharp bank shot.

All right, now I'm curious to see what kind of spin he'll put on his interpretation of the loser's personality. To my disappointment, we go on wandering around the house but the real estate agent never really shows his hand. He looks the loser up and down, he does his best to get a read on him, he even sighs in annoyance once or twice, he points out unconvincingly a couple of times that it would be possible to put an island in the kitchen with a stone countertop, but by the time the tour is over nothing solid has surfaced. Obviously, a guy like him has no dreams: he can't afford any.

At last, we all sit down at a table to talk over the terms of sale, and I begin to have a new appreciation for the bodybuilder. There had to be trick lurking somewhere, but the old chestnut of the wrong price printed in the classified ad certainly blindsided me. First thing, I feel like laughing; the loser, maybe because he has a nervous disorder of some kind, looks like he's about to burst into tears. The oaf just plants himself in front of the real estate agent and says: "Nice work, so what are you going to do about the forty euros worth of diesel fuel and the nine euros in highway tolls I spent to get out here?" Most people get started by launching into the lack of ethics, attempted fraud, the country that's going to the dogs because of a lack of personal integrity. But he's strictly pragmatic and goes straight to the point. Along with it, of course, there's the whole typically Italian pantomime of the threatening physical confrontation. Face to face, streaked highlights standing toe-to-toe with the bodybuilding oaf: a counterfeit Dolce & Gabbana business suit against full-regalia Armani outlet. It begins with "Don't raise your voice." The next step is "Get your hands off me." And it culminates with "What if I don't?"

I have to say that, even though "What if I don't?" might be one of the most pathetic comebacks out there, it's also one of the most difficult to respond to. I've had to deal with it periodically ever since I was eleven, and even so I've never really been able to untangle the riddle. If you answer, "Then I'll have to kick your ass black and blue," there's always the risk of using up that margin of safety that is the only thing that separates you from a full-blown fistfight. If you just say "Try it and see!" nine times out of ten the other guy'll put his hands on you again, and you're back to square one: "I told you to get your hands off me!" "What if I don't?" "Just try it again and see!" One time I played the card of pure mockery and in a tone of genuine disgust I replied: "And what if I do-o-on't? What are you, ten years old? Just cut it out!" It all went perfectly until I got up to the "Just cut it out!" an uncalled-for gloss that prompted a further "What if I don't?" from my challenger. One last possibility, which is very upper middle class, and therefore of little use with working class adversaries, is to respond "If you don't I'll call the police!" It's a line I use very infrequently and in any case never in front of women. Everyone knows, even if you're five foot two and you weigh 98 pounds, women want to be able to dream that they have a fearless hero by their sides, always ready to charge into the fray. Never undermine a woman's dreams.

After a couple of exploratory skirmishes, this is the exchange between the bodybuilder and the real estate agent:

"I don't give a damn if it was your secretary's mistake, you owe me forty-nine euros and I want that money now," says the oaf, stabbing a finger at the real estate agent's chest.

"Get that finger off me."

"What if I don't?"

When the tension has been cranked to the breaking point, when the two men are standing toe-to-toe with menacing expressions and clenched fists, suddenly the loser cuts a fart. A high-pitched, sharp fart, throttled at the end with a sudden belated clamp of the ass cheeks. We turn to look at him in disbelief, and he tries to justify:

"Sorry, you guys, but all this arguing . . . "

The sudden surreal glow that has been cast on the dispute gives the real estate agent an unexpected and welcome way out. He looks us up and down like the crowd of panhandlers he takes us for and sidesteps the inevitable "What if I don't?" with a simple: "Oh go on, get out of here!"

One thing the real estate agent said was true: the town really is just a ten-minute drive away. The historic center of the town is sweet, but the minute we leave the leafy tree-lined piazza, we're confronted with a succession of apartment buildings dating from the Seventies, each uglier than the last, thrown together with haste and no taste. One six-story office building was erected with its windows about a foot away from the balconies of a handsome palazzo from the 1920s. As we pass one dreadful pile after another, we pass by a bar and decide to stop in for a drink before undertaking our long drives home. Fausto and Claudio—respectively the bodybuilder and the loser—sit silently at an open-air table, chewing over the recent fight and fantasizing about magnificent put-downs they only thought of when it was already too late. I focus on a blackboard right behind Claudio's head where a short list of wines and beers is written out in chalk.

"It's *alopecia areata*," says Claudio with some annoyance.

It takes me a couple of seconds too long to figure out what he's talking about, so my explanation rings hollow once I get it out.

"I was looking at the day's specials," I say.

"It comes and goes, it's stress-induced. Do you guys mind if we move to another table?"

We follow his gaze, which seems to be focused on the roof of the building.

"Down here in the south, you never know how solid the construction is . . . and we're directly under the overhang," he informs us.

I meet Fausto's gaze, and it's steeped in that resigned criminal pity that must have been typical of the Nazis when they were dealing with the mentally ill. We move to a nearby table without comment and while Claudio shifts his chair, mentally calculating the trajectory of a possible falling chunk of plaster, I do my best to change the subject.

"Come on, don't dwell on it. We had a nice drive in the country!"

"What I don't get is what they thought they were doing! When you announce a price and then you tell the buyers it's three times that price, what exactly are you hoping to obtain?" Fausto snaps.

"Maybe it actually was an oversight," I say.

"That's even worse! If it really was an oversight it's worse! Because this is your fucking job and the reason this country's going to hell in a handbasket is because there's nobody left that knows how to do their job!"

The waiter brings our beer. I consider offering a toast, but they're already hoisting their goblets.

"Aaah, this beer is watery!" says Fausto to cap off his speech. Not even beer knows how to do its job anymore.

"But if you stop to think about it, it's worth the price. Sure, there are plenty of things that need to be fixed up, but it's still a bargain," I say.

"Not to my mind. It may be worth the money but I couldn't pay for it even with a thirty year fixed," says Claudio.

"Would you really move down here?" I ask him.

"It wouldn't be to live here. My idea was to open an agri-tourism bed and breakfast."

"I was thinking the same thing. But do you have any expe-rience? What kind of work do you do?" Fausto asks the loser.

"No, not really . . . my job has nothing to do with it, I work in supermarket retail. How about you?"

"I'm in television," says.

"Good evening, friends, good evening, timepiece connois-seurs! . . . that's you, right?" I ask.

Fausto smiles and winks an eye at me.

"Ah, that's right, late night home shopping . . . I've seen you before too," says Claudio.

What a lovely crew of insomniacs, I say to myself.

"What about you? What do you do for a living?" Fausto asks me.

"I'm in sales myself. Cars."

"What kind of cars?"

"Huge gas-guzzling lemons that get 18 mpg and cost you fifty euros to go a hundred miles."

"So what's a car salesman doing down here?"

"Taking a nice drive in the country," I say curtly.

Half joking, Fausto suggested we pool our savings and buy the farmhouse, and then we could run the bed-and-breakfast as a partnership. He started jotting down columns of figures on a scrap of paper, then he compared earnings against the ini-tial investment, and estimate after estimate the conversation turned serious. According to Fausto, the winning formula is the agritourism bed and breakfast with a beauty farm and day spa. All you'd need to do is set up a massage room and install Jacuzzis in all the bathrooms and you'd instantly double your potential revenue stream, at the very least, compared with a normal agritourism bed and breakfast.

I listened to him intently and gratified him with a few questions tossed in here and there, but the idea of going into business with those two guys undermined once and for all whatever credibility the already vague idea of changing the direction of my life by starting an agritourism bed and breakfast might ever have had. And Fausto in particular is the kind of person I trust least. He's the classic individual who's got a friend who's a lawyer and a friend who's an accountant, who'll take care of the publicity and PR himself, who'll arrange to bring in a steady stream of guests, and who knows famous people who'll get the operation off the ground. He's so used to lying that he's even started lying to himself. Claudio doesn't strike me as the kind of guy who'd pull a con game, but my God, I've never seen such a limp dishrag, so lackluster and apathetic. I wouldn't go out for dinner with him to a decent restaurant, much less start a business together. But just out of pure courtesy we exchanged phone numbers and we promised we'd give the matter some serious thought. As far as I'm concerned, the most serious thought I can give it is to avoid thinking about it entirely. And hurry back to my father.

4

It takes only a second or two to tell when a question is strictly perfunctory. Take a quick look in the person's eyes and you can see it: they don't really want an answer at all. They might be asking how your father's feeling, but they're already thinking about something else, inside their head they're mentally weighing the best approach to use when they inform you there's going to be another special promotional "Open House" event, so you're going to have to work this Sunday too. There's nothing worse than answering those questions, nothing more destructive in terms of the priorities that you've painstakingly constructed and the way that you've always put your work ahead of everything else. I put the needle on the spinning record and repeat for the umpteenth time that the old man is sinking fast, that it's a matter of days now, but at least there's the consolation that he's not really suffering anymore. They'll let me have another day or so of immunity, maybe two, and then they'll start getting sick and tired of hearing about dying fathers.

Oscar is one of those guys who give you the sneaking suspicion that if a gigantic meteorite were to strike the Earth full-on, resulting in the complete annihilation of the human race, it might not be such an unmitigated calamity after all. He asked me about my father, he listened with a pained expression to my brief response, and then he started talking about himself. About what he'd been through, and of course he'd been through much worse; about how hard it was, and of course it was much, much harder; about how he'd worked to make sure none of his co-workers noticed a thing and of course he'd succeeded far better than I had. This man has an overwhelming need to talk about himself, and not even a scrap of personal style. I wonder if people like him really think they're so crafty they can transmit their messages without anyone noticing a thing, or whether they know perfectly well what slimeballs they come off as, but they just don't give a good goddamn.

This kind of thing can just wreck your day, unless in the midst of personal tragedy you happen to develop a kind of peripheral vision that allows you to broaden your field of observation so that this kind of thing begins to seem piffling and insignificant. Dealing with death makes certain aspects of life suddenly much clearer. Your job, for example, and this exquisitely Italian point of view that you're very lucky to have a job at all, and that therefore everyone expects you to be willing to do anything to keep that job, even working much harder without any increase in salary. Because you're privileged and privileges need to be paid for.

Outside the plate glass windows it must be suffocatingly hot. A quick glance at the sidewalk is enough to tell me that the exodus to the beaches is about to reach its peak. There are no fewer than three available parking places, whereas up until a week ago there was a chaotic and unbroken line of cars, either crammed so close they were actually touching, or else with minimal spaces between them, spaces that would immediately fill up when someone squeezed their motorscooter into the spot left free. I wonder if the nurse has turned on the air conditioning. My father prefers the fan set on medium, about six feet away from the bed, but blowing diagonally, not just any six feet. Should I really be here today? Is my presence at the auto dealership really fundamental to the development of the human race? Does life really have to go on? Should I really be experiencing pangs of guilt for a man who only remembered me on his deathbed?

We're born with our hands full. That's why as newborns we clench our fists, because we've been given the most wonderful gifts anyone could ask for: innocence, curiosity, the will to live. Even this shithead sitting across from me was born clenching his tiny little fists. And he too opened those fists to grab one thing after another, each more meaningless than the last, and day by day he squandered his treasure trove. At age fifty, he's reduced to clenching a stack of paper that right now he's waving in my face. He's red in the face, his jugular vein is bulging, and his eyes are filling with tears of rage. The newborn, who once clutched the gift of innocence, is now brandishing a contract that speaks clearly: the door handles of his SUV were supposed to be black, not chrome. There comes a tactical moment when you can weigh in to calm a customer down, but this isn't it. You have to wait for him to push it too far, say more than he ought to, indulge in some oafishly offensive phrase, usually something on the order of "You're all just a pack of thieves."

At this point, you've got to be sufficiently cool and collected to let another few seconds go by, useful for letting him vent the last sparks of rage, such as "That's right, a pack of thieves, goddamn it!" and then finally launch a counterattack with a phrase that, in my case, is always the same: "You have every right to be angry! And how! In fact, I can only thank you for the courtesy you're kind enough to show us in this case!" Every word uttered with a conviction and an emphasis that are certain to throw them off guard. Guaranteed. Unfortunately, we're still a long way away from the misstep and this guy is determined to retrace his steps through the tragic misadventure with his door handles. This affords me the time to begin a serious examination of the superiority of western culture, based on freedom, equality, and door handles that match the body paint. A bulwark made of tensioactive materials, as hypnotic as a soap bubble, and precisely as solid.

I demonstrate my empathy during his heartfelt account by nodding at all of the crucial plot twists. People like this dissatisfied customer think it could never happen to them, and yet they know perfectly well that in summertime the rate of homicides due to temporary insanity rises sharply. The level of stress accumulated during the year combined with the suffocating heat can turn mild-mannered retirees, exemplary neighbors, and pillars of the community into vicious killers. Later, they'll say the same thing about me: "He was such a respectable person, always said good morning, good afternoon, good evening . . . generally kept to himself . . . " No doubt about it, I'm perfect fodder for a grim opening item for a summer news report, the man in the street who just grabbed an axe one day and chopped a ball-busting customer into little bits.

"You're all inept fools!" the guy finally shouts. I wait.

"Fucking inept fools!"

Okay, now the ball is in my court. "You, sir, have every right to be angry . . . "

5

My father is winning and likable. I've always known that, but the fact that he was so nice even during the brief moments of lucidity during his death throes came as a real surprise. Yesterday, he seemed to be feeling a little better so I got him into his wheelchair and wheeled him over to the table. Because I remember that he once told me that sitting at the dinner table with your own family is the most wonderful thing on earth, and since then I've done everything I can to make him happy. I tucked in his napkin as fast as I could because I know that he can't take sitting up for all that long. I zipped into the kitchen to get some plates and I turned the flame up to high underneath the pan of chicken noodle soup. When I got back I saw him, eyes shut tight, slurping the chicken noodle soup I hadn't served yet, raising an imaginary soup spoon to his lips. I stood there, motionless, riveted to the spot, until a shiver ran down my spine and rattled the stack of dishes, silverware, and glasses that I was holding. My father opened his eyes, looked at his hand, and then turned toward me, with a self-amused smile on his face, and asked: "Who am I? What am I doing?"

I feel like telling him that it's all been forgotten and forgiven. The inappropriate phrases, the absences, the phone calls never made, the birthday wishes overlooked, all the resentments accumulated over the years, all swept away by that stupid line, the sublime timing, and the stellar performance.

He hasn't touched his food today. I've been watching over his breathing for hours and I decide to take a break in front of the TV. After watching for not even half an hour, the programs that in theory are supposed to keep me company have made me feel even lonelier. There's a pair of politicians settling some personal feud, serenely indifferent about whether I understand a word of what they're saying. One of them keeps saying without stopping for breath "How dare you say such a thing! How dare you say such a thing! How dare you say such a thing!" while the other one, perched on the farthest useable half-inch of his chair, is shouting accusations about a short-sighted budget bill or maybe a flat-sided bucket mill, who can say, I certainly can't: it could be either one. Or else there's one of those TV series that, if you missed the first episode, four years ago, it's hopeless to try and understand the plot. Then there's the usual news program that wallows in a seamy slice-of-life interview with kids high on drugs outside of a disco. And a sober-sided documentary about the nonexistent American Big Foot. I channel-surf rapidly until I get to Channel 61. That's the channel my father recommended so strongly, but the screen is black. There is no such channel, or maybe it's just off the air right now. The blank screen makes me notice the silence that fills the apartment. I wish I had a little company right now, someone I could talk to and say: "This is a tough time."

In my time here, I haven't received a single phone call. I have no friends, I only have playmates, people who call me up to go out for a pizza or to play on the PlayStation. Even my automatic homecare dispensers have vanished. The minute they realized that my father is renting this apartment and that what money he has in his bank account is being drained to pay for caregivers and nurses, they started dreaming up excuses. That doesn't matter, my father and I no longer need anyone else. We're a closeknit couple. I change his IV like a professional nurse, I give him morphine injections with a delicate touch. My father does his part. Whenever he happens to regain consciousness for a few seconds, he always, unfailingly smiles at me.

I turn off the TV. I put on a rubber glove, I fill a basin with hot water, I dissolve a disinfectant in the water, and I go into the bedroom. I feel that I'm giving back. You can think about it for the rest of your life, but you'll never be able to understand what it feels like to clean your father's ass. There's no disgust, no shuddering, no reluctance. You're completing a circle. You're obliging yourself to perform an ineluctable act that leads to perfection.

In the morning, I open my eyes the instant the mechanism of the alarm clock clicks into gear and I bang it silent with the flat of my hand before it can even emit a sound. I get ready to go to work and when I walk into the old man's room to say goodbye and check in with the nurse, I notice that he's breathing irregularly. Long periods of apnea. I understand that we're coming to the end, but in certain situations understanding and actual awareness of the state of things travel on two different tracks.

At the dealership I perform work that is of fundamental importance to all mankind, such as unpacking the new brochures, masterpieces of the printer's art embellished with debossed covers. I arrange them carefully on the totem pole that stands next to the car and in stacks of twenty underneath every desk. Then I do my part to make this world a better place by doing a progress report on the orders now underway. I note with satisfaction that a batch of black door handles is on its way from Germany. And it's with a smile of anticipation that I answer the phone, guessing that this must be the fifty-year-old who had the temper tantrum. Instead, it's the nurse. I hang up, I put on my jacket, I tell Oscar that my father has died, and I leave without noticing any particular reaction on his part. As far as I can tell, one second later I'm home, standing by the old man's bed.

He's a beautiful man, like hell I resemble him. He doesn't look a bit like an eighty-year-old who's just died of cancer. His face is a little hollowed-out, but there's something miraculous about his skin, completely unlined. The deterioration of age is more pronounced in his legs: his knees are wider across than his thighs. Otherwise, it's a relief to look at him. I strip him bare and while I wash him carefully I tell him the three or four little things that I'd like to get off my chest now, rather than hold them in for the rest of my life. I dress him in a pair of dark trousers, a white shirt, and a good pair of dress shoes. I brush what little hair remains on his head, I pull the bandages off his arms, and I shut his mouth. That's it, there's nothing left to be done but to stop and look at him.

"Who am I? What am I doing?" I ask myself.

6

In our way, we're a very tolerant society. Not toward the needy, however; we're tolerant of the privileged. Millions of citizens ought to pour into the streets demanding the heads of whoever organized the nightmarish bureaucratic machinery that grinds into motion after every death, but nobody does. I've heard so many people run down the funeral parlors, but in my case they were the only ones who actually helped out, took care of things, and worked. Aside from them, all my dealings were with diseased bureaucratic procedures, dreamed up by deeply diseased minds that had been corrupted by the special priority access lanes, enervated by the right to a pension after just a few years on the job, asphyxiated by the sheer volume of privilege. On the death certificate there's an expiration date. I am therefore authorized to hope that my father may yet come back to life. If people who earn eight times my salary, and who I therefore assume are much smarter than me, tell me that there's a possibility of a change in my father's state of death, by God, I believe them.

But that's just the beginning. To access my father's bank account I have to submit a certificate that attests to my being alive and existing. It ought to be sufficient for me to show up at the bank with a photo ID. The bank officer looks at the document, compares your face with the picture, yes, that's you, yes, you're actually alive, and therefore you exist, end of story. But that would be too simple. In order to get this certificate you have go to the office of vital statistics and there you find that all you need to do to get this certificate issued is to show them a photo ID. What the fuck!

Alice calls me again, for like the thousandth time. I had been hoping that just not answering her calls would have been sufficient. But no, the young woman obstinately demands her fair share of lies. What part of this doesn't she understand? If I left her and stopped coming around entirely it means I'm not in love anymore, right?

"Hello."

"Diego . . . have you gone crazy, just vanishing like this?"

"I haven't vanished, I walked out in plain sight, where you could see me clearly."

"Sure, but Jesus, you had your father's funeral and you didn't say a thing to me!"

"I didn't say a thing to anybody. It was just him and me."

"Oh my God, but why?"

"There was a wonderful echo in the church. My father had four services for the price of one."

"Why do you keep the people who love you at a distance?"

"Alice, please, don't make this all about you, I'm on the brink of the abyss, I just want to be alone."

"I'm not making this about me . . . you know that."

"Of course I do, that's the last thing you would do, but really, this just isn't about you, try to understand, it's just a tough time for me and I need some time alone. I'll be in touch, okay?"

"Okay," she says. She sniffs and hangs up.

Maybe that did it. Or maybe she'll call back again, in a couple of weeks. She'll find one of my socks, the navy blue sock that I love so much, and she'll insist on telling me that if I want to, I can come by and get it.

I ought to call the dealership. I've used up all my vacation time and there are a thousand things to take care of. The stock of black door handles is lost somewhere in a logistics center in Germany and now, no doubt, they're having a department meeting to decide on the thorny matter of etiquette, that thin line between professionalism and being sons-of-bitches: "Should we call now or wait another twenty-four hours? How about twelve hours and then we call?"

"What an idiot. For years I've waited for a signal from life and I failed to understand that it had already arrived, long ago, from my knees." That's what my father said to me as he was getting out of bed and all I thought was that he needed a nice vigorous walk up and down the hallway. My father is the last person you'd expect to deliver a great truth about life. In my mental archive I possess a great truth about silicone: "After you use the sealant gun to seal the edge of the sink, run a soapy wet finger over it. It'll come out much smoother than with a putty knife," nothing else. But now that I've gotten out of the car, after being stuck for forty minutes in a traffic jam, and I've felt that small twinge of pain from the side of the kneecaps, I have no doubts, it's the signal that time's winged chariot is hurrying near, that if I ever dreamed of doing anything special, well, the time to act has come.

The signal has come and I've decided not to ignore it. Maybe one day I'll think back on my life and I'll remember with anguish the time that my kneecaps told me to become partners with a boorish oaf and a pathetic loser whom I had met only once. Before common sense can get the upper hand, I turn on my cell phone and I call Fausto. After the first ring, I think to myself, "What the fuck am I doing?" after the second ring, I pray he won't pick up, after the third ring, ditto, after the fourth ring I tell myself, "One more ring and that's it," after the fifth ring, I tough it out with "One last ring," just to make it clear that I was making a serious, good-faith effort. On the sixth ring, he answers.

We're in luck, the farmhouse hasn't been sold yet and in fact the price has been lowered by a good 10 percent. All it takes is an informal meeting lasting not even an hour to come to terms on the partnership. Fausto is the most enthusiastic, Claudio allows himself to be dragged into it, and I just hope this attitude doesn't create problems later on, while I quite simply am not responsible for my own actions. When I tell them my father has just died and that I'm going through a crazy period, they volunteer to take care of all the paperwork. All I have to do is show up in a lawyer's office a couple of times and sign a series of documents that I don't even bother to read.

Concerning the purchase of the farmhouse Claudio seems very cautious, warning us about a thousand different pitfalls and potential cons. Fausto tries to reassure him, but Claudio only calms down when the settlement agent confirms that the documentation on the property is complete and trustworthy. There are no gray areas, no liens, no overriding claims. In less than ten days we deposit our down payment and a little more than a month later we sign the papers and pick up the keys.

I hand in my resignation with a very stiff email just three lines long. I return my company car and I leave without saying goodbye to anyone. For the closure of one of the longest chapters in my life, I had imagined a more laborious endgame.

7

I've been so absorbed in wrapping up all the details surrounding my father's death that I haven't had time to get to know my two new business partners. During the trip down to the farmhouse it dawns on me for the first time that I've just gone into business with a pair of perfect strangers. I figure they're probably already the best of friends, that my absence during this crucial period means that I'm permanently cut out of things, and that this will work to my detriment as soon as there's some decision to be put to a vote. Turns out I have no reason for concern. I soon figure out that there's already bad blood between them and, even though that puts my mind at ease about one set of worries, it's certainly not promising for the future. Taking advantage of a pit stop at a service plaza, Fausto tells me that Claudio is a complete incompetent, that the only reason he went into business with us is that he's at his wit's end after managing to bankrupt a company that was practically running itself. As for him, on the other hand, this idea of running an agritourism bed and breakfast is just a fling, something to take his mind off things, a new enterprise to fill his time after walking away from a very successful career in television home shopping sales.

A second pit stop proves to be the undoing of Fausto. Claudio tells me that a friend of a friend knows him well and that he's nothing more than a two-bit home shopping salesman weighed down by debt and problems with the law. He says nothing about his supermarket, he just says he suddenly felt the urge for a change of scenery. Actually, I need to use the restroom myself but I have no intention of becoming the next target. I prefer to stand there with an aching bladder thinking about how I've gone into business with an incompetent and a con artist. If I had any feelings available at this point, I could throw down a little fear or, as an alternative, depression. But my emotional palette is dry, and I watch my life going past as if, all things considered, it's none of my concern.

Pulling up in front of the farmhouse with the keys in hand is a nice sensation. The second week in September brings cool, luminous days that stir a welcome impulse to roll up our sleeves and get to work. The minute we throw open the front door, our heads start teeming with ideas. Unfortunately, all of those ideas are radically different. In the big double living room, we could put dining tables on one side and, on the other, sofas and armchairs for leisure time, I decide. Fausto is in agreement on the dining tables but: instead of the sofa and chairs, how about a pool table? Claudio is in favor of neither. With its magnificent vista over the countryside, the attic would be perfect as a massage room, I suggest. Perfect for a giant screen television for watching soccer matches in blessed peace, thinks Fausto. Claudio hedges his opinion. These minor disagreements do nothing to dampen our enthusiasm, we have plenty of work to do in any case, and we can come back to the issue of how to use the various rooms a few weeks from now. We survey all the rooms in the house for the third time, and very professionally take a complete set of notes on the work that needs to be done. Then we sit around the kitchen table, illuminated by a shaft of sunlight that almost serves as a mystical seal marking the beginning of this undertaking.

Fausto's father was a plumber, Claudio's dad was a carpenter, and mine knew a fair amount about electrical systems. For some reason recounting these details has always reassured us about our own ability to do most of the work ourselves. "Why not, we'll just hire an expert to do the work on the roof and we can do everything else on our own," we've said more than once. As if our fathers' expertise would automatically be handed down to their sons or it were enough to pronounce these words to a faucet—"You realize, I hope, that my father knew all about this sort of thing"—and the washer or threading would automatically self-repair.

We decide to start with the items that are fundamental to our basic survival. First item in terms of importance: make sure the television works properly. We go into the living room and, operating with perfect coordination, we snap into action as a team: Claudio turns on the set, I pick up the remote control, we observe and confirm that we see only gray static. Fausto takes a look at the back of the set, picks up the antenna cable and screws it into the proper receptacle. The channels appear instantly. We slap high-fives all around and go back to the kitchen.

Claudio checks off item one. We move on to the next item: the bathrooms. After a thorough inspection we've noticed a clogged toilet, two dripping faucets, a door that doesn't close right, one jammed door lock, a couple of ceiling lights that need to be replaced, and a few loose ceramic tiles. We decide to start with something easy: the clogged toilet, just for the satisfaction of quickly marking another item off the list.

Armed with a toilet plunger, we go downstairs to the bathroom in question, the half-bath of the *taverna*. As a good faith gesture, in hopes of speeding up the process of becoming a member of the group, I volunteer. I roll up my shirtsleeves, I pick up the plunger, and I place it over the drain hole.

"Not like that," Fausto says instantly.

I'm a normal human being, so the sudden surge of blood to my temples and the driving impulse to plunge his handsome face, glowing with anti-aging moisturizer, into the filthy water are perfectly understandable reactions. But in my resumé, I've always written "team player, works well with others," so I turn to look at him with a smile.

"Unless you place the plunger so it covers the drain hole completely, you'll get a stream of shit on yourself," he adds.

I move the plunger slightly.

"How's that?" I ask.

"Look to the right . . . there's a gap."

I shift the plunger by a subfraction of a millimeter, imperceptible to the human eye.

"There, that's perfect. Go ahead!"

I go ahead . . . A stream of water and toilet paper hits the fly of Claudio's trousers.

"Aaah, look at this! How disgusting!" Claudio shouts. He stands there, on tiptoe, arms and legs splayed wide, as if every part of his body were trying to run away from his bespattered crotch.

"Give it here, I'll do it!" says Fausto and grabs the toilet plunger out of my hand.

He rolls up the sleeve of his white shirt and with a series of wrist motions that are largely useless but still quite elegant he positions the plunger. He takes a deep breath, gets a mean look on his face, and thrusts downward, pumping, powerfully, twice. Two correspondingly powerful streams, this time a deep handsome brown, strike Claudio full in the chest.

We spend the next half hour consoling our partner. He's shut himself into another bathroom and amid the splashing of water in the sink, the shower, and the bidet, he tells us in a quavering voice that he's not overstating things, one of his mother's first cousins actually died of a streptococcal infection. We're standing around outside the door listening and every so often we have to bite our lips to keep from laughing out loud. We blame it on the toilet plunger which must have a worn lip.

Once we've restored our group consensus and harmony and we've regained our motivation, we go back to the bathroom, this time armed with a bottle of professional plumber's acid drain cleaner. While waiting for the liquid to take effect, we amuse ourselves by trying to come up with a name for our agritourism bed and breakfast.

"I've got it! FàClaDi!" says Fausto, spreading his hands out in both directions to indicate the scale of the sign.

"It sounds like the name of a Greek archipelago," I say, hoping that this harmless observation will be enough to put an end to the idea of acronyms.

"Or ClàFaDi," Claudio ventures.

Having noticed that in either case my name still brings up the rear, I decree, dismissively:

"No acronyms. It sounds like a professional cleaning service or a contracting company. We need a warm, evocative name, the kind of name you'd associate with an agritourism bed and breakfast."

"Villa Serenity?" suggests Claudio, once again sketching out the same imaginary sign.

"Yeah, okay, so what would that be? A hospice?" asks Fausto.

"The Olive Tree Inn!" says Claudio.

"There are no olive trees here," I point out.

"Not even the shadow of an olive tree," Fausto piles on.

"Well, we can plant olive trees if that's the only problem!"

Fausto grabs the bottle of acid I'm holding. He says that I didn't wait the three minutes before flushing. He pours it in and focuses on his name-brand chronograph. But three minutes is a long time to wait.

"The Hillside Inn?" Claudio ventures, by now fully immersed in his creative trance.

"There must be two thousand agritourism B & B's that are called The Hillside Inn, The Olive Tree Inn, The Old Well Inn, The Venerable Farmhouse, and The Dingy Dick!" Fausto snaps.

"The Dingy Dick is not bad at all!" I reply, prompting laughter from Fausto and a stricken gaze from Claudio, but I refuse to explain to him that it was just a joke.

After two hours of vain attempts we abandon the field of battle with our tails between our legs, just in time to watch the evening sports news on TV. Our intention was just to rest up for half an hour and move on to item three on the list. But once the sports news is over, a gossip program begins. Nobody takes the initiative to turn off the television set, so we allow ourselves to be instructed on the latest fashion trends, the top ten costliest divorces of the year, and the invaluable tips of a fashion model and new mother who manages, with great effort, to reconcile her work life and her family responsibilities, in part through her annual income of eight million euros and four full-time nannies. Hypnotized by the skin-tight shorts worn by the women's team, we then watch the third set of a volleyball match and then, through sheer inertia, we spill over into a quiz show. After the closing credits of the quiz show, we hear the theme song of the evening news, but at that point Fausto slaps his thigh and stands up. I pick up the punch list and follow him, while Claudio pantomimes his intention to catch up with us just as soon as the news is over.

Fausto and I withdraw to the kitchen and over a glass of wine we concur that it's late, that wisdom dictates a fresh start tomorrow morning, that we're a little rusty, and that we could do with some help from a plumber and an electrician, and that in the meantime, we can focus on the furnishing and layout of the farmhouse.

"What do you think about getting a consultation from a professional *interior designer*?" I ask, mouthing the exotic English term.

"A what?" Fausto asks.

I say *interior designer* again, but this time in Italian.

"What an international man of style you are! What, you never furnished an apartment on your own?"

In a split second my mind has flown backwards through time to the place we first met to discuss the details of our partnership. The living room in Fausto's apartment. Practically speaking, a scene of gang warfare between third-world imports and formica cabinets.

"Sure, of course I have, but what does that have to do with anything, interior design is an art, you can't just wing it," I say.

"Don't you worry, I'll take care of it. You'll see what a masterpiece I create. Who needs *interior designers?*"

He grabs a sheet of graph paper and with a dull pencil starts sketching out the perimeter of the farmhouse. After he finishes the first two sides he starts frantically fine-tuning a series of nonexistent corners that he can't manage to stitch together.

"Can we turn off that damned TV, please?" he shouts at Claudio.

I'm better than that. It would take me no more than thirty seconds to wrap a guy like him around my little finger, but right now I'm tired, and I have no desire to launch into any psychological chess matches. And anyway, I'm preoccupied, I can't quite remember what there was in his apartment, between the bamboo coffee table with the candles on it and the stereo console in black formica. Oh, yeah, that's right, there was a butt-shaping exercise machine.

8

In order to assign bedrooms, we turn to a technique that's especially common among high school students out on overnight field trips. At a previously agreed signal, everyone runs upstairs as fast as they can and throws their suitcase on the bed in the room they want, usually the biggest room or else the room that's closest to where the prettiest girl in the class will be staying. In our case, either the biggest room or the one with the nicest bathroom. I make a valiant stab at pretending to compete and I feign bitter disappointment when I find myself forced to choose one of the three remaining bed-rooms—in every detail identical to the rooms they chose for themselves. I walk through the closest doorway, shrugging off their mocking laughter like the loser that I am, and softly shut the door behind me.

There are times when you really shouldn't be alone, like when you've just made some crazy and reckless decision about your life . You shouldn't be alone because, no matter what, you already know how this is going to end, so you stretch out on your bed and you start staring at the ceiling. Your worst thoughts are lighter than air and somehow they all eventually float up to the ceiling.

It's only ten o'clock and I decide to put an end to my cell phone's sullen silence by calling someone. The only names that come to mind for a heartfelt conversation all belong to ex girlfriends. I immediately discard Alice, for obvious reasons, and instead opt for Giuliana. She's one of the less recent exes, so no complications, no chance of a misunderstanding, I tell myself. I'm glad to talk to her, her voice is familiar, and I immediately find myself feeling better. At first, she's surprised and then, suddenly, she seems strangely detached. Am I both-ering her? Does she have something else to do? She always responds after about a second's delay and forces me to repeat everything at least once, sometimes twice. Even though I can hear her perfectly, I ask if by some chance she has a bad con-nection and wants me to call her back. But after the first few questions she asks, it dawns on me that the reason she can't hear me is that she's sharing the phone with someone else, probably the man she lives with now. She asks me if I have a girlfriend now, and I tell her I don't. Then she asks me why I called her, and from her tone of voice I understand that she thinks I was trying to arrange a great big welcome home party. Once I figure out what's gone wrong, I start giving her dull, reassuring answers.

I tell her that I've taken some time off work for the first time in many years and that I just felt like talking to some people. I could always tell her about my father and clear up the misunderstanding in a flash—after all, that's why I called her in the first place—but I just don't feel like confiding in the stranger that I know is listening in. She must still be angry about the way I broke it off: just like that, one fine day, without warning. But what was I supposed to if I wasn't in love with her anymore? Would she have preferred something long and drawn out, a few months' worth of boredom and fighting? I was careful and considerate, I spared her the knowledge that I already had a new girlfriend, I told her that she was perfect and that she deserved someone better than me.

After a few moments of silence, which I imagine represent her confirming her next move with the man at her side, she tells me that she's married now. I take it calmly in stride and act as if I'm happy for her. Since I presume that according to their conspiracy theory my interest should now subside markedly, I launch into an interminable series of detailed questions about their wedding. I ask about her wedding gown, the church, the reception, the wedding gifts, the guests. I even ask her who caught the bouquet. Serves them right: they were expecting the horny advances of an old reprobate and instead they're forced to wade through the tedious questions of a garrulous and ineffectual friend, harmless as an elderly aunt. I can feel them withering under the onslaught, but I refuse to put them out of their misery until I've tormented them for a good solid hour.

By rights, I ought to be heartsick and disappointed in the human race. I should be reconsidering my entire life and wondering seriously about the emotional void I've managed to create around myself. Instead, I grab two miniature bottles of vodka I found in the living room and I drink to my narrow escape. I was actually in love with that monster and, Jesus, right now I could be the poor fool sentenced to spend evenings of boredom so crushingly intense that I'd be glad to eavesdrop on a phone call from an ex boyfriend.

I go back to staring at the ceiling and decide that this idea of starting an agritourism bed and breakfast is pure insanity, that we're a trio of incompetent wannabes, that I can't stand my two partners, that I've set up a company with people I don't even trust, that any guests we manage to lure out here are going to hate them too, and that that's the last of my problems, because we're never actually going to have any paying guests.

I've carefully considered, reviewed, and evaluated every single decision I've made in my life, but where has all this judicious planning gotten me? I've done easy work, an unambitious job that demanded nothing because I had a natural talent for it, I've made a few insignificant friendships, I've had relationships with women whose utter meaninglessness I've only appreciated after leaving them. So now, maybe, let's hear it for a reckless move, a little detour from this marvelous six-lane highway that I've been driving along, a highway that leads straight to a failed marriage, a retirement in an easy chair watching TV and, finally, the grave. And with this last thought, the clock strikes three.

I get up and leave my bedroom, heading for the kitchen. I take great care not to make even the slightest sound. I would expect Fausto in particular to be ripping out the virile snores of a truck driver, but not even a sigh emerges from the door of his room. I slowly descend the steps and, in the kitchen, I find Claudio sitting at the table with his hands cradling a mug, to the light of a flickering candle.

"Am I interrupting something? A romantic midnight cup of chamomile tea?" I ask. Considering the time of night, it strikes me as a pretty good wisecrack, but I can't manage to drag even the hint of a smile onto his face.

"I just can't seem to get to sleep tonight. It must have been the dinner," he replies, unmistakably irritated at my presence.

Since I couldn't care less about the mood he might or might not be in, I grab a cup and a chamomile teabag and sit down too. He's wearing a pair of sky-blue pajama bottoms that, by God's mercy, he mismatched with a white T-shirt branded with the logo of his supermarket.

"It's never easy to get to sleep when you're someplace new," I tell him.

"Huh, well Fausto doesn't seem to be having any trouble."

"Yeah, sure, my ass. With all the noise you guys are making!" says Fausto's shadow behind us.

Actually we had both been whispering and I have my doubts that the tinkling of the spoon stirring the cup reached all the way upstairs.

"Oh well, now that you guys have woken me up, I might as well have a cup of chamomile too."

Fausto's wearing a pair of camo boxer shorts and a white wifebeater. Scratching the tribal tatt on his left arm, he turns a chair around backwards and sits down, leaning his chest against the backrest. I hand him a chamomile teabag, and he holds up his hand, with index and middle finger extended in a V, like a tough guy ordering a double whiskey from his usual bartender. It doesn't seem to me that a guy like him is going to be eager to be the first to take off his mask and engage in an honest discussion of what the hell we're planning to do next. Maybe Claudio would. Already a couple of times today it struck me that he was on the verge of coming out with something. I pounce eagerly when I hear him sigh.

"What's wrong?" I ask him in a friendly tone of voice.

"Nothing, why?" he replies, instantly on his guard.

"You sighed."

"Me?"

"I thought you did."

"No no."

The full moon casts a spectral light on the pit where the pool was supposed to go. The pile of dirt seems to be ready to cover up a giant corpse.

"The last time I stayed up until three in the morning it was with a mulatto girl," says Fausto.

"A Caribbean girl? A Latin American girl?" Claudio asks.

"An SST," risponde.

He wants someone—anyone—to ask him what SST stands for. I make the sacrifice.

"SST?"

"Super Sexy Tart," Fausto explains.

"Ah," says Claudio, mentally verifying the accuracy of the acronym.

Unlike the average human being, I'm able to perform two different tasks simultaneously. Like watching a green lizard skitter rapidly up the window glass and pretending to be interested in Fausto's story, for instance.

"I mean, heart-attack material, seriously, an athletic physique and a couple of knockers on her like the Graf Zeppelin," says Fausto, sketching out with both hands a pair of mammaries that were unlikely occurrences in the animal kingdom of this planet.

The green lizard's padded feet are amazing. They never lose their grip. I could draw an existential metaphor of some kind from them, something to do with a life made up of vertical movement, always striving upwards. Not horizontally, back and forth on the same plane, like my life.

"You've had plenty of girls, haven't you?" I ask, moving my first pawn onto the board in my chess match with Fausto.

"Well, you know, I don't know if it was me who had all those girls or the personality they saw on TV, there's no point in denying it . . . " he replies.

You see, I think to myself, Fausto isn't so stupid after all, there's some depth to him, he's not just skin deep.

"But who the fuck cares!" he adds, with a burst of lewd laughter. In the meanwhile, the lizard has vanished.

9

We'll have to replace nearly all the furniture in the farmhouse. Nearly everything is old and, with the exception of the sofa, the armchairs, the beds, and a few armoires, we're forced to buy everything. We find a wholesale outlet for used furniture and we leave first thing in the morning so we can shop methodically and pick out the very best items.

We wander around in the dreary warehouse and Fausto immediately falls in love with an array of card tables that must have belonged to a gambling den or, perhaps more plausibly, an old people's social club.

"Throw a tablecloth on them and you can use them for breakfast, lunch, and dinner. Take off the tablecloth and they're perfect for leisure time. Brilliant!" he says.

I look at the tables, but I have a hard time imagining them in the farmhouse. I can't say whether his suggestion is the splendid intuition of a born interior decorator or a sublime piece of idiocy.

"The idea doesn't really work for me. What do you think about them, Claudio?" I ask, and immediately I bite my lip.

If there's one thing I've learned about Claudio, it's this: never ask his opinion. He rarely has one but if pushed, his policy is to support whatever view is being argued most vehemently.

"They seem perfect to me," he says.

Without any real conviction I nod and head off to find some garden furniture.

"Wait, I've already spotted something," Fausto tells me.

The something to which he's alluding is a stack of white plastic lawn tables and chairs.

"Wait a minute, sorry, but are you saying we should get a bunch of ratty plastic lawn chairs?" I ask.

"What do you think we ought to put outdoors, Louis XI side chairs?" Even though I doubt he's talking about the right Louis, I get his point. So I wave to an assortment of wooden chairs and tables.

"Why don't we get these? They're much nicer!"

Fausto takes the price tag dangling on a length of twine from the backrest of one of the chairs and examines it, and then shoots me a glare.

"Listen, baby, I don't know if you've looked at the prices. I say let's buy the plastic chairs and once we start taking in some money, a little at a time, we can afford to buy better furniture."

"That makes sense to me," Claudio comments when I ill-advisedly give him a quizzical glance.

"Let's try to think like businessmen, if you please, not like a bunch of hysterical girls. The investment should be commensurate with the prospective earnings," says Fausto.

I remember very well that, when he was trying to talk us into forming this partnership in the first place, Fausto gave us a presentation of the potential earnings that would easily have included Louis the Whatever side chairs, but I decide that this is no time to start a pointless debate so I just passively agree.

The theory of commensurate investments leads us to acquire six card tables with twenty-four matching chairs, four small white plastic garden tables with one large rectangular white plastic dining table with twenty chairs, two black leather armchairs with purple seat cushions, yellow formica kitchen cabinets, bookshelves and credenzas of various colors, twin-door armoires made of imitation mahogany and three single camp beds.

The site inspection with the building contractor is a demoralizing experience. He walks through every room in the farmhouse accompanied by two young Romanian immigrants who don't speak a word of Italian, and shakes his head grimly at everything he sees. The size of the farmhouse and the checklist of jobs, he tells us, are going to mean a significant cost increase. Now, to the wiring and the roof, expenses that we'd already budgeted for, we're forced to add the demolition of the floors in two of the bathrooms to fix a water infiltration problem that we'd overlooked, as well as a new water heater.

When he gives us the estimate we can only put on expressions of astonishment and chagrin, but we lack the expertise to be able to judge the extent and the specific points upon which we can bargain. So we try on a couple of well tested techniques used by housewives: we make a pot of coffee, we offer to barter in kind with free lunches and dinners once the agritourism bed and breakfast is up and running, and we appeal to his professional ethics. With this old song and dance we manage to cadge a pathetic discount on labor, but when it's all said and done, we're still bound to run through all the cash we've saved up. Our disappointed faces don't seem to chip at the contractor's emotions in the slightest, so we play our last card: we decide to turn the tables by telling him we don't have the cash to underwrite such an expensive project and that we'll be forced to turn to other suppliers to explore their pricing. He seems unconcerned. In fact, he brusquely tells us that we'd better make up our minds within a week because he's about to take on another job and he won't be able to fit us in after that. He sees us and raises us, the bastard.

As soon as he gets in his car and drives away up the dirt road, we wish him farewell with a chorus of fuck-yous and hooked forearms. Fausto grabs his cell phone and starts scrolling through his phone book. He says there's no way he's giving that thief a single euro, and that he has a buddy who can do the same work for half the price, and that they're practically blood-brothers.

"Hey dude!" he launches into the phone call.

Then he announces that it's Fausto. Fausto, the one who sells watches, he's forced to explain. Then he says other things, but I'm unable to hear them because the rest of the phone call takes place out in the yard, far from our prying ears.

"Well, okay, I see where that's going . . . " says Claudio.

He pulls out his cell phone and says that he knows a reliable, honest contractor who renovated his supermarket. He says that with all the work he gave this guy, he'll definitely give him a substantial discount.

"Guess who this is?" he says into the phone.

The reply shouldn't last much longer than a first and last name. Instead the guy on the phone says a series of things that make Claudio fall silent and then step outside into the yard, where he walks up and down in Fausto's general vicinity.

I watch them. They pace back and forth, they kick a little gravel, they scratch their asses, they realign a loose testicle, they nod. And at last, for a good long while, nobody says another word.

10

The next day, with the construction workers already busy inside the farmhouse, the delivery truck arrives with our furniture. It's about time. The sheer cost of the renovations has crushed our enthusiasm and even triggered some vicious quarrels. While the new furniture is being unloaded in the yard, we start carrying some of the old pieces out to the shed. We'll see if we can sell them or, worst case, we can use them for firewood during the winter. The sun is beating down hard, but there's a light breeze that at first seems to make work tolerable, but only at first: after wrestling the heavy wooden table out of the kitchen, we're already wrecked. We make three separate stops on the way to the shed and, once we're there, the idea of going back out into the hot sun strikes me as nightmarish. Claudio has carried down two nightstands, after which he volunteers to go keep an eye on the two young Romanians. It's a cowardly excuse, we know it, but in a way it's useful. When we accepted that cutthroat plumber's estimate for the work, we swore that we would keep an eagle eye on everything he did and not let him get away with a thing. In this kind of situation, Claudio can be a real pain in the ass. It's almost as if he's taking cruel pleasure in torturing the workers, showing an aspect of his personality you'd never suspect was there.

I glue my sweaty back to the naugahyde of one of the new armchairs, while Fausto gulps bottled mineral salts. He massages his belly to show off his sculpted and waxed abs and pecs. As much work as he does to keep his muscles pumped, I'm not surprised that he takes every possible opportunity to show them off.

I pick up the remote control and click the television on.

"Ten minute break?" asks Fausto.

We start channel surfing, determine that there's nothing worth watching, and to double-check this self-evident truth we run back through the entire channel lineup three times. After a solid hour, Claudio comes sprinting down from upstairs, taking the steps two at a time.

"What, are you already worn out?" he asks, with an asthmatic wheeze that undercuts the thrust of his wisecrack.

"Take it easy on us, we're not in fighting trim like you are," I respond.

Fausto grins and slips me a wink.

"Everything's under control upstairs, I'm on their tails like a bloodhound," Claudio says.

"Outstanding, I want them to sweat blood!" Fausto drives the point home.

"Let's take our cue from the bloodhound," I say, "it's time to move some furniture."

Fausto gives me a slap on the back. It's practically as if he's pinned a medal on my chest assigning me a rank in his corporate hierarchy, a foothold allowing me to begin undermining his role of self-proclaimed leadership.

When it's time for the fun part of the day's work, arranging the furniture, Claudio decides that the Romanians have been properly trained and instructed and he decides to join us. We start with the living room, and it isn't long before the fun begins to pall. No matter how we arrange the furniture, the rooms look depressing and bare. In the end, more out of exhaustion than any real conviction, we decide the following: in the section of the living room with the fireplace, we set up the sofa, two armchairs, and the larger bookcase; in the other half of the living room we arrange the six card tables with their matching chairs. They look horrible, but before emitting any definitive verdicts, I'd like at least to try and see how they look with tablecloths.

We move on to the kitchen. The cabinets are a nightmare. It takes us two full hours to hang them and barely two seconds to see that the old cabinets were much better in every way. After all, the rest of the farmhouse is rustic in style, everything's made of dark wood, and yellow formica fits in like a swear word in church. Only Fausto, who has already ventured to decorate his own apartment in this exact same style, seems to be pleased with the effect.

"These are just more practical," he says.

"Well sure, they're definitely practical," says Claudio.

"Yeah, right, they're practical," I sum up.

All that's left to furnish on the ground floor is the residential area. That's where we'll live when all the other bedrooms are occupied by paying guests, so we decide to take our time and do things right. We move some of the old furniture pretty much at random, then we carry in the three single camp beds and the two small bookshelves.

"A little bare," says Claudio.

"Spare, I'd say. Essential," Fausto responds.

"Can we agree on minimalist?" I ask.

We slap a round of high-fives as a sign of our satisfaction and get ready to lay waste to the second floor. The entire floor is bedrooms, each of which has double windows across from the door, exposed roof beams, a double bed on one side and a double-door armoire on the other. We carry up the missing nightstands and armoires, moving them carefully to keep from scratching the hardwood floor, and when we're done we flop down exhausted on the bed.

"We'll set up the garden furniture tomorrow morning, what do you say?" asks Claudio.

"That's fine, we've done more than our share today," says Fausto.

My eyes are clouded with little black spots. My blood pressure must be low. What I need is a bottle of wine and a lavish dinner. I wish I felt as enthusiastic as Fausto, but I'm frankly overwhelmed. I don't know how to furnish a house, I can't take a look at a piece of furniture and envision the way it will look once you get it inside the house. I can't say if I like a room until it's done. I can't say if I find it elegant, miserable, or what. And the farmhouse, well, it looks to me as if it had been invaded by a colony of alien furniture from a distant planet. But it's night time, the lighting is dim, and nothing looks good if the light is bad.

"Agreed," I say.

11

The morning light is comforting. I wander around with a cup of coffee in my hand and decide that once we've furnished the farmhouse thoroughly with standing lamps, paintings, and curtains, the place will be perfect. I run into Claudio, whose eyes are glued to the morning news report. He has a few mosquito bites on his head, evidently the work of mosquitoes with a highly developed sense of humor, right in the middle of his bald patches. We exchange a greeting without emission of sound and I head back to get ready for the day's work.

Fausto is deciding on which pair of running shoes go best with his skin-tight Nike shorts. He has the wardrobe of a serial killer. Hanging on his closet rod are fifteen or so shirts, all pure white and immaculate; between one shirt and the next hang trousers of various styles but all black, all perfectly pressed; in the back of the closet are twenty or so pairs of shoes, black, and virtually identical. But they're not right for him. First, he tries on a pair of gym shoes with a large M on the side, then another pair with a large H. He likes the H better. Or, so it seems. He tries on the pair with the M again, then no, he's made up his mind, he likes the ones with the H, but he needs to change his shorts. So over the boxer shorts with a big CK printed on the elastic band, he puts on a pair of tech Bermuda shorts, also emblazoned with a CK.

While Claudio plays around with the plastic garden chairs, Fausto and I go exploring in the garden. We notice a series of large water pipes partially covered with dirt leading toward the half-excavated pit of the swimming pool, and in an excess of optimism we decide to hook up the last two lengths of pipe that are still lying abandoned on the ground. We spit on our hands like a couple of manly construction workers who've been doing this sort of thing all their lives, and we pick up the first length of pipe.

"Careful how you touch the pipes. There could be some ungrounded electric current and that would be the end of you!" Claudio shouts to us.

I look Fausto in the eye and silently persuade him not to

react. We pick up the pipe and try to line it up with the ninety-degree elbow sunken beneath ground level. You'd think it would be easy, but it's an awkward location and the nearly six-foot length of pipe is incredibly heavy and we can't seem to manage to hold it steady. Bending double, legs braced wide, I can only hold it in place for a few seconds at a time. We try switching around, but the same thing keeps happening. The mouth of the ninety-degree elbow is tight and we're trying to hold the pipe perfectly in line.

"What the hell is he looking at?" says Fausto angrily.

"He who?"

"The negro!"

Now that I look around, there is an African, bent over the tomato plants in the adjoining field, and he's looking over at us and shaking his head. He's one of those coal-black Africans, with a taut, hollowed face and well-defined musculature, like a living anatomical chart. Fausto lifts the pipe, I try to ease it into the angled receptacle and screw it in with my wrench, but after just a couple of seconds the bodybuilder's hands start trembling and the end of the pipe pops loose.

"Goddamn it to filthy hell!" Fausto shouts.

The African gesticulates, waving his arms and trying to convey something in pantomime. What's he trying to tell me? That I need to hold the pipe higher? Higher how? I raise the pipe in accordance with his gestures and accidentally smack it against Fausto's head.

"What the fuck did you do that for?" he shouts.

"Sorry, I was just trying to follow his instructions . . . "

"The negro's instructions? What are you, stupid? Oh, no-o-o-o, here he comes now!" The man has walked across the dirt road and now he's striding purposefully in our direction. He could either be someone our age who hasn't taken good care of himself or maybe a guy in his fifties who's in pretty good shape for his age.

"Stop calling him 'the negro' . . . and what do you know, maybe he knows how to do it!" I say in a low voice.

"What—you think he's ever laid pipe in his life? In his little mud hut back home?"

The African walks up, wiping the dirt off his hands on his trousers. I assume he's doing it so he can shake hands so I promptly extend my hand in his direction.

"Ciao," I say.

He looks at me in surprise and only responds after hesitating long enough to make me feel uncomfortable in turn. But that's not the only thing that makes me feel like an outsider. His skin is tough as shoe leather and as rough as granite. Shit, this guy really has worked all his life. And God only knows what ran through his mind as he was shaking my silky hand.

"Higher," he says, and demonstrates by raising his arm.

"The pipe should be higher? Is it too high?" I ask.

"If they make it that length they must know what they're doing," Fausto says, with his usual sarcastic tone.

The African turns to look at him.

"Hold it higher."

He bends down, unscrews the mouth of the ninety-degree elbow and turns it so it's pointing straight up.

"Now, hold pipe up above."

"Oh, I see! That way we can just set the pipe right down on top of it and tighten it down without difficulty," I say.

"Well, it's bound to work if he says so," Fausto observes.

In fact, it works perfectly. It takes us just a second to tighten the pipe, then we lay it down, tighten the elbow, and we're done.

"My name is Diego," I say, pounding one hand on my chest, then I point to him and ask: "What's your name?"

From the stunned expression that greets my gesticulations I realize that what I've just done was ridiculous.

"Abu," he says.

Fausto breaks out laughing.

"Really? Just like Yogi Bear's little friend?"

"You asshole, he said Abu, not Boo-Boo!" I snarl at him without even realizing it. Then I add: "He's Fausto. Thanks for the help. Would you like something to drink? Something to eat?"

"If I want to eat, I'd better go back to work." Abu turns around and walks slowly back toward the fields.

"Thanks," I call after him.

"Oh, but do you really think you should call me an asshole in front of a guest?" Fausto asks me, tapping me on the shoulder with one finger.

"A guest? You think you treated him like a guest? All those stupid wisecracks, the snide laughter, you never even shook hands with him," I note calmly.

"Listen Diego, I've got my own ideas about him. You ask me, he's an illegal immigrant. I'll put in a phone call to the Carabinieri and I'd like to see if your little boyfriend Boo-Boo is still around tomorrow."

I hate people who say "I've got my own ideas." You can almost always bet those are someone else's ideas, lovingly fished out of the filthy pools of the most despicable minds mankind has managed to produce. But it's too late now, I've lit the fuse and I might as well let it burn all the way down to the keg of dynamite. The bodybuilder needs to be set back on his heels; it'll all work better around here if it's made clear to him that he can only play at being Il Duce, Jr. if he keeps it within a set of clearly defined boundaries.

"What a piece of shit you are . . . maybe I should call the tax authorities, and we'll see which of you gets hauled off in handcuffs," I shoot back.

"Oh, nice! You'd need to beef up by about twenty pounds if you want to call me a piece of shit to my face!" and he takes a step toward me and drops one shoulder.

"Let me remind you that we're business partners, and even

if you are an advocate of going back to the good old ways of the Neolithic Era, you're going to have to interact with me just as if you were a civilized human being!"

That leaves him speechless just long enough for me to turn my back on him and begin a highly dignified strategic withdrawal.

"Oh, aren't you all so smart!" he shouts after me.

When you shift into the plural, the class-action insult, there's no telling where things'll wind up.

"Right now he's just picking tomatoes, but later, when he's out of work, he'll be lurking around the corner with a switchblade in his hand, and I'd like to hear your Communist party line then! Fucking fair-weather Gandhis!"

Communists, Gandhis, he's lost his mind. We've come to the point in the conversation where I just stop answering. This is when I realize that after all there's not much left of Italy, this nation of saints, poets, and great thinkers.

12

At first I was sorry about my fight with Fausto, because I exacerbated a situation that was already uncomfortable, and moreover I did so for a damned illegal immigrant who means nothing to me. In the end, though, things went better than I expected. Fausto sulked around for half a day, then he made the first overture, telling me we should have a heart-to-heart and clear up what had happened and stake out our real philosophical positions. The discussion was a long tactical skirmish, a strategic minuet in which, with one step forward and two steps back, we tried to prove to one another that our belief systems aren't actually all that different after all, that all told, with some minor nuances, we both really see things in the same light, that we really can be friends. We scrutinized one another and rounded off the corners of our respective ideals, doing our best to make them fit with the other guy's. I have to admit, I did some pretty extreme rounding off and corner-shaving. In the end, we came to common ground that we can summarize as follows, to put it into words that Fausto might have used: negroes are okay, as long as they work hard, but the minute they pull something, back home they go, and on their own dime, not with charter flights underwritten by the Italian tax-payer; faggots are okay, because deep down they're people just like us, but all we ask is that they be faggots strictly in the comfort of their homes, and not to put on any exhibitionistic shows we'd just as soon not see, thank you very much; but the gypsies, unfortunately, are beyond salvaging, with all the benevolence in the world, sorry but they need to go back to wherever they came from, even if they were born in Italy. With an admirable show of good sense, we avoided taking the discussion onto religious territory, so the fate of Jews and Muslims was left to be determined at some later date.

After a morning of work that, to keep up our morale, we describe as 'not particularly productive,' we're slacking off for a few minutes on the plastic lounge chairs, enjoying a cigarette and the view. My lounge chair is tilting off to one side because one of the legs is collapsing, but I keep that to myself.

"Let me tell you, I'm feeling pretty good," Fausto says.

"I'm not," Claudio replies. This morning he woke up irritable.

"Oh come on, Claudio, this is what it means to believe in something . . . struggling, sweating, hanging on by your finger-tips to the things you care most about. We have to be ready to make any sacrifice in order to achieve our ultimate objective!"

It sounds like a deathless exchange of vows between two heroes of the Italian Risorgimento, but it's actually a conversation between a couple of idiots who failed to do some basic arithmetic and are now realizing that they'll have to sell their cars if they want to pay the contractors.

"Well, that may be. But I'm done with all this. We're out of money. And why don't you shove over . . . "

"What do you mean?"

"Shove over with your lounge chair, I'm crowded right under a branch loaded down with pine cones. A friend of mine got a concussion when one of those things fell on him."

"Yeah, okay . . . Anyway, even if we're going to have to sell our cars to pay for the roof job, we won't need any more money after that. In fact, that's when money will start pouring in," says Fausto, who throws himself back in his chair with a huge happy smile that's immediately interrupted by the loud crack of the plastic backrest.

By now, people's reactions are pretty subdued. Aside from Fausto's shortlived moments of enthusiasm, we're all just waiting for the moment when we're going to have to look each other in the eye and admit the truth.

"Let's just hope we don't have to pay to have the road repaved," I say as we watch a small red Renault come frantically jouncing and jerking up the dirt lane.

"There's nothing wrong with the road. Of course, the problem is that there are still people driving cars from the last century . . . I can't wait to meet this genius," Fausto says.

But his mocking smile fades quickly into disbelief and then dies out on a note of despair.

"What's the matter?" I ask him.

He stands up, dons an expression of overjoyed surprise, and walks over to the car, which has come to a stop, with both arms thrown wide open.

"Sergio! You have no idea how hard I've tried to get in touch with you!"

The first thing you notice about Sergio the minute he steps out of the car is that, compared to him, Fausto looks like a medium-sized dwarf. Curly red hair, overgrown beard, long-shoreman's shoulders, and a prominent belly, the kind of belly that on a guy like that is much scarier than a rack of ripped abs. The hasty smile that the man flashes at me and Claudio, before making a beeline for Fausto, isn't exactly reassuring.

"You tried to get in touch with me, eh? You son of a god-damned . . . " Those are the last words we hear before the two of them disappear behind the veranda. They walk along taking turns grabbing each other's neck and punching each other in the ribs like a couple of rough-hewn burly friends. Or at least that's what Fausto's body language is trying desperately to convey to us.

Seated around the kitchen table, we listen to Fausto, seated next to Sergio, as he solemnly addresses us.

"For years, Sergio has supervised production on all the television broadcasts of my home shopping shows and he's much more than a friend to me. We've been through a lot together . . . handkerchief, please."

Without taking my eyes off his face, I hand him a kleenex. Fausto grabs it and uses it to stanch the blood flowing out of his nose, which is purple and swollen as an eggplant.

"Thanks. So, I was saying . . . in other words, Sergio is going to be a partner in our little enterprise with 50 percent of my share . . . "

He pauses briefly, just long enough to swallow a clump of clotting blood, sip some water, and resume his speech.

"He's going to give us a hand until opening day, then, since we have only a limited amount of living space here, he'll just come down from time to time to lend a hand and see how things are going . . . "

Sergio nods at every word, and so do Claudio and I.

"Well, anyway, if you have any questions for him . . . " Fausto trails off, sick of talking by now, and tilts his head back to stop the bleeding.

"Any problems?" Sergio asks us.

I'm not in the habit of having problems with people who weigh a good seventy pounds more than me. And after all, it's an extra pair of strong arms that will only cost us a share of Fausto's profits. So I decide to give voice to Claudio's nervous head-shaking.

"No," I say.

"No no, absolutely not," Claudio says.

"Of course not," Fausto says, caustically. And once he sees us looking at him, he adds: "My nose . . . you watch, it'll probably bleed for the rest of the day."

13

We show Sergio around the farmhouse. Like so many tour guides, we accompany him up and down the hallways and stairs and through every room in the place, telling him about our projects and showing him the work that's being done. The whole time, Fausto raises expectations for the living room. "We're saving the living room for last!" he says, and then, when we're finally about to enter, he shouts: "Close your eyes and only open them once you're in the middle of the room!"

Sergio goes along with the game, closing both eyes for a second and then opening them again when Fausto throws the doors open. I'm standing behind him so I can't see the expression on his face, but I do detect a sinister stiffening of his whole body. Then he finally takes a step forward and starts wandering among the tables, grazing the tabletops with one finger, and finally takes up a stance in a corner to study the overall effect of the room.

"I feel right at home . . . it looks exactly like a community center," he says.

With a grimace of bewilderment, Sergio lowers the curtain

on our careers as interior designers and demands the punch list of work to be done. He slowly leafs through the pages and shakes his head sadly more than once.

"What's wrong?" I ask.

"Eh, what's wrong? . . . what's wrong is you're just throwing away a lot of money." Fausto takes the list out of Sergio's hand and starts reading it again as if he didn't already know it by heart.

"None of these projects are so big that we would have to call a plumber. The electric system needs to be brought up to code, okay, but you're wasting thousands of euros on work that we can easily do ourselves," says Sergio.

"But what about jackhammering the floors and installing new pipes?" asks Fausto.

"There's no leak. Those stains in the ceiling have been there for years. All you need to do is put your hand against them and you can feel for yourself!"

"We believed what the plumber told us," I say.

"He's a con artist. When you showed me the bathroom where they're doing the work, didn't you notice that the pipes are brand new? They probably just poured some water on them right before we walked in," says Sergio.

Fausto slaps the stack of paper down on the table.

"The fact is there aren't any Italian plumbers left, not one! You can't believe a thing these guys tell you, they take advantage of you, they know exactly what they're doing . . . and they stick it to you every time. I wish they'd go back to their own country to stick it to their own people!" he says, his voice gradually rising to a shriek.

I flash Fausto a disgusted glance, from one Neo-Nazi comrade to another, and turn my back on him. Then I turn to Sergio and give him a glance that contains all my disdain for Fausto's unfortunate outburst.

"And what about you, Claudio, what the hell have you been

keeping your eyes on for the past few days? Weren't you supposed to be a human bloodhound?" shouts Fausto.

"Me-e-e?" cries Claudio hitting a high note in his falsetto.

"What the hell's the matter with you all? You ought to be glad you're going to save a bunch of money," says Sergio.

"He's right. If he's confident that we can take on all these projects then we can just tell the contractor that we've changed our minds and we only want him to bring the electrical system up to code," I suggest.

"Of course I'm confident, I rebuilt three community centers single-handed, for practically no money at all," Sergio says.

I stop to ponder two words at a time. First of all, "community" and "centers," and I feel a surge of anxiety, then "no" followed by "money," and the anxiety vanishes like morning dew.

Before we decide to call off the contractor officially, we decide to put Sergio to the test. Fausto opens the door that leads into the *taverna*, mentions a simple little chore that needs to be done, and I immediately guess that he's referring to the clogged toilet. Sergio walks ahead of us and I take advantage of the opportunity to flash my partner a playful grimace.

"Nice simple little chore! You're such a bastard," I whisper.

Fausto smiles wickedly as if I'd just paid him the finest compliment in the world, and heaps it on a little higher.

"It's child's play, Claudio was going to take care of it . . . " he tells Sergio.

We walk into the bathroom in the *taverna* and Sergio looks around with a quizzical expression.

"If you don't think you can do it, we'll take care of it ourselves," I say, strictly for Fausto's enjoyment.

"What are you saying to me? For something this stupid?" he responds.

Working with the toilet plunger and several bottles of muriatic acid, the three of us have already spent a total of at least six hours on this toilet. Now we're eager to savor a minor moral victory, so we elbow for prime viewing position. Just watching Sergio roll up his sleeves brings a smile to our faces. I hand him the plunger but he holds up one hand flat and refuses it. He picks up a rubber glove and slips it on, holding his hand high as if he were a surgeon. Then he wraps a floor rag around his clenched fist. When he lowers his forearm into the toilet, we all take a step backward and start snickering. Then Sergio delivers a powerful piston-like thrust without splashing so much as a drop of water. The roar of flushing water sweeps away the residual slime and toilet paper, all spinning away neatly down the drain.

"Let me go tell those two Romanians to stop working right now," Fausto says.

Like a group of interns, we follow the new head physician up and down the hallways of the farmhouse, watching in awe as he replaces the gaskets on leaky faucets, unblocks a sticky lock, and replaces rusty radiator valves. In less than four hours' time, Claudio checks off roughly one third of the items on our punch list. They're all minor items, it's true, but the psychological aspect of the situation is fundamental. We're so recharged with enthusiasm that when the name of the plumbing contractor appears on the display of Fausto's cell phone, we all rush to be the first to answer.

The telephone call unfolds in three acts. In Act One, also called "The Surprise," the plumber expresses his amazement at our decision. We explain to him that we figured out about the fraudulent leak and that we can't consider continuing to work with a contractor we no longer trust. The man tries say that it's impossible, that there's definitely a leak, and so at Sergio's suggestion we tell him that we'll let the pipe dry out, then we'll turn on the water and he can come see for himself. Act One ends with him putting all the blame on his Romanian workers. In Act Two, also called "The Threat," the plumber talks about penalties we'll have to pay for canceling his contract, other jobs he's turned down, materials he's already purchased. We tell him that we have no intention of paying his penalties because the work that was done was done badly, and we offer to cover 50 percent of the cost of materials, but only after he presents us with invoices proving that he actually purchased the building materials. The plumber tells us there are no invoices because, in an attempt to help us out and lower his costs, he bought everything off the books. Act Two ends with the plumber putting all the blame on the manufacturers of building materials and their skyrocketing prices. Act Three, also called "The Agreement," witnesses us striking a hard-fought compromise according to which we'll pay for the work done so far, reimburse him for the materials acquired, but at cost, and honor the contract for the work on the electrical system. On his end, he agrees to redo the bathroom floor, which was wrongly demolished, cancel the order for the new water heater without penalties, and give us a 10 percent discount on his price for the work on the electrical system.

We raise our glasses to the successful outcome of the phone call and we start recalculating our accounts. The way we reckon things up, if we manage to do the work on the roof ourselves and keep the hot water heater limping along without replacing it entirely, there's a decent chance we'll actually manage to cover all our expenses and avoid having to sell our cars.

14

We're all on our feet bright and early, eager to get busy and scratch more items off our punch list. With the building materials that we have on hand, the only project that we can undertake is the work that needs to be done on the wooden shutters.

A job that in Claudio's new punch list is classified with a triple underlining, and therefore "Extremely Demanding." As always, before beginning work on an Extremely Demanding project, we try to attain the proper level of concentration by turning on the television set.

"Well?" says Sergio.

"We'll be there soon," I say.

"You go on ahead," Fausto reassures him.

But he doesn't budge. In fact, he stops and stares as if he'd never seen three grown men sitting in front of a television in his life. He's trying to make us feel ridiculous, but it's too late for that. The morning TV programming, which involves puppet shows for children and cooking shows for housewives, has already taken care of that.

The hinges are all rusty. We have to dismount the shutters so we can replace the hinges. Then we have to sand the wood and repaint the shutters. The whole wooden shutter affair becomes the terrain for Sergio and Fausto to resume their long-running feud. While Claudio and I work in a team on the same shutter without managing to impose our will, Fausto grabs one with both hands and, grunting, gets his shoulder under it, finally managing to separate the hinges in a matter of seconds. Sergio watches the operation and then grabs the other shutter and, with a simple smack of the hand, dismounts it. In an attempt to catch up with the rival team, I start spraying WD-40 onto the hinges while Claudio tries out the hand-smack technique. By the time we finally get the first shutter dismounted, Sergio and Fausto have already piled up all the second-story shutters in front of us, and have moved off toward a large dead tree that the wind knocked over. We get busy with the sandpaper and as we work, we watch a duel between the two ax men. The guiding rule appears to be unmistakable: taking more than one stroke of the ax to remove a branch means you're a sissy. In the time it takes us to sand four shutters apiece, a thirteen-foot-tall tree has been reduced to an orderly stack of wood ready for burning in the fireplace.

Fausto stops to catch his breath. He's dripping with sweat and could stand a little wringing out. His hands are covered with blisters. Sergio takes this opportunity to shred his adversary once and for all. He strides over to the wooden palisade that rises out of the tall grass. He uproots the posts by clutching them to his chest and then bracing his legs to jerk them out of the earth. Then he separates the palings, nailed solidly into place, as if they were so many chopsticks from some sushi restaurant. Every action this man takes could be broadcast as a commercial for sheer manliness

"Good idea, you get started, in a little while I'll relieve you!" Fausto shouts at him.

"If it weren't for this damned hernia of mine . . . " he adds, gingerly touching his back.

Fausto the contractor-in-chief has handed over his scepter. Sergio is a born leader. And his leadership is rendered annoyingly easy by our total collective incompetence.

It seems as if we're at Fort Apache: the arrival of any car driving up the dirt road is heralded by a cloud of dust.

The car that's coming up the road this time is an old dark green Alfa Romeo Giulia 1300. It's a car we've seen in hundreds of movies, sometimes being driven by cops, other times by criminals. The car pulls to a halt, and at first glance the man driving would appear to be a farmer. Classical music comes wafting out of the half-open car windows. The impression conveyed is that a film editor has made a mistake, mismatching the sound track with the film. The music I'd expect to hear wafting out of the windows of that car would either be snatches of Neomelodic music, or perhaps a tarantella. My God, how the peasantry has changed over the years. I walk over to the car expecting to see a musclebound guy sitting behind the wheel, with a wrinkle-creased face, and a checkered shirt. Instead, what I see through the windshield is a musclebound guy with a wrinkle-creased face sporting a pair of wrap-around sunglasses, a manila-brown suit, and a white shirt with a collar sprawling out over the jacket. A mix of Mario Merola and Tony Manero.

The man switches off the radio, gets out of the car, and slams the door. The radio comes back on by itself and the man silences it with a flat-handed smack to the dashboard through the open window. He stands poised for a few seconds, glaring at the radio, and then, when he's finally sure he's stunned it into a coma, he turns to look at me.

The two alpha males barely deign to glance in my direction, and then they go back to the challenge of dealing with what's left of the palisade. Claudio, on the other hand, is busily sand-papering away, head down, eager to avoid involvement in the drudgery of interacting with a neighbor. I smile at the elderly peasant, bracing myself to turn down an offer to purchase an array of local cheeses. The man walks over to me with an overly theatrical display of cordiality and shakes hands. They must not even know what Nivea Cream is around here, I think to myself.

"You guyz noo aroun' heah?" the old man asks.

"Yes, we just moved here a couple of weeks ago. Are you a neighbor?"

"This's a small town, we're all neighbors, know what I mean? You starting some kind of business?"

He looks around circumspectly.

"That's right, an agritourism bed and breakfast . . . "

"So, you got all your permits and everything, huh?"

I'll bet he's a plainclothes cop.

"Yes, certainly, we only need a certificate of occupancy from town hall, but they only issue that when construction is complete."

"Those guys don't count for shit. You want permits, you gotta ask the people who really count."

I must have misunderstood the meaning of his words because, despite the arrogance in his voice, the man's face is still sunny and encouraging.

"So who really counts?" I ask.

"There's people that have been living here for, oh, about a hundred years. Very old families, my frien'."

The word "families" sends a shiver down my back. And suddenly the suit, which I was having a hard time reconciling with my image of a peasant, now dovetails perfectly with my concept of a *camorrista*, a Mafioso in the Camorra network of crime families indigenous to Campania, the region surrounding Naples.

"This land belongs to us, we bought it with our own money," I say.

"Of course it's your proppity, you're in charge. You're in charge of living the way God commands, you're in charge of living with a world of problems, hell, you're in charge of living or dying as you t'ink best."

I stand there, speechless. Sergio notices my blank gaze and hurries over looking worried. Seeing him striding toward me reassures me. His face is completely sun-scorched but he mops the sweat from his brow with a coarse rag, without the slightest sign of pain. My interlocutor doesn't seem to be particularly impressed.

"*Buon giorno*," Sergio says to the fake peasant. "What's up?" he asks me.

"Are you a partner?" asks the *camorrista*.

"And just who would you be?"

"I'm just a friend who's dropped by to offer a little friendly advice."

"What kind of advice?"

The guy, who doesn't seem to like spending time in the warm

sunshine, puts on a weary expression and provides Sergio with an abridged Reader's Digest version of the little speech he just delivered to me.

"You ain't from heah, you can't be expected to know the way things work in this part of the world. There's a lot of bad people heah. I can offer you protection."

"Are you a security guard?" Sergio asks.

"No, see, what he's saying . . . " I start to say, and then trail off without knowing exactly how to put it.

The *camorrista* laughs in a way that makes my flesh crawl.

"A policeman, a Carabiniere, who the fuck is he?" Sergio goes on, his voice growing louder.

"Let's do this: you take the night to think over what I've just explained to you, and tomorrow morning we talk it over again. Ah, and tomorrow morning, let's see if we can come to another concloosion. In this part of the world, you're just a crew of new arrivals," he says, pointing his finger disdainfully at Sergio.

And here the man has miscounted his cards. I'm an asshole who has a hard time controlling his bladder when someone raises their voice. But Sergio is an asshole who has perfect control of his bladder. What he has trouble controlling is his fists.

The *camorrista* flies backward. Without embroidering too fancifully on the straightarmed smack that Sergio gave him, I would still be willing to swear that the man rose straight up a good eight inches from the ground before spinning around in midair and landing face-first.

There's a second of silence, followed by a series of shouts:

"You piece of shit! I'll drop-kick your ass all the way back to town!" (Sergio)

"You fucking shithead. You're a dead man!" (The *camorrista*).

"Stop it, Sergio! Stop!" (Fausto)

"Oh! Oh-oh-oh! What the . . . !" (Claudio)

I leap onto Sergio's back, but I'm completely ineffectual in my efforts to keep him from smacking the guy again. As if all he were carrying on his back was a rucksack instead of an overweight adult male, he leans over to grab the *camorrista*. He stands up, foaming at the mouth, and with one hand clutches at his waistband. His handgun is lying on the ground but before he can pick it up we pile onto him.

"Let's get him out of here, hustle him inside!" Sergio shouts.

"Lemme go, you piece-a shit! You're all dead men!"

We haul him bodily into the kitchen and we thrust him into a chair. With trembling hands, Claudio pulls open a drawer, pulls out a length of string for trussing a roast, and starts to tie up his wrists.

"What the hell are you doing? Go get the duct tape!" Sergio shouts.

Claudio jerks in alarm at the sound, grabs the duct tape, and puts it into Sergio's hands before crumpling to the floor.

"Claudio!" I shout in fright.

"Now what's wrong with him?" Fausto shouts, more in annoyance than concern. While I tend to the faintee, holding his legs up to help his circulation, Sergio, with practiced and slightly sinister expertise, ties the *camorrista*'s hands together at the wrist.

"What do you think you're doing, you bunch of little faggots! When they come looking for me, you're going to be a roomful of corpses!"

Other threats follow, but we manage to muffle them with a dish sponge and a length of duct tape.

I drag Claudio out of the kitchen, I raise his legs onto the armrest of an easy chair, and I flop down onto the sofa. My own legs are shaking and I'm afraid that if I remain standing the others will notice. Fausto sits down next to me, cradling his head in his hands. Sergio paces back and forth.

"We've fucked up, my God, we've fucked up completely!" I say.

"No, it's Sergio who has fucked up. Now, Sergio, you go in there, say you're sorry, and we'll resolve everything!" says Fausto.

We sit there looking at each other for a few minutes. We gradually start saying things that make better sense. We immediately agree that apologizing to somebody like this guy isn't likely to do the trick. I venture the idea of calling the police, but Sergio and Fausto disagree. I imagine they both have problems with the law in their past, so I don't push the point, in part because it's clear to me that if we report the attempted extortion, we might have to enter a government witness protection program, and in any case that would put an end to our plan to start an agritourism bed and breakfast. We'd also spend the rest of our lives worrying that one day they'd find a way to settle the score with us. In that case, we might as well just walk away from the farmhouse immediately, leaving the keys in the door.

That last thought makes it clear to us why the farmhouse sold at the rock-bottom price and why the previous owners walked away from it immediately after undertaking a series of costly renovations. We rack our brains for other solutions, but we can't seem to come up with any way of living without fear and completing the project we've begun. I feel helpless, but that's an experience I just went through, and the last thing I want is to relive it. I'm filled with a growing wave of anger, and Sergio seems to be aware of it.

"We're not leaving here. If anything, we can arrange for him to disappear," he says.

"Fuck you, Sergio, I'm not arranging for anyone to disappear! Who the hell have you taken us for?" I ask.

"I mean, we'll make him disappear into the *taverna*! We'll lock him up in there!" he explains.

Fausto shakes his head and smiles nervously. But it strikes me as a good idea. It's insane, of course, but it's also the only idea so far that doesn't involve buckling under and accepting what's happened to us.

"Sergio's right . . . we'll open the agritourism bed and breakfast and as soon as we've made all our money back we'll get out of here. Sell the place. And then we'll let him go," I say.

"Are you crazy? That'll take at least . . . " says Fausto.

"It'll take as long as it takes. I'm not going bankrupt just because of some fucking Mafioso!" I say.

"They'll come looking for him, you know that, right?"

"We'll just say that we've never seen him, that he never came around here!"

"What about his car?"

"We'll roll it down a gorge somewhere!"

"Oh, sure . . . they'd find it immediately!"

"Okay, then, we'll burn it . . . "

"Great, a huge fire with lots of smoke, that way no one'll notice a thing!"

"Now that's enough!" says Sergio. "If we've all made up our minds that we're not going to let the first Mafioso punk who wanders by ass-fuck us royally, then you can rest assured that we'll be able to come up with a way of getting rid of the car. Are we agreed?"

Fausto doesn't look convinced, and I try to imagine what the right button to push would be with a guy like him. Just what would trigger his pride. Fatherland and honor, I venture to guess.

"Fausto, this land belongs to us, let's take it back, for God's sake!" I whisper.

He closes both eyes and takes a deep, deep breath.

"Yes," he says to Sergio.

"Yes," I say.

We turn to look at Claudio who's lying there unconscious,

with the tip of his tongue protruding from the corner of his mouth.

"Excellent, 100 percent of the electorate that is currently conscious has voted in favor of the motion to hold out against all odds!" says Sergio, holding up his clenched fist.

15

Convincing Claudio wasn't easy. After blocking him twice at the front door, suitcases in hand, it's not until early evening that we succeed in persuading him to say. Part of the process is writing out a statement in longhand, signed by both me and Fausto, in which we state that he took no part in coming up with the plan. To make up for that, we have quickly come up with a way of making the Giulia disappear.

At sunset we walk down in the swimming pool pit and start digging into one of the sides in order to create a ramp down which we'll be able to roll the car. We dig with determination and, I feel pretty sure, the whole time every one of us is mentally repeating the same six words: we, are, doing, something, incredibly, stupid.

The dirt is soft, it's easy to shovel, but after an hour we've barely scratched the vertical face of the wall and we're already tired as dogs. To make the situation even more complicated, Abu shows up out of the darkness with his lazy gazelle gait and heads straight toward us. We just have enough time to agree on a lie to stick to when the African appears, looking down from the edge of the pit.

"Ciao Abu," I say. "Sergio, this is Abu, he works in the fields around here . . . "

Before I can even finish the introductions, the African has leapt into the pit, grabbed the shovel out of my hands, and started digging.

"What the fuck are you doing?" Fausto asks him.

"I'm helping you," says Abu.

"It's not necessary," I cut in. "We won't need the pool until summer, there's plenty of time . . . "

"I saw everything. Better finish this tonight," says Abu.

"Who else saw?" Sergio asks.

"Them," the African replies, pointing out into the fields. In the distance, we see two other Africans coming toward us. They're younger than Abu, twenty or so, and they're dressed like rappers, with baggy jeans and T-shirts. They too jump down into the pit and start digging.

"What is this, an invasion? Did we declare war on Nigeria and no one thought to tell us?" Fausto asks us.

"We are from Ghana," one of the young men replies without even looking at us.

"This is taking longer than I expected, we'd better lock up the prisoner," says Sergio, and gestures for me to follow him.

"Hey, where are you going? What are you, leaving me with the . . . eh?" calls Fausto.

The word "prisoner" has traumatized me. I follow Sergio like a robot, indifferent to Fausto's complaints and Claudio's astonished gaze.

We untie the *camorrista*, we lock arms with him, and we drag him down into the *taverna*. The minute we ungag him, the old man starts shouting. His attitude seems to have changed, he seems bewildered, disoriented. He can't seem to place our reaction or figure out what we intend to do with him. Words, gestures, hints, and sarcastic smiles that have worked successfully for a lifetime have suddenly and inexplicably malfunctioned, and now he's at a loss. He can't think of anything to do but yell. We inspect the *taverna* for any dangerous objects, but aside from two empty bottles that we remove, there's nothing.

We take advantage of his wild screams to do a test. We shut

and lock the door of the *taverna*: his voice echoes terrifyingly. Then, after we climb the stairs and close the kitchen door as well, you can hardly hear a thing. Of all the words he's shouting, we can barely make out an "I'm-a kill you all!"

"It could work," says Sergio. "If we soundproof the doors with phonoabsorbent insulation, we don't have to worry about a thing."

Incredibly, I actually find the idea reassuring.

At three in the morning we're done shoveling and we throw ourselves down panting onto the grass. Sergio climbs aboard the Giulia, starts the engine and, in first gear, riding the brake, he drives it down the ramp. Then he turns off the engine, wipes the steering wheel clean of fingerprints with his handkerchief, and gets out of the car with a waterproof tarp in one hand. He tosses it over the roof of the car and starts stretching it down over the sides carefully. A little too carefully.

"He's crazy," Fausto whispers to me.

"Well, as long as he's at it . . . " I say.

The Africans pull their T-shirts over their sweaty skin and, just as unhurriedly as they arrived, they depart back toward the tomato fields.

"You have two and a half hours to fill in hole," says Abu. We nod in agreement, but we waste a few precious minutes standing there, watching the strong slender figures vanishing into the darkness.

"He could even blackmail us," Fausto says.

We're too weary to start a serious conversation about all the potential risks involved in Abu's involvement, so we go back to gripping the handles of our shovels with our blistered hands. The fear of letting the sun rise with the Giulia still above ground gives us the strength to go on working, heads down, uncomplaining despite the intense pain.

At 4:30 A.M. the job is almost finished and we're seized with a wave of unjustified enthusiasm.

"We've done it!" I say.

"Great work!" says Sergio.

"Tomorrow we'll buy grass seed and in two weeks, no more, we'll have a handsome new lawn here."

The two musclebound men scatter the extra dirt into the hollows. Claudio and I take care of compacting it by jumping up and down on it and smacking it with the backs of our shovels. The sky is abnormally star-spangled, like the ceiling of a planetarium. It seems like a good omen. Nothing bad can happen under a sky that looks like that. Sergio tosses the last shovelful of dirt onto a pothole and I pound it down with a couple of vertical leaps, both feet joined at the ankle.

"Done!" I say, and emphasize the completion of the job by smacking my shovel down onto the soil.

If at that very moment, a spring of fresh water had bubbled from the ground, I think our amazement would have been relatively restrained. But instead, what begins to rise from the earth directly beneath my feet are the carefree notes of a well played violin.

"What did you do, leave the radio on?" Fausto asks in a small, frightened voice.

"I never even touched it," Sergio replies.

Bone-weary and frightened, we let ourselves drop to the ground one after the other. The music, muffled and diffused evenly over the terrain, envelops us. There's something surreal about this situation. And beautiful, in an odd way. The stars overhead, the music rising from beneath us. We lie there stretched out on the grass until the first light of dawn, perhaps out of animal weariness, or maybe just in the hope that the battery might run down any minute.

16

The notes from a triumphal march filtering up from the Giulia and its anything-but-run-down battery convince us to turn our minds to a more lucid consideration of our situation. We take advantage of Sergio's absence—he's gone into town to buy tools—and we take seats around the table. We agree that we can't be held hostage by a lunatic who has already taken a dangerous criminal prisoner. We have to give peace a chance and see if we can come to some sort of reasonable terms with the *camorrista*.

"It won't be easy. He's arrogant. He thinks he's stronger than us. After all, people like him are in charge here," I say.

"It's not that they're stronger, it's just that they have nothing to lose," says Fausto.

He stands up, he massages his abs, and he adjusts his Rolex, a gesture that, as I've learned by now, is a prelude to another one of his tirades.

"Then come on, let's analyze these *camorristi*? That's what we do, right? We look at them, we understand who they are, and in a flash we figure out how to con them," he says.

Claudio stares, open-mouthed.

"All right, then, let's analyze us some *camorristi*," I say, confident that no one will detect the irony.

In fact, Claudio nods and Fausto starts pacing back and forth.

"Low levels of education, working-class culture, living the good life . . . " I toss out, just to get the lesson started.

"Wrong!" says Fausto, leveling his index finger straight at me. Claudio shakes his head, exactly the way a treacherous bastard classmate would have done at school.

"What good life? These people aren't living the good life. The good life is the mirage that keeps them locked into the organization . . . this is multilevel marketing, my friends!"

I don't know whether to laugh in his face or agree with him, and my momentary hesitation proves fatal.

"Multilevel, guys! A pyramid scheme, a hierarchical organization! They all dream of easy money, but the only ones who really see any cash are at the tip of the pyramid. All the others, in a cascading hierarchy, make less and less in direct proportion to increasing levels of risk, the lower you go."

"And so?" I ask.

"And so the guy who came down here today is at the base of the pyramid, did you see the car he drives? He's not living the good life, he's just dreaming about it."

"Okay, so?"

"So now we know our enemy. All we have to do is find his weak spot!"

Fausto sits down across from us, elbows on the table and hands joined, pressed against his mouth. Claudio takes over Fabio's shift, standing up and pacing around the room while looking at the ceiling with both hands interlocked behind his back. I can't seem to think clearly. It strikes me that reexamining our situation is certainly the right thing to do, but deep down the only thing I hope is that we don't decide to fold our hand and mildly accept defeat. I'm a man who has wiped my father's ass, goddamnit, not just any idiot off the street. The role of powerless spectator is not one I choose to accept any more. So I try to concentrate, because this time, at least, I want to work to find a solution. Still, nothing illuminating pops into my head, but I'm ready to do anything to kick them into line. Okay, now, he's an old man, he's being held against his will at the bottom of a pyramid, which means he's working to enrich other people, he's living on the crumbs they toss him, and, unlike a young man, by now he's figured out how the thing works, and the only thing he really wants now is to find a way to go off quietly into a peaceful retirement.

"I've got it!" Claudio exclaims, interrupting my train of thought.

"Go on," Fausto encourages him.

"This guy is at the base of the pyramid, so they just throw him some scraps . . . what do you think his cut could be? You think 5 percent? Ten percent? Well, we'll just double the offer!"

"I'm not sure I follow you," I say.

"We just pay him, it'll cost us a few hundred euros instead of several thousand. Not bad, right?"

"And how is he supposed to go back to his boss without the money?"

"That's his problem, we give him twice what he would normally get just so that he can dream up some excuse. Now it's his problem," Claudio reiterates the point.

"We can do better than that," says Fausto, to keep up the troops' morale. And he resumes his meditative pose.

"These are people who have nothing to lose . . . nothing to lose . . . " Fausto mutters to himself under his breath.

Shitty lives, shitty families, shitty friends. It's true, these people have nothing to lose. Never go up against someone who has nothing to lose. That's the real point. They face off regularly with people who don't want to lose their comfortable evenings watching TV, their enjoyable Saturday afternoons at the trattoria, their two weeks paid holiday at the beach, and that's enough to make them seem invincible. I can't see a solution, but a thought does begin to surface. A *camorrista* should never take on someone else who, like him, has nothing to lose. He should never take on, for instance, us.

In the middle of the night with the door shut tight, in Claudio's room because it's the room that's farthest from Sergio's, we go on with our conspiratorial brainstorming session. There are lengthy silences during which it's extremely difficult not to drop off to sleep, the already infrequent suggestions grow worse as time goes on, and morale is steadily declining. Around two in the morning we decide to summarize our results. Aside from Claudio's initial proposal, we've come up with an "incentive" program that rewards the *camorristi* according to the number of guests they manage to bring to the agritourism bed and breakfast, along with an offer to barter, whereby we'd take care of wedding, first communion, and confirmation dinners for the local *camorristi*, up to a maximum of four annually. Then comes a series of fanciful ideas designed to discourage the gangsters, such as offering special discounts for Carabinieri and policemen, or else hosting national judo meets. Fausto, even though his only active contribution has been the incentive program, is disgusted and he writes the best proposals on a sheet of paper with a clear attitude of disappointment in us, his partners. When we have the complete list drawn up, we decide to sleep on it and review the suggestions when our minds are clearer.

Not even twenty minutes later, the minute I've finally turned off the light and settled in, our own personal Red Army sergeant wakes us up for a field exercise.

"Come on, on your feet! Soundproofing tests!" he says, pounding on our bedroom doors.

Even if the rude awakening shakes up our nervous system, we decide to go along with it. After all, he worked in the *taverna* all day long, without any help from any of us.

Claudio in an upstairs bathroom, Fausto in the living room, and me out in the yard all listen carefully for the horrifying roars and snarls that Sergio is bellowing out in the room where we've imprisoned the *camorrista*. I can't hear a thing, and neither can Claudio, but Fausto heard something, however muffled.

"Really?" Sergio asks. "You're sure you weren't imagining it?"

"You sang that old partisan anthem, *Bandiera rossa*," Fausto replies in disgust. We go back to bed, leaving Sergio to mutter something about the flimsy wooden doors and the acoustic resonance effect.

17

We allow ourselves a few extra hours of sleep and around ten the next morning we shamble downstairs to the kitchen, pale and silent as a troupe of zombies. I see at a glance that in the clear light of day, Fausto and Claudio have also glimpsed our brainstorming session for what it really was: a state of temporary insanity.

In the kitchen, we find Sergio and, sitting next to him, Abu, who is studying our punch list of the jobs still left to be done.

Mistakenly, I'm more surprised by the sight of Abu than by the ugly grimace on Sergio's face.

"We've got to instill a little discipline around here," says Sergio. "The work isn't going to do itself, you can't wake up at ten o'clock in the morning like a bunch of jaded noblewomen!"

"I'm not taking orders from you," Fausto replies harshly. But then he clearly has a hard time meeting Sergio's glance and he sidles off in the direction of the espresso pot. I feel as if I ought to say something conciliatory, but I'm still pretty sleepy, so I leave the two of them to thrash it out between them.

"Look me in the eye when you talk to me," says Sergio.

"Let me remind you that you're only a temporary partner here. In fact, let's get one thing perfectly clear. The minute you've been paid what you're due, you're kindly invited to go away and be the straw boss of some other work crew!" Fausto shouts.

They stand there for a little while: the two of them, eye to eye, like a couple of pistoleros, and the rest of us, all agog, like a crowd of rubberneckers at the door to the saloon. Suddenly there's a thump, so unexpected that it takes us a couple of seconds to realize what's happened and rush to help Claudio, who's fallen face down onto the floor.

"Oh hell, now what!" says Fausto.

"Claudio! Oh, Claudio," I say shaking him by the shoulder.

Abu looks quizzically at Sergio. Our fearless leader shakes his head dismissively.

"And we're trying to wage war against the Camorra! Fuck this, my God!" says Fausto.

Then he steps over Claudio's body and storms out of the room. In the meanwhile, the faintee gurgles and rolls over onto his back, with one eye open and alert and the other eye rolled completely back up into his head. The alert eye takes a look around.

"Sorry . . . sorry about that . . . " he says.

"Are you okay? How do you feel?" I ask him.

"Sorry . . . it's just the tension. I can't take all this tension," he says, sitting up.

We help him to his feet. He's wobbly at first, then he shakes off our helping hands and marches off unsteadily to his room.

"All this tension is killing me!" he shouts from the stairs. We stand there watching him with worried expressions until he vanishes around the corner.

"Oh, this is just great," says Sergio.

"But he does have a point, all this tension isn't helping anyone. If this is how it's going to be, we might as well throw in the towel right away," I say.

The words come out of my mouth with an authoritarian tone of voice that is completely out of place. I'm already on the verge of apologizing but Sergio beats me to it with a friendly pat on the back. He tells me that this is no time to get discouraged. During the night, he says, he's already taken care of the problem with the noise, and moreover we will no longer have any problems with construction workers wandering all over the house. Abu has offered to help us with the work, which will mean getting it done faster and much, much cheaper. Their confidence encourages me, and it reinforces my determination not to give up, which is actually just dictated by mere desperation. Now that I feel I can leave the reins in more experienced hands, I feel more at ease. My life is so complicated that it's not something I feel I have any ability to handle personally.

18

I need to get out of the house, so I volunteer to go to the post office to pay some of the overdue bills. I feel the need for a little time alone to think about my father and find the proper motivations to keep on going, but Fausto intercepts me and tells to wait for him. While I'm waiting, I take a walk on top of the Giulia. No music is rising from the earth, and this apparent normality brings a smile to my face. I can't seem to change my life, I think to myself. In the end, I always have been and always will be the kind of guy who can't solve problems, so he just conceals them.

This is the first time that I've gone into town, except for that one stop at the bar on the provincial road with Fausto and Claudio. My idea of a small town is narrow streets, very little traffic, and lots of people walking or riding bikes. The streets actually are narrow, but they're filled with cars. No one's riding bikes and the few people not blocking the thoroughfare with idling automobiles are zipping along on giant motorscooters the size of a compact car. This is no place for me, that much is clear the instant I get there. I was born in the city and so I'm used to noise and confusion, bad manners and devious behavior, but always restrained below a certain, and to my mind extremely generous, threshold of tolerance.

When we reach the outskirts of town, we're welcomed by the first swarms of people without helmets zigzagging around on motorscooters and mopeds. I do my best to keep from being an asshole straightaway and I plaster a smile on my face. I try to keep from thinking too hard about this idiotic conceit of refusing to wear a helmet because it's uncomfortable, inconvenient, because it ruins your hairstyle, or just because the police will never ticket you anyway. One thing I know is that, just because they choose not to wear a helmet, every year hundreds of people are crippled, and then they become dependents of the national health system, and therefore on my tab. I know one thing: I wear a helmet even if I'm just moving my scooter fifty feet. When we come to the first intersection, all my good resolutions go down in flames. We come close to colliding with a moped driven by two enormous women with a little girl—she can't be more than six—standing on the running board and holding onto the handlebars. Even though they're coming from the left, and we therefore have the right of way, Fausto still jams on the brakes to let them pass. The fact that we had to brake at the last minute offends the sensibilities of the two women. They shoot us menacing glances, while the little girl signals the family's disgust, waving her little hands angrily in our direction.

Fausto's already on the verge of a breakdown. He can't seem to grasp the idea that his normally bullying driving style seems to have lost all its usual efficacy in this new and unfamiliar setting. When we get to the piazza in the center of town we witness a scene that we've probably already watched in at least a dozen television news reports: a traffic cop waving directions at motorists who roundly ignore him. Three people go sailing past him on a single motorscooter, and he does nothing. People honk their horns, and he does nothing. People fail to respect the right of way, and he does nothing. What the hell does this cop do for a living? Is he just a mime standing in an intersection? That's why we pay his salary? Witnessing this scene puts the kibosh on any hope I might have felt that there could be a lawful solution to our problem. If the police have no authority with motorists, then you can bet they have no authority with *camorristi*.

The traffic is jammed solid and to get out of the vise grip of stalled cars, we try turning down a narrow lane. Ah, now, this is truly romantic. The blackened and encrusted facades of the buildings face off across a thoroughfare barely ten feet wide. All that's holding the buildings up, to an untrained eye, are the spindly clotheslines from which brilliant white sheets are hung out to dry. We round a curve and are confronted with an old woman sitting at a table. The street has become an extension of her home. She sees us coming but remains seated. Inch by inch, we begin the delicate operation of making our way around her. Our side-view mirror just misses, by an inch, no more, the hair gathered into a bun on the back of her head. Once we get past the old woman, we discover that this is just the beginning. Shops and households seem to have detonated into the narrow alley, with armchairs, bookshelves, flower stands, and television sets dotting the cement. As we make our way through the obstacle course, Fausto starts ranting about law and order. Then he ratchets up to strongmen, rules, and respect. Soon, he's moved on to social control and long prison terms. Finally he's calling for tanks and napalm. But I'm beginning to feel a sneaking admiration for this city full of reckless mutineers who live their lives in utter indifference to the rest of the world, scornful of people like us—a carful of sly moralists from some Swiss canton to the north, preaching from a prayerbook of rules that serve only to mask lives based on other, subtler, more diabolical scams and con games.

A young boy, not even twelve, on a souped-up motorscooter pulls up next to Fausto's SUV. He's wearing wooden clogs and when he stops, he can barely reach the ground with the toe of just one clog-shod foot. I smile at him. He winks an eye at me and roars away, pulling a wheelie.

19

Even though we have a handgun, Sergio chooses to go in armed with a billhook. He throws open the door of the *taverna* and walks through without taking any particular precautions. In contrast, I have to screw my courage to the sticking point. The man is sitting on the bench in total unconcern. At least, that's the impression I get, since I can't actually get a glance at his face. We carry in the cot and the mattress. Then, while Sergio is drilling a hole in the door and installing a peephole, I make the bed. I lavish loving care on the bed, naively hoping that an impeccably tucked blanket and a nicely fluffed pillow will persuade him to go easy on us. Once Sergio has finished with the peephole, he retouches a few details on the external soundproofing on the door. I take every opportunity to go upstairs and escape the old man's cringe-inducing gaze. A bar of soap, a disposable razor, and a hand towel require three separate trips. When I come downstairs carrying an air freshener, I hear Sergio's voice.

"What's your name?" he asks the man while he's hammering.

I walk in and see the old man stretched out on the bed, his eyes on the ceiling.

"No answer?"

The *camorrista* flashes a smile that makes my blood run cold. Sergio asks his questions in a conciliatory tone of voice and the thought that even he is afraid and is doing his best to ingratiate himself with the *camorrista* makes me shiver.

"Fock, you're a very interesting clinical case, you are," the old man suddenly says.

Sergio stops hammering.

"Oh, I am?" he replies, waiting for an answer that is not forthcoming. Then he says: "How so?"

"You're already dead, but you're still talking," he replies in a mocking tone. "The doctors should really take a look at you."

When I was a young man I took an acting class, so I have an appreciation for the importance of timing: the old man is using his pauses to make everything he says that much more stark and dramatic.

Sergio goes back to hammering with nonchalance. I escape into the bathroom to set up the air freshener. Then I take a scrub brush and set about making the filthy sink gleam. I remind myself of my mother when she was in a mood. Every now and then I hear a snatch of conversation and I stop.

"My name's Vito. What's yours?" says the old man.

I stand there with the sponge in midair, waiting for a reply.

"What was your name?" the *camorrista* goes on, picking up the motif of the dead man talking again.

Sergio's silence gives me a touch of heartburn and I go back to scrubbing energetically.

"Everybody's good at asking questions, but it takes a big pair of balls to give the answers," the old man says.

I unleash my zeal on the calcium deposits on the faucet.

"Did it ever occur to you that we might actually be right about things? That workers have every right to defend themselves from their exploiters?" asks Sergio.

What, really? Really? Is Sergio asking a *camorrista* such an elementary question?

"No," Vito replies in a bored tone of voice. "Actually, yes, if you want to know the truth. I've thought about it."

"And what did you decide?"

"Nothing . . . because then I decided, what the fock do I care? Look, no matter where you turn, everyone's a *camorrista*, everyone twists the laws to their own benefit, like there's some who erase the date on their bus tickets and use them more than once, there's others who have a tiny accident with their car and then walk around with an orthopedic collar for fifteen days, people who punch the time clock in a government office and then go grocery shopping—they're *camorristi*, let me tell you.

The difference is that you're all amateurs and I'm a professional. And professionalism is nuttin' to be ashamed of . . . "

Sergio goes back to hammering, I resume my scrubbing. It's all pointless, a *camorrista* doesn't give a damn, and you're certainly not going to make an impression on him with a gleaming sink. After all, how can a man destroy families, make children orphans, and leave old people penniless unless he's capable of not giving a damn about anything? Vito has built a wall for himself, a safe house where he can sleep through the night, proof against anything.

We go upstairs and Claudio's head appears in the door for a moment. When we enter the kitchen we find him sitting at the table with Fausto.

"How is he doing?" he asks us.

"How do you think he's doing?" Sergio replies.

"Is he depressed?"

"Depressed my ass! He's royally pissed off!" says Sergio.

As obvious as the answer might be, it upsets Claudio all the same. I sit down at the table next to Fausto, while Sergio picks up the punch list and starts muttering under his breath, carrying on a muttered conversation with the remaining items.

"They're going to come looking for him, you realize that?" says Claudio.

Sergio ignores him. He's busy barking something at "Item Six: fix roof tiles."

"And who's going to have the courage to lie to people like that?" he adds.

"I built my career on spouting bullshit, if you guys don't want to do it, I'll take care of it. A man? Here? No, we haven't seen any man. We're still closed, we don't expect any customers until Christmas. What do you think? Convincing?" I say.

I look for a little approval from Sergio but he's too busy

laughing sarcastically at "Item Eleven: replace rain gutter on north side of farmhouse."

Sergio puts down the sheets of paper, slams his fist on the table with satisfaction, and stands up. He's filled with enthusiasm and when he glimpses our gloomy mugs he gapes in astonishment.

"Come on, guys, snap out of it! This is war! There's no turning back now! We have to take back what belongs to us and fight for it, goddamn it!" he shouts.

His head jerks up as if he's possessed and his call to arms, meant to galvanize us, just scares us.

"You've lost your mind . . . " says Fausto.

"Fausto, come to your senses! You've spent your whole life fighting motorists who wanted to steal your parking place, angry customers, and nonfunctional remote controls! At last you can fight for something that really matters! Wake up: it's us against them!"

Too many things are happening at once. I go outside to get a little time to myself and I take advantage of the opportunity to see whether the Giulia has finally fallen silent once and for all. There's a gentle breeze, the tall dry grass rattles under the light gusts. I pace back and forth for a few minutes until I hear the echoing note of a flute in my head. I turn and stand motionless, but now there's only the noise of wind in the dry grass. Then there it is again, the flute, three ascending notes, the last one drawn out and ending on a dying fall. I stretch out on the ground and I hear a majestic array of brass instruments add their voices to the flauto crescendo. I begin to relax and it dawns on me that maybe the psychopathic Communist isn't entirely wrong. Of course, it's not really news to me that the life I've been leading was pretty shitty. Now, perhaps laying down a challenge to the Camorra is not the most logical solution to that problem but still, deep down, I've always wanted to take on some larger issue, deal with something that makes my own dissatisfaction look relatively insignificant. Now a string section furiously joins the brass and, over that, the voices of my partners as they come outside to go back to work.

"Item Eleven!" Claudio shouts to me.

"Rain gutter on the north side!" Fausto adds.

"Has the battery died?" asks Sergio.

20

I thought that by this point I'd have started to miss my life, the city, all my old habits. I was wrong, though I have to say that down here I haven't found any of the things I was looking for. I wanted a quiet, untroubled life, but instead I'm facing one problem after the other; I wanted to break free of a life of mediocrity but, at least for now, I haven't built anything to be proud of; I wanted adventure and, fair enough, it's not like there's any shortage of excitement here, but I'd definitely had something different in mind. And yet, I don't miss a thing. Maybe it's because there's always so much to do and I still haven't had time or a chance to linger in front of the bathroom mirror. Without the happy accident of the agritourism bed and breakfast, by this time of day I'd be sitting at a café table in a bar downtown ordering an aperitif. A little conversation with my friends, a couple of lewd comments about some passing blonde, and I'd head home feeling like I'd had a pretty good evening. Instead, here I sit once again at the table with three guys I barely know. Four glasses of wine from a huge demijohn, a plate of bread and olive oil, and a bag of peanuts emptied onto the table, without a shred of choreography. So why don't I miss the colorful cocktails, the fruit slices perched on the rim of the glass, the savory tarts and the couscous?

Fausto tosses a peanut into the air and tips his head back,

mouth wide open, waiting for it to land. The peanut lands on his nose and bounces off onto the floor. Fausto looks down on it scornfully, as if it was the peanut's fault for botching its landing, not his fault for tossing it wrong.

"The important thing, if we want to make sure nothing takes us by surprise, is to consider all the possible scenarios," Sergio points out.

"That's your line of work, Claudio. Come on, give us a rundown on all the disasters that are likely to befall us," says Fausto, as he tries his trick with another peanut.

It sounds like a wisecrack, but it's a perfectly serious request. Lately, we've started to appreciate Claudio's constant apprehensive fear, and we've decided it's a God-given talent. In practical terms, he's become our shaman, our witch doctor, and we consult him for a couple of reasons: because there's always some catastrophic scenario that we hadn't thought of, and in part because of the sheer fun of the thing. When he starts to have an anxiety attack and begins prophesying calamities, he trembles, sweats, and stammers. Sometimes, if he's really upset, he even changes voice.

"I've already thought it through carefully," says Claudio, turning a piece of bread over and over in his hands. "Someone will come looking for him. Maybe they'll even believe us when we tell them that we haven't seen this person they're looking for, but then after a little while they'll come back for the shakedown. At that point, we'll have no choice but to pay . . . and with the protection money it'll take us at least three years to pay off our expenses and have a chance to leave here. And if we keep that poor devil in the cellar for three years, it's not like we'll be able to go to the police and say that we just locked up a criminal. It'll become kidnapping. In fact, it *already is kidnapping.* And that's without considering that the prisoner's an old man and he could get sick on us. Or else, since he's not exactly a feeble old man, he might try to escape. We're going to have to watch his health and keep an eye on him, which means that he'll slow down our work on the farmhouse. Considering our financial situation, we can't afford not to be open for paying guests by Christmas."

"First class analysis, comrade!" says Sergio, in an onslaught of unjustified satisfaction.

"But can't we count on the fact that after all we're just small fry and they're probably going to forget about us?" I ask.

"*Camorristi* with Alzheimer's?" says Fausto.

"I wouldn't be so optimistic. Sure, we're not a big deal for them and they might not come after us full bore, but sooner or later they'll show up again," says Sergio.

"In any case, the way I see it, the situation will definitely get out of control. And it'll happen when we least expect it," Claudio concludes.

There's a limit to everything, even the respect we're willing to show for our witch doctor, so we decide to heel-toe it away from the table in silence, our hands clutching the crotch of our pants to ward off evil. We go back to work on "Item Thirty-Six: pulling off ivy." As I hold the ladder for Sergio, I watch Abu picking tomatoes, the farmhouse taking shape, and Fausto and Claudio sticking the branches they've cut into a trash bag without noticing that it has a hole in it. And, in perfect isolation, I wonder why I fail to note or mind the absence of yet another in my succession of blond girlfriends.

21

For the past week we've been working at night as well. Abu, Samuel, and Alex show up around ten o'clock and they do repairs on the roof until two in the morning. By that time we really could use some rest, but no one objects, the simple awareness that at six the next morning these miserable wretches are going to have to be back at work in the tomato fields is enough to give us the strength to keep working. They work tirelessly in exchange for the daily wage of a farm worker, such a tiny sum that it aroused Fausto's suspicion. For the first few days he did surprise management checks but failed to turn up any slacking or malingering. To his intense disappointment, the repairs are proceeding efficiently and all the work is done to the highest standards. The work on the electrical system is finished and, as agreed, we immediately paid the contractor. Now, what with the purchase of insulation for the roof, gravel for the courtyard, and paint and electric appliances for the kitchen, we're completely out of money. And the issue of the water heater remains to be solved. To scrimp and save, we've changed our diet. Farewell sausages, farewell steaks, so long cheeses; now we subsist on pasta alone, for lunch and for dinner, and our wine comes in a tetra pak.

The tournaments of knightly jousting between Sergio and Fausto are staged on a daily basis, and all that's left over for me and Claudio are odd jobs and chores. Claudio takes care of housecleaning in general, while I wander through the farmhouse with a bucket of plaster looking for cracks and holes to fill in. I like this kind of work. I plunge my finger into the cool plaster, push the goo into the cracks and holes, and then run my spatula over the surface to smooth it down. If only I'd been able to do this kind of work on my father, if only someone had been able to suggest a treatment of some kind to fix his illness, I could have gone on for years, fingerful, push, spatula stroke, fingerful, push, spatula stroke, fingerful, push, spatula stroke. I see a small crack near the sill of a window on the second floor. I reach into my bucket and get a good solid fingerful of plaster and, when I lean closer to apply my finishing touches, a trail of dust bursts into my field of view.

"Someone's coming!" I shout.

Sergio, who's directly beneath me in the yard, turns around

and waves for me to relax. But, if he's involved, I feel anything but relaxed. I run headlong downstairs and in the living room I run into Claudio who's looking out the window.

"Who's that?" he asks in a faint, frightened voice.

"I'll take care of it, you go upstairs . . . I left the can of putty open," I say.

"So I should go upstairs?"

"Go on, go upstairs."

I wait until I see him climbing the stairs and then I head for the door. In the courtyard, a powerful motorscooter carrying two young men has rolled to a stop. Sergio is already walking up to them so, to give a purpose to my appearance, I grab a copy of the *Gazzetta dello Sport* and head for a chair.

"*Buon giorno,*" says Sergio.

"*Bona jurnata,*" says the skinnier one of the pair.

He's in his early twenties and all skin and bones, with bags under his eyes that not even the oversized sunglasses manage to conceal; he has a super-close buzz cut and his cheekbones are so hollowed out that you would think he had some terminal disease if it weren't for his hyperkinetic activity. He dismounts from the motorscooter and says hello, then he performs an astonishing series of nervous acts: he folds down his collar from one side to the other, he sniffs like a cokehead, he adjusts the lapel of his jacket, he hikes up his pants, he scratches his chin, and then he shakes first one foot then the other, as if they'd fallen asleep and he was trying to stimulate his circulation.

"You guys had any visitors, past few days?" he asks.

"Nobody's been around so far," Sergio replies.

"We're not open yet," Fausto explains, from atop a ladder that's leaning against the wall.

The skinny guy turns and gives his comrade a disbelieving glance. He's a young man aged about twenty-five, with a slight scar on his right eyebrow and a chipped incisor that give him an especially sinister appearance. Unlike his friend, he stands motionless and scrutinizes us with a narrow-eyed squint, holding his sunglasses in one hand.

"A old guy drivin' a green Alfa Romeo Giulia," adds the skinny guy.

"You're the first people to come by," says Sergio.

The skinny guy looks us in the eye, one by one. It makes me shiver, but I must have played my role successfully because he jerks his head at his partner and climbs aboard the motorscooter.

"Take it easy, we'll be back."

"*Arrivederci*," says Sergio.

As soon as the pair of them are out of earshot, we cluster around Sergio. I see Abu watching us from the tomato field, and then he resumes his stoop labor.

"Do you think they went for it?" I ask.

"Of course they went for it. All these guys understand is the usual business . . . they send their guys out to threaten someone and they expect him to come back with the money. We've screwed up their script and now they don't what the fuck to do anymore. We've outsmarted them!" says Sergio.

22

I walk down into the *taverna* carrying a tray, with Sergio as my bodyguard, armed with a billhook. We've decided to try to have a conversation with Vito. The situation is getting complicated and we hope he can help us figure it out.

Vito is sitting quietly and obediently on his bed. When I hand him the tray he uncovers the bowl and digs in, head lowered. The harmless attitude of the old men convinces Sergio to pull up a chair and sit across from him. I stand there, staring at the bowl. It may not be the most important issue right now, but we're testing out our culinary skills and I'm interested in seeing what he thinks of it. Vito eats silently, with a vacant expression, so I take my chance.

"How is it?" I ask.

Sergio and Vito both turn to stare at me. Both of them are having a hard time believing that I'm actually talking about the pasta.

"Complete horseshit," Vito says with disdain.

"What's wrong with it?" I ask.

"What the fuck?" Sergio says to me.

"We need to find out what our guests think, don't we?"

It only occurs to me that I used the word "guests" after I've said it. Sergio shakes his head in amazement. Vito snickers.

"The pasta's overcooked. And then . . . who da hell puts onions in a bowl of carbonara?" he asks.

"There's no onion in carbonara?" I ask Sergio.

"Of course there's no onion! I told you that! Anyway, who gives a crap about carbonara recipes . . . today two guys came by here on a motorscooter: one of them's skinny, the other one's a little tougher—looking with chipped teeth, you know them?"

"Course I know them boys," Vito replies.

"Who are they? Big shots?"

Vito goes off into peals of coarse laughter and coughs out a clump of egg that splats onto the floor.

"Dontchoo worry. When a big shot comes around heah, fock if you don't notice!"

"So who are these two? Are they likely to come back?"

"Theyz just two guys that don't count for shit, just like me. And don't worry, they'll be back."

The old man finishes his bowl of pasta, shoving to the edge all the limp pieces of onion. Then he takes a piece of bread and starts scooping up the remaining pieces of egg and bacon. I decide we should serve larger portions. After all, we're an agritourism bed and breakfast, not a chic little restaurant in down-town Rome.

"I don't understand . . . " says Sergio as he leans toward Vito. "Instead of working in an organization where you count for nothing, why didn't you start a business of your own where you don't have to answer to a boss?"

Vito drops the clump of bread, eggs, and bacon that he had so painstakingly assembled.

"Lookie what we got heah . . . we got a Communist, a dreamer," he says, looking at me. Then he turns to Sergio.

"We all got bosses! All you got to do is make up your mind if you want more of 'em or less of 'em. I give respect to my capo and no one else. You, on the other hand, have to show respect to the first asshole who crosses your path wearing a uniform."

I hate it when I'm left speechless. I hate playing the part of the moron who can't think of a word to say in response to an apparently sensible but deeply rotten argument.

Sergio smiles confidently. After all, at least he said some-thing. In contrast, I actually waste some time thinking, "Well, he does have a point." It takes me a while to consider that there are bosses and there are bosses. My boss, for instance, is never going to tell me to go shake someone down for protec-tion money or shoot the third cousin once removed of an investigating magistrate.

"But now, really, explain this to me," says Vito, pulling me out of my thought process. "Is this kidnapping? You lookin' for ransom or what? I gotta say, I don't really follow your plan."

Instinctively my gaze shifts over to Sergio, which amounts to an implicit admission that we don't have a specific plan of any kind, or at least that if there is, I haven't been told about it.

"We're defending our rights as workers, the right to be exempt from exploitation, first and foremost. That's our plan."

Vito stares at him in disbelief, then he turns to look at me in hopes of an explanation. I pick up the tray and with an undignified posture I trudge out of the *taverna*. Sergio follows me, closing the door behind him.

"I don't get a focking thing you're talking! You want to tell me what yo' fockin' plan is?" Vito shouts at us.

23

Our first attempt to make grass grow over the Giulia was a failure. The few grass seeds that survived the banqueting birds just withered and dried out in the hot sunshine. But Fausto knows how it's done. "So do it yourself," I tell him, and step aside with manly self-restraint. There's nothing more dangerous than someone who makes false claims of competence. That much has become clear to me. I've chosen to take up sanding the deck of the veranda, a position from which I can properly admire the lawn-developing technique orchestrated by Fausto, the mastermind, and executed by Claudio, the menial laborer. First of all, it is necessary to scratch up the dry soil with a metal rake and pile up a fair amount of dirt to one side. Next, scatter an abundant quantity of grass seeds and cover them by broadcasting fistfuls of the dirt previously referenced. Final trick: go back over the ground on all fours and beat down the surface of the soil with the heel end of an old rubber beach sandal. Quite a show.

In the meantime, Sergio has been scattering gravel over the courtyard. He handles fifty-pound bags as if they were nothing. A sudden cascade of gravel interrupts our work. Sergio is standing motionless, his gaze riveted on a motorscooter coming up the dirt road. For days, we've been wondering how long it would take them to regroup. Here's the answer: exactly ten days.

"Should I go upstairs?" Claudio asks.

"Go upstairs, go upstairs," we practically chorus in reply. I catch up with Sergio.

"I'll take care of it," I say.

Sergio says nothing. In fact, he doesn't even look at me. I'd like to say something more to him, but the two guys are already here. So I just put on a broad welcoming smile, hoping that he'll do the same thing. The skinny guy gets off the scooter and gives us a brief reprise of his behavioral tics.

"Who's in charge roun' heah?" he asks Sergio.

"There are no bosses here," he replies.

In response to his glowering expression, I decide to weigh in with a smile.

"We're partners. Is there something we can help you with?"

"We're heah to talk abou' business."

"Come on in, let's sit down. It's much more comfortable under the pergola."

As we walk toward the table, the duo looks around.

"Listen," the skinny guy says, "you wouldn't happen t've seen that guy we said, the guy wit'the Giulia?"

"No, nobody," I reply.

"A green Giulia," says the other one, describing its outline with his hands.

"No one, you're the first people to come by since we moved in."

"What kind of business?" asks Sergio, pulling up a chair.

The skinny guy sits down across from him. The other guy remains standing, leaning against a wooden post.

"You're not from round heah are ya?" asks the skinny guy.

"No," says Sergio.

"You starting a business operation a some kind?"

Unlike Vito, the kid expends no effort to make his dialect understandable and it takes us a while to figure out the meaning of each phrase.

"Yes, an agritourism bed and breakfast," Sergio replies.

"You got all your permits?"

"Sure, we have them all. Except for the one from the local cops."

"They don't count for shit. There's families round heah that have been in charge since long before they first thought of cops."

The young man talks fast, whole sections of sentences emerge from his mouth as gummy as extended yawns, but luckily we know the script by heart and we're able to follow his drift in a general fashion.

"There's families that could constitute a kind of interference with your little business."

"And so?" Sergio asks.

"You need proteckshun." We sit in silence.

"Widdout proteckshun you'd be in danger, both you and your business," the young man adds.

"And just how much would this protection cost us?" I ask in an interested voice, as if I were thinking about buying a washing machine.

"T'ree t'ousand."

"Ah, three thousand," I say, sincerely relieved at the figure.

"T'ree t'ousand around the first of the yeah and another t'ree t'ousand around the Maronna Assunta," the skinny guy explains.

I don't have the slightest idea of what the Maronna Assunta might be, but that doesn't really matter, it's the total that counts.

"And that's it?" Sergio asks.

"It makes a difference to us that your business goes well for you. We'll take our share when you've got plenty of business. Just twice a year, that's all."

"And we wouldn't have to pay anyone else?"

"Who else would you have to pay? You pay us and then you work in blessed peace. No one'll touch you. And if you need a little help getting permits or licenses, well you just let us know."

"Well, sure, why not!" I say to distract their attention from Sergio's glowering face.

My ploy works perfectly. The young man turns to look at me and never sees Sergio's fist coming. He jerks back against his chair and then slumps face-first onto the wooden surface of the table. The punch, thrown so suddenly, makes me leap to my feet and stagger a step or two backwards. The guy leaning against the wooden pillar, after a moment's astonishment, flicks open a switchblade knife and lunges toward Sergio. The gleaming blade of a butcher's knife from the kitchen that looks like the meaner big brother on steroids of the knife he's clutching in his hand persuades the kid to halt his charge.

"Drop it or I'll slice you down the middle!" he shouts.

Then, when he sees that Sergio isn't dropping the knife, he shouts his friend's name in a frightened voice:

"Saverio!" He shakes the body, which doesn't move, and he starts to step carefully backward.

"The fock you doon?! You're a dead man, piece-a shit!"

This time, when Sergio heads for him, the guy doesn't even think of taking him on. He turns and runs. Sergio cuts off his escape route toward the scooter so he takes off in a headlong dash toward the fields. Only then do I manage to snap out of my paralysis.

"Holy crap, those guys are going to kill us!" I shout at Fausto. Together we start racing after Sergio. By now, completely out of breath, he's losing ground on the kid. I overtake him, but when I realize that Fausto's Prada thong sandals are slowing him down, I pull up. I'm not the kind of guy who takes on a knife-swinging criminal all by myself.

"Now we'll never catch him!" I shout.

Sergio comes to a halt, panting and holding his side. The kid, in the distance, turns and with a mocking smile, aims his hand at us, finger extended and thumb cocked like a revolver. It's the last thing he does before collapsing in a heap, after being decked by a shovel blow to the head by Abu. The African looks around. The heads of dozens of tomato harvesters swivel right and left. Abu throws the unconscious boy over his shoulder as if he were a ragdoll and comes walking toward us.

"He just saved our asses," I tell Fausto, panting.

"He didn't save our asses out of the goodness of his heart, you can be sure of that," he replies.

The expression on Vito's face when we walk into the *taverna* with the two young men bound hand and foot would have made a fantastic photograph. Sitting on his bed, he stares at us open-mouthed and follows our every move without saying a word. Then, I couldn't really say, but at a certain point it strikes me that an incredulous smile flickered across his face. But I could be wrong.

As the sun sets, Abu and I start digging a pit to bury the motorscooter. This time we dig next to the shed and the Alfa Romeo Giulia, from a distance, plays a few hiccupping notes to us, a sort of wheezing admonishment.

"Let's not fuck up, eh? Let's make sure this thing doesn't have an anti-theft device with an alarm!" says Fausto.

"Of course, *camorristi* are worried that someone might steal their motorscooter!" says Sergio.

Abu smiles.

"What have you got to laugh about?" asks Fausto, rude as usual.

"This people, bad. Very bad."

"So what's so funny?"

"You . . . "

We look at one another. And it's anything but reassuring. Maybe Sergio has some vague credibility, but Fausto? Claudio? And especially, me? We're warriors fit for a condominium board meeting. We're a cluster of wise guys who bury a *camorrista*'s motorscooter, taking great care not to scratch it, whereas if you actually want to go up against these people the very least you should do is dissolve it in acid.

"Now you're getting yourself into the same mess we're in," Sergio says to Abu.

The African looks at him, but he doesn't stop digging.

24

We have an appointment with Abu near where he lives. We leave Claudio behind to guard the farmhouse, not because we trust him, but because we gave our prisoners a triple ration of beer and when we left they were all three sawing logs. Plus there's Samuel and Alex, who are working on the roof.

We walk through the tomato fields, we follow a narrow trail barely lit by a dim half moon, and we cut across the provincial road, heading for a cluster of low hovels, the farthest edge of town before the outskirts fade into open countryside. The road is unpaved and only two of the many streetlamps work, far from Abu's house. At the end, we're walking in total darkness, but then a door swings open and lights our way. To avoid attracting attention, we wait for Abu to come out and then we fall into line behind him without a word. Not until we've left the road and we're in the middle of a field does Sergio walk up next to the African.

"No rumors, everything quiet for now," says Abu.

Abu is our infiltrator in town. Thanks to him and his contacts, we can keep up to date in real time on the mood in the village, the gossip in the bar, and the mutterings of the seediest circles.

"The guy you hit with a shovel doesn't remember a thing . . . but you have to stop taking risks, you've already done too much," says Sergio.

"You have choice but still you risk. Why not go to another place?"

"We can't now, we're up to our necks in debt."

"What kind of work did you do back home where you come from?" asks Fausto.

"No work."

"You couldn't find a job?"

"No, I was . . . how do you say it? . . . a prince. I had people working for me."

"A prince? And you come all the way here to become a bum?" Fausto, ignoring our furious glares.

"If I'd stayed, I'd be dead prince."

"Listen, prince, next thing you're going to tell us is that you have a college degree."

"No, I am warrior, I never studied."

A warrior. Of course, he's a warrior, a warrior prince. It's unmistakable, it's sculpted in his DNA. We exchange a series of rapid glances. Sergio's gloating joyfully, proud of his new friendship; Fausto is still thinking it over, trying to decide whether or not to believe it; I don't know what to say, but there is one thing I know: walking through the dark fields suddenly doesn't scare me anymore.

We cross the fields and skirt a handsome brand-new four lane road, with towering powerful streetlamps.

"We could have taken the car," says Fausto.

After a kilometer or so, the road is blocked by a dirt rampart about a yard high and there's no more lighting. After another half-mile of abandoned fields, in the middle of nowhere, Abu stops.

"We're here," he says.

Looming before us, barely perceptible in the darkness, is the shape of a large oval structure made of reinforced concrete. It's the classic cathedral in the desert, one of those bridges to nowhere that serves to ensure the continued vigor of Italy's anti-southern Lega movement. It was built to serve as a town sports facility, then it was repurposed as a structure for CONI, the Italian National Olympic Committee, and then it was inaugurated as a senior center, and finally put into use as public access center providing services for the differently abled. Now the building stands abandoned, clearly decrepit and deteriorating. We make our way through the tall grass and walk in through the front gate, past the guard's booth. It's no problem getting in, since all that remains of the perimeter fence are the poles and here and there a few shreds of rusty wire fencing. A dog barks somewhere in the distance, and Fausto jerks around as if he's just felt someone place a hand on his ass.

The front door is half open. Abu kicks it all the way open with his foot. The interior, barely illuminated by the moonlight filtering in through the shattered windows, is stark and ransacked. Abu flicks on a flashlight. We're walking on concrete. All that remains of the linoleum floor covering is an isolated tile here and there. The wooden benches have been ripped out of their moorings and nothing remains of the bleachers but the metal framework. We cross what looks like a volleyball court and walk into the locker rooms. We stare at a puddle of water at least three inches deep, and the echoing splash of a falling drop of water gives me the shivers. In the restrooms, someone has made off with all the toilets and all the sinks, the mirrors have all been shattered, and likewise the ceiling lamps and the panels of the drop ceiling.

"Are you sure it's still there? In here it looks like they've carried off everything . . . " says Sergio.

It's hard to imagine that anything could have survived the systematic plundering. Around here, whatever they can't carry off they generally destroy. Abu's flashlight illuminates a stack of white tiles that were detached from the walls of the showers.

"Can you use them?" he asks.

"What do you guys think? For the bathroom of the residential area?" I say. No one answers so I add: "After all, they're free!"

"What the fuck are you saying? You sound like my ex at Ikea!" says Fausto. We file into a hallway and head down a narrow flight of steps. I start thinking about uttering lines like "You guys go on ahead, I'll stand watch right here" or else "I think I heard a noise, I'd better go check on it." I definitely have to come up with something, because there's no way I'm going down there.

"There it is," says Abu.

"Incredible, they left it here . . . " says Sergio.

Curiosity pushes me down the stairs. On tiptoe I move past Abu and I see the hot water heater, in bad shape but still exactly where it's supposed to be.

"Too big for ordinary house, that's why still here," says Abu.

He's right; it's the size of a small double-door armoire. Of course, since they couldn't haul it away, they whanged away at it with sticks and bricks, but aside from the bent access hatch, it doesn't seem to have suffered any permanent damage.

In less than an hour, we have it pulled off the wall. Then we unscrew the pipes and jury rig a stretcher that allows us to carry it.

From Abu's house to the farmhouse, we have to carry the thing without Abu's help. Sergio walks in front while Fausto and I, bringing up the rear, share the weight between us. We immediately notice Abu's absence, as well as that of the moon, now that it's gone behind the cloud cover. My arms are numb and I stagger forward with unsteady footing. I listen to Sergio's grunts, and I use them to find my way, like a form of sonar.

"Well, they're fucked now," Sergio mutters under his breath.

"They who?" I ask.

"We have a warrior prince on our side. We'll kick their asses black and blue."

"What are you saying, you believe that guy? He tells you he's a prince and you believe him? He's probably just a common criminal, not a warrior at all," says Fausto.

"Sure, if he was blond and had a British accent, you wouldn't have any doubts. But since he's black, you assume he's a criminal. And after all, excuse me very much, he's never asked us for anything in return, so why should he lie to us?"

"We already have enough trouble without getting a warrior prince involved. Do you think those three are going to be good and stay quiet down in the cellar? They're probably already plotting something, and the first false move we make . . . " says Fausto.

"Then we'll just have to make sure we don't make any false moves!" Sergio breaks in.

Sergio's exalted state persuades me to stay out of the argument, in part because I just put my foot into a mud puddle and I'm covered with mud up to my ankle. On the way there, we didn't run into any high grass or mud, so it's obvious that we're lost. I shake my foot and get most of the heaviest mud off it; it drops off the sole of my shoe in large, compact clumps. I look around in all directions. The situation is pretty discouraging. I can't spot landmarks of any kind. Uniform darkness seems to have swallowed up the landscape.

"There it is," says Sergio from the head of the group.

"Of course," says Fausto.

"What else!" I say.

A piano concerto announces in unequivocal terms that we have reached the farmhouse. The Giulia had remained silent for the past couple of days and, once again, this had rekindled our hopes that its battery had finally died.

Fausto's bizarre grass-planting method has achieved some noteworthy results: a dense lawn has sprung up over the old pit of the swimming pool. We slowly set down the water heater and sink to our knees, exhausted. I caress the grass with one hand. Fausto takes out his lighter and with the flame set on high he illuminates small sections of the lawn, rescuing them from the darkness. He really did a good job. I lie down on the grass and a few seconds later I sense the bodies of my two companions stretching out near me. The grass has a wonderful scent. There's a faint breeze and it tickles my ankles.

"This place belongs to us," says Fausto.

25

Now that there are three people being held captive in the cellar, we've established an ironbound procedure to be followed in every case. Item one: order the *camorristi* to go into the bathroom and close the door behind them. Item two: check to make sure that item one has been properly implemented by looking through the peephole. Item three: at least two people enter the room, armed with billhooks. Sergio first, followed by Fausto. Item four: securely lock the bathroom door. Last of all, item five, I enter the picture carrying their lunch tray.

Under our breaths, we recapitulate the proper procedure to follow, then Sergio takes up his position outside the door of the *taverna*.

"All of you go into the bathroom and shut the door behind you!" he says.

"We're not focking doing what you tell us for shit!" says the skinny guy.

There's a moment of disorientation, then Sergio points to the peephole. I squint and look in. I see the two young men stretched out on their beds in an arrogant manner. Vito, who had stood up, sits back down on his cot, shaking his head. I report what I've seen in a low voice.

"If you don't get in there, no lunch for you!" shouts Sergio.

"You can stick lunch up your ass!"

"These bastards planned this out," says Sergio.

"That's fine, go on a diet, it'll do you good!" he shouts to them.

Through the peephole, I can see that the two young men are still stretched out on their beds without any sign of concern. Vito on the other hand slaps his thigh and goes on shaking his head. I follow Sergio and Fausto back upstairs with a bad feeling inside. This first act of open rebellion strikes a hard blow against any hopes we might have of a growing normalization of relations.

Back in the kitchen, we run into Claudio. He immediately notices the tray I'm carrying.

"What? They're refusing to eat?" he says.

"They're acting tough, but they'll get over it," says Sergio.

"What do you know about it?" asks Fausto.

"Do you think those guys are Indian gurus? Do you think they have the determination to carry out a serious hunger strike?"

"What do you know about it?" I ask him.

"Those guys grew up on snack food and fast food . . . if they don't gulp down their daily dose of artificial color and preservatives, they'll go out of their minds!"

"Well, it was certainly too much to hope that they'd behave and cooperate," I say.

"Sure, if you look at it from their point of view, we're just keeping those kids in a cage when they have their whole lives waiting for them out there . . . " Fausto points out.

"What I don't understand is exactly what kind of lives guys like this must lead," I say.

The question leads us to sit down around the table to explore the matter in depth. We decide that in all probability a couple of guys like them spend the day riding around town on their motorscooters, wasting their money on videopoker machines; on Saturdays they go to the disco to pick up girls, and on Sundays they go to the soccer stadiums to toss tear gas and fight opposing fans, or else they stay at home overdosing on television and PlayStation.

"We could get them a television set and a videopoker console," Claudio suggests.

"Yeah well maybe, and a jacuzzi too!" says Fausto. Actually, I think to myself, that's not a bad idea. The more we can manage to distract them the less time they'll have to plan an escape. An idea is fluttering around in my head. It seems crazy, but if I play my cards right and bring Sergio in on my side, maybe I can persuade them.

"We need to adopt the same strategy that the government uses against us," I tell Sergio.

Fausto looks at me with a blank expression waiting for the punchline because up till now he hasn't heard anything that makes him laugh.

"The economy is in the tank . . . we're losing our jobs and our houses are being foreclosed, while the bankers that started it all are just collecting bigger bonuses; the politicians tell us that retirement is farther and farther away while they give themselves a lavish pension after serving just five short years in parliament . . . We all ought to be pissed off and fighting in the street. But we aren't, and why not?" I say.

"Why not?" asks Fausto, baffled.

"Because they're drugging us . . . they're drugging us with false hopes with the state lotteries! People think that the best way to get through an economic meltdown isn't to go protest in the streets. They need to scratch—and win! So we need to do the same thing, just like the government!" I say, triggering a glitter in Sergio's eyes that may not be true love, but it's certainly something close to it.

"With scratch and win?" asks Fausto.

"Certainly, with scratch and win!" says Sergio.

26

For the first time, our lives are so full of surprises and challenges that we feel no need to pack our days with ersatz emotions and substitute thrills. Only Claudio stubbornly goes on turning the television on at the same times every day, as required by the news broadcasts.

We walk into the living room and there he is, with his eyes glued to a report about a fight between neighbors in an apartment building that has resulted in tragic mayhem. He looks like a toddler hypnotized by toy commercials.

"Look at him, and we wonder why he's such a paranoid freak!" Fausto says to me.

"That's it, Claudio, turn off the TV!" I shout at him.

He turns his head ever so slightly, but his eyes never leave the screen. The report on the apartment house killings gives way to another report about a mother who has killed herself with her three-month-old newborn baby girl. The female news reporter recounts the facts to the heartbreaking notes of a sad piece of music. We sit down next to Claudio, but he only glances at us fleetingly and distractedly.

"Why do you do it?" I ask.

"What?" he asks.

"Why do you watch these news reports? You're doing yourself harm!"

"It's valuable information, I need to know what it's like out there in the world," he answers me in astonishment.

"But that's not the world."

"Look, let me hear!" Claudio tells me.

On the screen we see images of a shattered automobile and

pieces of metal scattered across the asphalt for a good hundred yards or so. The news reporter is talking about a drunk driver and an entire family slaughtered.

"Claudio, that isn't the world, that's just the world that makes the news! There's an important difference!"

"Look, these things really happen, it's better to know about it, right?"

"Okay, but now that you know, what's the point of you sitting in here everyday getting high on disasters!" says Fausto.

"I'm not getting high on disasters!"

"That's exactly what you're doing!" shouts Fausto.

"All you do is watch news broadcasts, endlessly. I've never seen you watch a movie or a documentary!" I say.

"Or even a soccer match!" adds Fausto.

"I like real life!"

"Real life also consists of Eagle Scouts, upright citizens, acts of generosity, volunteers who go on humanitarian missions to the Congo. Have you ever wondered why they don't make the evening news?" I ask him.

Fausto grabs the remote control and briskly punches in a three-digit channel that he seems to know quite well.

"No!" shouts Claudio.

On the screen the image of a brutally beaten lapdog gives way to a young blond woman, completely nude, masturbating with a hot pink vibrator.

"This is real life too! Come on, Claudio, stop poisoning yourself! Have some fun!"

"That's disgusting, get this stuff off my TV screen!"

He tries to grab the remote control but Fausto hides it by sitting on it. In the meanwhile, a brunette appears on screen who seems to be very interested in understanding how the garishly colored electric device works.

"All right, then, can we please change the channel now?" asks Claudio, pronouncing each word very distinctly.

"So you actually prefer murder victims to pussy? What's the matter with you?" Claudio mimes the classic *vaffanculo,* left hand bracing his right elbow, jumps up from the sofa, and stomps off huffing and puffing.

"Come on, Claudio, Fausto's right!" I insist.

"Leave him be, leave him be, he's a hopeless case!" says Fausto.

And he vindictively raises the volume to maximum, filling the farmhouse with panting and sighing so patently fake that even a man would know it.

"But just don't ask us why your wife left you!"

"Fausto!" I say, doing my best to make him shut up.

Claudio comes storming back and I leap to my feet, ready to defuse a potential brawl. He stops at the door to the living room and starts shaking his head with hatred. It looks as if he's about to explode and I'm afraid of what he might be about to do right now. He levels his finger angrily at Fausto. His mouth twists into a grimace of disgust, he takes a deep breath, and then he thrusts his finger to and fro like a mini-piston. Then he turns on his heel and stalks off.

Fausto and I look at each other. We shake our heads in disappointment.

27

I purchase a stack of scratch and win tickets so we can get started on the lottery. I buy twenty-seven, to be exact. Naively, I thought at first that someone might find such a large purchase suspicious, but I soon discovered that, given the turnover of that newsstand, that number of tickets was actually average.

Coming to an agreement about the prizes to award the prisoners hasn't been easy. Fausto and Claudio don't see the value of this project and they've decided to just agree to anything we propose, including the idea of adding to the cash prizes an assortment of supplementary prizes in the form of consumer goods that we've decided to throw into the pot. A little ploy to ameliorate their sense of frustration and increase their general satisfaction at a moderate cost.

When we go downstairs with the lunch tray and three lottery tickets for each prisoner, just seeing their amazement is a spectacle that is worth every penny we paid for the tickets. Billhook in hand, Sergio explains the rules to the astonished prisoners. The cash prizes they win will be split evenly, half for them and half for us. That prompts some skeptical smirks, but all Sergio has to do is raise the billhook and it becomes clear to them that, after all, we're buying the tickets, so a fifty-fifty split is more than reasonable. Their share of the winnings will be set aside in a crate and put somewhere safe in the house. More ironic smirks, which vanish when they are informed that, in turn, without advance warning, they can ask to see that the crate is where it's supposed to be and that the contents are intact. Saverio, the skinny guy, asks why they can't have their share right away. Sergio has no problem telling him that we dismissed that idea immediately, because we knew they'd gamble their shares away immediately among themselves, and that the odds were good that fighting and bad blood would ensue. That seems to strike the three of them as eminently logical. Renato, the other guy, asks us whether we'd really put five hundred thousand euros into the crate if they won the first prize.

"If you win first prize, you'll get your five hundred thousand euros and we'll set you free," Sergio replies.

That catches me by surprise, because we'd never really considered the possibility that they might win first prize. The three of them stare at us for a second. Then they turn skeptical again and they start making fun of each other for having swallowed it hook, line, and sinker. They stretch out on their cots without paying the slightest attention to what Sergio is saying, and I wonder how he'll win them over. But Sergio doesn't even try. As if it were the most natural thing in the world, he just starts talking about the intermediate prizes, extremely easy to win, which include: bottles of beer, time outside for exercise, new PlayStation games, and half an hour with a prostitute. The last-mentioned prize catches the attention of the three men for a moment, but they hold firm and ask no questions, even though it's evident that they're dying to.

We go back upstairs to the kitchen and I think about what just happened.

"At first they believed you, but certainly the idea of hitting the first prize is highly unlikely," I say.

"What's so unlikely about it?" Sergio asks.

"They know perfectly well that we aren't going to set them free no matter what happens."

"Oh yes we will. If we have five hundred thousand euros in our wallets, we can sell off the farmhouse for a ridiculous pittance and we can get out of here at the speed of light."

The fact that he said five hundred thousand and not a million astonishes me. It means that he really does intend to give the prisoners their share.

"Even if they believe it, they know that first prize is practically impossible, there must one chance in a . . . . "

"Even if it were one chance in a billion, it would work all the same. It's always worked. All the TV has to say is that winning is easy and people fall for it. Maybe they know it isn't true and, right then and there, they tell their television and that commercial to go fuck themselves, but later they go ahead and buy the scratch and win all the same, because deep inside there's a tiny voice convincing them that it's possible, that deep down they deserve it, that life never gave them a thing for free, and so they're ideal candidates for a triumphant victory."

I hate knowing that I match the portrait of the average idiot. But I have to admit it: I've sneered ironically at lottery commercials, only to go out and buy scratch and win tickets, and I've also heard that tiny voice. I sit there mulling over the thought, with a bitter look on my face that Sergio completely misreads.

"If you don't believe me, go take a look through the peephole, why don't you!" he tells me.

I don't need to see it. I follow him out into the yard. I can imagine them perfectly, sitting on their beds, hunched over and scratching away at those damned lottery tickets.

28

A quick phone call from Abu gives us ten minutes' warning that a black BMW is on its way. That's just enough time to assign the roles we are to play and to keep Sergio safely on ice, where he can't cause trouble. This time, Fausto and I will form the welcoming committee, and Sergio will have a walk-on role but only at a safe distance. Claudio demanded a role of some kind, so we decided to cast him as the man reading a newspaper on the sofa. If he happens to faint, they'll just assume he's fallen asleep, we decide.

Two men wearing sunglasses step out of the car. The one behind the wheel surveys the scene warily, while the one riding shotgun walks back to open the rear passenger door without giving us so much as a glance. Gripping the man's arm, a man in his seventies emerges from the car. He's in a terrible state of repair. He's well groomed but his face is hollow and wrinkled. He has an oxygen tube taped to his nostril, running from a little portable hanging on a strap around his neck.

"Don't pull any of your stupid fucked up moves this time," I hiss at Sergio as he goes to take his position.

The man comes over to us while the two other guys stand by the car. Now they're looking at us, and how.

"Forgive the intrusion," the man says, to our surprise.

"*Buon giorno*," I say, holding my hand out to shake his.

I expected his hand to be callused, but it's smooth as a woman's hand.

"You must be the new arrivals . . . "

"We've just been here for a couple of months," Fausto replies.

The questions follow the usual direction. The old man asks if we're starting a business and nods courteously to all our answers. Now he's going to ask if we have our permits, I think to myself. Instead, his expression suddenly changes and he raises his index finger as if he wanted to point something out to us that he's afraid will slip his mind.

"Forgive me, but by any chance, did a man come by here . . . 'bout sixty, short and fat?"

"No, we haven't opened for business yet, no one has any reason to come by here," I say.

In order to make my answer more persuasive, I look over at Fausto for confirmation. He nods his head.

"Not even a coupl'a kids on a motorbike, either?"

"Absolutely not, you're the first people to come by," I say.

The old man turns to look at the two men and shakes his head ever so slightly. The two men nod back sternly.

After this brief digression, the conversation runs according to the script. There's a slightly different performance, but the words themselves, with a very few minor variations, are identical. We listen with a hint of boredom, a feeling that in this sort of situation is actually quite unlikely. Only a concluding personalization of the usual script attracts our attention.

"Round heah the government deserves no credit for anything. If anything's been done around heah, you can thank the families, and no one else . . . so it's really as if you were just paying your taxes but, instead of giving your money to the people who ain't done a thing . . . " he says to us, leaving the phrase unfinished.

We agree on the figure that we already know all too well, to be paid in two installments as we've already been told. The one who will come to collect the amount due is Franco, as the old man tells us and then gestures in the direction of the man with the soul patch. Massive, in his mid-forties, furious with the world as a matter of general principle. If he weren't already a *camorrista*, he'd be extremely believable playing the part of a bouncer or a leatherneck. The conversation is so friendly and genial that when the time comes to say goodbye, I almost feel as if I've just spent some time with a kindly uncle.

The car heads away up the dirt road and Sergio walks toward me with a smile on his face, with an attitude that I find comforting. I'm about to tell him "See? It's not so bad after all," but he beats me to the punch.

"Did you hear that?"

"What?"

"There'll be just one man coming for the pick up."

"Sergio, don't even think about it!"

Sergio turns his back on me and walks snickering into the house. I try to catch Fausto's eye but he too turns around and goes back to work. I follow Sergio with the full awareness that, despite my warning, for a split second there I too was thinking that we could arrange for this Franco to wind up with all the others. But it was only for an instant. Four prisoners would no longer be manageable, and that's not even counting the fact that Franco hardly seems like a two-bit pawn in this game, and that if he vanished it would probably unleash a world of trouble.

Claudio waits for us in a tizzy of barely concealed excitement like a newlywed bride. We tell him that this guy must have been a big gun, that he doesn't suspect a thing about our prisoners, and that he actually seemed to be fairly friendly. If we pay him, we shouldn't have any more problems.

"So we're going to pay . . . " says Claudio.

"Well yeah, let's just pay and stop living with all this fear," I say brusquely, cutting short the discussion.

I expected to see an expression of relief, but instead Claudio just nods somberly. What the hell's the matter with everyone?

29

We decide that it's time to have a conversation with Vito without the two snot-noses listening in. When we go downstairs to take them their lunch, we intimate to the old man that he has to come with us.

"Whaddya gonna do to him!?" the skinny guy yelled in alarm.

"He'll be back right away," says Sergio, grabbing the old man by the lapel and shoving him out the door.

The minute we walk into the kitchen Vito covers his eyes with one hand and tears roll down his cheeks. He pulls his sunglasses out of his shirt pocket and hurries to put them on. Even with his sunglasses on, he's blinded and we have to lead him to the table that we've set for his lunch.

Vito eats his stew while we hang from his lips, figuratively speaking.

"The old guy wit' th' oxygen tank, okay, he's someone that counts. It's unusual at best for him to come around in person."

"Do they suspect us?" says Sergio.

"From the bottom of my heart, it's kind of hard to think you've done anyt'ing wrong. Don't take it wrong, but there's lots more dangerous guys 'n you guys around heah . . . "

"Has it ever happened that one of you just up and leaves, to start a new life somewhere else, maybe?" I ask.

"Every once in a while . . . someone'll steal some drugs or throw some cash in a bag and take off. You've heard those stories, haven't you, about people gettin' knocked off in Belgium or Germany?"

"And the two young guys, for instance, couldn't they have run away?"

"The first thing they'll do, they'll check to see if there's nothing missing, a drug shipment, a suitcase full of money . . . if everything's where it ought to be, then they'll figure they got wacked. There's no other way to figure it, this ain't people that run away to go start an agritourism bed and breakfast. And even if they did, you want to bet they wouldn't get word to their mothers or sweethearts?"

"Do you think that if a message reached their mothers they'd stop looking for them?"

"For a bit. I think so . . . but whaddo I know, that kind of thing never happens round heah!"

With Vito, we're on much better terms. He seems to want to talk to us, to spend time in our company. At least that's the impression we get. He must be hungry, but he eats slowly, he knows that the minute he's done we'll take him back down to the *taverna*. He's well behaved, far too well behaved for someone who really feels like he's in a cage. I have the feeling that he's taking his imprisonment as something like a holiday. In spite of what he says, I think he actually hates the life he leads.

"How was it?" I ask as he takes the last bite.

"Sonny, don't take this wrong. Cooking ain't your skill. A self-respecting stew should make way for a fork, melt in your mouth. This is all tough . . . "

"I thought it was excellent," Sergio, the chef who prepared the delicacy in question, replies in an irritated voice.

We sit under the pergola with Claudio and Fausto. Sergio places an old cookie tin on the table. In the tin we've hidden the *camorristi*'s gun, switchblade knives, and cell phones.

"We've come up with a diversion. Two of us are going to drive a long way and then send text messages to the families of the two kids," says Sergio.

Thinking that this was just yet another of our sergeant-at-arms' many pipe dreams, Fausto and Claudio look at me with amused smiles.

"If we let their families know that they've just run away and they're fine, we can keep them from reporting their disappearance to the police and, even more important, we can keep their bosses from getting suspicious about us," I say.

"Where would we have to go?" asks Fausto.

"Far away. The cell phones emit a trackable signal every time they're turned on. The last signal would be from two days ago, here. It's not enough just to leave the town. We'd have to go further. At least to Umbria," says Sergio.

"Where in Umbria?"

"I don't know, even in Tuscany if you'd rather."

"And who would we have to write to?"

"It's going to take some imagination. The cell phones can only be turned on once, wherever it is you go. That should be long enough to read a few text messages and identify a parent, a sibling, a girlfriend."

"What if we don't find anything?" asks Claudio with his customary optimism.

"All we really need to do is keep it turned on for a few minutes, or else maybe make a phone call to someone and just hang up once they answer. We just need to leave a trace, give them a clue. But the text message would be best. It'll keep them chewing on it a little longer."

"Okay, but exactly what are we going to write?" Fausto asks.

"I don't know, maybe it's enough to write 'I can't take this life anymore. Don't come looking for me, I'll get in touch with you in good time.' Something like that."

"Yeah, that seems good," I say.

"But you've heard the way they talk. How the hell do you think they write! They'll figure out immediately that they didn't write the text messages," says Fausto.

"Listen, Diego, you take care of it. When you turn on the cell phones, read their text messages, try to figure out how they write, copy some passages here and there, and try to put together a sentence that more or less corresponds to what we said," he tells me.

The assignment, which amounts to a battlefield promotion, makes me forget that until just a moment ago I was trying to come up with some excuse to get out of going on the trip.

"Sure, don't worry, I'll take care of it," I reply.

"I'll go too, that way we can all rest easy," says Fausto, putting an end to my moment of personal glory.

30

Even though it's only going to be a day trip, I've packed a backpack. I've put in the usual things: a pack of Kleenex, a chapstick, headache pills, a collapsible umbrella, and a light fleece. This is my way of making sure that I'm not going to need any of the things I bring with me. So I can be sure it's not going to rain, it won't be cold, and I won't have a headache. I meet Fausto in the hallway and together we walk downstairs to the kitchen. It's four in the morning and we only have a few minutes to eat breakfast. I set about making a pot of coffee while he sits down at the table without even bothering to get out the coffee cups. Claudio appears in the doorway.

"Ha, ha, ha!" he cries, clapping his hands theatrically.

I'm not entirely verbal yet at this time of the morning, so I emit nothing but a guttural grunt.

"Funny, funny, look what a funny prank we pulled!" he goes on.

"What's wrong?" I ask.

"And now the little smartypants is going to march right into the living room and put the television channels back the way they were. A television set that, need I remind you, belongs to all of us!"

"Nobody touched the television set!" I say.

"You see," says Fausto turning to look at me, "watching the news is the first thing he thinks of when he wakes up! He's a fucking drug addict and he needs his morning dose!"

"Ah, okay, so this is the little smartypants. Listen, you worthless so-called therapist, now you march in there and fix the channels!"

"No no, I'm not doing any such thing."

To keep Claudio from watching television news broadcasts while we're away, Fausto has put parental controls on all the main channels and has only left the erotic and pornographic channels unrestricted. I have to say that channel surfing is now a fairly unsettling experience. We've progressed from: cooking shows, documentaries, old reruns, gossip shows, incredibly old reruns, television news, and old comedies starring the classic Neapolitan comedian Totò, to: stripteases, group sex, lesbian shower scenes, vintage group sex, sado-maso, bondage, and multiethnic group sex.

"Leave them the way they are," Fausto tells me.

"Oh come on, that might be a little too much. Let's give him a few documentaries, at least," I say.

"Yeah well maybe: that'd be like trying to cure a cocaine hound with chamomile tea!"

He grabs the remote control out of my hand and turns up the volume.

"It takes strong medicine!"

Claudio starts rummaging around on the shelves underneath the television set and grabs the instruction manual.

"Don't worry about a thing, I'll put the set back the way it was," he says.

He leafs frantically through the instruction manual in search of the Italian version. It takes him a while because, given the international prestige our country commands, it's the last section, after Arabic and Korean.

"I'd like to see how he manages without this," Fausto whispers to me as he slips the remote control into my backpack.

"Broadcast the stop hour remembers to broadcast the position, the some channel orders to a time while broadcast the some catalogue up is shut down, switch on after then park the last time of time order—play order to start broadcast from now on?" Claudio reads aloud from the instruction manual.

Sergio comes down from upstairs and stares at the welter of thighs and tits. He walks over to me in complete bafflement.

"What the hell are you guys doing?"

"Nothing . . . it's just a little therapy to cure Claudio's TV news addiction," I say.

"Ah," he says, "good idea." And he leaves.

31

We set out without any exact idea of where we were going. I asked Fausto if he knew any places in Umbria or Tuscany and, to my amazement, he said that he didn't, that he'd never been up there. The only places he'd ever visited in Italy were Rimini, Riccione, and Forte dei Marmi. Then, once he had enough money, he always went abroad. Specifically, to the beach resorts of Ibiza and Sharm el-Sheikh.

By the time we hit the highway, all conversation has long

since died out and Fausto starts nodding off. As usual, I concentrate on the ribbon of asphalt and the hypnotic divider lines. But something's changed. I no longer feel the usual urge to run away and leave everything behind me. I enjoy the trip without dissatisfaction or anxiety. I focus on the scattered houses that whip past me, though not so fast that I don't have time to think about the people who live there and what might be happening in those illuminated rooms.

I turn on the radio at low volume to keep from waking my traveling companion. I switch around from one station with wobbly reception to another, and without really thinking it through, I settle on a religious station. I put the blame on a woman's voice that I find particularly soothing, even though it's easy to guess that her intention is to come across as a little shepherd girl in the throes of inspiration in the presence of a vision of the Madonna. I imagine her as angelic, with blond hair, green eyes, and incredibly fair complexion. The young woman is talking about the Sentinelle del Mattino, the Baywatch lifeguards of the Catholic faith. I turn the volume up slightly because I can't figure out what the hell she's talking about. Completely captivated by the sound of her voice, I drink in the incredible news that a number of dioceses across Italy have organized a service that spreads the Word of Christ among beach-goers. If it weren't for the intuitive respect I feel for the beautiful babe I imagine to be speaking into the microphone, I'd switch to another station with a hearty fuck-you. "Hundreds of young people, organized into small groups, have approached vacationing young people on beaches to spread the light of the Gospel," the woman says. I can just picture the scene: first a coconut vender goes past, followed by a Pakistani selling necklaces and earrings, then the Chinese woman who gives massages, then an African selling CD's, and finally the Sentinella del Mattino bringing the Word of Christ.

"What the hell are you listening to?" says Fausto, jerking awake to the sound of one of the woman's joyous high notes.

"I don't even know. I was listening to some music and the radio just changed stations all by itself . . . "

Fausto shoots me a worried glare and goes back to sleep. I turn the volume up ever so slightly, but on the frequency of the religious station now there's only weather reports and commercial rock. After the funeral, the parish priest asked me whether I wished to reserve any holy masses for the dearly departed. Masses in suffrage for my father's soul, he explained when I said nothing. Inside, I was angry, as usual. A mass shouldn't be like a table in a restaurant or a lounge chair at a beach resort. I mean, after all, if a man dies alone, without anyone to reserve a mass for him, does he have to pay for that misfortune by spending extra years in purgatory? I'm sick and tired of the church, I'm sick of this garbage that undermines the comfort I get from believing in God, the hope I have that one day I'll be able to see my father again.

It's almost nine in the morning when we get to the hills over Piana di Castelluccio. As long as we had to take a long trip, I figured we should go someplace I love, a place I haven't seen for years. Before heading downhill, the provincial road looks down on the valley from a vantage point high above. As soon as I see a place to pull off, I park and shake Fausto awake. Beneath us is a sea of fog and, in the far distance, the little town perched high on its hill, just barely breaking through the mist.

"Where the hell have you brought me?" says Fausto.

"It's not always like this. You'll see how pretty it is when the fog clears away."

"It's wonderful, I've never seen anything like it . . . " he says. I glance over at his dazed expression and it dawns on me, oddly enough, that he's not making fun of me. We get out of the car and sit on the hood, where we can enjoy the spectacular view with warm butts.

"If those assholes would stick their noses just once outside of their little villages and take a look at a view like this, goodbye Camorra, goodbye Mafia," says Fausto.

In the time that I've known him, I think this is the first reasonable thing I've heard him say. I have the urge to give him an encouraging hug, but I doubt he'd take it the right way, so I tone it down to a slap on the back. We sit there enjoying the view for another couple of minutes and then, when the fog starts melting away, we get down to work. We have very little time to read the messages and put together a believable phrase.

Enveloped in complete silence, we turn on Saverio's cell phone and immediately a carnival of sounds, the messages being downloaded from memory, adds a surreal touch to the atmosphere. We open the queue of sent text messages and amid the welter of incomprehensible phrasing we manage to find something we can use. The text message, translated into proper Italian, says: "I'm sick of this party, I'm leaving to see if I can find some pussy." By replacing "party" with "life" and "some pussy" with "myself," we have the phrase we need. We punch it in and we send it to a certain Rino, who seems to have been the recipient of most of the text messages sent. We turn off that cell phone and move on to the other device. This time too there's a lovely concert of missed text messages and phone calls. As for the text message itself, this time it's child's play. Renato wrote at least thirty heartbreaking text messages to a girl named Valentina who, as far as we can tell from his inbox, never even bothered to write back once. First he threatened to kill himself, then to kill her, and then to kill some guy named Daniel and finally, what the hell, to just go away for awhile. We took that last text message and rewrote it with just a few minor changes, taking great care to insert at least five exclamation marks at the end of each sentence, to remain true to the young man's style.

We had agreed to head straight home after sending the messages but, once we turn off the second cell phone, we notice that the fog has almost completely burned off. There are just a few dissolving wraiths of mist here and there, which only makes the valley even prettier, with its colorful mosaic of cultivated fields. A road runs straight through the middle of the valley floor, as direct as one of the roads you see in American movies. We decide we deserve a reward.

We take turns driving, me on the way down, Fausto on the return trip. I wasn't expecting him to be so comfortable with a long stretch of silence. I'd taken him for the kind of guy who feels obliged to fill in every second of silence with some idiotic wisecrack. Instead, as we go rocketing down through the empty valley, I'm the first one to speak.

"Nice, right?"

"Fuck, the coolest."

Fausto lowers the window all the way and we let a blast of cool morning air wash over us.

"This is liv-v-v-i-i-ing!" he yells into the wind.

Yup, that's exactly what this is, this is living, I think to myself.

32

With help from Abu, Samuel, and Alex, construction moves along briskly. As soon as we see them work, we realize we could never have gotten this done without them, not even in six months. In about a week's time, I manage to become fairly competent at mudding walls and laying tile. All credit to Alex, who has done every imaginable kind of work since he first come to Italy, and who is a patient teacher. Samuel, on the other hand, is a funny guy. He'll read anything he sees. Billboards, scraps of newspaper, the back of a shampoo bottle. Abu told me that his arrival in Italy was traumatic. The landing was terrifying, the crew just unloaded them way offshore, in the middle of the night, in stormy seas, into small inflatable boats. He got separated from his immediate group and was unable to find out what had happened to his brother. He speaks excellent English and he assumed that that would prove helpful, but instead he wandered around in vain for a whole day asking for help. Only after he met a group of fellow Ghanians did he learn that his brother had been drowned, along with eight other people. He came to believe that it was somehow his fault, that his brother died because he had taken too long to ask for help. He won't admit it. If you ask him to his face, he'll tell you that he blames the crew members who unloaded them into stormy seas in the middle of the night too far from shore, but since that day he has studied Italian obsessively. He reads and memorizes anything that comes to hand.

In this anarchic, multiracial, partisan oasis, Sergio is living his own personal dream come true. He's working shoulder-to-shoulder with his African comrades, sharing meals with them and putting every decision to a vote.

"Comrades, let's take a vote on the next job: should we install the hot water heater or lay insulation panels in the attic?"

Four hands go up in favor of laying in the insulation. Comrade Sergio takes note of the people's will.

"Glass of beer before we begin?" The same four hands go up.

After the grand success of Operation Text Message, Fausto has roared back, just as motivated and annoying as in the good old days. All by himself, he scythed a five-acre field and he would have gone back over the whole thing with a pair of nail clippers for a final trim if we hadn't pulled him off the project to work on the website.

The designer who's building our webpage has asked us to send him the text. I sit down at the keyboard and write a caption to go with the photograph of one of the bedrooms. "Double room, panoramic view, with bath."

"Aren't we saying anything more than 'double room'?" Fausto asks.

"Should I add 'big'?"

"Yeah, I mean, it all seems just a little measly . . . and 'panoramic view,' somehow, strikes me as kind of . . . "

"Should I add 'very'?"

"Sure, but let's really lay it on, adjectives help people to dream. Obviously, you don't know much about advertising."

I let him take my place at the keyboard because, really, it's true, I don't know a thing about it. Advertising language is something I can't get worked up about. In the catalogues I used to display in the auto dealership, I constantly read the same idiotic things: the engines are the latest generation, the performance is at the top of its category, the driving experience is unmatched, and let's not even talk about the level of comfort, to say nothing of the extraordinary one-time offers. We live in a society where adjectives are on steroids. "Ciao beautiful," "ciao magnificent," even the way we say hello is hypertrophic.

With one last stab at the keyboard, executed with the flourish of a professional concert pianist, Fausto is ready to show me the copy. "Enormous wedding double suite, with a magnificently panoramic view, and an elegantly luxurious and surprisingly commodious private full bathroom equipped with a prestigious bathtub in magnificent white porcelain."

"Excellent copy with a magnificent flow and endowed with much extraordinary trenchancy," I say, hoping that on the rebound he might yet pick up on the irony.

But Fausto doesn't pick up on a damn thing and he goes back to work with the air of someone who is weary of being so exceedingly unstoppable and wonderful and every once in a while just wishes he could be an ordinary person—someone like me, for example.

Sergio calls me. He tells me that we've got to let Vito out to get a little fresh air. Unfortunately, since he isn't African and doesn't belong to any oppressed subcategory, the decision isn't put to a vote.

In the *taverna*, we interrupt the soccer match of the century. Showing on the old television set now set up as a monitor for videogames is Caserta vs. Manchester United, halted with a score of 4 to 2. We let the old man out of the bathroom and, in consideration of the young men's urgent impatience, we lead him away immediately.

This time Vito immediately puts on his sunglasses and goes straight over to the kitchen table. He starts eating forkful after forkful of rigatoni with ragu and as he does, he moves a few inches to one side, bouncing in his chair, to catch a ray of lovely sunlight angling in through the window.

"What the hell happened to the car?" he asks me.

Even if the question is innocent, I give Sergio a glance before answering.

"We hid it," I say.

"Take good care of it, you don't mind, it's a cherished keep-sake and all."

"Did you buy it with the earnings from your first shake-down?" Sergio asks.

"You can tell it's been well cared for," I say.

"In fact, if it's not too much trouble, there's a tarp under the front seat . . . "

"We already found it and used it, don't worry," Sergio says.

"If something happened to it, it would really be a shame. I just put new tires, the clutch . . . and the battery is brand new," says Vito.

"The battery's new?" I ask.

"Yessir, I've got a little problem with the radio, it's a short or sumpin', nothing serious, so I had to get a brand new battery. You want to buy the car? I'll give you a good price."

"But wasn't it a cherished keepsake?" I ask.

"Sure, it belonged to my father . . . but I'll never forget my father. Otherwise, what kind of shitty son would I be?"

It seems like a comic skit, but Vito's peremptory tone of voice eliminates any doubt that he means what he says. And that we haven't the slightest chance of understanding the world he grew up in.

"You like classical music?" Sergio asks.

"I grew up on it. My father was a music teacher."

"What about you?"

"I had to support my family when he died, he was young and full of debts."

"Is that why you joined the Camorra?"

"Boys, boys, don't use words you don't understand. The only thing you know about the Camorra is what you see on television, here we breathe Camorra from the day we're born and most of the time, it's the only organization that can help you out."

We both nod. I don't know about Sergio, but I know I'm nodding because I've heard this phrase at least a hundred times in just as many television news reports and documentaries, but only now, for the first time, do I actually feel as if I understand it.

"I don't know what you've got in mind, but it's not going to work. It's going to be a disaster," Vito adds.

33

I try lying on my belly and focusing on my breathing. Then I change position, turn over on my side, and wrap my arms around my pillow. I look at the time on my cell phone: the glare from the screen blinds me and it takes me a few seconds to realize that it's two in the morning. I turn on the lamp and try reading a book. There's nothing I find more boring than reading a book. I generally fall asleep after just a page, some-times half a page; if it's the right book, it can work miracles. Instead, this attempt is just irritating me. I read a sentence and then, with my eyes already sliding to the next one, I realize I was completely distracted and I have to start over. I concentrate furiously, but by midway through the sentence, my brain has already left the room. I close the book and get up from the bed.

From atop the stairs, I can see the flickering light illuminat-ing the living room. Claudio is sitting in front of the TV, turned on but with the volume muted. He's sprawled out, head tipped back, mouth agape. He's snoring intermittently while on the screen in front of him, a young Japanese girl is kneeling down and winking serenely into the camera as if the body that some guy with jailhouse tats behind her is working on furiously weren't her own. Out of modesty, I do my best to turn off the television, by feeling along the monolithic side of the set. I accidentally turn up the volume for a fraction of a second and Claudio wakes up with a start.

"What are you doing?" he says.

"No, what are you doing? Does this strike you as the time of night for your therapy?"

"I can't get to sleep unless I watch some TV," says Claudio, who fails to react to my wisecrack with the proper surge of shame.

Two seconds later, his head starts lurching forward again and he falls back asleep in the same position I first found him in. I sit down on the opposite side of the couch and, aside from a little creaking from the backrest, I don't hear another sound. The countryside is just too quiet. Maybe that's why I have trouble get-ting to sleep. I could try to create a more familiar nocturnal soundscape. I could mix and master a CD with a nice compila-tion of car horns, roaring engines, distant car alarms, garbage trucks with hydraulic hoists and banging dumpsters, squad cars with sirens wailing. It could be a piece of "urban new age" music.

My father would have enjoyed it here. Every so often I can imagine him sitting on the veranda or by my side in front of the fire. I don't know why, but I can only picture him as an ailing patient, with an IV in his arm and an oxygen tank invariably at his side. After all, that's the father I really got to know, the one that sticks out clearly in my memory. The other father, the one who was always running away from me, left only a few blurry images in my mind.

34

It's one of those days that seems heavensent for the local news broadcasts. There's a weather emergency. It's been pouring down without a break for thirty-six hours and cities are flooding, rivers are overflowing their banks, hillsides are giving way to mudslides, and television newscasters are wallowing in it all. Even though news broadcasts have been banned from our house, the footage of the reports, which haven't varied in the slightest for at least the past fifteen years, unspools automatically in my head.

Setting foot outside is impossible, so we're forced to devote ourselves to projects inside the house. I hate working in a team. Whenever we try to do it, this is more or less the way things go: I get a ladder and a screwdriver to hang a light fixture and the minute I climb onto the first step of the ladder, Claudio shows up and says:

"Look out, a cousin of mine fell down with a screwdriver in his hand and he punctured one of his lungs." As soon as I touch the light fixture, Fausto shows up and says: "You'd better let me do that." And the second Fausto pulls out the first wire, Sergio comes along and says: "What the fuck are you doing, you're going to destroy the whole house."

We decide to whitewash the attic. After the work on the

roof, it's really in pitiful shape. To avoid conflict, we split the room up into four sectors. Each of us gets a wall. As we're painting, we listen to a radio program that's seems to consist of songs prefaced by call-in dedications. We chanced upon it while surfing the dial and now it's our favorite show, hands down. The DJ is a kid in his late twenties who deals admirably with a daily stream of phone calls from garrulous old women, lonely and mostly depressed. I'd be willing to swear that since we started listening to the show, we've never once heard a call from anyone younger than sixty. When a dedication from a certain Anita begins, we all noisily hush one another and listen in silence. The woman's voice is gloomy and irate. "This is Anita from Colle Brunito, I wanted to dedicate this song to Tonio because it's our song and I still don't know why he left me." By now we're familiar with the format, so we know that the dedication, pitiful as it is, will only be embellished by the ensuing choice of song, so we restrain our catcalls and laughter until we can identify the first few notes. The whiny old thing who still can't get over Tonio's abandonment has requested *How Sad Venice Can Be* by Charles Aznavour.

"Oh happy day!" shouts Fausto.

"If that doesn't bring Tonio running back home, nothing will," Sergio observes.

Laughing and joking together is good for us. It's at the expense of poor old people like Signora Anita, but at least we manage to forget the distances separating us from one another. Laughter at the misfortunes of others helps us to bring together the Communist Sergio and the Fascist Fausto. And both of them with the fearful Claudio and the feckless Diego.

Once the hilarity over the Aznavour fan dies down, we wait for the next dedication. While the DJ yaks on, trying to move the show along, Sergio's cell phone beeps twice.

"It's a text message from Abu . . . 'There's been shooting, watch television news'," he says.

"There's been shooting? Who's been shot?" Fausto asks.

"That's all he wrote."

We hurry down to the living room and turn on the television set. It's not until we're confronted by a pair of sudsy tits in a 16:9 aspect ratio that we remember that we'll have to remove the channel restrictions.

"Fausto! The manual!" I say.

"The radio, damn it! Let's try to find a radio news broadcast!" shouts Sergio.

Like a galloping herd of idiots we rush back up to the attic and Claudio frantically starts turning the tuning knob. There aren't a lot of stations around here and we only hear static and snatches of Neomelodic songs.

"When was the shooting?" Fausto asks.

"What do I know, it doesn't say in his text message!" Sergio says.

"Well, call him, why don't you?"

"I'm out of credit or I would have called him already!"

"Give me the number, I'll call him myself . . . " says Fausto impatiently.

He punches in the number, hits send, then fires off a light curse, without a subject.

"Night . . . viterno . . . fired twenty-two shots . . . Camorr . . . " says the voice of a news anchor that emerges by fits and starts from the static. I put my ear up to the radio and wave the others silent with one hand. "The ambush of Priviterno can probably be blamed on a feud between rival crime families," the radio news announcer comments.

"Priviterno isn't far away," I say.

"They're not kidding around, I wonder if those thugs from the other day have anything to do with it," says Fausto.

"A fine mess. Of course they have something to do with it,

and in particular the thugs we have locked up in the cellar have something to do with it," says Claudio.

"Vito said this would happen. If you were a mob boss and three of your men vanished into thin air, what would you assume? That they're being held prisoner in an agritourism bed and breakfast or that they've been murdered by a rival crime family?" I say.

"That's our fucking problem," says Claudio.

"No," Fausto breaks in. "It's their fucking problem. This report means that our plan is working perfectly. They don't suspect a thing and they're cutting each others' throats . . . and what the hell does that matter to us?"

"Until some innocent bystander gets killed," says Claudio.

"Don't jinx this thing!" Fausto shouts.

"But that's how it works, in the end someone always gets hurt who has nothing to do with it," says Claudio.

"Listen, for the moment they've just wounded a *camorrista*. Let me repeat: just wounded . . . so they're not even all that efficient. So let's just relax a little bit," says Fausto.

35

We listen to the afternoon news broadcast with Vito. Our ears glued to the radio, we sit around the kitchen table listening to the report on the shootout, scrutinizing each and every twitch on the old man's face.

"I knew it," he says.

"Is all this mess breaking out over you?" I ask.

"You think they give a damn about us? Old men like me, kids like them, they're a dime a dozen . . . no, it's the disrespect shown to the clan. They think someone's tangling with their business, challenging them," Vito continues.

"But anyway, they don't suspect us . . . " says Fausto.

"Like I already tole you once, around here there's people much worse than you. I think you can live in blessed peace for awhile."

I stand up and pace back and forth in front of him.

"What's that on your shoe?" he asks.

I look down and notice two smears of a wooly white substance on the tip of my right shoe.

"This stuff? I don't know. It's on the grapevines, I must have brushed against them and it stuck to me."

"It's on the vines down low? On the vine proper?"

"Yes, it's on just about all the vines, it must be normal."

"Normal my ass, that's armillaria."

"What's armillaria?"

"I can see that you've never cleared away the weeds and the fallen leaves. The dirt underneath a grapevine needs to be clean, always clean, otherwise the water puddles up and you get this mold."

"And how do you know about these things?" Sergio asks.

"I come from a family of farmers."

"I thought you said musicians?" says Sergio.

"On my daddy's side. On mama's side, they were all farmers." It would be interesting to delve deeper into the matter, but for now all I really care about is the health of my vineyard.

"So what do I do?" I ask.

"If it's not too bad, all you need to do is keep the ground clean. Then the sunshine'll do the rest. Or maybe you'll have to use some product."

"And how can I tell whether or not it's spreading?"

I didn't have to argue much to convince the others to let him out. Maybe because of the friendly conversations we'd had over the last few days, it never dawned on me that it was a risky thing to do. It just seemed to me that the poor old man deserved a walk and a breath of fresh air. Claudio outlined a couple of catastrophic scenarios for us, but it was nothing that couldn't be taken care of by keeping careful watch on him and making sure that he wore a straw hat, so that there was no danger of prying eyes recognizing him.

Vito walks along, hemmed in between Sergio and Fausto, with me in front of him Claudio bringing up the rear. Under careful guard, he walks along the rows of vines and starts examining the plants. Just as he's picking up a piece of bark, I notice him catch sight of the farmhouse.

"Look at that," he says.

"At what?" I say.

"Look what you've done. It's byoo-tee-ful."

When we first locked him up, work had just begun and only now does it dawn on me how much progress we've made. Maybe it's because he's looking into direct sunlight, but Vito's eyes are glistening with moisture.

"Nice work you done," he says, putting the straw hat back on his head. "I really never thought."

He crumbles the piece of bark between his fingers, then he tells us that maybe we've been lucky and all we need to do is thoroughly clean up the plants and soil.

"If you want, I could take care of that," he says.

We don't say a word. His offer immediately arouses our suspicions. A clarinet and a violin worm their way into our disapproving silence. Before we can say anything, Vito stops short, a smile on his face, cocking his head to hear better. He waves the index finger of his right hand in the air. He knows the music's coming from his car but, hemmed in by grapevines, he has no idea of where it is.

"*Flute Concerto in A Minor* by Michel Blavet," he says.

Vito tries to catch our eyes and uses his finger to punctuate each passage.

"Listen, listen, you hear how the flute talks to the violins?" he asks.

Okay, so it wasn't a clarinet. And, in fact, it does seem like a conversation: the flute speaks and the violins respond.

"We'd better get back inside," says Sergio.

He links arms with the old man and, escorted by Fausto, leads him toward the farmhouse. Vito follows willingly but never stops listening to the music. He turns to look at me.

"To turn off the radio . . . a sharp smack of the hand on the dashboard! Not hard really, just a short, sharp rap'll do it."

"Right, right, a sharp rap," I reply.

That evening, the discussion is tense. We're exhausted from the long days of work and the noise of the nocturnal labors of Abu's work crew has put us all on edge. We talk about Vito for more than half an hour without coming to any conclusion or making the slightest progress. The only thing that everyone cares about is finally getting to bed.

"I don't trust him," says Fausto.

"Me neither," says Claudio.

"He's a man without family or friends, he has a shitty life, he can't possibly prefer to go back to a gang of thugs rather than stay here. Did you see the expression on his face when he was looking at the farmhouse?" I say.

"Sure, but you're thinking about it as if he were one of us. For those people, a hand at videopoker would be worth selling off the whole property, along with the farmhouse and us inside it," Fausto replies.

"You're right, they're pretty different from us," says Sergio.

"Of course, if he turned out to be reliable, it would make it a lot easier to handle the situation with our prisoners. Three prisoners is definitely too many," I say.

"That's true. We could put him on a sort of parole. We could let him work with us for a few hours every day. After that, though, he's going back to sleep in the cellar," says Sergio.

Claudio listens thoughtfully.

"If one of us has to stand watch on him all day long, we'll save the vineyard but we'll delay all the other projects. I say we put him to the test," he says.

36

We come up with an admirably simple plan. We'll take Vito out to work in the vineyard. Once they're outside, Sergio, who will be guarding him, will be called away urgently by Claudio, who'll pretend to need help because a scaffolding has collapsed inside the farmhouse. Fausto and I will lie hidden in the tall grass, ready to cut off his escape route if he bolts. As a last barrier, in the unlikely event that he actually does manage to shake us, Abu will take care of intercepting him before he can get out to the road.

Excited to be part of a cunning plan, we take our positions. Sergio goes down to get Vito and, the minute the two of them are out of the cellar, Claudio starts acting out his end of a loud but imaginary conversation to make Vito think that the rest of us are at work with him upstairs.

Crouching in the tall grass, we watch as the two men walk out into the courtyard. Vito is wearing a broad-brimmed straw hat that covers his face, while Sergio is carrying handfuls of tools.

Vito carefully studies the vines, then he gets down to work. He works hard, with great focus, showing certain grapeleaves to Sergio, evidently explaining things to him that we're unable to catch at our distance. He seems absorbed. Then, from inside the house, we hear a loud crash and Claudio starts yelling.

"Holy crap, the scaffolding collapsed! Sergio, come give us a hand!"

It's a little wooden in terms of delivery, but the old man doesn't seem to notice a thing.

"I'd better go see what those idiots have gotten up to," says Sergio.

"Yeah, yeah, you go," Vito replies.

There's something about his response that I don't like one little bit, and I signal Fausto to be ready to grab him. Vito follows Sergio with a suspicious eye, and he takes a few peeks at the farmhouse. Just as Sergio steps through the front door we brace for Vito to cut and run, but in that exact moment the situation spins out of control. A car appears on the dirt lane.

"Stay down, stay down!" I say to Fausto.

"Oh hell, now we're really screwed!"

"We have to get our hands on Vito!"

But the minute we turn around we see that he's vanished.

"We've fucked up, but good!" I say.

The car comes nearer and I expect to see Vito leap out into the open any second.

"We've got to get out of here, this isn't going to be good!" says Fausto.

"You're crazy, you want to just abandon Sergio and Claudio like this?"

When he hears the car coming up the lane, Sergio sticks his head out the front door. His worried gaze turns instantly to the vineyard and then toward us, but we have to remain stretched out on the ground to keep from being spotted by the occupants of the vehicle.

Just the sight of the car, a beat-up old black VW Golf, makes chills run down my spine. It swerves to a halt right in front of Sergio, who leans down to talk into the driver's side window. In a frenzy of panic by now, I do my best not to meet Fausto's gaze. I can tell he's even more freaked out than I am. I shift my gaze to Abu. From a distance, the African watches me out of the corner of his eye and goes on gathering tomatoes. I gesture an inquiry about Vito, but he just shrugs his shoulders.

Then the car backs up, turns around, and heads away down

the dirt road the way it came. Only now do I have the presence of mind to focus clearly enough to see that there are two young women in the car, and that one of them is holding a road map.

"Fucking hell," I say to Fausto.

"What's happening?"

"It was a couple of girls who took a wrong turn."

"Wha-a-at? . . . " Fausto responds in a panicky voice.

Once the car disappears down the road, we emerge from the grass and go over to Sergio who's still squatting with his hands braced against his knees.

"Vito?" he asks us.

"Vanished," I say.

"Shit . . . let's alert Abu that he's escaped and then we've better get ready to run for it," says Sergio.

I've never drawn up a top ten of the worst moments in my life, but I'm pretty sure that this silent stroll through the vineyard would either win, place, or show.

We're just passing the last row of grapevines when a cluster of leaves speaks to us.

"Have they went away?"

We had all been lost in thought, and even the manliest member of the group jumps two feet in the air. Vito's face emerges from the dense foliage, blackened like Rambo's face when he's fleeing the paranoid sheriff in the forest.

"Hey, have they went away or not, I'm getting ate alive by ants in heah!"

"It was just a couple girls who took a wrong turn, come on out," says Sergio.

Vito stands up, and we help him brush off the dirt and leaves that cover his clothes. The dusting and brushing gradually turns into slaps on the back and then ecstatic hugs.

"Hey, boys, boys, hey, should I be worried? This ain't one of those communes where you screw each other in the ass and such, is it?"

37

To keep the kids from guessing that we have a side understanding, we decide that Vito is going to have to go on sleeping in the cellar. In the morning, we'll haul him out as if we're
marching him off to forced labor, and we'll bring him back
down at night. The old man will have to put on a show, as if
he's being crushed by all the hard labor we force him to do. We
have to make sure that the *camorristi* have not the slightest
doubt, otherwise it could be fatal to Vito's health. It's also crucial to our security: having a mole in the cellar will protect us
against potential escape attempts.

The old man also collaborates with us in this capacity. For
our benefit, he reenacts a couple of versions of his evening
return to the *taverna*, including one with artificially induced
tears, highly theatrical but still quite convincing. Then, he
offers to embroider somewhat on Sergio's life story to keep the
young men well behaved.

"Don't take it the wrong way, ya know," he says to Fausto
and me. "But Sergio is definitely the most believable of youse."

He's going to tell them that he's heard a few things about
Sergio: that he's not someone you'd want to fool around with,
that he has at least a couple of political mass murders on his
conscience from the stormy years of the 1970s. And if the boys
don't do their arithmetic too carefully, and try to calculate
Sergio's age, he's pretty sure they'll fall for it.

"Youngsters respect that kind of thing," he tells us. "Kids,
you want them to stay in line, you gotta make sure they're
scared."

Vito is the first to agree that he should limit his activity outside of the farmhouse to a minimum, because there's a very real
risk that someone might be keeping us under surveillance.
He'll have complete freedom to go where he pleases and do as
he wishes inside the house but, in any case, when guests arrive,

it'll be best for him to remain out of sight. There's always a chance that someone in town might start asking questions, and if they heard about an old man in the farmhouse, suspicions could be aroused.

Vito then eagerly begins listing all the ways he can help out. He can look after the vineyard, he can take care of routine carpentry, and he can be especially useful in the kitchen.

"I come from a family of cooks," he tells us.

"Didn't you say they were farmers?" I ask.

"And musicians?" Fausto adds.

"Two uncles of mine were cooks on cruise ships. One even cooked on Agnelli's yacht!"

We're all baffled.

"And really, no offense, I can appreciate you're doing your best, but your cooking tastes like it was made in a sewer, you might give me a chance to cook something, no?"

Seeing Vito actually take an interest in things surprises me. Until just a few weeks ago, it was impossible to get beyond his "what the fuck do I care" façade. He seemed to be so steeped in that Mafioso way of life that we assumed it was unthinkable that anything we said could make a breach in the wall around him. Instead, something seems to have worked. I'd give a tidy sum to know exactly what it was that did it, what act or what phrase.

He's calm and even-tempered. He sits drinking with us as if he were a member of the group, his gaze is softened and gentle. The thought that he might have killed people troubles me and gives me the shivers. Even I, who launched myself into this adventure in hope of changing my life, still have a hard time accepting the idea that a man like him might be driven by the same desire. But maybe the truth is terribly simple. We are accustomed to saying that the Mafia still exists just because it always has, and that it's basically invulnerable. But maybe the truth is much worse than we think, maybe it's eminently possi-

176 · FABIO BARTOLOMEI

ble to defeat the Mafia. The Mafia is incapable of staking out and occupying a space of its own, it can only prosper where society leaves it a gaping void in which to operate. If our families leave it space, if the schools leave it space, if the government leaves it space, then sure, the Mafia will gain ground. The thing is, though, that the Mafia, too, leaves gaping holes that we could fill in if we only tried. And in this war of position, the Mafia ought to be at a natural disadvantage, because its gaping spaces can be filled not only by families, schools, and governments, they can be filled by much, much less, by just the slightest shred of an alternative. Say, an agritourism bed and breakfast that's bound to go bankrupt, for example.

38

The kid who's building our website starts pressing us for the official name of our farmhouse B&B. Up till now, we've just told him to use The Farmhouse as a temporary name, but this problem has been dragging on for weeks now and so far we haven't come up with a thing. We leave Vito cleaning the grout in the kitchen tiles with a toothbrush and we start leafing through the list of names from our last brainstorming session to try to whittle it down to the finalists.

"So these are the ones we kept: The Inglenook, Hilltop Inn, The Haven, The Rockpile, The Three Chimneys, and L'Asinara," says Sergio.

Actually, we'd rejected L'Asinara. It was one of Sergio's incendiary suggestions, that we name the farmhouse after the old maximum security prison used to house convicted Mafiosi, considering the guests we have in our *taverna*. But no one told him to keep that name on the list, so we do nothing but smile and move on.

"I think we should come up with something better," I say.

We decide to go outside and set up a table and chairs on top of where the Giulia is buried. A little music could serve as an inspiration. Sergio gets a demijohn of red wine and four glasses. The lawn is silent, but after a few coordinated group jumps—we make sure that Vito's not watching—we manage to get the radio to play. The notes of a piano concerto rise from the bowels of the earth. Maybe there's some other instrument, but I can't distinguish the sound. We'd need our *camorrista*/musicologist for that. When you can recognize the instruments and imagine the physical movements that produce the separate sounds, then you're really listening to music. The foolish smile emblazoned on my face has given me away. An angry grimace from Sergio persuades me to start focusing on the name. After the second round of red wine, I finally feel my brain freeing itself. The only problem is that it frees itself a little too thoroughly, in fact, it frees itself of any and all ideas. The same thing seems to have happened to the other three, who all strike various poses designed to force them to concentrate to the greatest degree possible: Fausto, elbows on the table and hands clasped; Sergio, hands behind his head gazing at the sky; Claudio, forehead on the tabletop and eyes on his feet. Then comes a third round of wine, followed a few minutes later by a fourth. Sergio stamps on the ground a couple of times to get the now-silent radio going again.

Fausto laughs and we all look at him hopefully.

"No, no, it was nothing . . . " he says.

We all sit there staring at him.

"Come on, really, it was nothing, I was just thinking . . . "

"What?" I ask him.

"No, nothing, really, it was stupid . . . "

"What is it?" Sergio demands, impatiently.

"Really, nothing, I was just reminded of the name of the part of town where I was born . . . "

"And so?" says Claudio to make him go on.

"Oh, it's just silly, but it would be a perfect name . . . "

"What the fuck! Are you going to tell us?" Sergio shouts.

Now I'm the one with my forehead on the tabletop. As if the situation weren't already irritating enough, the two begin the usual sissy fight. You watch the way you talk. I'll talk however I please. You arrogant Communist. You spoiled little Fascist. Apologize. Apologize for what? Apologize or I'm leaving. Well what the fuck just go on and leave. Oh, you'd like that wouldn't you? Then, I'll just stay.

"Well, all right, I'll tell you! Casal de' Pazzi. You know the place: Lunatic Hill!" Fausto finally says. We exchange glances.

"It just occurred to me, that's all. I'm not saying it's the name we should use, I just think it kind of fits perfectly, is all."

"Well, yeah, it's pretty fitting," I say.

"True enough," says Sergio.

We take to the idea. The wrong idea, though. We let ourselves be carried away by the desire to sign off on the matter once and for all. And even though we're by no means convinced that we've come up with the right name, we let the conversation wane and die. We let our attention wander off in search of the right catch phrase to put an end to the brainstorming session. As I gaze idly around the room, I notice that Vito is watching us from over by the kitchen window. Actually, to be exact, he's listening to us.

I walk over to the window and, without looking at me, he points at the lawn.

"There was no other solution," I say.

Vito looks at me and nods his head. He seems a little overwhelmed.

"Anyway, we put the tarp over it very carefully," I add.

Even though he nodded, I don't think he heard a word I said. Sergio and Fausto act indifferent, Claudio shrugs his shoulders.

"Okay, then," I say with a glance at my watch. And the meeting is adjourned.

39

As agreed, we take advantage of a rainy day to draw up a list of friends, family, and acquaintances we can contact to promote our establishment. For days on end, we've retailed encouraging numbers: Claudio said a hundred fifty names; oh, a hundred I think, I ventured, keeping it vague; at least five hundred, Fausto said, seeing us and raising us with the expression of someone making a very conservative estimate. He also boasted very important friendships, the kind of people that could give the golden touch to any business. Who? We asked him, and he responded with an enigmatic smile. Soccer players, rock stars, actors, fashion models? we insisted. And he gave us a conspiratorial wink, timed to coincide with "fashion models," I seemed to gather.

Sergio refused to take part in the meeting, telling us that between friends and coworkers he might be able to come up with fifteen names, no more, and there's no need for him to draw up a list. "That's okay," we told him. "Even just fifteen names would help," we added, to keep from making him feel bad about it. But Sergio is a pretty arrogant guy, he never feels bad about anything, as far as I can tell. He looked at us as if we were the losers and he walked off with Vito.

"Did you see his face?" Fausto comments.

"I tell you, there are times when I feel like slapping him around," says Claudio with all the confidence of his 5' 5" physique. According to his driver's license, actually, 5' 7".

"If there are really fifteen people in the world who can stand being around him, it's a minor miracle," says Fausto.

"Maybe he included us," I say.

Nobody else got the involuntary irony of the phrase. Claudio and Fausto laugh with gusto.

We sit down around the table with paper and pens and we're off, at a gallop. After the twelfth name—that is, once I've run through my relatives and three or four PlayStation friends—my enthusiasm subsides and I run out of steam. I look over at Claudio, who strikes me as the adversary I have the best chance of beating, or at least coming within striking distance, and I see that he's starting to slow down too. Fausto is charging along like an express train, so I decide to just empty my whole historic archive: I start with Oscar, confident in the reassuring certainty that he'll never come down here in any case. Then I move on to my other coworkers, followed by the complete list in alphabetical order of all my classmates from high school. This burst of twenty-five names gives me a solid headstart on Claudio, who's staring at his own sheet of paper with his pen poised in midair. Then I gleefully throw in the names of a few old girlfriends, just because I like the idea of showing them I'm no longer the awkward boy they once knew, but a man with a plan in life. I throw in the names of all my neighbors, a couple of guys I knew in the army, and even a guy who rear-ended me at a stop light. Claudio is in the depths of depression, he looks over at my sheet of paper and smiles nervously when he sees me finish my second column, filled with the last names only of my father's apartment house neighbors, but how is he supposed to know that? Alice has been whirring around in my head from the very start. She hasn't called me again, which is a sign that she's feeling miserable and can't bring herself to call, or else that she's thriving and having a great time and has completely forgotten about me. I'm not looking for trouble, but when it comes to money I can't afford to be squeamish. Maybe I could get word to her indirectly, by inviting all her girlfriends, for example.

We go on writing for another half hour or so, then we tote up our list of names. We have a total of two hundred ninety-one names. Including Alice.

"I only included the names I can definitely count on," says Fausto, attempting to justify himself. Then he scans the sheets of paper rapidly.

"Signora Fernanda, Signora Rosalba, Signora Maria . . . what kind of list is this?" he asks Claudio.

"They were customers at my supermarket. I might not know their last names but, actually . . . I do know them," he responds.

This triggers a brief but animated discussion over the importance of putting together a serious list because "the launch of the agritourism bed and breakfast," as Fausto puts it, "is fundamental." As I listen to the argument without much interest my eye happens to fall on one name in Fausto's list.

"Cruise, Tom?" I ask.

"That's right," Fausto says, dismissively, as if it were just one more name on the list.

"Tom Cruise . . . on the list of people you can definitely count on?" I reiterate the point.

"Believe me, Tom is a really nice guy, you'll see. If he's in Italy he'll definitely drop by."

The fact that he calls him by his first name drives me crazy. This is the kind of thing I thought only happened in Italian-style comedies, but here he is, in flesh and blood, a social-climbing con artist. Now I really ought to ask him: "Have you ever actually met him?" but I don't have the stomach for the miserable puppet show that would ineluctably ensue.

"But are you saying you've actually met him?" Claudio asks.

"When you're on TV one or way or another you wind up meeting just about everyone . . . we had dinner together once."

"And you think he'd remember?"

"I introduced him to *carciofi alla giudia*: nobody forgets the first time they eat fried artichokes," Fausto responds in a tone of voice that clearly conveys that there is nothing more to be said on the subject.

After sending out nearly two hundred invitations, in the form of emails and text messages, I would have expected at least twenty or so responses right away. Instead, two come in, with some vague compliments, plus one more from the server reporting that the address is unknown and undeliverable. To keep from losing heart entirely, we turn off the computer and start assigning the tasks that remain.

"I'll head into town and go to the butcher's while you take care of the firewood," says Fausto, who as usual has stuck me with the most challenging task.

"I think we're going to have to take turns with the firewood . . . it's pretty grueling," I say.

Claudio, meanwhile, is zapping through channels, and the pinwheeling scenes of flesh and silicone on the screen are undermining my concentration. I grab Fausto by one arm and I shove him outside. "If you ask me, this isn't good for him," I say.

"Have you heard him ask even once for a television news show?"

"No, but . . . " and I spread out my arms.

"Don't worry about it, let's just get through the next few weeks and then maybe we can replace this with soccer," he says in a professorial tone of voice.

I'm nonplussed. Something that started out as a game is starting to take on the dimensions of an actual detox cure.

"Okay, well I'd better get into town before the old ladies can grab all the best cuts of meat," he says.

I nod without saying anything. In fact, up until two weeks ago, it had been impossible to drag Claudio away from his television news shows. Now he turns the television set on much less frequently, and even if he still seems to hear the irresistible siren song every day around one and again at eight in the evening, he gets tired of watching after just a few minutes.

40

As expected, the lottery has worked perfectly. Thanks to the idea of supplementary prizes, the guys manage to win something practically every day. What I find most surprising is that they continue to barter their hour of exercise and fresh air for beer, cigarettes, and joints. They haven't set foot outdoors for weeks, they're frighteningly pale, but the one thing that would have been at the top of my list of priorities is beneath their consideration. They've even won some money, five hundred euros to be exact, and after we cashed in their tickets we went down into the *taverna* with an old wooden crate, which once held wine bottles, containing the two hundred fifty euros they were due. They were happy, though of course they concealed their joy behind a wall of sarcasm and scorn and veiled threats about what they'd do if they figured out we were ripping them off. But that's part of who they are and we don't really even notice it anymore.

I walk downstairs with Sergio as my bodyguard. When they emerge from the bathroom they hurl themselves on the tickets first thing. Before Renato scratches his ticket, he gives it a kiss. Saverio on the other hand rubs his ticket on his ass.

"Yes!" Renato shouts.

He slaps the ticket with the back of his hand, then he waves it in the air so we can see it. Emerging from beneath the gold latex coating are two cherry clusters.

"What do you win with two cherries?" I ask Sergio.

"A woman!" says Renato. I'd forgotten about that.

"So what do you want instead?" I ask.

"Nothing, we want a woman!" he reiterates in a threatening voice.

Sergio takes the ticket.

"This is a respectable lottery, you'll have your prize."

Sergio had already taken this eventuality into consideration and through Abu he had reached out and made a deal with a Nigerian sex worker. Sex deprivation is one of the strongest driving forces behind most escape attempts, he tells me, so it's a good idea to throw them their prize when they win. The idea seems self-evident to me, but when we broach the subject with Fausto and Claudio perhaps we fail to lay the groundwork properly. There's an outburst of shouts, insults, slamming doors, and even a couple of "*What if I don't?*'s"

But around nightfall, when the doorbell rings, we all gather in the living room. Fausto hurries down from upstairs trailing an unseemly whiff of cologne, Claudio hastens to turn off his 8 o'clock pornocast and grabs a magazine. I condemn them both with a scornful glance in Sergio's direction, but in spite of myself I give my bangs a quick brush and pat.

The woman at the front door is enormous and must weigh in at roughly 200 pounds. She isn't fat, it's just that she has an abnormal mass of flesh and muscle distributed uniformly over her 5-foot-5-inch frame. My first thought goes to those two pale young men who are probably dreaming of a slender young prostitute from Eastern Europe, with cherry-red lips and champagne-glass breasts. We welcome Claretta—that's the discus thrower's name—with the uneasy courtesy you'd expect of a group of well-brought-up young men in that situation.

"Would you like something to drink before you—eh . . . " says Fausto.

"Nice touch, the miniskirt . . . with this hot weather," I venture. Claretta smiles at us but says nothing. Sergio takes her aside to discuss a few ethical matters. While I while away my embarrassment by smoking a cigarette with Fausto, I hear our fearless leader whispering a series of questions including: "Did anyone take your passport away from you in order to blackmail you?" "Are you here against your will?" and "Did you come to Italy because you were promised work as a dancer?" Once she's been certified as an authentic DOC prostitute, Sergio sets his mind at rest and heads downstairs to inform the guys that their winnings have arrived. Security considerations demand that their hands be tied securely to the headboard of their bed, and considerations of privacy dictate that a sheet be hung between them, to serve as a rudimentary curtain.

A few minutes later Sergio returns to the kitchen and gallantly offers his arm to Claretta who, wobbling on her towering heels, walks downstairs with him. Her thudding steps resound throughout the tunnel-hallway. I can just imagine the looks on the faces of those two right now.

"You know, I have to say that I'm almost tempted to have a go with her myself," says Fausto.

"What, really?" asks Claudio.

"You think I'd go with a whore! The minute this place opens we'll be getting so much pussy we could use it to upholster the sofa!"

Claudio, who has one hand resting on the back of the sofa, yanks it away and then pretends to examine his fingernails.

We start pacing back and forth in loose array. Fausto lights another cigarette and sits on a windowsill. Claudio sits down and picks up the remote control.

"I don't think that's a very good idea," I say.

So he puts it back and then moves it over to the coffee table.

Then he lines it up with his finger next to the neat stack of magazines. I go into the kitchen to drink a glass of water, then I pick up a recipe book and sit down next to the fireplace and start leafing through it. Fausto crumples up a sheet of newspaper and starts dribbling and juggling it.

"Guys!" Sergio says as he comes upstairs from the cellar. "Claretta's leaving . . . "

The Nigerian appears behind him with a makeup mirror in one hand and a lipstick in the other. Instinctively, I look at my watch, but since I have no idea what time it was when she got here, that provides me with no useful information.

"Ciao, Claretta," Fausto says.

"Goodbye, thanks for coming," says Claudio.

I do nothing more than to smile and raise one hand.

"So long boys," Claretta says, kissing Sergio on the cheek on her way out.

The minute the door swings shut, we cluster around him.

"Well, how did it go?" Fausto asks.

"How would I know, I didn't stay to watch!"

"Sure, of course not, but the guys? Were they happy?" I ask.

"You should have seen their faces . . . "

41

After spending the morning painting one of the exterior walls of the farmhouse, we all meet in the kitchen to reckon up all our culinary expertise. We determine that, putting all four of us together, we know how to make Spaghetti with Olive Oil and Garlic, Spaghetti alla Carbonara with Onion, Spaghetti all'Amatriciana, various kinds of frittatas, a simple stew, and grilled meat. Vito, who in the past few days has proven to have a far greater variety of abilities than any of us, could certainly put together an attractive and appetizing meal, but we can't run the risk of showing him off to our guests, because among other things we expect a fair amount of our business to be coming from the village. In this line of business, it's the extras that really bring in the money. The fee for the room alone hardly begins to cover our expenses, but if you factor in lunch and dinner, massages and other items, such as bike rentals, then you really start to see some profits.

"We have to get a masseuse, absolutely, but I don't think we can afford a cook," says Claudio.

"Don't talk nonsense, that's where you make all your profit. In the rosiest imaginable scenario, we could throw together a bowl of spaghetti for a group of not-particularly demanding friends. What we are going to be expected to do, on the other hand, is to satisfy the palates of discerning guests with varying tastes, and—most important of all—convince them to stay here to eat rather than venture out in search of some charming little local restaurant," says Fausto.

"That's true, but chefs are incredibly expensive. Plus, we'll have to get a sous-chef," says Claudio.

"That's where we can save some money. We'll take turns helping out in the kitchen," says Fausto.

"He's right, a masseuse and a chef are indispensable. Do you have any ideas?" I ask.

"Hold everything, we're forgetting an important detail. The guys in the cellar," say Sergio.

"You think they know how to cook?" asks Claudio.

"Christ, I mean, how are we going to find a cook and a masseuse willing to work in a prison for *camorristi*?"

Obviously, we won't be able to. Silence falls over the little group. Vito looks at each of us in turn; he seems the most eager of us all to find a solution. When Sergio clears his throat he immediately turns toward him with a smile on his face.

"The guests aren't a problem, all we need to do is keep them out of the kitchen . . . and I'd say the same thing applies to the masseuse, but what are we going to do about the chef? Should we tell him? Should we just warn him never to go downstairs to the *taverna*?"

"Oh, don't be silly, we have no choice but to tell him. And who can we find that would be willing to accept that kind of a risk? It would take a desperado," I say.

For the first time in a long while I find myself thinking once again that this is all just madness. We fooled ourselves into thinking we could do it and, now that I consider matters carefully, maybe the *camorristi* we're holding prisoner aren't even the biggest problem. We couldn't have pulled it off anyway. We just don't have what it takes.

"I might have the right person," says Claudio, attracting our mistrustful gazes.

"As a chef or as a masseuse?" I ask.

"Both."

"And who are they? How do you know them?"

"It's just one person, a young woman who used to work for me . . . and she's one of the hardest working and most reliable workers I ever had. I know she took a massage course and I also know that she's a fabulous cook because she invited lots of her colleagues to dinner and they all spoke very highly of the food."

"And you've never . . . "

"So she never asked you to dinner, eh?" says Fausto.

"Of course she asked me to dinner! I just always preferred to keep my relations with my employees on a professional footing," Claudio replies.

"Well, do you think she'd accept the risk?" I ask.

"I don't know, but I can tell you for sure that when we went out of business, she was pretty upset. If you like, I can give her a call and ask her to come for a tryout. Then we can decide how much to tell her."

42

We may not be any good at dealing with clogged toilets, but when it comes to persuading other people to do things, we're past masters. We have a reassuring array of fairytales ready to retail the cook-qua-masseuse, ranging from a rehabilitation program for young *camorristi* all the way up to an overarching general anti-Mafia plan for the intelligence services. We'll decide which fairytale to trot out when we have a better idea of what kind of person she is.

Vito will introduce himself as Pietro and say that he's one of our partners. To gain an extra advantage in terms of time before we actually have to level with the girl, Sergio has come up with a brilliant idea: conceal the door that leads down to the *taverna*. He took an old credenza, installed rollers from an office chair behind the legs, and then nailed it to the door. It's perfectly camouflaged and now we have a genuine secret passageway that might prove to be useful in other circumstances as well. The problem of our musical lawn, on the other hand, is proving to be intractable. We have yet to come up with a solution for that one, and in fact the Giulia hasn't made itself heard for a few days now, so we've decided to take on our various problems one at a time. First and foremost, let's see if she's the right person, then we'll deal with the issue of our prisoners. Once we've done that, the buried automobile will just be a last niggling detail.

Sergio and Claudio come back from the train station carrying a precious human cargo. Fausto, Vito, and I gather in the courtyard to welcome her to the farmhouse. We've been men living with other men for a long time now, and it doesn't take a genius to see that a burden of expectations is riding on the new arrival.

When the car stops, a petite young woman steps out, with delicate features and a cheerful expression. She has a shock of bright red hair dangling over her forehead, and as she gets closer I notice a daunting array of piercings, orphaned of what must once have been an equally impressive array of metal rings and spheres. This is probably not exactly the girl we were dreaming of, I'm willing to bet.

"This place is straight out of a fairy tale! . . . Elisa," she says, extending her hand.

"Diego," I introduce myself.

"Elisa," she says, holding her hand out to Vito.

"Pietro."

"Elisa," she repeats to Fausto.

"A pleasure, Fausto Maria."

Sergio slams the door of the car hard, and the Giulia comes to life. The musical notes arrive faintly, vaguely, but the girl only seems to notice our awkward silence.

"Mozart . . . *Piano Sonata*," Vito whispers to me.

"Come on, Elisa, let me show you around," says Sergio, leading her into the farmhouse.

After mentally telling the Giulia to go fuck itself, we follow.

"I didn't know your name was Fausto Maria," I say, when the girl is out of earshot.

"Well, actually I'm just called Fausto, but women like men with a feminine side. So I add Maria . . . it's a form of pussy bait."

The first thing Elisa says when she walks into the living room is: "Well, there's certainly plenty of work still to do."

We're all left speechless because, after so much time, we'd become accustomed to the furnishings.

"Actually, we're almost finished fixing the place up," says Fausto.

"What about these?" she asks, pointing at the poker tables.

"They were a real bargain! Just picture them covered with beautiful tablecloths." Elisa stands there, speechless. She seems to be on the verge of saying something. Then she smiles briefly and asks:

"Well, should we do this audition? Shall I make you something to eat?"

In less than forty minutes, working with the few items we have in our pantry, the young woman has put together a meal with a first course, an entrée, and side dishes. The spaghetti has a variation on the standard pesto that she invented herself: no garlic, but with the addition of walnuts and sesame seeds. The cutlets are garnished with an eggplant and yogurt sauce. As a side dish, she made roast potatoes, with a perfectly crunchy exterior and a flaky soft interior. The food is not only delicious; it is also beautifully presented. The cutlets, for instance, are garnished with eggplant skins sliced very thin and fried. On the plate, the skins form a crunchy mattress of purplish wool. Our stern façade as so many exacting connoisseurs crumbles into a symphony of moans and sighs of pure enjoyment.

The first salient result is that such an excellent lunch restores our good humor. We exchange smiles and knowing looks and we praise Claudio for his excellent idea. Elisa is the right person, for us and for the bed and breakfast. Because for too long we've been eating in haste, without appetite, and in shifts, living with the constant nightmare of having to cook without knowing how.

"With what was in the pantry, I couldn't come up with anything better," says Elisa, who already knows she holds us in the palm of her hand.

"Everything was first rate, I don't think I've ever eaten so well in my life," says Sergio.

"Super," I say.

"Quite acceptable," says Fausto, but he undercuts his show of self-restraint by displaying half a sprig of parsley smeared across one of his incisors.

"I knew you'd be impressed," says Claudio. "So if we're all in agreement . . . "

"First of all, there's something I'd like to discuss with you," Elisa breaks in. Sure enough, it was all going too smoothly. We should have known that there would be problems when it came to the matter of salary. Considering our financial situation, all we can offer are poverty wages plus a generous percentage of the revenue from meals and especially from massages. As we all gather in the living room, a mist of disappointment glazes our eyes.

"Fifty euros more per month, tops," Fausto whispers to me.

"Then we can kiss her goodbye immediately," I say.

"You did the figures!" he hisses at me bitterly.

"Come on guys, let's just promise her something, higher percentages based on what we bring in . . . " says Claudio.

"Sure, let's get a list of things to say without actually promising anything," I suggest.

Two minutes later we're all sitting on the sofa, rapt and respectful, while Elisa strides back and forth waving an old interior decorating magazine. We aren't talking about money, we're talking about style, color combinations, room identities, space allocation, and coordination and consistency. We don't actually follow most of what she's saying and, like children, what we focus on are the pictures. Those are unmistakable and clear. The interiors of the houses are warm, colorful, and cozy. There are details, like the fact that the window curtains all seem to be same color, that give the interiors a much more elegant appearance. We hang our heads as we tour the farmhouse upstairs and downstairs, and suddenly there isn't a single thing that looks right. At the top of the punch list we once again have a new heading, "Interior Decoration." We'll have to scrimp on what little money we still have, but none of us has the slightest doubt that, unless we want to open an agritourism bed and breakfast that doubles as a gambling den for unaccompanied men, we'd better get busy, and fast.

43

She may not be stunningly beautiful, but there's something very special about this girl. The more I look at her, the more

I'm captivated by her understated charm. Right now, for instance, I'm watching her from a distance as she sits down on the sofa to watch a little television. She's not exactly elegant, but she has a natural, unselfconscious sensuality. I take a step back to vanish into the shadows of the kitchen so I can watch her unobserved. Just what is that expression on her face? She seems like a little girl. That's right, she looks like a little girl watching television for the first time in her life. Or maybe it's just the fact that, for the first time in her life, she's watching television on a set that refuses to show anything other than porno movies, damn it to hell! I take two more steps backward in a desperate attempt to vanish entirely into the darkness. I see Fausto come in from the yard. He's chilly and he walks over to Elisa without fully realizing what's happening. Perfect, I'm happy that he's the one to walk into this situation unawares. He smiles at the young woman but it's not until it's entirely too late, when he's just a few steps away from her, that it dawns on him. Elisa turns an indecipherable gaze on him—she's not embarrassed, she's not appalled, she's not even mad. But one thing I do know: I'm glad not to be in that room.

"Now you just tell me what's going on here!" Fausto shouts.

His voice is filled with exasperation, and the girl is nonplussed.

"We followed the instructions step-by-step to block these disgusting channels . . . and now they're the only channels you can see!" he rants with a note of distaste in his voice.

Elisa doesn't doubt him for a second. She takes him at his word. So he picks up the instruction manual and let's fly with his last parry and thrust.

"You take a look and tell me if you can figure it out. I must have tried a dozen times at least!" he says, and he walks out of the room, heading furiously straight for me. The minute he walks into the kitchen I throw my arms around him and I hail the conquering hero. He's exhausted.

"Superb, Fausto, you were absolutely su-perb!" I tell him.

"Thank you, thank you . . . anyway, starting tomorrow we're going to move on to the next phase in Claudio's detox therapy—soccer," he says, panting.

It takes us nearly a week to cart all the furniture back and buy replacement furniture. Happily, we've been able to limit our expenses because Elisa saw all the furniture that we put in storage in the shed and, to make a long story short, she decided that it was all wonderful. To make that story a little longer: first she was surprised, then nonplussed, and then practically furious, after which she treated us like a herd of drooling idiots unable to see that these were valuable antiques and that with a bit of tender loving care they would be just as good as new. So we abandoned all our various occupations and turned into a team of improvised furniture restorers.

Taking shifts, we also had an opportunity to experience Elisa's bravura as a masseuse. The health and fitness room that she set up in the attic is already the loveliest room in the house. The massage bed is turned to face the window so that the guest can enjoy the magnificent panoramic view. Candles and scented essential oils tinge the atmosphere evocatively. And that's to say nothing of the massages themselves. I'm certainly no expert, I'm just a guy who would happily become a gigolo in exchange for having my back scratched. So, after a fifty-minute massage, I've become a faithful slave in her hands. What I feel isn't just gratitude, it's an oath of eternal loyalty issuing from each and every relaxed and languid fiber of my body.

In the kitchen, Vito has proven to be a first-rate sous-chef. Together, he and Elisa manage to serve up a varied and astonishing menu. We go crazy over the details, such as the vegetable gratins with poppy seeds, linseeds, and sesame seeds, or toasted pine nuts tossed into a tomato and basil sauce as a surprise ingredient. Well fed and massaged, we work in concert with all the harmony of a Hare Krishna commune. Sergio spends the evenings stitching the hems of the new window curtains; Vito, with his oversized hands, made to strangle deadbeat debtors, spends the evenings applying beautifully inked calligraphic labels to the mason jars that contain our preserved foods; Fausto and Claudio string beads on the fringe of a lampshade; I braid straw to make placemats.

We're all so extremely relaxed that we completely forget to tell her about what we're hiding in the cellar. Once or twice, to tell the truth, we've considered telling her how things stand. For instance, one time when she was in the kitchen and a triumphal march performed by some demented German philharmonic orchestra wafted in through the window, but she just assumed that the music was coming from upstairs and we convinced ourselves that there was no real hurry, that the right time would just present itself and then it would be easy to win her over.

When the delivery truck shows up with the new furniture, we immediately spring into action like so many orchestra members obedient to the orders of our new conductor, Elisa. We start arranging tables and chairs, lifting and carrying credenzas, sofas, and armchairs, hanging paintings, placing vases and carpets, hanging curtains, installing consoles and bookshelves, and we warm up the setting with lamps, plants, and books. We are all such supine victims of the enchantment of those slender hands that even when she's using them to show us where to move a piece of furniture we fall into an adoring trance. The discreet charm of Elisa is no longer a secret to anyone. We've all fallen under its sway. Aside from Claudio, who seems to be interested only in watching soccer matches on TV, everyone else has started to court and spark. Vito relies on old-fashioned gallantry, well aware of the age gap between him and her, but also of the fact that you can never tell in life. Fausto and Sergio have gone back to their knightly jousting and they're doing their best to impress her, singlehandedly carrying pieces of furniture that would normally require at least another pair of arms. End result: by midnight, the interior decoration is almost complete.

After the Elisa cure, the farmhouse is a worthy rival to the interiors depicted in the design magazines. All it took was a series of minor tweaks. For instance, in the living room, we turned the sofa toward the fireplace instead of toward the TV, the window curtains are all the same color, the card tables have all been replaced by rustic tables, the chilly white light of the halogen spotlights has given way to a warmer illumination from artfully deployed standing lamps. The kitchen has been restored to its former splendor and the formica cabinets have been abolished. The bedrooms have been embellished with nightstands in the same style as the armoires and brightened with colorful fabrics. Out in the yard, the white plastic has vanished, replaced by the wooden lawn furniture I had futilely pointed out to Fausto. As for the plants, it couldn't have been simpler. The garden is full of plants, but it never occurred to us to bring any inside. Now there are plants in every corner and yes, taken as a whole, the farmhouse looks like a first-class establishment.

"It's marvelous," I say.

"This is the loveliest agritourism bed and breakfast I've ever seen," says Claudio.

"We'll be able to raise the room rate by a good 30 percent," Fausto concludes.

44

Fate has a way all its own of restoring the balance of things. After properly celebrating the completion of work on the inside of the farmhouse and dropping into our beds dead drunk, we woke up the next morning to the sound of cascading water. During the night, the pressure of the new water heater broke a radiator pipe in the attic, and we didn't notice a thing until the house had been flooded.

It's only about a month till Christmas and once again we're out of money. With the help of Sergio, Abu, and the others, we've saved a lot of money, but the building materials for the work on the roof along with the groceries to feed eight mouths, seven of which are connected to ravenous appetites, have bled us white. After an inspection to determine the extent of damages, we sit down around the kitchen table and decide that in order to meet the new expenses, we're going to have to establish an emergency fund. Fausto and Claudio will sell their cars, while my contribution will be to pitch in my savings, including my last paycheck and my tiny inheritance.

"Could you give me the address of a good car dealership?" Fausto asks me.

"You really ought to just sell the car yourself. It's quicker and you save the thirty percent commission on the price," I say.

"What do you think, should I have some work done on the car first? Get the clutch fixed, maybe?"

"Wash the car thoroughly, inside and out, and clean the engine until it sparkles like your grandmother's silverware."

"The engine?"

"That's right, wash the engine. It has to gleam. Then put a vanilla-scented air freshener in the car for two days."

"Vanilla-scented?" asks Sergio, who is being drawn into the conversation.

"That's right, none of the other scents work properly. Keep it in the car for two full days, then get rid of it. Then three hours before the potential buyer is scheduled to come, clean the dashboard with an anti-static gloss spray."

"Everytime someone comes to see the car, I have to clean the dashboard?" Fausto asks.

"It's not because the dashboard needs to be clean, it's because of the smell. The spray, mixed with vanilla air freshener, leaves a scent that's very close to new-car smell. Trust me."

Fausto scrutinizes me. He doesn't know whether he should throw his arms around me or dismiss me as a bullshit artist. Everyone's eyes are on me. Even Vito is very interested and Elisa is giving me an incredulous stare. I feel I owe my audience an encore.

"Listen, you don't have any wiggle room on tires and clutches . . . if it's somebody who knows about cars, he'll notice, and in that case your only option is to replace everything and lay out a huge wad of cash. But the ones you want aren't the guys who know about cars. The ones you want are the people who know nothing about cars and who just show up hoping that they've finally come to the right place, that you're the seller of their dreams. They see the gleaming bodywork and they fall into a reverie . . . at which point it's enough to make sure that they don't think of driving over to a mechanic friend of theirs to get the car checked out, and that's where the sparkling clean motor comes in. Then you let them sit in the car and the fake new-car smell will deliver the knockout blow."

"What a fantastic son of a bitch you are . . . " Fausto says to me, finally won over heart and soul.

I revel in Elisa's look of amazement and decide to go for the cherry on top of the cake.

"If you want, we can even try the old car inspector gag . . . " I say.

"What's that?" asks Sergio.

"When they come to see the car, I'll be there . . . with my head under the hood."

It's my own invention. I've staged this scenario a couple of times to help out friends of mine and I find it endlessly amusing. I dress up as a real nitpicker, an obsessive, unfashionable geek, and when the prospective buyer shows up, I'm under the hood with my head in the engine compartment, eyeglasses perched on the tip of my nose, pocket flashlight in hand. While the guy is standing there, I peer around at this and that, flashing the beam here and there, and then I extract myself as if I've been bent over like that for a long time, and I stretch as if my back is aching. I flick off the flashlight, I slip it into its plastic case, and I put it carefully away in a tool bag. Then I say, "Well, you're obviously a car lover, there aren't many people around anymore as conscientious and scrupulous as you seem to be. I'll let you have my answer by the end of the day." Then I shake hands with formal good manners and I leave. With the reassurance of the nitpicking rival buyer, the unfortunate sucker has no alternative but to be swept away by the gleaming bodywork and to hasten to put in a competitive offer.

"This man is a genius!" says Fausto as he wraps me in a bear hug. I never thought I'd be able to worm my way into Fausto's heart. Instead, it was the easiest thing in the world to win his esteem and respect. All I needed to do was show him what a skilled con artist I am. I try to catch Elisa's eye, but all I see is her back. Probably, she hasn't fully grasped the plan. After all, she's a woman, so what can she know about cars?

45

We sell Fausto's car to the first person who comes to look at it, and Claudio's to the third. The stratagem of the car inspector worked brilliantly and now we can get back to work and recover the time we've wasted, and fix the damage from the leak.

We'll need to replace the broken pipe and check the seals on all the radiators. Then, once we've tested the heating system, we'll have to replace the hardwood flooring on the second story, plus there's a nice long list of ceilings and walls to scrape and sand and repaint. Since the only ones who have any experience with the first part of the job are Sergio and Vito, and since they already have two assistants to help them, I take advantage of the opportunity to catch up with Elisa in the garden.

It's a bright sunshiny day, but for the first time, I need to put on a wool sweater and a jacket to go outside. The grounds of the farmhouse are so big that every chore becomes a grueling undertaking. Even just to gather rocks to mark the boundary between the courtyard and the garden. I push a wheelbarrow back and forth in search of stones and pebbles. Unless they're sufficiently large and white, Elisa isn't happy. Just to line the perimeter takes twelve trips with a full wheelbarrow load. But as always, the result is spectacular to behold.

"They put our website online!" Fausto shouts out the window.

We hurry inside and cluster around the computer. We give the place of honor to Elisa and we hold our breath as we watch the webpage open. First there's a brief animation sequence: a panoramic photograph of the farmhouse, with a blue sky and two small white clouds that sail slowly from right to left. Okay, I think. Then a horrible musical jingle starts up that seems to be played by a kid's electric organ, and okay again. Then comes a biplane pulling an advertising banner behind it, and okay for the third time. As the banner slides into view, the name of the farmhouse appears, and no, no, no, what the fuck!

"Lunatic Hill?" asks Sergio.

Fausto turns toward us, extinguishing his pleased smile a little too late.

"What, have you lost your mind?" I say.

"What's the matter?" Fausto asks. Elisa looks around at us in bewilderment.

"Didn't we say we were going to call it the Hilltop Inn?" asks Claudio.

"What Hilltop Inn! We said L'Asinara!"

Fausto pulls the records from our brainstorming session out of a drawer and nervously shows them around the room.

"No, my friends! The last name on the list was Lunatic Hill and you all said yes!"

"I never said yes, I just smiled!" Sergio points out.

"I just said 'huh,'" I add.

The usual skirmishing ensues. Each of us seems to be certain that we unanimously voted for a different name, but the truth is that we never came up with anything good and the work of creative brainstorming is incredibly boring.

"I don't actually think the name's all that bad . . . " says Elisa.

We turn to look at her, as she's scrolling through the pages of the website.

"There's a much more serious problem here, it seems to me." Our quarrel comes to a sudden halt.

"What problem?" asks Fausto.

"The photographs are the most important thing . . . and the ones you've used totally suck."

She scrolls rapidly past the pictures before our eyes. And she's right: they're poorly lighted, the rooms look tiny, and that's to say nothing of the fact that they were all taken before her arrival, when the interior decoration was frankly revolting.

"To say nothing of the captions and texts . . . " she adds.

We decide to abandon our argument over the name. Under Elisa's supervision we set about re-photographing every room in the farmhouse. After just the first few shots in the living room, the difference is stark.

When I throw open a window to improve the lighting in the dining area, we hear the sound of a car pulling up slowly in the courtyard. Peeking out from behind a curtain I glimpse a town police patrol car parking just a few yards from the front door, parallel to the front of the house.

"Town police," I say.

There's a moment of panic. We all assume that their arrival has something to do with the missing *camorristi*. Even Sergio loses his proverbial icy cool for a second.

"Vito, go downstairs!" he says.

"Who's Vito?" Elisa asks in some confusion.

"Fausto, go with Elisa and Claudio and turn on the TV. Diego, you come with me!" he adds.

"What's happening?" Elisa asks.

"Oh, it's nothing, they're probably just here about a parking ticket . . . " says Fausto as he drags her over to the sofa and pulls her down, seated, next to him.

The minute Vito vanishes into the kitchen, we open the front door and walk smiling toward the patrol car.

"You hear anything?" Sergio asks me out of the side of his mouth.

"God, that damned car does it on purpose!" I say through clenched teeth.

A fine thumping drum roll comes gusting up from the Giulia to greet the arrival of the town policemen, both of them in their mid-fifties. The one who gets out on the driver's side has salt-and-pepper hair and a mustache that hasn't been fashionable for at least thirty years; the other one seems to outrank him, and his hair is dyed a raven black with ridiculous steel-blue highlights glinting in the bright sunshine. They stop to look at the farmhouse and it's at least a full minute before they decide to respond to our welcoming smiles.

"Haven't I seen you before at the police station?" says the senior officer.

As he extends his hand, he displays three gold bracelets as thick as handcuffs.

"I don't remember. It's certainly possible. I came in to notify you that we were starting construction," I say.

In the meantime, the other police officer takes a stroll around the garden, just as another drum roll comes booming across the yard. The way the two policemen are scrutinizing the farmhouse is reassuring. They seem to be here for a routine inspection.

"Would you care to step inside?" I ask, eager to keep them from noticing where the music is coming from.

"If it doesn't get your nose outta joint, I think we'll take a look around at the work you've done outside."

"Of course, be our guests. I'll show you around."

We walk around the house, following in the footsteps of the other town police officer who, as if by instinct, is heading straight for the Giulia. The sound of music is growing clearer. I start yammering in my urge to distract them.

"As you can see, we haven't done any construction on the exterior of the building," I say, pointing at one of the walls of the farmhouse in hope of deflecting their gazes, which are starting to turn toward the lawn. "We just replastered here and there and touched up the paint. There were some climbing vines that were damaging the plaster so we took them down. Then there was a dead tree that looked like it might be about to fall, so, you can imagine, to avoid any risks we chopped it down . . . "

"Oh, that's where it's coming from!" says the town police officer.

My blood runs cold until I have the presence of mind to follow the finger he's pointing toward the kitchen window. Claudio is a genius. He's put the radio, unplugged, on the window sill, and as he washes a sinkful of spanking clean pots and pans, he conducts the imaginary orchestra, with one hand waving in the hair.

"He just loves classical music," I say, and immediately change the subject.

Once they're inside the farmhouse, they ask to see all our permits and other documents. They let us lead them from one room to another with the fixed smiles and the fake benevolent demeanor that are starting to become all too familiar. The wheeled credenza that we nailed to the door to fool Elisa seems to take them in as well. The whole time I'm sweating bullets and I'd have to guess that my partners are all feeling the same level of anxiety. Still, not a sound comes from downstairs. The whole time, the two town policemen take notes furiously. Once they've finished their inspection the conversation takes the same direction as the ones we've had with all the other gangsters.

"There are a few irregularities in these bathrooms," the senior officer points out.

"But we did everything strictly to code," I say with a disarming smile.

"What code?"

"We came to the police station to get the building guidelines . . . "

"Ah, the building guidelines. In the building guidelines it's written that the walls have to terminate at the base with a slight outward bulge, to avoid unhygienic accumulations of garbage. Some of my colleagues don't pay attention to that detail . . . but I do."

The town policemen start noticing plenty of other things, such as the height off the floor of some of the beds and the absence of emergency fire exit markings. I leave Sergio with them—he seems to be maintaining his calm—and I hurry to the kitchen to get the file with the inspector's certification of the electrical system. Vito peeks out from behind the door.

"How's it going?" he asks in a whisper.

"They're reaming us out, but good!" I hiss back and wave frantically for him to shut the door.

"Stay calm, it's all under control . . . at a certain point, they'll ask you if you need something new, like a air conditioner or a refrigerator, you say yes and ask them if there's a place they can recommend. That's where it's all heading. That's the bribe they're looking for . . . "

"But wasn't paying protection supposed to ensure we wouldn't have this kind of problem?"

"Sure, you've got no problem, this is just a one-time payout."

Just as Vito predicted, the town policemen completely ignore the stack of papers that I bring them and after tsk-tsking at the umpteenth not-to-code irregularity they walk into the living room. There's a brief round of introductions with Fausto, Claudio, and Elisa, who pretend to be engrossed in a Uruguayan championship match. Then the town policeman walks over to me.

"It's a little old, this television, don't you want a nice big 42-inch plasma screen set?"

"Of course!" I say, to Sergio's bafflement. "Do you have any idea where we could get one?"

"I'm perfectly satisfied with this one," says Sergio, clearly determined to put an end to that line of inquiry.

The cop acts offended and snatches back the business card he was about to hand me.

"He might be satisfied but I'm not. A 42-inch plasma screen TV is better than seeing it at the movies, right guys?" I shout at the trio sitting on the sofa.

"Eh?" says Elisa.

"Yes, definitely," says Fausto.

"You go to this shop, the owner'll take good care of you. If I were you, I'd try to get by this week sometime . . . "

"The day after tomorrow at the very latest, because there's a game on Wednesday, right?"

Sergio watches the puppet show in evident amazement, but luckily keeps his mouth closed.

"All right, my friend, we'd better get going, we've got a lot of things to take care of today."

"What about the citations?" Sergio asks, putting an end to the miracle of his temporary silence.

"The citations? What do you take us for—jackals? We want your business to prosper, why would we get you started with a 2,000 euro fine? We pointed out the things that aren't up to code, you fix them, and we're all set."

Sergio stands expressionless and the town policeman, who clearly lacks some basic instinct for self-preservation, walks over to him and pats him affectionately on the cheek.

"We're all nice folks around here . . . you be good now," he says to him.

46

The arrival of Abu helps us to stanch Elisa's curiosity after the puppet show with the town policemen. He's in pitiful condition, frighteningly worn out and skinny. His employer short-changed him on his paycheck and, when Abu objected, the bastard had the African beaten badly by his henchmen. Abu hasn't been able to do any work for two weeks now. He tells us these things without any intention of making us feel sorry for him. He's just giving straightforward answers to Sergio's questions about why he hasn't come around for the last little while. Vito and Elisa immediately bustle around the kitchen preparing something for him to eat, and I feel a pang in my stomach at the sight of his ravenous hunger as he wolfs down the food.

Claudio, Sergio, and I have withdrawn into the living room to talk the matter over in private. The whole time, the background noise is Fausto, who's been arguing furiously on the phone with the guy who put the website together for him. This web designer is supposed to be a friend of his but he's absolutely refusing to upload the new photographs without charging us extra.

"We ought to pay Abu right away for the work he did on the roof," Sergio says.

"How much money do we have left?" I ask Claudio.

"If we take out the money for the plasma screen television set . . . for the new washing machine and the lawn mower, then what's left is the grocery budget, the advertising fund, and the fund for the opening day party."

"That's it?" I ask.

Fausto strides into the living room, evidently furious.

"That bastard wants another three thousand euros . . . and that's not all, he's demanding immediate payment of the first installment now!"

"Hold on, Fausto, we have another problem. Abu is here. He needs some money," Sergio says.

"So now he's trying to get his hands in the till too. Just as I expected!" he says with a mocking smile.

I turn my head and look toward the kitchen, directing Fausto's eyes toward Abu. The African is eating with his head just inches above his plate. He uses his fingers to snatch a piece of meat that fell onto the tablecloth and quickly lifts it to his mouth.

"What the hell happened to him?" Fausto asks. The smile has vanished from his face.

"They beat him up and they haven't given him any more work for the past few weeks," I say.

"So why didn't he come to us before this?"

"Maybe he was afraid that one of us would take it the wrong way . . ."

Fausto takes my point. It's not like him, though. Usually he'd have some fast retort, aggressive and sarcastic in direct proportion to how far wrong he actually was. He looks at me without a word, nods once, and heads for the kitchen.

"Guys, Abu has come up with a wonderful idea!" says Elisa the minute we walk in.

"Why didn't you come to us sooner?" Fausto asks Abu. The African smiles up at him without a word.

"Don't you want to hear his idea?" Elisa asks us.

"Of course," I say.

"Since we're spending too much money on groceries, Abu has suggested we could start a vegetable garden!"

Our blank faces and total silence say all you need to know about us. There is no doubt that for thousands of years the first thought that would have crossed the mind of any biped with opposable thumbs at the sight of farmland like ours would have been to get busy planting a vegetable garden. Logical enough, since for thousands of years the first thought was always that of sheer survival. But all it's taken is a few decades of madness to change what ought to be an essential part of our DNA. We looked out over the farmland that we now owned and thought to ourselves: "Ah, this is a perfect place to build a nice parking lot."

"A vegetable garden . . . " says Fausto.

"So, what do you think?" Elisa insists. "He would do the gardening and we could split the harvest with him."

"It's just my idea, land belongs to you . . . " Abu says apologetically in response to our silence.

"It strikes me as an outstanding idea. We'd become self-sufficient and maybe we could even sell some of the produce," Sergio says.

"I'm for it," I say.

"Me too," says Claudio.

We all turn to look at Fausto, but he's gone.

Fausto is all by himself, sitting outside on the grass and smoking a cigarette. We peek out discreetly at him through the window, and then we decide to head out, tentatively, with a bottle of wine as an offering.

When we all sit down on the grass around him, he hardly

looks up. We sit in silence looking out over the woods, where he seems to be staring, transfixed. Sergio takes a long gulp from the bottle and passes it to Fausto. He takes a slug and hands it to me. The wine seems to oil the mechanisms of his mouth.

"It'd take someone smarter than me to understand it all . . . " he says.

Instead of answering or asking what he's talking about, I just pass him back the bottle.

"What kind of world do we live in? A guy spends his life looking for friends, believing in his friends, always making sure that he's there for them when they need him." He takes another drink. "The next thing you know he's turned forty and he realizes that the best friends he's known longest he doesn't even really know at all . . . "

I exchange a rapid glance with Sergio. He's as baffled as I am.

"Let's look reality straight in the eye!" he says, turning to look first at Sergio and then at me. "Where are my friends? That bastard of a web designer has been telling me for years that he's like a brother to me . . . and all the people I invited to come down here? How many of them even bothered to write back or call?"

He looks at me when he asks the question, but at this point I'm as curious as anyone to know just how many of his rock-solid friends we can count on to show up.

"If I look around with eyes wide open right now, I have to say that my only friends are an African immigrant and a *camorrista*!" He takes another gloomy swig of wine. "Present company excepted, of course."

"Of course," says Sergio.

"Of course, of course," I confirm.

"Actually, it's pretty funny . . . an African immigrant, a *camorrista*, two losers, and a fucking Communist! What's that? The lead-in to a joke?"

Through a process of exclusion, I realize that I'm one of the two losers. But I don't take it personally. This is our first real conversation in two months of living together, and I choose to empathize with his pain without arguing, just nodding silently.

"It'd take someone smarter than me to understand it all, no two ways about it . . . " We sit there in silence, enjoying this moment. Witnessing the dark night of the soul of our fascist buddy Fausto is at least as unforgettable experience as my growing awareness that the realization that has just dawned on him could just as easily be applied to me.

47

Once again, the scratch and win has revealed two cherry clusters and now Saverio and Renato demand their prize. They want Claretta, no one else, not just some prostitute off the street. What's more, they tell us that the *taverna* is a miserable hovel, that not even a dog would live in it. We suggest giving them a table and two chairs, so they can dine more comfortably, and a bigger television set and more blankets. But we've missed the point. The two *camorristi* want scented candles, a vase of fresh-cut flowers, and some new clothes.

"And a bottle of Passiòn," Saverio adds.

"Passiòn?" I ask.

"Eh, Passiòn, the perfume, right?"

Really, we ought to thrash out the details of this, but no one seems to feel like saying anything. Any human being, reduced to the status of a chattel slave and confined 24-7 in a 3 by 5 foot room, would start to go a little nutty. Not them. Aside from the circles under their eyes and their pallor, they seem to have been reborn. Saverio's put on weight and now he looks like a normal kid, and that's not to mention the fact that he's lost all his nervous tics; Renato, I couldn't say—physically, he looks the same, but he's more relaxed and every so often he even seems contented.

Sergio, who just put in a call to Claretta, says that the woman will be here within the hour. Fausto sets out immediately to go grocery shopping in town and I volunteer to distract Elisa. I suggest we go out and take a walk around the garden. She gives me a suspicious glance, and I add that I'd like to get her opinion about a few improvement projects I have in mind.

We walk toward the area behind the farmhouse and I start talking about the idea of planting fruit trees to cover up our view of the industrial sheds. I walk her all the way to the boundary of the property, ostensibly to show her the exact site where we'd like to plant the orchard. After fifteen minutes or so, however, we've run out of things to talk about and so we walk on in silence.

Elisa seems to be waiting for something. I know this attitude very well. She's expecting me to make some kind of move, and quite likely she'd be willing and happy to reward it. We've already been strolling aimlessly for a while but she isn't showing the slightest intention of heading back. An unmistakable message: she wants me to do something. But for the moment I prefer to study her. I'll launch one of my conversational gambits as a test and, without her even suspecting a thing I'll have a better idea of just what she's like. On the provincial road, just a few hundred yards ahead of us, there's a small religious procession straggling along behind a priest carrying a crucifix on his shoulder and encouraging twenty or so children in two lines of ten to prayer. At least ten of them are risking their lives at every bend. I point the group out to Elisa and take advantage of it to start the conversation back up. Children are a crucial topic, you can understand a lot of things about a woman, her view of life, and especially whether you have any hopes of getting her into bed without sticky complications.

"You like children?" I ask.

"Are you sizing me up?" she replies.

Since I'm not exactly a new arrival on the planet Earth, I manage to slap a surprised smile on my face in less than a second.

"No . . . I'm just asking you if you like children. It's just something to say, I guess."

"Aaah. Now I see. No, it's just that certain questions strike me as Rorschach tests . . . like if I tell you 'Sure, I adore children,' then in your mental filing system I'm tucked away under the heading 'Romantic,' that is, a girl who won't go to bed with you unless we're talking about marriage. But if I answer with a wisecrack, like 'Yeah, I like other people's children,' then I'm filed away as an easy lay, a one-night stand and then it's over."

I hold the surprised smile in place, because her tone of voice has me stumped. She's not angry and she's not being sarcastic, she's just straightforward. I don't want to give in so I just nod in agreement with her analysis, as if it had nothing at all to do with me.

"So let's hear it, do you want to have children?" she asks.

"If I tell you that I don't really know, what heading does my name go under?"

"Somebody who at age forty tells you that it's never crossed his mind whether or not he wants to have children? Where do you think it goes? On the longest, most crowded list of all, the list of liars."

"Are you mad at me?"

"Are you kidding? I'm crazy about guys who stare at my piercings and don't have the nerve to ask the questions they're secretly dying to ask."

"I wasn't staring at your piercings, and in any case they don't make me think of any particular questions."

"Oh, well then, I must be mistaken. I could have sworn that any minute now you were about to ask me how many I had. A question that would only have been a pretext, obviously, a way of testing the ground to figure out whether or not you could ask the next question, the one that's really buzzing around in your head: "Why on earth did you get those piercings in the first place?'"

I stall for time with a smile.

"Piercings aren't such a disturbing topic . . . they're basically just cosmetics for the soul. Like lipstick or a little eye liner, but with the addition of an extra little bit of pain that makes the beautification a little more profound and significant," I say.

Sometimes I surprise myself. Where did that last line pop out of? I've actually always assumed that piercings and tattoos were the signage of desperate souls. Well, whatever the explanation, it was the right thing to say. The girl seems to have come out of her nose dive.

"Okay, so it never crossed your mind to wonder just how many hidden piercings I might have?" she asks point-blank.

"Frankly, no."

"That's a pity."

"Why, do you have others?"

"See?"

Once again, she's not bitter or sarcastic, nor is she even angry. She speaks and replies in the most unaffected manner imaginable, and this leaves me nonplussed. Actually, it kind of pisses me off. I realize that I've fantasized a little too much about her. I can't stand people who respond blow for blow and don't let you get away with a thing. I'm the kind of person who needs understanding. We walk along in silence for a few minutes. We look around in all directions, taking care only to ensure that our glances never meet. Then, fortunately, my cell phone rings: it's the all-clear signal from Sergio.

48

The first gas bill has arrived and, until we can get our first paying guests, we've decided to rely on the fireplaces to heat the house. In just a few days, we've already burned all the firewood we gathered in the past few months, and now we're going to have to take time and effort away from the work on the farmhouse to build up a new supply. Claudio and I spend a whole morning pruning the lower branches of our trees and filling the trunk of the Renault. My arms are so sore that I have a hard time even gripping the steering wheel, and the whole short drive I dream of lying immersed in a hot bath right up to my chin. We get back to the farmhouse just in time to see a group of young men and women piling out of two cars parked in the courtyard. Sergio is standing at the front door and he welcomes the new arrivals with a broad smile. There's nine of them, plus two dogs. From the Rastafarian haircuts and the flea market couture, it's not hard to guess that these are friends of his. The hugs are affectionate, the dogs sniff the air excitedly, looking for affectionate pats on the head.

The group of visitors includes a pair of guys the size of refrigerators who may actually be as big as or bigger than Sergio; a tall gangly guy leading a dog on a rope leash—a dog that outweighs him by at least twenty pounds; and the intellectual of the group, with an unkempt beard and round eyeglasses. All the others are women. Five women and four men: it's been many months since I've had company with such a favorable ratio.

"Look at this sweet little place!" one of the girls squeaks.

I put on my best smile and walk toward the group but I remain invisible to them until Sergio makes up his mind to introduce me. The most expansive member of the group is a girl that if you took her home would break any mother's heart. What with the chains hooked to her trousers and the earrings punctuating her face at random, she's clearly risking her entire epidermis every time there's lightning. She tells me her name but I immediately deep-six it down the nearest memory hole, the opposite of what happens when I'm introduced to the next girl, Eva, who not only shakes hands but looks me in the eye that extra two seconds that immediately triggers a series of fantasies about celestial lovemaking, with fluttering clouds of butterflies and choreographic gusts of pollen. While one of the dogs takes a dump undisturbed right in the middle of the garden, another one goes in search of a little friendly scritchy-scratch in exactly the wrong place: from Fausto. Standing expressionless at the door, dressed in his impeccable suit like the bourgeois capitalist that he is, he has the glassy-eyed glare of someone who's trapped in his own worst nightmare.

"Why don't you go take a stroll in the garden while we whip up a bite to eat for you?" says Sergio.

We walk into the kitchen and while Sergio and Elisa get busy cooking, we start pelting Sergio with questions.

"Who are these people?" Claudio asks.

"They're friends of mine, who the hell do you think they are?"

"Why didn't you tell us they were coming?" Fausto asks.

"Guys, this is a drill! If a carful of guests show up without calling ahead, how are we supposed to make them feel welcome?" Sergio replies.

"Yeah, good question! How are we supposed to make them feel welcome?" I ask.

"Oh! What the hell is the matter with you people? You ought to be happy! At least, we're actually doing something for real, we can put ourselves and this place to the test! You wanted guests? Here they are!"

"I was thinking of a different class of guests," says Fausto.

"Then bring them!"

I think of a marvelous wisecrack that involves Tom Cruise,

but I decide to keep it to myself since it's already a pretty tense situation. Sergio goes back to his prepwork while I give Fausto a pep talk sotto voce.

"Well, if you stop to think about it, we did need a dry run sooner or later . . . better if we do it with these guys as a test subject, right?"

My argument penetrates Fausto's black heart, and in fact, he immediately starts looking around for something helpful to do.

The hospitality test has immediately evidenced a number of our shortcomings. First and foremost, we don't seem to be able to keep the guests from wandering out onto the exact spot where we buried the Giulia and where the grass has grown back at its thickest and most inviting. Luckily, the radio has remained silent the whole time, except perhaps for a couple of brief moments, when I saw one of the dogs stop suddenly and point. Our young guests are all very pleased with Elisa's delicacies, but I have to say that even the cooking we guys could do might have impressed them: to compete with the cooking you get in the community centers isn't much of a challenge. Vito, whom we can present to these people without any concerns, is a perfect sous-chef and the dishes are served promptly. A couple of times we forget to call him Pietro, but Fausto, who's the biggest source of slips of the tongue, explains it away by telling Elisa that it's just his middle name.

The conversation of today's guests focuses primarily of the looming threat that they'll be kicked out of the community center they've taken over as squatters. Fausto, completely exasperated, has secluded himself in the kitchen. In one of my rapid trips back there to get more wine I notice him chopping carrots with a meat cleaver.

After lunch, while we're all sitting around on the carpet in front of the fireplace, the first joints begin to sprout here and there. Claudio leaves the group, stating in a hushed whisper that he'd better go tend to his organic gardening. He might just as well have said that he was heading off to desecrate Lenin's tomb: nobody was paying him any attention anyway. Eva hands me the joint and, even though I haven't smoked since my high school days, I take it without the slightest hesitation. The girl smiles at me, it's evident that she thinks I'm funny and, who knows, maybe she's one of those girls who'll take you to bed just to reward you for being likable. I'd like to talk to her, but that one puff on the joint has interfered with my ability to control my jaw. I stretch out on the carpet. Eva strokes my hair and lets me rest my head in her lap. It's soft and warm, and her dress smells good. I close my eyes. Her long necklace tickles my forehead. I reach up to touch it with my fingertips to feel what it's made of and my hand inadvertently brushes her breast. She makes absolutely no objection and so I feel authorized to venture a little further with this game. I go on for countless minutes in this state of beatific joy. Then I hear her whisper to me "What are you laughing at?" I wish I could answer her but instead all I can do is go on grinning. "What the fuck are you laughing at?" she whispers again and then, strange to say, she does a perfect imitation of Fausto's voice.

"Would you very much mind telling me what the fuck you're laughing at?"

I must have done something odd when I woke up because Fausto walks away swearing.

"Well would you look at the shape this guy is in!" he says.

I look around me and all I see are scattered dishes and glasses. I struggle to my feet and I go to the window. The cars are no longer parked in the courtyard. I see Elisa standing motionless in the middle of the lawn, directly on top of the Giulia. I want to warn the others, but my head is spinning and I'm forced to sit on the sofa. Elisa comes back into the house and walks past me without saying a thing, chiefly interested in the shouts that are emerging from the kitchen.

"What did you want, did you want me to make my friends pay for dinner?" Sergio shouts.

"I could understand a discount, but feeding nine people dinner free of charge is insanity! What are we, the Royal Society for the Protection of Freeloaders?" Fausto retorts.

Elisa snorts and goes upstairs. I lie down and meditate on the boundaries between dream and reality.

49

This time, the four of us set out to gather firewood. The farmhouse is damp and we're going to need a good supply if we want to keep the fireplaces burning for more hours every day. We drive the Renault through the fields and come to a dead tree. It's the last dead tree around here. After that, we'll have to venture into the little forest. Maybe it's just an impression, but it strikes me that as a work crew we've made considerable progress. In just a couple of hours, we strip the tree of its branches, without taking any breaks and without complaining about the hard work. On each hand I have four small calluses and I'm proud of them.

We load the trunk with firewood and head back toward the farmhouse. Maybe it would be more efficient to split up, with two of us transporting the wood and the other two staying behind to cut up the trunk of the tree, but the thing is this: it's fun to drive across the fields and no one wants to miss the experience. Before we unload the firewood we go into the kitchen to get some water and there we run into Vito. He's terribly upset and the minute he sees us he starts gesticulating.

"What's wrong?" Sergio asks.

"She left . . . she knows everything," Vito says.

The news catches us off guard. It takes us a second or two to realize that he's actually talking about Elisa.

"How'd she find out?" asks Sergio.

"I found the kitchen door left open, I went downstairs, and there she was, looking in the peephole of the *taverna* . . . she saw it all."

"When did she leave?" Sergio asks.

"About an hour ago, more or less . . . she left without a word. I tried to stop her but she was in a freaking hysterical frenzy."

"Come on, let's get to the station fast. Unless someone gave her a ride she may not even have gotten there yet!" I say.

We hop into the car and set off at full speed, bouncing crazily over every bump on the dirt road. The minute we round the bend we see Elisa walking toward us. Sergio jams on the brakes about thirty feet short of her. Fausto leans out the window.

"Oh, good thing you came back, Elisa . . . there's an explanation, you know," he says.

I gather my courage and get out of the car. I take a few steps in her direction and try unsuccessfully to look her in the eye.

"Elisa . . . "

"Sssh!" she silences me.

With exaggerated facial expressions that even an idiot could read the three guys in the car are urging me to go after her.

"Elisa?"

"Mmmh!"

She keeps on walking at a brisk pace. I trail along a few yards behind her. Sergio and the others creep along slowly at a safe distance behind us.

"I don't want to know a thing!" she shouts at me and goes on walking. "Nothing!"

"Elisa, look it's just that . . . " I start to explain.

"Actually yes! There is one thing that I'd really like to understand! . . . Where the hell does that music come from?"

I smile in a reassuring way even if she turns her back on me and can't see me at all.

"It's simple, the music . . . "

"Ssssh! I told you I don't want to know a thing!" she shouts in a fury.

Behind me, the guys are gesticulating, asking how it's going. Irritated by the sheer idiocy of the question, I respond sarcastically with a thumbs-up à la Fonzie, and they're all immediately wreathed in smiles, heaving big sighs of relief. My God, what a gaggle of morons.

50

"It's Dvořák's *Serenade for Strings in E major*, Op. 22," Vito tells me.

After spending the whole day in her bedroom with the door shut, Elisa is sitting in the middle of the lawn, out in the cold. Vito and I spy on her through the kitchen window, hiding behind the curtains like a couple of old housewives.

"How beautiful," I say.

"It's wonderful, a heartbreaking piece in lovely waltz time signature," he replies. Sure, the music's beautiful too, I think to myself. It's certainly making an impression on her too, I'm willing to bet. The notes linger inside me, they echo in a way that trails after me even now that I'm leaving the kitchen and my ears can no longer hear them. A part of my soul is reverberating to them in a way that I thought could only be prompted by the human breast, or rather breasts. I open the door and the chilly air locks the muscles of my belly into a cramp. I hug my arms close to my chest and walk, head lowered, straight toward Elisa. My footsteps crunch noisily on the gravel, but she shows no sign whatever of having heard them. I start listening to the waltz again and out of respect I lighten my footsteps, barely brushing the ground. When I'm just a few feet away from her I hesitate. Only a gust of wind persuades me to crouch down beside her. There are times when you manage to think a number of different things in the space of a split second. First, I think that maybe I should have thought out something to say to her before I left the house, and then I think that it's much better just to sit next to her in silence, and then that she could still rudely tell me to get away from her, and then, no, I think that with such a beautiful piece of music playing, her heart must have softened and maybe it'll occur to her that I'm freezing to death, and she might even decide to throw her arms around me. In this split second, so crowded with thoughts and expectations, she simply stands up and walks away.

At first, answering the phone or checking our mail was fun, we were confident and we never took it the wrong way if the inbox was empty or the hit counter on our website showed no signs of noteworthy progress. But ten days before Christmas, the atmosphere in the farmhouse starts to turn a little grim. We start quarreling over the name of the agritourism bed and breakfast that the young man who built our website refuses to change until we pay him, and we fight about the fact that once again we're penniless, except for the fund set aside to pay the basic bills. With our advertising budget flickering dimly, we decide to go ahead and print a thousand flyers and hand them out around town, but the response is zero. Vito explains to us, after the fact, that the people in that town aren't likely to want to go to an agritourism bed and breakfast in the first place, and the few townspeople who might would want to go somewhere new, somewhere different. They certainly aren't going to pay for a room with a view of their own backyard. He is right, of course, but what we were actually hoping for was a few reservations for dinner, at least on Saturday night. But what we get is nothing. Zip, zero, nada.

We desperately need to throw a big opening night party in

grand style but, leaving aside the minor question of money, we've left it too late, the holidays are upon us.

Sergio calls a meeting in the kitchen, by the fireplace, over a relaxing glass of wine. He tells us that there's no point to all of us staying at the farmhouse, that it's Christmas and it'll do us good to have some time away. We look at him quizzically but he reassures us: with Abu and Vito to help him, he's perfectly capable to taking care of everything. Elisa is the first to take the offer. I realize that we'll never see her again and the idea makes me sadder than I ever would have imagined.

"Why, sure, I guess I'll go. That'll give me a chance to do a little promotion for our agritourism bed and breakfast," say Fausto.

"I'll take advantage of the opportunity to go see some relatives," says Claudio.

"If something seems to be happening, just give us a call and we'll be back here lickety-split, okay?" I say to Sergio.

"Certainly, I'll text you," he responds without much conviction.

51

The two guys in the cellar are in a gloomy mood. The impending arrival of Christmas and the awareness that they're going to be spending the holiday far from their families for the first time has awakened them from the state of torpor into which we had managed to lull them. We do our best, but we can hardly hope to console them with promises of a spectacular banquet or by giving them extra scratch and win tickets. We've thought about maybe driving them somewhere far away and letting them call home at least once. But the risk is too great, the situation would be impossible to control. Then it occurs to us that the guys could write letters and we could arrange to have them delivered. Even though it's obvious that the idea doesn't thrill them, still they start writing. After a half day of groans, crumpled balls of writing paper, and embarrassing questions about how to spell simple words, they give up on the idea.

While I'm packing my suitcase, Sergio and Vito are pacing back and forth in my room trying to come up with a solution.

"Maybe we could find a way of letting them get news about their families," says Vito. "If I had any close relatives I'd be anxious to know that they're all okay," he adds.

"Sure, but how could we do it? Go ask around in town?" asks Sergio.

I'd like to come up with a good idea, if for no other reason than to get them out of my hair, but my mind is elsewhere. I try tossing out a gambit.

"If you ask me, we should adopt another tactic developed by the police state we live in," I say.

"Eh? What would that be?" asks Sergio.

"A bunch of young people locked into a small living space, confined but with a chance at winning a final grand prize that will change their lives . . . remind you of anything?"

"Holy crap, a reality show!"

I don't actually have any specific ideas, I'm just thinking aloud in the hope that a lightbulb will blink on in his head.

"Exactly, and what do they do on a reality show when the contestants start going stir crazy or becoming apathetic? What do they come up with as a way of re-exerting control?"

A gleam of light appears in Sergio's eyes.

"Brilliant! That's absolutely brilliant!"

Vito looks at us as if we'd both lost our minds. He doesn't understand a word that we're saying and frankly I don't have the slightest idea of what Sergio has glimpsed in my vague and allusive words. All I know is that he gives me a glance of frank admiration and leaves the room with Vito, finally leaving me alone to think.

*

The trip to the station is wordless, and even more so the train trip itself. Elisa spends the whole time talking on her phone, isolated from us. At first, I wait for her to finish her phone call so that I can have a chance to approach her, to say something to her. Then it dawns on me that the unbroken succession of phone calls is designed specifically to dissuade me from attempting any such thing. I decide to go to the bathroom. I walk up the corridor toward where Elisa is laughing on the phone with a girlfriend, at least that's my guess, and as soon as she sees me coming she leans against the window, turning her back on me. To show her that there was no need for such a theatrical gesture, I duck into the bathroom without so much as a glance in her direction. The bathroom is a disgusting mess. While I listen to Elisa's voice through the door, I try to muster the courage necessary to piss into the hillock of filthy toilet paper that fills the toilet practically to the rim. Incredible to say, I manage to find something strangely romantic about it: that foul sight brings a memory bobbing to the surface of my consciousness, an important moment in my own personal evolution. I'm six years old and I'm pouring bath foam into the toilet. I add a little toothpaste, a shot of spray deodorant, and then my favorite ingredient of all, shaving cream. I squirt in an abundant spurt, a handsome cream pie that rests on the surface of the water and gradually builds up, dense and compact, to a towering height of at least eight inches. It reminds me a lemon meringue pie and I decide that I ought to garnish it with a few drops of my grandmother's hair dye. I'm standing there with the bottle in hand when, to my horror, my mother swings open the bathroom door and comes in.

"What on earth are you doing?"

Mistake number one, I should have locked the door. Mistake number two, I was too quiet, and as anyone can tell you, if you behave yourself and make no noise for more than ten minutes, that inevitably arouses your parent's suspicions.

"Nothing," I reply.

"What do you mean, nothing? What is that mess, what the devil are you doing?"

"Nothing, I told you!"

"Would you be so good as to tell me why you put all that junk in the toilet?"

It finally dawns on me that she actually wants an answer to her question. Absurd though it is, she really expects me to explain why I'm brewing my chemical slushes. And at age six I'm not grownup enough to say: what kind of a stupid question is that? I'm a child and colorful foul-smelling messes just fascinate me. So I say the first thing that pops into my head:

"I'm experimenting."

"What are you experimenting?" she asks me.

"I just wanted to see how products react in water."

My answer intrigues my mother who, then and there, says nothing, but the next day, bursting with pride, gives me a My First Chemistry Set. Obviously, like all children, what I was really interested in was chaos. The chaos of a set of Lego building blocks exploding across the floor of a neat and tidy room, the chaos of liquids and creams contaminating the immaculate surface of the porcelain toilet, the chaos of a small flame deforming the curving line of a brand new plastic scale model Ferrari. In any case, in my memory, the gift of the My First Chemistry Set put the seal of approval on a theory that was already taking form inside me: lying simplifies your life, lying makes both you and other people happier. I'm not an out-of-control pathological liar, not one of those intolerable people who invent lies just to feel cool or impress others. My lies are part of a partisan resistance campaign, my way of fighting the power.

"Utter bullshit!" I hear Elisa say ironically, still talking on the phone.

That's right, I think to myself.

52

The minute the front door of the apartment swings shut behind me, I ask myself what the hell I think I'm doing here. Everyone goes home for Christmas, sure, but if you don't have a family, what's the point of going home?

I wander from one room to the next and everywhere I go I see my father. I see him in bed, on the sofa, in the bathroom, I see him all around the apartment, in his wheelchair. I call a couple of aunts and a few cousins, just to break the overwhelming sense of Christmas at an orphanage. No one asks me how I'm doing. I tell them about the agritourism bed and breakfast, but I keep it short, because they don't ask any questions and it's hard to miss the fact that they don't care in the slightest.

Fausto's right. All of a sudden, I can see clearly, and I understand that my family consists of a Fascist, a Communist, a *camorrista*, and a loser. And a dead father. What's called for right now is to tie one on. I rummage around in the kitchen, but I find nothing. In the living room, all I manage to dig up is a bottle with a couple of fingers of Limoncello and a mason jar of brandied cherries.

To my surprise, I also find a cardboard box with all the pieces of a manger scene. And not just any manger scene: this is the manger scene that I used to set up when I was a kid. Not all that much is left of the lavish display that once was. A balsawood stall, a fragment of a starry night sky, a paper shooting star covered with glitter, a peasant's house without a roof. The best thing though are the little figurines. St. Joseph has a gunfighter's belt and a six-shooter glued to his robe. The shepherd standing watch by the flock of sheep is a Sioux Indian brave. I can't find the ox, as best I can remember he got the losing end

of a *corrida* with Big Jim. And so, next to the donkey with just
one ear, I put a string of lambs. Baby Jesus should be long
gone, but I don't think my father could stand the idea of the
figurines of Joseph and Mary standing there with open arms
and adoring gazes around an empty manger. The Three Wise
Men are long lost, I can't remember whether I burned them or
used them for target practice with my BB gun. I replace them
with three peasants. To make the manger scene look a little
more up to date, I adorn the face of each of the peasants with
a pair of tiny sunglasses fashioned out of aluminum foil.
Instead of bringing gold, myrrh, and frankincense, they have
come to provide an offer of protection. Because, see, the owners of the stable are part of a group of ancient families and
around heah—for instance, King Herod doesn't count for shit.

A strange blend of three-ring circus and medieval court of
miracles, the manger scene is finished, and so is the jar of
brandied cherries. I turn on the twinkling Christmas lights and
let their repetitive blinking hypnotize me. I have an urge to call
Sergio and find out how it's going, but I can't seem to drag my
eyes away from a tiny red light that blinks on and blinks off,
blinks on and blinks off, blinks on and I blink off.

53

At 11 P.M. I receive a text message from Sergio. I tell myself
that it doesn't matter, that it might make me look like a total
loser, but I pack my bags and leave immediately, without so
much as a minute's hesitation. The joy of witnessing the arrival
of ten paying guests is just too wonderful to miss. We'll have a
full house from the 28th until the 2nd and I want to hurry back
to the farmhouse immediately to make sure that everything is
in its place, that there's no dust under the beds, that the rooms
are toasty warm, and that the garden is tidy and well tended.

I rush to the station and catch the last train. Most of the passengers are commuters and immigrant laborers. Everyone's asleep. I ride standing by a window in the corridor. I can't see the countryside we're passing through, just the reflection of the compartment behind me, with two Africans curled up on the bench seats. I think about the odd jobs still left to do and especially the doors that still need to be painted, doors that in a moment of weariness I persuaded the others to leave unfinished. What the hell was I thinking? Everything has to be perfect now.

By the time the train pulls into the station I'm completely mesmerized by my stream of thoughts and without thinking twice about it I start walking home along the provincial road. The idea of nearly an hour's walk doesn't frighten me in the least. I think about the vegetable garden and wonder if anything's sprouted. Seeing it groaning with eggplants and zucchini would make an excellent impression on our guests. We could even invite them to go out themselves and pick the fresh vegetables that we'd cook and serve them that day. I'll have to make a note of that, it's not a bad idea at all. A compact car tricked out as a sports car whips past me at high speed, swerving dangerously close to hitting me. I decide that it's probably better to walk facing traffic. I see another car coming toward me, a black Mercedes ravaged by spoilers and rear wings. I'm on a stretch of road that's practically all tight curves, a road that I wouldn't take at more than 30 mph and these criminals are zipping along in the opposite lane as if the prospect of an oncoming truck, all things considered, was just their idea of fun. The curves are tight here and I don't even feel all that safe walking on the side of the road, even facing traffic. I take advantage of a short stretch of straightaway to cross over to the other side of the road again. When I reach the opposite guardrail, I find the carcass of a dead dog to welcome me. It's baring its teeth as if it had spent the last instant of its life snarling at the radiator of the oncoming car. I force back an urge to vomit and decide to turn my thoughts back to the egg-plants and zucchini in our vegetable garden. Not even a second later, I hear the roar of a souped-up engine and the compact car that passed me earlier whips by again, grazing me at top speed. My sense of uncomfortable familiarity with that car jerks a loud and heartfelt "Asshole!" out of me.

If a car is driving aimlessly back and forth on the provincial road in the middle of the night, there's usually a good reason. The driver and passengers are probably a gang of kids bored out of their skulls and I ought to know better than to give them an excuse to liven up an otherwise dull evening. A split second after my shouted insult the car comes screeching to a halt, lay-ing down an impressive patch of black rubber. The white light of the backup signal illuminates my terrified expression. I rap-idly evaluate the wisdom of just continuing on my way, confi-dent that I'm in the right, and challenging that carful of idiots. In the next instant, I've already hopped over the guardrail and I'm engaged in some frantic open-field running, silently pray-ing that the muddy terrain will dissuade them from dirtying the shiny new shoes that they probably bought with the take from their last purse-snatching. Turns out, they must all be wearing heavy boots because they come running after me without any hesitation at all. The bastards don't even shout. They're pro-fessionals, and they're saving their breath so they can grab me and still be in good enough shape to kick and punch the fool out of me. It's probably been a good five years since the last time I ran really fast and hard, and I start to wonder how long I can hold out. My legs are starting to give me that answer: another hundred yards or so, tops. The thudding footsteps behind me draw nearer and nearer, now I can even hear the panting breath of my closest pursuer. He's practically caught up with me and I start to think that I need to grab a stick or a bottle or anything else I can use in my last-ditch defense. If he catches me here, in the dark, barehanded, things can really turn ugly.

"Go on, run, run, sooner or later we'll catch you!" he shouts after me.

His voice is hoarse with exhaustion, he comes to a stop and stands there panting. That gives me renewed energy to sprint up the hillside ahead of me.

"You'd better not let us catch youse!" another voice shouts from much farther away.

Clearly, I'm no Charles Bronson, but I still relish my victory as a long-distance runner, looking down as my adversaries retreat to their car.

I get back at two in the morning, and the farmhouse is all lit up. Sergio's car is parked outside the front door and I hear Fausto's and Claudio's voices filtering out from the living room windows. Good, at least I won't be the only one to look like a pathetic loser.

The minute I walk in, they look up from the table where they're sitting, sheets of paper and pens in hand. Everyone smiles. Elisa's there too, with the biggest smile of all. An exchange of questions and answers begins, and even though I'm involved in it, I am completely unaware of the things I say.

"Diego! How did you get here?" says Sergio.

"Train," I say.

"Same as us . . . what train did you catch?" asks Fausto.

"You could have called me, I would have come to pick you up at the station," says Sergio.

"Just walked," I say.

"What's the matter with you? Did you actually take this train or did you run the whole way back from the city?" says Fausto.

"Shortcut."

"Anyway, I have to say, damn if you guys didn't all hurry back the minute I texted you, eh?" says Sergio.

As people start telling their first tall tales, I untie my mud-caked shoes. Fausto says he was staying with a friend just twenty-five miles away, otherwise there's no way he would have come back in such a hurry; Claudio tries to make us believe that, when he got the text message, he just happened to be over near the train station so it seemed convenient to take advantage of the fact. By the time I get the second shoe untied and set on a piece of newspaper to dry, I have my own tall tale ready to recount. But then I happen to exchange a glance with Elisa.

"I couldn't wait to get back . . . " I say.

"Shitty Christmas, huh?" says Fausto.

54

"What about the boys? How was their Christmas?" I ask, confident that I've touched on a sore subject.

Sergio says nothing but gestures with a jerk of the head for me to follow him, and with his hand he enjoins my silence. We swing open the kitchen door, and halfway down the stairs I hear a swelling chaotic din of sobs and laments coming muffled through the walls. The dolorous moans suddenly give way to peals of laughter. A shiver goes down my back. I have the impression I've wandered into an asylum for the criminally insane.

"What the hell is going on?" I say.

"They've been like this since this morning . . . " says Sergio.

He invites me to take a look through the peephole. I see the guys with their backs to me, sitting in front of the television set. On the screen home movie images flicker past to the soundtrack of Velvet Underground's *Sunday Morning*. The young men are clearly excited, they point out people on the screen and then burst into tears; they laugh tenderly when they see a toddler trip over a soccer ball. A girl walking by herself with a sad expression plucks a sigh out of Saverio; a mother looking sadly out a window makes his partner in captivity break down sobbing.

"That was a brilliant idea you had," Sergio tells me. "I knew it would work, but not like this. But just take a look! You keep people locked up somewhere, you drug them with a thousand useless things, and then every once in a while you show them a well made movie, a picture window thrown open on real life, and cue the tears!"

"But how did you manage to film it?" I ask.

"Vito gave us all the practical information. I had Abu, Samuel, and Alex stake out the people in question and film them with their cell phones. That took half a day, then a couple more hours at most to edit all the footage and smear some high-production tear-jerking music over it all as a soundtrack."

"It's insane . . . But . . . you're saying they've been like this since this morning?"

"I swear. They just keep rerunning it. And that's not all: they even begged us to make another one . . . "

55

The house is in an uproar. With the help of Abu, Samuel, and Alex we clear all the upstairs bedrooms of furniture and carry everything into the residential area. Fausto walks outside massaging his face. There are streaks of some orange cream under his eyes, and he delicately smears it over his face with a semicircular movement ranging from his nose to his temples. His mouth, which theoretically has nothing to do with this careful operation, accompanies his hand motions, frozen into a theatrical expression of astonishment.

"What are you doing?" I ask.

"Nothing . . . just a little moistener," he replies.

Behind him, I see Samuel walking toward me. When Samuel sees me looking at Fausto, he whispers:

"This self-tanning gel will let you achieve a sublime, stain-free, streak-free natural glow in just a few hours while enjoying the cooling sensation and light citrus scent. Continue to use until you have achieved your desired bronzing level."

Samuel must have read the back of the bottle, and now we finally hold the key to the mystery of Fausto's perennial tan. He's not naturally bronzed, after all.

"The only thing I don't understand is the *bronzing* . . . " Samuel continues. "Do you mean like: 'Your baby's first steps happen only once. Preserve that memory for a lifetime by having your little one's first baby shoes bronzed today.'?"

A loud burst of laughter distracts us. After so many days of simmering frustration, we're all eager to let off some steam and the only thing that really bothers me is the fact that Elisa has decided to let off steam with Sergio. They're having a pillow fight and laughing about nonsense, nothing, anything. I try to worm my way into their game, but I sense a barrier and wind up butting heads for a privileged position with Claudio and Fausto.

Once the initial frenzy of excitement has subsided, we split up the last assignments before the arrival of our scheduled guests. I'm in charge of getting the fucking firewood, as usual, but I accept the task without argument and the minute everyone else gets to work I set off in search of Elisa. After a couple of fruitless scouting expeditions to her bedroom and into the kitchen I realize that she is outside, sitting on the grass, smoking a cigarette. It seems as if she wants to be left alone, but after seeing her so sunny and untroubled, I somehow manage to get up my courage to walk outside. I put on my jacket and only once I step outside do I pretend to notice her, after a suitable and fraudulent delay. I walk over to her as if I were doing it purely out of good manners. Given the results of the last interaction, I don't bother trying to sit down.

"You know, I never thought you'd come back," I say.

She smiles at me and then goes back to looking straight ahead of her.

"I don't know whether Sergio explained . . . " I say.

"No, listen . . . I really don't want to know a thing," she says, turning suddenly serious.

Right now a little music would be perfect, but the Giulia remains silent. I start stamping my feet on the ground as if I were trying to get warm. I even start hopping up and down, but it seems to annoy Elisa so I give that up.

"What do you think of Sergio?" I ask.

"What is this? Opposition analysis?"

"I'm tired today, why don't we just take the question at face value?"

"Sergio's a very interesting man."

"Do you like him?"

"If you really were all that tired, you could have just gone ahead and asked me that in first place, right?"

"Do you like him?"

"What do you think?"

I sit down next to her. "I don't know, he's a man with a past. Women like men with a past."

"Well, yes, that's true, women do like men with a past. But I can't see myself getting involved with a man who thinks he knows everything and who wants to teach you how to live your life. I'm not interested in having a mentor and a guru. To say nothing of the fact that half of his personal history is invented out of whole cloth."

"Right," I reply, unable to keep from heaving a sigh of relief.

"Oh happy man! He got the answer he was looking for!" Elisa says, as she tousles my hair.

56

A car comes up the drive. Our previous experiences with cars arriving keep us from rejoicing the way we'd like to, until we are able to make out the silhouettes of four happy young people. The car pulls up, an old beat-up Fiat Panda with one red door panel, and a young man and three young women get out. They don't seem like troublesome guests, they have friendly expressions, they're wearing inexpensive but tasteful clothing, and it occurs to me immediately that these are exactly the kind of guests I'd always like to welcome to my bed and breakfast. Fausto feels differently.

"We can forget about extra charges with these people, they clearly don't have any money," he says.

"Well, let's hope the others do," says Claudio.

Unfortunately, we never find out about the others. Someone forgot to call ahead and tell us they wouldn't be able to make it.

Morale is at an all-time low, but still they're our first paying guests and we decide to do our very best. The welcoming celebration is a big success. The young people relax, drink cheerfully, and ask for the recipe of every course. Elisa immediately makes friends and invites them into the kitchen to share a few professional secrets, and from there into the garden to show them the vegetable patch. We follow them at a discreet distance, smiling, without saying a word. We only realize that our behavior is ridiculous when our cook gives us a sharp glare and asks us whether the rooms are ready. Still, after all, we've been waiting months now for our first guests and it's hard to drag ourselves away.

Once they've dropped their suitcases in their rooms, the young people hurry back downstairs to Elisa. Hurt by the unmistakable snub, we decide that we've got plenty of other things to do. Sergio heads out to rake the yard, Claudio straightens books on the bookshelves, I discover with horror a sloppy woodpile and get to work creating a handsome, nicely tapered pyramid. Taken as a group, we seem like so many extras in a crappy B movie.

57

The young people's enthusiasm quickly wanes. On the morning of the 31st, they wander listlessly around in the garden and from the way they're muttering amongst themselves, we're afraid they might be about to pull up stakes and decamp.

Elisa has kept them well fed, pampered, and amused. The real problem is us. Fausto ruined a couple of evenings by starting a poker game in front of the fireplace, Claudio is constantly underfoot, asking if everything's okay and whether anyone needs anything. To make up for my partners, I do my best to avoid them as much as possible, with the result, I'm afraid, that they must assume that it's me who doesn't want them underfoot. The extracurricular activities that we've come up with so far have proven to be inadequate. The bike trip was a disaster: fifty yards down the dirt road, two of them already had flat tires. The tour of the town was an experience that lasted a couple of hours at best: once they'd wandered around the little piazzetta, taken a look at the poor-quality fresco above the main altar of the church, and taken photographs from a distance of the picturesque lanes and alleys of the working class parts of town, they were ready to come home. Gathered in the kitchen, we look out the window and try to think of what to suggest next.

"What we need is a volleyball net," Fausto suggests.

"Or a couple of soccer goalposts," says Claudio.

"We could have a mini-indie film festival with a good collection of independent films," Sergio fires back.

"No-o-o . . . now look at them, they're having a lover's quarrel," I say.

We cluster behind the kitchen curtains and watch as one of the girls strides angrily away from her boyfriend.

"Forget about the New Year's Eve banquet. Another half hour and these guys'll be clearing out of here, take my word for it," I say.

"We need a brilliant idea, pronto!" says Sergio.

It's hard to imagine that the same great minds that just came up with the volleyball net are capable of engendering a brilliant idea about anything. In fact, blank expressions appear on everyone's faces. Fausto paces up and down. Sergio strokes his beard. Claudio shakes his head.

"Now we definitely need to come up with an idea . . . " says Elisa, pointing to the little group in the garden.

The girl ferociously hushes her boyfriend and looks around her. The other young women, their curiosity aroused, follow her as she takes a few steps first in one direction and then the opposite way. Before long, all of them are searching the lawn. One of the girls drops to one knee and lays her ear against the ground.

"Didn't we say we were going to keep them away from there, goddamnit?" says Sergio.

"How are we supposed to do that? We can hardly prohibit them from taking a walk in the garden!" Fausto retorts.

"We've just spent two days coming up with the evening's menu! We could have just dug a hole and unhooked that goddamned battery once and for all!" I say.

Elisa watches us argue, wide-eyed, for a while, then she goes back to watching the young people outside. One of them is pressing his ear to a tree, and he waves the others over. They all try listening to the bark but they shake their heads no, that's not where the music is coming from. They get back on their knees and press their ears to the grass.

This is it, I think to myself, it's over. All our hard work, the calluses on our hands, the drives over the fields in the old Renault, Claudio's fainting spells, the long conversations with Elisa. Even though I don't know exactly what I hope to accomplish, I leave the others clustering around the kitchen window and go outside. When I first meet the eyes of the young people, I feel lost, I can't imagine what kind of story I can tell them. And yet, the minute they ask the first question, something starts to flow inside me. I begin talking, I pick up a clear thread, and I fluidly untangle the skein of a short history. Their interested expressions stoke my courage and I make it all the way to the end of the story without allowing myself to be derailed by the blank looks of astonishment on the four faces in the kitchen window. I end my story and there's a brief moment of suspense, the four young people stare at me without uttering a word. Elisa walks up behind me and the young woman who was furious at her boyfriend until just a few minutes ago flashes her a big enthusiastic smile.

"Why didn't you tell us about it?"

"The music? . . . " Elisa says, taking a stab in the dark.

"He told us about the legend. What a beautiful story!"

I observe Elisa, who maintains an impeccable sangfroid.

"Well, it's only a legend, obviously there's a scientific explanation," I say.

"What's the scientific explanation?" the young man asks.

Elisa turns to look at me.

"Well, they're actually still working on a few hypotheses . . . "

"Maybe it's just a radio buried in the ground," he replies with a skeptical air.

"Okay, since you're so smart, you just assume that if you bury a radio underground, with all the dampness, the rainwater, and everything else, it's going to go on working? And another thing, the sound never comes from one single point . . . " his girlfriend snaps at him. She clearly has no interest in letting him ruin that magic moment.

A hail of questions follows and, in my best professional voice, I start to embroider a series of answers.

"Why doesn't anyone talk about it in town?"

"There's a folk tradition that talking about it brings bad luck."

"Why didn't we notice it before this?"

"The music comes and goes in cycles that pass all human understanding."

"Why is the grass so thick right here? Is it because of the music?"

"A group of Swedish agronomists will be coming back later this spring to study the phenomenon."

"Why don't you mention it on the website?"

"It would make the place a pilgrimage destination for mystics, fanatics, and journalists. We just want to be left in peace here."

The confidence with which I answer their questions placates the young people entirely and seems to attract an indecipherable gaze from Elisa.

"You've got a gift, no question about it, congratulations," she whispers.

"It's wonderful to be out here. Let's go get some chairs and enjoy the panorama with musical accompaniment," one of the girls suggests.

"We can do better than that. Tonight we'll celebrate the legend," says Elisa, with a flash of genius.

The big New Years' Eve dinner is a spectacular success. We set a lovely table for our guests in front of the fireplace and another table for ourselves in the kitchen. But the young people insist with such determination that in the end we give in and set one big table for everyone. The whole topic of the music is the central theme of conversation throughout the meal and, aside from a couple of contradictory answers, on the whole we acquit ourselves admirably. We eat and drink convivially, but the young people's eagerness to get back outdoors is unmistakable. We've stacked a mighty heap of firewood for a bonfire on the lawn, and right after dinner we set the chairs up in a circle and light the fire. In minutes the flames are leaping high into the night air, casting a reddish glow over the garden. The Giulia remains silent, but the starry sky, the wine, and the sense of anticipation just make the situation even more exciting.

The only one who seems to be anxious is Fausto. Standing just a few paces away from the bonfire, his face red from the gusting heat, he starts jumping up and down in place.

"It's a little chilly, isn't it?" he says, to keep the young people from looking at him.

"Cut it out, damn it!" I whisper as I walk behind him.

If the music starts up just as he bouncing up and down the kids would be able to figure out the trick: so long legend, so long magic.

Midnight rolls around and we pop the corks a few seconds late, because we're all tipsy and the corks seem to be refusing to cooperate. The town is lit up like it's high noon; every so often it looks like an ammunition dump blowing sky high. The series of sharp cracking shots strike me as sinister, and my first thought is that someone is taking advantage of the confusion to settle some old feud.

The spumante that Claudio brought us is flat and the flavor is miserable, but in the euphoria of the moment, no one notices. It's not until we've drained our last toast, with the reports of a few isolated firecrackers echoing mournfully across the countryside, that we notice that a string quartet is buoying up our euphoria.

"Handel . . . *Suite in F major* . . . for flute, two oboes, bassoon, two horns, two trumpets, strings and basso continuo," says Vito.

Silence falls.

"Yo, youse guys, it's a minuet!" he adds.

He makes a gallant bow to Elisa and then sweeps her into a dance worthy of the court of the Sun King. Wavering steps, curtseys, flourishes of the hand. The young people break into couples and begin imitating their steps. Elisa moves clumsily: with one hand she holds Vito's hand, with the other she wobbles back and forth without a shred of grace. Fantastic. Fausto takes the plunge and invites one of the girls to dance. Claudio cuts in and steals Vito's mademoiselle. Vito steps away with a baroque bow and joins me. The minuet continues round the fire and at the sight of that image, my small personal collection of happy moments is once again open and accepting new material after a long hiatus.

"Vito . . . tell me, which are the oboes?" I ask without taking my eyes off Elisa.

"Listen . . . they come in after the horns . . . pararara-pa-pah . . . there!"

I don't know what he's talking about, but that doesn't matter, it's all perfect just the same. I feed the fire while the others march around the field to the notes of Haydn's *Symphony No. 100*, and then go spinning and twirling to a string and violin concerto by some composer I can't even remember.

The Giulia isn't just a hunk of metal buried underground, it's a sentient being. When dawn appears on the horizon, the waltzes, minuets, and triumphal marches give way to the sad and moving sound of a slow upwelling of strings.

"*Suite No. 1, opus 46* . . . Grieg," Vito tells me.

One young woman takes a deep sigh and stretches out on the ground. Her boyfriend and the two other girls lie down beside her. No one says a word. There is only the faint sound of stringed instruments and the crackling of the fire. As hard as it is to walk away from this spectacle, we slowly file back into the farmhouse.

58

After waving goodbye to our guests, we gather in the kitchen to review our situation. After all, it turns out our inaugural event was a success. When the young people left, it was almost an emotional departure, with big hugs all around and promises to tell their friends all about the place and urge them to come, and to come back themselves in the spring. Concerning the issue of the buried Alfa Romeo Giulia, we all feel reassured. The battery can't last forever, and in any case, our worries have proven to be overblown. Any fairytale we choose to palm off will in any case be more believable than the truth.

We talk about the wonderful evening and by popular demand I'm obliged to recount the legend that I dreamed up on the spot. Since Abu is there too, and he knows nothing about it, I decide to tell it with all the trimmings.

"Mario was an ambitious young conductor, penniless but rich in talent. Giulia was a young noblewoman. For years, the two young people had been secretly in love, meeting infrequently but bound together by the music that, every night, he wafted up to the windows of his beloved. Soon, however, Giulia was married off to a coarse and authoritarian landowner who made her little more than his household slave. Weary of her mistreatment and eagerly hoping to embrace once again her only true love, Giulia stabbed her husband to death in his sleep. Before she could flee, however, she was in her turn murdered by her brothers-in-law and sent straight to hell. Mario, brokenhearted over his lost love, wanted to join his beloved in the infernal depths. Since he was a goodhearted soul who had never done anyone harm, he decided the one sure way was to murder the brothers-in-law of his beloved and then commit suicide, and so he did. To his surprise, however, when he arrived in hell he found that his beloved was nowhere to be seen. In fact, when she stabbed her husband, he was not sleeping, he was already dead, murdered by the hand of one of his brothers. From that day on, nearly every day Mario wafts his music up through the earth to the winds in the hope that it might somehow reach his beloved high in the heavens."

Abu applauds wholeheartedly. Elisa is still gazing at me in disbelief, while the others smile and nod their heads.

"Mario and Giulia?" says Fausto.

"I know, I know, but I had to dream up the names at the beginning . . . I hadn't warmed up yet," I say.

"Incredible that they went for it, hook line and sinker."

"It's just a legend, and with an extra touch here and there it turned out very nicely."

"It's revolting!"

"I disagree, it worked beautifully. In fact, we ought to put it on the website and publicize it," Elisa says.

"Mario and Giulia . . . " Fausto says again. "Mario isn't a composer's name."

"Neither is Giuseppe, and yet . . . " I say.

"And yet what?" he replies.

"Nothing, nothing . . . "

Unfortunately, the thrill is short-lived, just long enough for us to add up some figures. We've earned seven hundred euros and in just a few days we're going to have to pay three thousand euros for the first installment on our protection shakedown. For the moment, there are no reservations in our inbox and we can't reasonably expect to take in much revenue until at least Easter.

"Vito, do you think that we can ask him if we can put off paying him until after Easter?" Fausto asks.

"Do you want to know what he'll say?" Vito says.

The old man gets to his feet, walks off before our eyes, and exits through the door. A second later he returns, wearing the mocking bitter smile that was on his face the day he first showed up at the farmhouse. We stare at him in disbelief as he swaggers over to Fausto and takes a seat across from him, leaning back in his chair and swinging his feet up onto the table.

"So dey tell me that business has been good for you guys. I'm happy to hear it," says Vito.

Fausto looks at him in disbelief, and then decides to go along with the charade.

"Actually, we only had four guests . . . two young couples."

"You just need to put out a little more advertising, what can I tell you? You're the businessmen."

"That's right, and in fact we were wondering if you could give us a little more time to pay our installment, say until after Easter."

"So what are you saying, you want us to pay for your advertising? It's your business, you have to pay."

"We only earned seven hundred euros, if you factor in our expenses. We'd go bankrupt!"

"What are you talking about, four smart boys like youse. And I told you already, we're not animals, we want you to make your business a success. For just this once, we can shut an eye."

"Thank you!" says Fausto, who's completely absorbed in the part by now. His voice throbs with emotion.

"Gimme seven hundred euros now . . . and you can give me the rest after Easter."

The scene is bloodcurdling and Sergio vents his frustration by slamming his fist down on the table.

"Oh, oh, calm down . . . that's the way it's gonna go, boys, you'd better face up to it," says Vito.

Maybe we're still feeling the effect of the magical night's entertainment, but we don't react like a group of brink-of-bankruptcy entrepreneurs. We're annoyed, no question, but I'm not seeing any of the hysterical scenes from the good old days, with Claudio whining, and Fausto and Sergio skirmishing and nearly coming to blows. Who can say: maybe they're still hoping that our two hundred fifty friends will show up.

59

Elisa and I have no intention of ruining our New Year's Day. The bonfire has left a large charred patch on our favorite lawn, and we decide to commemorate the event by creating a handsome border of white cobblestones around it.

"Do you have someone waiting for you?" I ask.

"God what a disaster you are . . . "

I roll my eyes, and I do it so that she can see.

"You have a lovely way of putting things," she continues.

"Could you just let one go by without comment every once in a while?"

"Of course, why do you think I would care? I was just saying, to help you out. Obviously, you understand that if you say something that stupid you're going to get a stupid answer back, right?"

"Can't you just tell me the truth?"

Elisa smiles at me. Unintentionally, I put my finger on the crucial point.

"Of course there's someone. My mother's waiting for me, and so's my sister, a dozen or so cousins, a couple of close girl-friends, and my dog."

We arrange a few more cobblestones. But she focuses on rearranging the one's that I've just arranged. She does it to annoy me, but I hang back.

"Do you have a girlfriend? Sorry if I'm too straightforward, eh? Maybe you would have preferred it if I'd beaten around the bush for half an hour or so," she says.

"Oh why don't you go fry your head!"

I walk off, my face twisted into an angry grimace, even if I'm not really angry at all. I don't really even know what I am right now. All I know is that I hate bad-tempered women, but she's not bad tempered in the slightest. I hate bitter women, but she's calm and joyful. And I hate argumentative women, except for her. All things considered, maybe I'm just in love.

60

We've decided to take off a whole day and go for a nice long bike ride and explore the surrounding countryside. In all the time we've been here, we've been so wrapped up in our work that we've never once ventured down the dirt road that leads into the open countryside. While on the other three sides of the farmhouse, you immediately run into roads, other farmhouses, and villages and towns, in the fourth direction there is nothing but fields and trails that invite you to set out on long strolls through the unspoiled nature of the countryside. Abu is at work on the vegetable patch along with Elisa. Where until just two days ago there was nothing but rows of piled dirt and a few sprouts, now there are vigorous young artichokes, broccoli, green, red, and yellow pepper plants, and zucchinis, already tall and thriving. It's a day off and I don't want to ask too many questions. I just want to believe that the soil around here is incredibly fertile. At least as fertile as Abu's hard work can make it.

We climb on our bikes and set off in search of potential itineraries to suggest to our guests. Claudio brought a camera to start developing a chart of the local fauna. With a little internet research, he hopes to create a tipsheet to the species that can be found in the various seasons. As we ride slowly along, we take pleasure in the panorama that opens out before our appreciative eyes. Looking back at our farmhouse offers an equally lovely view, and it gives us a sense of satisfaction at the work we've done.

We ride through a wild, untilled patch of land where sheep graze. Claudio photographs the sheep. Further along, there's a small herd of black cattle, probably water buffalo. Claudio photographs the water buffalo. We ride around the hill along the road that seems to lead toward the forest. In the middle of the curve, we brake to a halt, one after another.

"What's this?" asks Fausto with a smile.

In front of us, square in the middle of the road, stands a white bidet with faucets intact. It's set so solidly in the road and seems like such an integral part of the scenery that we almost expect it to work, with jets of water spraying into the air from the rusty spout.

"Photograph that, too!" I tell Claudio. Claudio gets off his bike and actually starts to take the picture.

"Wait, wait!" Fausto shouts.

In the throes of congenital idiocy, he drops his trousers and sits on the bidet. Claudio steps back a few feet and snaps a picture.

"Come on boys, all together now!" shouts Fausto, standing next to the bidet with his ass in full view.

This kind of thing always embarrasses me, my personal sense of aesthetics prevents me from getting naked in public. But at this point even Sergio is dropping his trousers and I can't bring myself to be a spoilsport.

"Come on, come on!" I say, egging on myself more than anybody else.

Claudio moves off down the dirt road a few yards to get us all into his viewfinder, while the three of us, bent over with our asses in the breeze, snicker like teenagers.

"Go Claudio, now!" shouts Sergio the minute he sees me posing.

"Are you done?" I ask, anxious to get my clothes back on.

"Oh, Rembrandt! You going to take this picture?" Fausto puts in his two cents.

We have one last guffaw, then Sergio turns toward Claudio and suddenly gets to his feet. There's a serious expression on his face. With our pants still down around our ankles, we instinctively follow his gaze. Claudio turns his back to his and silently stares at something on the road, around the curve.

"What is it?" Sergio asks, without getting an answer. We dogtrot over to Claudio and there we discover that the bidet is just an outpost of a large and distinctly illegal dump. Along the side of the road, for roughly the next two hundred yards, there are tons and tons of garbage and waste piled up.

We take our bikes and walk them wordlessly past this burial ground for refrigerators, washing machines, television sets, water heaters, broken toilets, heaps of rubble, cans of paint, and automobile batteries. Then our eyes turn to our farmhouse, which is a little less than a mile away, as the crow flies.

"These people live like animals. Damn it, they have no respect for anything!" Fausto snarls.

"Disgusting pigs, what filthy swine they are," Claudio adds. A sheep grazes among black plastic garbage bags, full of who knows what.

"The next time we're in town and someone offers us a taste of the local cheese, please, let's tell them to go fuck themselves!" Sergio says.

No one feels like continuing our bike ride. Obviously, with that illegal dump square across the road, we can't suggest that our guests take hikes or bike excursions, much less boast about the unspoiled countryside. We wonder whether it's worth reporting it to the Carabinieri, but after the visit we received from the town police, the last thing we want to do is go look-ing for interaction with the local authorities. And we do still have a few captive *camorristi* hidden in the cellar, so we're not interested in attracting attention. We wonder how much it would cost to have someone clean it up, but Sergio has a point, considering our situation, we can't think of spending a single euro. We agree to report it to a local environmental associa-tion. We look on the internet and we discover that there's only one in the area. We call their number, but get an answering machine. We leave a message but we don't expect much to come of it.

After dinner we look out the window, standing guard. We figured it would take nights at a time of stakeouts but at ten o'clock that same first night, we see a flat-bed truck pull up. It rolls slowly along the dirt road and, out of our line of sight, it stops around the curve, right where the dump is. From the window we see Sergio run into the yard. We're worried, we're afraid he's going to start a confrontation, but none of us dares to go outside. In the meantime, the truck makes a three-point turn and comes back. For a moment, the headlights sweep the lawn where Sergio is running. His silhouette, lit from behind, is like a rapidly moving ghost. We see him as he clumsily throws himself to the ground. He lets the truck go past, and it rumbles away up the dirt road, heading for the provincial road. Only after that do we decide to emerge into the open and walk to meet him. As soon as we're outside, Claudio starts swearing at the truck, which we can't even see anymore.

We catch up with Sergio, who is covered with mud like a soldier returning from heavy action at the front.

"I got their license number," he says, with the sound of someone who has a plan.

61

Now that the giddy intoxication of the night of the bonfire is waning and we've gotten over our initial hysteria about the dump, we gather around the kitchen table to have a serious discussion about what to do next. There's a sense of resignation but also of confidence. The extraordinary loveliness of that night has given us a clear understanding that after all, we too are capable of doing great things.

"Say perhaps that they lacked good fortune, but never courage," Fausto decreed, quoting a plaque placed by the Italian army at the site of the Battle of El Alamein.

Sergio looks baffled for a second, and then, incredibly, flashes him a smile.

None of us feels defeated. We start taking into consideration the idea of exploring the local real estate market, getting an appraisal on the farmhouse, taking a reasonable loss on the whole deal. A series of concentric circles revolving around the unspoken idea of throwing in the towel. Only Vito seems to be ill at ease and keeps trying to find a way of bolstering our morale. In the end, surprising to say, Vito seems to be more frightened than any of us at the idea of going back to his old life.

While Sergio and Fausto look around for the phone number of the real estate agency, Abu and Elisa pick up a basket and head for the vegetable patch. Claudio turns on the television set and, even though they're showing his favorite program, a rerun of the 1982 World Cup (Italy trounced West Germany), he soon snorts in annoyance and turns it off. I turn and walk rudely away from Vito because I just don't know what to say to him anymore, and I don't want to hear any more unlikely solutions.

The documents from the real estate agency aren't where they're supposed to be and Sergio starts getting agitated. When his cell phone rings in his trouser pocket, he leaps up like a man possessed.

"Hello? . . . Yes!" he replies, gruffly. Then his tone softens. "No, what email? . . . Aaah, I'm sorry, we must have missed . . . " and he waves for Fausto to go turn on the computer immediately.

"Weren't you supposed to check the mail three times a day?" Claudio asks him.

"Nobody ever sends us mail, it was really starting to depress me!"

"Well, okay, fine, how many in your party?" Sergio asks, attracting our attention. "Ah, understood . . . " he says, sadly holding up the first two fingers of his left hand.

"Oh boy . . . " says Fausto, losing his already faint enthusiasm and giving me his place at the computer.

"Listen, I can definitely assure you that we can take your reservation, in any case we'll send you an email with all the details in just a few minutes . . . certainly, of course . . . thanks very much . . . goodbye . . . "

In the meanwhile, I type in Fausto's password, *DuceDuce-Duce136*, and I wait for the page to load.

"Of course . . . of course . . . " Sergio keeps saying. He can't seem to put an end to the phone conversation.

When I open the inbox, I see a page full of email all in bold.

"What the hell does this pain in the ass want from us? There's nothing here," I say. Fausto leans over the computer and grabs the mouse out of my hand.

"Great, that's just what we needed . . . let me see . . . "

In the time it takes to click the mouse, he practically screams into my ear. I try to get up and give him the chair but instead he just sits down on my legs and starts clicking away savagely. Abu and Elisa stick their heads curiously through the door, Sergio briskly terminates the phone call and walks over to us in annoyance. Fausto is in a frenzy of confusion, he curses the computer's slow performance even as we watch one window after another opening on the screen.

"Would you please calm down?" says Sergio.

"It's full of mail . . . guests, customers . . . a couple for this weekend, six people for next weekend!"

The thing is that really, for the longest time, no one ever wrote us at all, and when I saw a page full of messages in bold, I had a moment's dyslexia, I thought the solid queue of new emails were all old messages, marked read.

"Let me take a look," says Sergio, evicting both of us from the chair.

"These people want to know if the music effect only occurs during full moons and, if so, what phase the moon will be in next weekend . . . " says Sergio.

"What are they talking about?" I ask.

"What the hell do you care, tell them yes, tell them it happens with full moon, half moon, quarter moon, and no moon," says Fausto.

There are fifteen or so reservations, and all of them received in the past couple of days. Even if it isn't really ethical, we need to take in as much money as possible so we give preferential treatment to bigger parties. To all the others we write back, with enormous satisfaction, explaining that we have a problem with overbooking for the moment and there are no vacancies in the immediate future. Two people respond straightaway, telling us to just go ahead and put them down for the first available weekend.

After we've read and answered the very last email, we celebrate. We carry armloads of wood out to the lawn and light a bonfire. Then we open a demijohn of wine and start bouncing up and down on the grass to wake up the Giulia. When the music starts up, we all look toward Vito.

"It's *Autumn* by Vivaldi—from the *Four Seasons!*" he says.

"Vivaldi!" says Fausto, who's finally able to pin down a name he's heard before.

We drink to Vivaldi. We drink to the Giulia. We drink to Lunatic Hill. We drink to the young people who spread the word. Finally, sprawled out on the grass, we drink to us.

62

Abu, our secret agent in town, has managed to track down the identity of the man who owns the flat-bed truck that's been transporting scrap metal and trash to the dump. It's actually two middle-aged men, possibly brothers, who run a small moving company and basement cleaning service out of an isolated property on the edge of town.

As usual, Sergio brings Fausto and me up to speed on his plan and then, with our modifications and fine tunings, it's submitted for the approval of the Delphic oracle.

"So, Claudio, here's the plan. We're going to rent a dump truck, we're going to pile most of the contents of the dump in it, and we're going to dump the whole thing right out front of the house where these two filthy pigs live," says Sergio.

"If we rent a dump truck, they'll be able to identify us immediately," says Claudio.

"True, so we'll rent it a safe distance from here," Sergio responds.

"But what if someone sees us?" Claudio points out.

"We'll do it all in the middle of the night and with a dump truck we'll be able to dump the whole load in seconds, we won't even have to get out to do it. The worst they'll be able to do is take our license number, but we can cover it up or even modify the numbers with duct tape," Sergio replies.

"But what if they hop in their car and follow us?"

"We've checked them out. They only have that old flatbed truck and we can lose them easily. In any case, if we want to avoid that risk, we can always deflate their tires."

"You realize that we'll be the prime suspects, right?"

"I doubt that, we've never complained or reported them, and there are plenty of farmers around here that have trucks, while we don't even own cars anymore."

"Well, what can I say? . . . it seems like a pretty good plan to me," says Claudio.

With a series of gestures, he mimes a self-congratulation for the excellent idea, followed by a hand-puppet enactment of the dump truck tipping its load as he walks away.

"The oracle seems a little off his game, wouldn't you say?" I ask.

"He didn't put up much of a fight," Fausto agrees bitterly.

63

Sergio shows up with the dump truck right after sundown. It takes us almost five hours to load the truck with all the bulkiest items. Fausto, Abu, Samuel, and Alex lift everything onto the bed of the truck, while Sergio and I organize it to maximize the use of space. Claudio takes care of moving the truck as needed, while Elisa fills the refrigerators and washing machines with smaller objects. Vito, watching from the attic window, serves as our lookout.

Once we're done, we have five minutes to gulp down a glass of water and say goodbye to the three Africans as they head home. As agreed, Claudio, Elisa, and I head back to the farmhouse.

"Wait!" Sergio shouts. And he points to Fausto, twisting on the ground in pain.

"What's happened? What's wrong with him?" Claudio asks.

"It's my hernia, damn it! I've been putting off that operation for months now . . . " Fausto says through clenched teeth.

With the mountain of garbage that he's just hoisted onto the truck, it's entirely plausible, but we still have a hard time believing that the man who introduced Tom Cruise to Roman-style fried artichokes has a hernia.

"Diego, will you come instead?" Sergio asks me.

"Hey, that's not necessary, I'm fine, I just need half an hour or so to get my strength back!" Fausto shouts.

"We don't have a minute to spare, we should be there already. Well?" What tips the balance for me isn't so much the look that Sergio gives me as the fact that Elisa is watching.

"Okay, I'll come. But let's get going," I reply.

"Claudio, you come too!" Sergio calls.

For a moment, Claudio is nonplussed, but then he's the first one to climb into the cab of the truck.

"What, have you lost your mind?" I whisper to Sergio.

"It'll do him good," he says.

As soon as I climb into the truck, I start hoping a series of things. I hope the truck won't start. The engine turns over immediately. I hope it'll break its rear axle on the dirt road. We make it to the provincial road smooth as silk. I hope the police pull us over for a routine check. The provincial road is deserted.

"I might as well let you know right now that the most dangerous criminal act of my career was when I duct-taped the buzzers on an apartment house intercom," I tell Sergio.

"Actually, I've seen you steal a water heater," Claudio points out.

Sergio gives me a wry glance.

"Tonight, you're going to add an equally serious exploit to your rap sheet: you're going to let the air out of a truck tire. I'm not talking about punching a hole: you're going to deflate the tire! You think you're up to it?"

"Didn't you say something about not even getting out of the truck?" I say.

"I'll put the truck in position and operate the dumper

mechanism. But we need somebody to open the rear hatch and deflate one of the tires of their truck."

"You want me to open the rear hatch AND deflate the truck tire?"

"Jesus, Diego! What kind of life have you lived up till now?"

I want to make these bastards pay for what they've done just as much as he does, and really I'd be fine if I'd just had a little longer to brace myself psychologically. But no, that circus strongman Fausto decides to throw himself writhing to the ground and from one minute to the next I find myself recruited without warning. That's really all that's the matter, but I'm kind of out of control and so I go on a rant.

"Oh, excuse me? Excuse me very much if I've never thrown a Molotov cocktail! Excuse me if I didn't grow up with the scent of teargas in my nostrils and if I've never fired a handgun in action! I was busy, you know what it's like: I had to earn a living!"

"What the hell are you thinking? I was earning a living too! The only thing is, when I got off work, I didn't just flop down in an armchair in front of the television! I got my ass up and out on the street, where it was a fat target for riot clubs and rubber bullets!"

I usually do my best to avoid talking about politics. To avoid hysterical diatribes about budget bills or immigration laws, I've learned to say that I vote for the Green Party. It works beautifully, because nobody can think of how to start an argument with a Green Party supporter. But right now I feel an overwhelming need to let off steam, so I continue my end of the quarrel. Our vicious back-and-forth only dies down once we turn onto the road that runs past the garage that those two pigs run their business out of. Sergio switches off the headlights and slowly maneuvers the truck into position, so that the dumper deck will drop its load right outside their front gate. I look out the passenger-side window, watching him maneuver with bated breath. Claudio, who's been sitting rigidly between us since he got in the truck, starts breathing like a woman going into labor. I turn to see what the hell is going on with him and through Sergio's window I catch a glimpse of the truck whose tire I'm slated to deflate. My anxiety surges and I go off on a new tirade.

"And while we're at it, those days are gone forever! Now the real heroes are old people who manage to get by on the tiny pensions the state gives them! The real heroes are the young people battling against a society that denies them a future by organizing peaceful rallies! You're finished! No one cares about you anymore!"

I step out of the truck to keep him from getting in a retort and I head around back to open the rear hatch. But he rolls down his window and shouts back me in an undertone: "*No one cares about you anymore*? In whose name do you think you're speaking, eh? Who the fuck do you represent?"

"Well, just who do you think *you* represent? Who gives you the right to break the plate glass windows of the bank where I keep my savings?" I hiss back at him, walking halfway back to the front of the truck.

"Ah, the truth is that you have the luxury of sitting at your comfortable desk because you can rest assured that there are people like me who are willing to risk jail for our beliefs!"

This time I decide not to dignify his words with a response. I head back to the rear hatch and I unfasten the first safety hook. But before I know it, my rage begins to boil over. It's ridiculous, these people think they're somehow essential to the good of the nation and they throw it in my face that I actually do some of the working and building and saving around here. I walk around to Sergio's side of the truck and look in his window.

"No, I think you've got it backwards, my friend. You can thank people like me who go to work every day, pay their taxes,

and make this country run, so that you can play at being revo-
lutionaries and act like clowns running wild in the streets!" I
say to him. I go back to the rear of the truck.

"You come back here, you asshole!" Sergio shouts through
the side window. "Go tell that to the relatives of the kids killed
by the police during protest marches! Go tell them to their
faces that their sons and brothers were just a bunch of clowns!"

I avoid looking him in the eye because this time I'm afraid
things could really turn ugly, but I'm not about to take this
lying down. I walk back to the passenger-side door, get in, and
slam the door shut behind me. Claudio jerks in his seat but
doesn't say a word.

"Fine, what a moving speech! So why don't you go tell the
son of a policeman killed at one of your rallies everything you
just said . . . Oh, just go fuck yourself, why don't you!" I say.

While Sergio is chewing over the devastating retort he's
about to fire off, he smacks the lever that operates the dumper
deck. The hydraulic mechanism starts tipping the back of the
truck up into the air with a steady hiss.

"Well, that's odd, because you strike me as an otherwise
intelligent young man . . . " he says, but suddenly his voice
dies out.

He stops talking because, instead of the road ahead of us,
the windshield is suddenly filled with a view of the starry night
sky. The entire front of the truck is rising off the asphalt.

"You fucking moron, the hatch!" Sergio shouts, immediately yanking the lever back into place.

I forgot to unhook the main fastener on the rear hatch and
now, instead of sliding out the back, the entire load is just
jammed against the back of the truck. I slowly crane my head
out the window and look out. I see that we're balanced pre-
cariously, with the front tires poised nearly a yard off the surface of the road.

"Now what?" I ask.

Sergio tries opening the driver-side door, but every tiny move he makes shifts his weight and makes the truck wobble dangerously in the air. Claudio is frozen like a pillar of salt.

"Holy crap, we've got to find some way of moving our weight forward . . . do you think you can climb out the window and get your feet on the front bumper?"

"Why don't you just lower the cargo deck?"

"I can't lower it! Unless we can get the front wheels gently back onto the asphalt, we'll break the rear axle! Get out there on that bumper!"

"How the fuck am I supposed to do that?"

"It was your fuck-up, it's going to have be your solution!"

Sergio has a pretty persuasive look in his eye. But what's even more persuasive is the idea that someone might notice us parked out here and call the police. I very slowly push my head and shoulders out the side window, then I manage to sit on the sill and, supporting my weight with one hand on the outside mirror, I inch my right leg out the window. The truck sways and I freeze in place.

"It's moving!" I say.

"You need to shift your weight forward, otherwise we're going to flip over!"

I manage to get the other leg out the window and I slowly lower my feet onto the running board. I shift my full weight like a crewman hiking out off the side of a racing yacht sailing on a bowline. The truck seems to tilt a few degrees closer to the ground. I stretch out one leg and with the tip of my toe I feel around for the bumper. Then I slither over the side-view mirror, I clutch one of the windshield wipers, and I manage to get my other foot onto the front bumper. As I swing around, the truck sways upward, and then finally begins to settle forward and down. Once the tires are almost in contact with the asphalt, we exchange a satisfied smile through the windshield. Sergio starts the engine again and is about to pull the lever to lower the cargo deck when he suddenly hunches forward over the steering wheel and switches off the ignition. From inside he gestures to me to shut up and to look around behind me. A car is rocketing down the street toward us at top speed. Our cover is blown. Maybe we can dream up some explanation, but the cargo we're carrying and the position of the dumper deck both offer fairly eloquent testimonials to our criminal intent.

When the car zips past us and I'm no longer blinded by its headlights, any hope that we might get out of this situation dies in my chest: I know this car. It's the guys who chased me across the fields. It screeches to a halt not ten feet away from us. Because of the ridiculous position I've been holding, my legs start to shake. I can just imagine their baffled expressions, their dawning smiles of cruel mockery, the grim satisfaction at once again finding a victim to enliven an otherwise dull evening. I do my best to keep from looking around because I don't want them to recognize my face. I limit myself to peeking out of the corner of my eye. Just one young man steps out of the souped-up compact car. From his physique, I'd guess it's the same guy who almost caught me. He stands there, resting his weight for a few seconds on the open car door, then he slams it and heads straight for me. Without a sound I mime a desperate plea to Sergio for guidance. The guy must be drunk or wrecked on drugs. He walks right past the front of the truck, not two feet from my face, our eyes lock momentarily, but his gaze is blank.

"Yo, you gotta cigarette?" he asks.

He tries to come to a halt, but the effort makes him lose his balance, and to keep from falling he starts a funny little shuffling trot that takes him away from the truck. He is unable to stop until he almost hits the door of the house and there he collapses in a heap, but only after spewing loudly. Sergio starts the truck engine and lowers the cargo deck. The truck goes back down on all four tires and I can finally jump down off the bumper. I run around back, unhook the rear hatch, and give Sergio the signal. Almost immediately a cascade of washing machines, kitchen sinks, and rusty refrigerators starts crashing to the pavement with an unexpected crash that startles and frightens me.

"Deflate the tire!" Sergio shouts at me out the window.

The bulk of the load hits the ground all at once with a huge metallic roar.

"The tire!" Sergio shouts again.

I'm all confused, I see lights coming on in the houses all around us. Once I've gathered my wits and lunge toward the flatbed truck I see that Claudio is already kneeling by the tire. I climb back into the cab of the dump truck and a second later Claudio piles in behind me. Sergio stomps down hard on the accelerator and we peel out at top speed, lowering the cargo deck as we swerve down the street. We sit tense and focused until we finally tear out at high speed onto the provincial road.

"Yes! Yes! We did it! Did you see the mountain of crap that we left on their doorstep? Vic-c-c-TORY!"

Sergio drives practically slumped over the wheel, his eyes reddened and weary. Every once in a while he bursts out with a laugh or a curse. I smile too, but I only really begin to savor our victory after we return the rented dump truck and we head back to the farmhouse in Sergio's old red Renault. As a peace-making gesture after our savage fight, I start singing at the top of my lungs: old anthems of the left-wing resistance movement like *Bella ciao* and *Bandiera rossa*, in chorus with Sergio. We try to cajole Claudio into singing along, but he prefers to just sit there, with a strange smile playing across his lips as he stares out the window.

"I let the air out of a tire, holy shit . . . I let the air out of a tire," he keeps reciting to himself.

64

Fausto, Vito, and Elisa are waiting for us at the front door of the farmhouse. They're jumping out of their skins with anxiety. When we pull up, waving clenched fists out the windows in a gesture of triumph, they wave their fists in the air with the same gesture. I pull my cell phone out of my pocket and take a great picture of Fausto.

We haven't eaten for hours and we lunge at a baguette and a plate of prosciutto. We're exhausted and the first glass or two of wine triggers attacks of the giggles that I can only remember experiencing once or twice before in my life. We've got plenty of stories to tell: how we snuck up on the garage, how we started to argue, how the truck reared up like a stallion, how I inched my way out over the hood, how the drugged-out hoodlum asked me for a cigarette, then how all the scrap metal and garbage came down with a roar followed by our escape into the night. We put great emphasis on Claudio's daring exploit, and we have to egg him on repeatedly before he finally agrees to tell the tale of his duel with the air valve of the truck tire. We're overheated, we talk over one another constantly, we share the tastiest morsels, and as I listen to Sergio with a gnawing urge to interrupt him, it dawns on me that in some sense he has a point. Right now I wish I knew the scent of tear gas in my nostrils, I wish I'd had a bruise from a billy club to show off, or a night spent in jail to tell my friends about. You never tell us about yourself, girls often tell me, intrigued by the aura of mystery that emanates from my deep silences. The truth is, I don't talk much about myself because over the past twenty years I've watched way too much TV.

As I tell my part of the evening's events, I notice their gazes riveted on me and I realize why I've never really had many friends. Friendship requires stories, shared adventures, tales to be told around a rapt tableful of people, lots of new things to justify drinking new toasts. We laugh and laugh and my belly, subjected to this relatively unfamiliar form of exercise, starts to hurt. You see, I tell myself, friendship is even good for your abdominals.

Elisa goes over and sits down on the sofa, and a second later I hear her start to snore. The adjective "sensual" can be extended to cover some fairly bizarre territory. Sensual doesn't just mean a breast glimpsed through the buttons of a blouse, or a certain way of crossing one's legs, or the imperceptible movement of the hip when you sit down. Sensual can also describe having such a strong personality that you don't think twice about snoring in front of a roomful of people.

I'm a lucky guy, in that I really can't hold my alcohol and I've never tried to pretend that I could. Fausto's talking as if he had wet rag stuffed into his mouth, but he keeps insisting that he can handle the wine magnificently, that it'd take more than this to put him out of operation, that he still remembers the time he drank a Marine under the table. Claudio, too, feels called upon to act as if he's steady as a rock, and for the past half hour he's been sitting practically motionless, with a foolish smile carved onto his face. Sergio, I couldn't say. I'm willing to bet that he's holding it in to keep from giving Fausto any sort of moral victory.

"To our shucksheshezh!" cries Fausto, raising the umpteenth glass.

"To our wha'?" Claudio manages to say before collapsing in a terminal case of the giggles.

"To our . . . successes!" Fausto repeats more carefully.

"No, not to our successes, we haven't really had any . . . and anyway that's bad luck," says Sergio.

"Okay, then to your failures, you mob of losers!"

"To all *our* failures," Claudio chimes in.

We ring our wineglasses with forks and knives before Fausto has a chance to retort.

"Well, okay, why the fuck not," he says. "Two full truck-loads of defective wristwatches sold in every corner of Italy, plus a third truckload, of which I never managed to sell a single item!" he says proudly.

There's a moment of silence, and since I don't want Fausto's risky venture out into the open to go over like a lead balloon, I take up the challenge.

"Competely unsuccessful relationships with family, colleagues, friends, and women. Result: Family? Zero. Job? Zero. Love life? Zero," I say, and with that I drain my glass.

My declaration of failure ignites a challenging smile on Claudio's face. *Piker*, he seems to be saying to me. *Amateur.*

"I brought about the collapse of a supermarket that was the pride of my family for almost a century, and with the same determination I undermined a wonderful marriage. And believe you me, I had to devote so much time and energy to both those undertakings that I had no chance to make any friends at all . . . "

"Here's to failure!" cries Fausto with his glass raised high.

Only Sergio has failed to report in on his failures, but no one puts any pressure on him. We sip our wine and let his moment come to him. As we kill time, we engage in an odd array of pastimes. I squeeze the white crumb from the interior of the baguette into tiny balls and I line them up along one of the red stripes on the tablecloth. Claudio scrapes the blade of his knife along the fabric of the tablecloth, with and against the grain, gathering little windrows of scattered food. Fausto obsessively smooths out the creases on the tablecloth with the palm of one hand. Sergio stares fixedly at the center of the table. All he needs to do is clear his throat for all our eyes to be locked eagerly on his face.

"Well . . . there was the failure of the armed revolutionary struggle, the failure of the militant labor movement . . . " he says.

Disappointed, we go back to our various hobbies and diversions.

"But on top of those, let's add my failure as a husband, so that now my wife is living with a guy who belongs to the national manufacturers' association! And my failure as a father, now that my daughter has turned in an essay at school listing David Hasselhoff as one of the most important figures in our nation's history! And my own personal ideological failure—me, from the great revolutionary that I was, come down in the world to working as a producer for a private television network with a former Fascist stooge and street enforcer."

"Cin cin!" we cry practically in chorus. "Here's to that!"

65

Samuel must have come up with an Italian grammar book from somewhere, because for days he's been asking us difficult questions. He asked Fausto what an oxymoron was, and Fausto—I can just see him doing it—refused to admit defeat and bravely came up with an explanation that involved oxyacetylene, oxycontin, and oxymorons. I hate making things up, but it's stronger than me, I hate admitting that I don't know something even more. So when he asks me what anacoluthon means I shush him emphatically and look around me with embarrassment.

"Samuel, you need to be careful how you talk! Anacoluthon is a very dirty word!" I say.

"No, that's not possible, I read it in . . . " he replies, mortified.

"Well, you'll just have to be a little more careful about the things you read. Anacoluthon: No! You mustn't ever say that word!"

From a bookshelf, I pull down a copy of an anthology of twentieth-century Italian literature that we found in the back of one of the antique armoires, a big heavy book four hundred pages long.

"Read this, carefully and from cover to cover. Take as long as you like. Then, once you're finished, you can ask me all the questions you like."

Samuel takes the book and holds it in his hands, turning it over and hefting it admiringly to feel its bulk.

"This is 'an unparalleled anthology, unequalled in its field'? A 'deathless literary collection'?" he asks.

"That's right, Samuel."

My problem is I never do things for the right reasons. The only reason I gave him that book was to get him off my back. It's too bad. If only I'd done it to make him happy, I could thoroughly enjoy the magnificent smile that's spreading across his face right now.

Elisa has decided on the menu for our guests and she calls us all together. While Abu heads out to gather vegetables in the garden, we split up the various assignments. I ignore the snickers of the three idiots after I offer to drive into town with her. I get in the car roundly ignoring the smiles and winks wreathing their faces. When we drive off, I don't even look in the rear-view mirror.

The drive into town has many of the hallmarks of a field trip. We sing in the car, we laugh at the chaotic traffic, and we honk the horn for no good reason, much like all the other cars around us. At an intersection we pay exaggerated respect to the traffic cop with his hand in the air by coming to a full stop immediately at his command and, ignoring the shouted insults of all the other motorists, starting up again only when he gestures us forward.

While we're waiting for the butcher to finish preparing our lamb chops, Elisa puts her hand on my shoulder. It's friendly, innocent contact, possibly involuntary, but I decide to remember it. This is the first time she's ever touched me. If I think about all the time we've spent together, it seems absurd. I've never talked so much with a woman in my life and, in particular, never so much with a woman I desire and with whom I'd like to make love. With women I've always said and done no more than was necessary to get them into bed with me. It wasn't out of hypocrisy, I just played by the rules of a game that calls for a specific modicum of moves, a threshold past which a woman can feel unencumbered by remorse if she chooses to give in.

Till now, I've systematically made every wrong move. I implemented the same tactics I used on all the others without realizing how different she is from all the others. She doesn't scrutinize me, she doesn't put me to the test, she never asks trick questions. She speaks, she listens—nothing else. No, wait, there is one more thing: she strips me bare. And for someone like me, whose only goal with women was always to get their clothes off, that's a pretty unsettling turnabout.

The butcher brings his meat cleaver down on a section of bone with a crunching thud. Elisa notices the way I jump and smiles at me in amusement.

66

The first guests to arrive are a young couple driving a beat-up jeep. This time, not even Fausto has any objections. Tomorrow eight more people are scheduled to arrive and there will be no vacancies. It's the first time that's ever happened.

To keep from being cloying and invasive, we've done a better job of assigning tasks. Sergio and Elisa will take care of the guests directly, Vito, due to security considerations, will remain in the residential area while Fausto, Claudio, and I see to all the various jobs, with a general aim of livening things up at our agritourism bed and breakfast.

After the welcome buffet, the assignment of rooms, and a lavish breakfast, the young people stroll impatiently on the lawn. After an hour without results, Elisa tries to distract them by inviting them to visit the vegetable garden to pick their own food for lunch. The gambit works for half an hour or so, but they're soon back on the lawn. All it takes is a few seconds of music to ignite their enthusiasm and allow us to heave a sigh of relief.

The young couple spend the day taking photographs of each other and strolling in the garden, awaiting a new miracle. It's not until evening, with dinner already served, that we manage to get them to come back in. We've set a special little table for them in front of the fireplace. They eat dinner looking at the fire, holding hands the whole time.

Sergio takes advantage of dinner to go out and smack the ground with the back of a shovel. The technique proves effective and when the kids go back out for a last attempt, they are stuck dumb. An all-enveloping piece of music and a magnificent starry night together persuade them to sit on the grass. It's the first movement of Bach's third *Brandenburg Concerto*, Vito suggests to Sergio.

I come out with a few lengths of firewood, and Sergio carries a couple of glasses of wine.

"It's the third movement . . . from the . . . *Strasburg Concerto* . . . I think, but anyway, it's Bach, that much I know," he tells the kids.

We turn and go, leaving them sitting by the fire, arms around each other.

The next morning, they've come down with a fever. The most enthusiastically feverish hotel guests I've ever seen in my life. They get on their cell phones and, in a storm of sneezes and ring tones, inform us that a group of friends of theirs will be coming around lunchtime, twelve or maybe fourteen, they say.

Half an hour later, the group of eight guests that we were

expecting shows up as well. To Fausto's delight, they pull up in two BMWs. We take turns admiring the unaccustomed sight of every one of our rooms booked and full, and then we foregather to discuss how we're going to be able to put together a meal for more than twenty people, not counting us and the *camorristi*. As a first step in that direction we decide to take five minutes to drink a toast to the first full house at Lunatic Hill.

The new arrivals are deeply curious. The earth remains silent but we're not especially concerned. We've figured out that the waiting is a fundamental component of the experience. It's like the northern lights, you have to start with a clear understanding that you just might not get an actual glimpse of the aurora borealis. Working diligently under Elisa's orders, we produce a lunch that leaves them all open-mouthed in astonishment. That earns us reservations for dinner as well. One young woman requests a massage and when she comes downstairs she has such a contented expression on her face that two young men sign up immediately for massages. Fausto and Claudio have become human cash registers. They calculate and recalculate our profits in real time, then they make long-term estimates by multiplying the current profits ratio by the number of reservations that keep pouring into our email inbox.

After half a day of ducking into the kitchen to help Elisa and drink a little wine as long as they're there, the two of them are completely stinking drunk, and they start shouting out astronomical sums, which no longer penetrate my mind. Right now, my body is downstairs but my head is up in the attic. The first of the two young men is upstairs getting his massage and the idea that Elisa is placing her hands on a stranger's body is driving me crazy. I try to get my mind off it by taking a stroll in the garden. While awaiting the miracle Abu, Samuel, and Alex are entertaining our guests with Ghanaian chants and music. This idea of the ethnic concert was an extemporaneous suggestion of Elisa's; she had a pretty good idea of how many dinners she would have to prepare and the delay that was likely to ensue in serving dinner. Once again, it was a spectacular success.

Such an atmosphere has developed around the place that even if we put on a children's puppet show, our guests would still be over the moon with delight. I do my best to enjoy the performance, but I can't hold out for more than five minutes before I'm heading upstairs to the attic. On the steps, I see the young man leaving the massage room with an expression on his face that I don't like one bit. When he passes me on the stairs, he gives me a wink and comes closer than he'll ever know to being hurled bodily downstairs.

"What are you doing up here?" Elisa asks me.

She's leaning on her elbows against the message bed. Her expression cheers me up. She doesn't look like someone who's been having fun of any kind. She looks completely beat, in fact.

"Why on earth did you come up here?" she asks me again.

I just came up to see if you needed something, I formulate in my mind.

"I was just going through a few minutes of jealousy," I find myself saying. What the devil am I doing?

"More than a few, quite a few," I add grumpily.

"Oh, how nice, so why don't you go downstairs and beat up the second guy? I don't think I have it in me to give him a massage, too. Rescue me!"

"May I?" says a voice behind me.

The second young man is here for his massage. I give Elisa a smile and head downstairs. I never thought that a staircase could look so beautiful, but these are special stairs, with wonderful steps and marvelous risers, and at the top, a young woman unlike any other.

I walk into the kitchen and notice Sergio stepping discreetly through the secret door down to the *taverna*, carrying a tray. I notice that there are three plates on the tray.

"Why three plates?" I ask with a broad smile.

"Don't worry about it," Sergio says.

Right then and there I don't worry about it. Then, I think back to his tense face and I decide to follow him down. I walk in and he's already inside the *taverna* and I come mighty close to dying of a heartache on the spot when I see that, along with the usual two kids, we also have Franco, the leatherneck *camorrista* as an involuntary guest. Sergio has a handgun drawn on them and he sets down the lunch tray on the floor, keeping them covered at all times. He doesn't even notice me until he's ready to leave. He immediately yells at me:

"The door!"

I'd left the door to the kitchen wide open and Franco, quicker than the other two to spot an opportunity, starts screaming help at the top of his lungs. Sergio slams shut the door to the *taverna* and together we run upstairs to the kitchen. Only after we close the second door are Franco's screams drowned out entirely. We peek discreetly out the window. The singing of Abu, Samuel, and Alex has saved us from certain disaster.

"If I say not to worry about it, then that means don't worry about it, goddamn it!" Sergio shouts.

"Like hell I won't worry about it! When did this happen?"

"When you were in town."

"And everyone else knows about it? Why didn't you tell me?"

"Yeah, I know, you're right, we should have told you earlier, but there were all these guests . . . and you're always following Elisa around, and she doesn't want to hear anything about all this."

"We said we were going to pay them and forget about it, not cause any more trouble . . . "

"There it is, there it is!" shouts one of the young people in the garden. We go back to the window and we see twenty-five people sitting motionless on the lawn. Some people crouch down, others lay their ear on the ground, and others still slowly begin to sit down in religious silence.

"This belongs to us," says Sergio.

He's right, but it still doesn't make sense to me. I leave the kitchen; I need some time to think this over. Common sense suggests that now that business is thriving, the right thing to do would be to pay the protection money, that all things considered, six thousand euros a year is a trifling sum compared with the potential earnings that have suddenly appeared on the horizon. We could enjoy our success and live without worries. But that's exactly the point. Living without worries is exactly what I've done for all these years. I lived without worries until one day I wondered if I was even alive anymore.

When our guests finally leave, Elisa collapses on the sofa. It's just a few hours until our next group of guests are scheduled to arrive, and we decide to let her rest. We'll take care of everything for her, but first we need to withdraw to the kitchen to have a talk with Vito. The old man knows what we want from him, and he comes straight to the point.

"It's a disaster now but it was already one before. I'm alone, but the minute you guys took those two young guns, you were in trouble deep," he tells us.

"Now what'll happen?" I ask.

"What do I know, this is the first time anyone's gone around kidnapping local *camorristi*."

This is also the first time we've ever heard Vito use the word *camorristi*. He accompanies it with a jerk of the head to indicate the *taverna*, as if that word no longer had anything to do with him.

"Up till now, there's been a shootout and they set fire to a warehouse, chump change. In the end, evidently, they believe the kids ran away. But with Franco, everything's different . . .

the families are going to start accusing each other of being involved."

"Will they start up the gang warfare again?" Sergio asks.

"For a while, yeah, for sure, and they might even forget about us . . . that is, about youse. Then, when the police step in, the capos will meet around a table. They'll talk it over and they'll have to find an explanation for the mysterious disappearances somewhere else."

"How much time do you think we have?" I ask.

"What do I know? First there'll be some killings, then one signal might be the arrival of an investigating magistrate from outside. This might mean that the government is tightening its grip and that the families might have some explaining to do."

"Maybe we could try the old text message trick."

"With Franco? I don't see that working. He's an important soldier in terms of business, he was trying to build a position, everyone around here knew that."

I don't know about the others, but I at least don't seem capable of being as worried as I probably ought to be. More than anything else, I'm resigned. We're doing the right thing and if we can keep some kind of control over all the potential consequences, then it doesn't much matter.

"Plus, Franco's got family," Vito says.

"Family in the sense that . . . " I start to say.

"He's got a wife! A total ballbuster. She'll turn the town inside out and upside down until she finds him."

It seemed so easy at first. The *camorristi* show up, we imprison them in the cellar, problem resolved. Whenever I get a clear picture of what we've done, I get cold chills.

"Plus, he had a girlfriend in Munich. Maybe we could leave his cell phone turned on up there. It would get them off our tail, at least for a while."

"So, what, we're going to have to drive all the way to Munich?" Fausto asks.

"Then we could just leave a clue of some kind on the provincial road, like his jacket. But we all know what that would mean."

Sergio nods. Fausto and I, reevaluating the possibility of a drive to Munich, remain expressionless. Sergio notices.

"They'll think he's been murdered!" he says to us.

"There'll be a gang war, some people'll probably die."

"But those guys are already killing each other all the time," Fausto says, with the candor of a small child.

"True enough," says Sergio.

Vito senses our loss of initiative and intensity. We no longer have the adrenaline of the early meetings. For instance, I wander off track, suggesting that maybe we ought to build a tunnel of our own. Like the ones Mafia bosses have under their houses, but not as an escape route, as a place to lock up *camorristi*, one by one, as they show up.

"Let's do it this way, it might work. Give me a road map, and I'll show you guys exactly where to drop the jacket. It's a boundary between the territories of two friendly clans that respect each other. The thing could turn out to be pretty drawn out and maybe nobody even gets killed."

67

The setting sun brings with it an orange sky that turns magenta around the few clouds stretched out in a high steady breeze. I consider that at this time of day I could be working in the auto dealership, showing a customer the leather trim on a power seat, while behind our backs we'd be missing this spectacular sunset. There are certain decisions from which there's no turning back.

Elisa's hand is moving ever so slightly, caressing the grass. It's half an inch away from mine. A gap I could easily close.

"Should I assume your hand is grazing mine accidentally?" she asks.

"Do you always have to ruin everything?"

"If you think that making things more real means ruining them . . ."

"I mean that every once in a while you could just take even a clumsy gesture as something romantic. You could assume that it's a primordial need in human beings, that it's something boys and girls have been doing ever since elementary school, and that no one would dream of fucking up such a naïve and innocent thing."

"Okay okay, let's not fuck it up."

"So, yes, damn it, I'm grazing your hand intentionally. I do it because I'm trying to figure out if it might be something you'd like. I'll wait to see if you make a gesture in return, something imperceptible that I can take as either a yes or a no. It's the pleasure of the wait, of the suspense."

"Yes."

"Yes what?"

"Yes. That's your answer. Yes I like it, go ahead, graze my hand all you like, we're here watching the sun set . . . you think I don't have anything better to do?"

68

Business is starting to thrive, and before long it's booming. In no more than two weeks' time we have a waiting list that'll cover us for the next six months. We still get a solid trade in young couples, but word of mouth has started to bring in a more refined and well-to-do clientele as well. We're no longer just busy on the weekends, many of our guests stay for a week at a time, and when they leave they make a reservation for the same week the following year.

The mystical aura attached to the place is bringing us yoga aficionados, former hippies, and practicing Buddhists, as well as the inevitable army of successful businessmen and executives looking for a charming setting in which to seduce their secretaries. We're experiencing that magic moment when everything is going perfectly. Everything we do seems to turn out perfectly. Elisa has become a money factory. We have an endless stream of reservations for lunch and dinner, and she's had to train Claudio to help her out with the massages. Abu's vegetable patch is a smash hit: the guests love seeing where their food is grown, and at least a third of the clientele returns home with a bag full of produce. Our bicycle rental business is a little less lucrative, because practically everyone prefers to stay around the farmhouse, waiting to witness the miracle of the Alfa Romeo Giulia.

The truth is that it doesn't take much to create a paradise. Since we come from the city, we understand that immediately. There, no one really knows how to do their job, no one works with joy in their heart. Sales clerks in shops refuse to smile at you, and they lose their tempers if you ask more than one question. When you eat out, you're served rudely and it's become a rarity to eat a bowl of pasta cooked properly—*al dente*. If I'd enjoyed selling cars, I would have loved all my customers for asking questions. If someone had asked me about the engine's horsepower, I would have gladly and promptly told them the HP rating, and I would have gone on to tell them about the power-to-weight ratio, which is the only number that really matters. Then I would have told them about Newton meters (or foot pounds) of torque, and I would have taken great personal enjoyment in explaining just what this ostensibly incomprehensible parameter really is. But I hated my job, just like everyone else, and I preferred staring at the ceiling for eight hours a day instead of willingly answering questions.

So here it is: our paradise. We welcome our guests because we're glad they've come; we cook with love because we want them to be satisfied with their meals and we want them to ask us for the recipes of the delicacies we feed them; we reassure anyone who tells us they're allergic to garlic and, if requested, we prepare special menus within minutes. We make ourselves scarce if a guest wants privacy, or we sit chatting until the wee hours if someone is looking for company. We throw open the doors to the kitchen because—aside from two or three *camorristi* in close confinement—we have nothing to hide, the ingredients that we use are fresh-picked, local, and organic. We don't set any rigid schedules for breakfast, lunch, and dinner. If our guests come back tired and hungry from a hike in the countryside, we make sure there's a snack left out for them and we don't charge them a penny extra.

It's a pleasure to take care of them. Our guests smile at us, display their astonishment, and thank us from the heart. Actually, at first they're vaguely suspicious, they always assume there's some hidden trick. Then, however, they finally relax, and that's when we get the smiles and all the rest.

We started this business to make money; now, it's the least of our concerns. It was enough to know that we weren't in danger of going out of business any time soon. Once that happened, we stopped worrying about profits and devoted ourselves heart and soul to improving our hospitality and accommodations. Claudio woke us all up at two in the morning to tell us that we should get an assortment of picnic blankets for our guests. A brilliant idea. Lying stretched out on a soft quilt in the middle of musical field, by a crackling fire, gazing up at the starry night sky. That's my idea of paradise.

69

The first few days of spring are transforming the countryside. Color is appearing everywhere, on the lawn, in the trees, across the fields surrounding the farmhouse. I'd go so far as to say that a thin layer of hair is springing up on Claudio's bald spots.

We're enjoying one of our all-too-rare days off, and we decide to take the whole afternoon for ourselves, but only after tending properly to the vegetable patch. The idea of putting in plants in the name of certain guests has proved successful, and now we're planning to expand the vegetable garden by at least a good sixty feet. There are guests who'll drive more than a hundred miles just to eat lunch here and drive home with a basketful of produce from their own personal plants. Elisa is busier all the time, and now Abu and Fausto are in charge of the vegetable patch. They're constantly working together, they study horticulture on the internet, they rejoice at every new bud and shoot, they worry about hail and strong winds. Fausto, who only got interested in gardening once he realized it was a brilliant conversational gambit with attractive female guests, has actually spent a whole night standing over his young lettuce plants with an umbrella.

It's time to take lunch down to our prisoners and I volunteer to go down with Claudio. Sergio offers to come with us, but then he decides to go on hoeing the garden. He glances over at Fausto. Even if our security mechanism is well oiled, it's always better for there to be a third person at meals.

Outside the cellar door, armed with billhooks, we perform our assigned tasks. Fausto, who has the most powerful voice, will order the *camorristi* to go into the bathroom, I'm in charge of locking the bathroom door, next it's Claudio turn to walk in with the lunch tray. Fausto is supposed to guard the door.

"Get in the bathroom and shut the door behind you, you pieces of shit!" Fausto shouts, prompting a scolding from me and Claudio.

"You always have to overdo it!" I say.

I ignore Fausto's sigh and eye roll. I peer through the peephole. The three *camorristi* troop sadly into the bathroom and close the door behind them.

"I'm going in," I say.

I walk in, gripping the billhook, and with a brisk stride I cross the room to the bathroom door. I turn the key twice to double-lock it.

"Done," I say.

Claudio walks in with the tray. I step closer to grab the carafe of milk which was about to tip over, and suddenly I hear a noise behind me. An arm wraps roughly around my throat.

"Let us out of heah, or I'll kill him!" Franco shouts.

I have a shard of broken glass pressed against my throat and my heart is racing wildly. I'm confused, but Claudio and Fausto have reacted promptly, leaping out of the *taverna*.

"I'll kill him!" Franco shouts. And he's still talking about me. I want to tell Claudio and Fausto to do what Franco says, but I can't get a breath in or out of my throat, which is clamped tight under Franco's arm.

"We're fucked!" Fausto shouts from the other side of the door.

I don't hear a word from Claudio and I have to imagine him lying senseless on the floor.

"Who's a piece of shit, now, yo? Come here . . . that way your friends can get a nice cleah look at you," Franco says, dragging me over in front of the peephole.

The two younger *camorristi* are still standing behind him, and they seem fairly passive and uninvolved.

"He's turning purple . . . " Saverio says to Franco, pointing to my face. I wish I could express my gratitude for his concern, but right now the blood pressure is pounding in my temples and I feel as if my head's about to explode. I hear footsteps galloping down the stairs.

"What's happening?" Sergio says.

"They've got him!" Fausto says.

"Let us out of heah, or I'll kill him," Franco says again, this time in a normal voice.

"We're fucked," Fausto says.

"What the hell are you talking about . . . " Sergio replies with a tone of annoyance that hardly seems appropriate, given the situation.

I hear the door swing open and Franco clamps my throat even tighter. Sergio walks in carrying a hatchet. Behind him is Claudio, who has not in fact fainted, and Fausto, both brandishing billhooks in plain view.

"Drop your weapons and let us through!" Franco says.

"No," says Sergio.

The two young men, baffled, look to Franco, eager to hear his reply.

"Look, I'm not kidding around heah, one more or one less dead man doesn't mean much to me!"

"Then go ahead and kill him," says Sergio as if I didn't exist. "Then see if you can guess what'll happen to you . . . "

This is all wrong. In the movies, whenever someone takes a hostage, he just holds something sharp to his throat, yells out for everyone to drop their weapons, and everybody does what he says. We are always taught that that's what happens, there are no alternatives.

"You're not playing the right way! It'd just take me a second to kill this guy!"

"That's not how I'd do it. I'd take my time. I'll kill you one limb at a time!" Sergio smiles.

Incredible. So what they showed us on TV all those years was just so much bullshit. Sergio has refused to drop his weapon and now we're in the middle of a standoff.

"Take his hatchet away, this guy's probably never even killed a chicken," Franco says to his people.

The kids look at each other and take an uncertain step toward Sergio. All he has to do to discourage them is swing the hatchet hard against the door. Claudio takes fright and drops his billhook for a second, but he picks it right back up again.

"So we want to see who's tougher in here? Let's see! Let's see how long your friend can last without breathing!"

I think of my father and a general sensation of letting go starts to sweep over me. Suffocating to death isn't such a bad way to die after all, there's no real pain. I just feel as if I'm slipping away. And the idea that at the bottom of the slide down which I'm slipping, my father is waiting for me, is somehow a welcome one. With my last remaining strength, without Franco noticing a thing, I manage to signal to Sergio that everything's okay. And he waves to Fausto to hand him a chair. Before the startled eyes of the two young men he sits down and makes himself comfortable, directly in front of me and Franco. That's the way matters remain for a few minutes. I can feel Franco's grip becoming less and less intense, and I can slowly begin to see things more clearly. I stop sliding away.

"You know this doesn't end here, right?" Franco says through clenched teeth as he pushed me into the arms of my friends.

Sergio stands up from the chair, walks over to him with the hatchet raised threateningly, and he takes the piece of broken glass out of his hand. Franco doesn't retreat and he glares scornfully back at Sergio. We leave the room without ever turning our backs on him, and we close and lock the door. After the key clicks around for the last turn, a hail of backslaps rains down on Sergio.

"You were magnificent," says Fausto.

"Mythical," says Claudio.

I'm too busy massaging my throat and trying to fathom this sense of disappointment that I feel at having survived. We walk upstairs like a platoon of triumphant victors. Our heads are held high, our eyes are fierce and proud. We're heroes and the only thing missing that would have made our entrance into the kitchen perfect is a nice handheld slow-motion pan.

70

"I swear I locked the door."

I must have said it at least six times, but in the end they finally believed me. We went back down armed to the teeth. Claudio insisted on carrying Franco's pistol. True professional that he is, he put on a glove before picking up the gun. A pink rubber kitchen glove, to be exact. We tied the three men to the beds until we were able to determine that they had managed to disable the lock on the bathroom door.

"Well, look at that!" I said.

"Nice work," Sergio said to the *camorristi*.

Saverio and Renato responded with an imperceptible movement of their heads to indicate Franco.

Elisa refused to be told anything about it, but the fact that she'd figured out what had happened, or at least that I had narrowly escaped death, is clear from the look in her eyes. She glances at me from time to time with a look of motherly concern. I ignore those glances, because I've assumed the stance of a mighty warrior who gazes intensely into the distance after the battle, scanning the horizon.

Meanwhile, between one worried glance and another, Elisa begins working on Vito's makeup. The man is the picture of health, but we've decided to make him look sickly and under the weather by accentuating the circles under his eyes and making his complexion look wan and ashen. This is a crucial safeguard. After the *camorristi*'s escape attempt, he can't sleep upstairs with us anymore. We have to take him back downstairs to make it clear to them that he's just as much a prisoner as they are, and that he's certainly not living the good life. We're sorry to have to do it, but the old man clearly understands the importance of having an infiltrator so we can avoid having more trouble with Franco.

Elisa's makeup job doesn't convince Vito, who asks us if we could arrange to mess up his face for real to some extent.

"He has a point," Sergio says. "They have to believe that he tried to take part in the uprising too."

We look around for a volunteer.

"Don't sweat it, this could prolly save my life, ya know," Vito says. Claudio nerves himself to strike the blow, stands in front of his chair, and slaps him in the face. The old man's cheek twitches slightly.

"Ah, hold on a second, that was just a test," Claudio says in response to our critical glances.

He tries again, swinging his arm in another slap, just slightly harder than the first one, followed by three more blows in rapid succession, each delivered with growing intensity. A small pink circle appears on the old man's cheekbone.

"We keep diss up, we could be here all night . . . " Vito says.

"Here, I'll take care of this," says Fausto.

He shoves Claudio out of the way and asks for some room. Vito closes his eyes and braces for impact. Fausto winds up for a tremendous smack but at the last minute he loses his conviction and the palm of his hand strikes the old man's cheek, producing nothing more than a flat crack.

"Done?" Vito asks, with a hopeful note in his voice.

"Not even . . . " I say.

Cut to the quick, Fausto defends his honor by launching immediately into another roundhouse smack. This one too is very loud but not especially effective.

"Come on, guys! We're doing this for him!" says Sergio, rolling up his sleeves and shoving Fausto aside.

"Maronna . . . " Vito whispers.

Sergio lets loose with a clenched fist and a determined swing, and he rocks Vito's head back on its gimbals. Vito lurches backward and lolls helpless on his side.

"Vito!" Elisa shouts.

"What, have you lost your mind?" I say.

We rush to his side. We cradle his head in our hands and slap his cheeks lightly to bring him to. One of his cheekbones is purple and there are flecks of blood on his lips. He slowly opens his eyes and looks at us in bewilderment for a few seconds before regaining consciousness.

"Now you're perfect . . . " says Sergio.

Vito responds with a dazed smile. We help him to his feet and once we're sure he's okay we lead him downstairs. Sergio orders the three *camorristi* to lock themselves into the bathroom, then we walk in and leave the old man stretched out on one of the beds. He winks an eye at us and begins to moan. We unlock the bathroom door, we leave the *taverna*, and clustering around the peephole, we witness the ensuing scene.

"Vito, what in the world have they did to you?" says Saverio.

"Dat guy's a stone killer," says Vito.

"Who? Da fatso?" asks Franco.

Sergio jerks in shock. Fausto, who can't help but snicker, is exiled to the kitchen.

"Yeah, dat fat guy's a sick fuck . . . he'll kill us all if we don't be careful," Vito replies.

71

The new group of guests is one of the most challenging yet, ten people ranging in age from seven to eighty. For today, I'm assigned to be Elisa's sous-chef. Taken individually, we're really not worth much, but as a group we can cover any situation that comes up.

Fausto is a perfect conversationalist when it comes to the clientele of a sports bar. From soccer to curling, he's an expert, or at least a self-proclaimed expert, on strategy and regulations. He has an encyclopedic knowledge and a monumental memory for dates, formations, and world records.

Sergio is an idol for left-wing intellectuals. He was mentored by leading personalities from the left-wing militant organizations *Potere Operaio* and *Lotta Continua*, he knows all the major speeches of Enrico Berlinguer by heart, and he does a pretty good imitation of Il Duce. He holds the keys to a number of dangerous truths, including the names of the masterminds behind the 1974 Italicus train bombing and the 1969 Piazza Fontana bank bombing. Concerning the downed civilian DC9 that vanished into the Mediterranean Sea off Ustica in 1980, he has own personal theory that involves the CIA, Mossad, and the Vatican.

Claudio is a heart throb for the over-sixty set. When they start talking about hospital stays and violent deaths, he eagerly joins in with his enormous repertory of emergency room horror stories, with a special focus on malpractice and medical incompetence.

Elisa is a wild card. Everybody likes her. She's a queen of improvisation, she can entertain children for hours. Painting lessons, gardening lessons, and workshops in salt-dough modeling clay pop out at a moment's notice, as needed.

I'm not sure exactly where I fit in. I just smile and say nothing. So people assume I'm very intelligent. Some kind of artist.

A fair number of single young women begin showing up, so Fausto has resumed his ab crunches. I've never given too much credence to his bedroom war stories, but now I have to hand it to him: he's quite the conquistador. Even though what really seems to pay off is the single-minded relentlessness with which he sets out to stalk every unattached female guest, his achievements have earned my wholehearted admiration. His pickup lines are distinguished by a disarming simplicity, and at times they verge on the slovenly. "Haven't we met somewhere before?" he asks, utterly shameless. I could never pull it off. No one takes that phrase seriously anymore; it's become a sort of emblem for dick-headed male vulgarity. But he throws caution to the winds and, over time, it occasionally works. Sometimes, someone even recognizes him. "Wait, aren't you the guy that . . . " We've learned to tremble when we hear those words. Most of the time, it's just people who've seen his face on TV when they were doing a little late-night channel surfing, but one time the person who recognized him was a dissatisfied—a deeply dissatisfied—customer. It took a lot to calm him down: a lot of time and a lot of money. Complete reimbursement of the money paid for the defective wristwatch, plus free room and board, as a form of moral restitution.

Not all our guests are so easily won over. In fact, with more than one, it's been pretty much impossible. Some people were just born to cause trouble. The room is drafty; I was told there was no garlic but I definitely taste garlic in this dish; what the hell kind of resort is this, it's always raining; I paid for a garden with classical music and so far I haven't heard a single note. Then there are people who think that spewing an endless succession of complaints is somehow chic, to say nothing of those men who feel virile only when they're testing some point, standing up to mistreatment, showing the world that it can't take advantage of *them*. These people are hopeless, they want to escape from the city, but when they leave they pack all their mental cages and bring them along for the ride.

The musical meadow, for example, is always a spectacular hit with the guests. Some guests are enchanted by the legend, others are fascinated by the possible scientific explanations, and then there are the very rare cases of individuals who can't seem to help wanting to show the rest of mankind just how smart they are, who make a point of refusing to have the wool pulled over their eyes. Like this one woman who stood up in front of a dozen or so people stretched out on their picnic blankets, all of them delighted by the musical miracle, and couldn't think of anything better to do than to start shouting: "What's the matter with you all? Didn't you notice that the piece didn't even start from the beginning? This is the radio, not some dead conductor!" Or the other guy who started jumping up and down on the lawn until he managed to make the music stop. No big deal, anyway: most of our guests are on our side, and in fact when the woman who shouted went inside, her departure was greeted with a chorus of Bronx cheers, while the guy who jumped up and down came closer than he ever knew to being strung up from a tree branch.

People who come here have no interest in staring reality in the face. They prefer to cherish a dream and say to hell with everything else.

I do my best to take Vito's place, even though when it comes to cooking I know little or nothing. More nothing, actually, than little. In her kitchen domain, Elisa is extremely organized and a bit of a martinet. I try to be useful, but I often have the impression that I'm more trouble than help, so I move quickly around the kitchen to stay out of her way, obsessively washing every single pot, pan, or utensil that's been sitting in the sink for any longer than fifteen seconds, getting down anything she needs from the higher shelves, and grating parmesan cheese whenever possible. I know, it's grunt work, but in the end, when we pull a steaming rabbit stew or an eggplant parmesan out of the oven, I feel as if I've done my part and it makes me happy.

"Doesn't this situation frighten you?" she asks me out of the blue.

"Should I answer you as a man?"

"Sure, go ahead."

"What are you talking about, frightened? Me? Ha!"

"Okay, now try answering me as a man who's not a jerk."

"Well, yes, maybe it frightens me a little."

"Really?"

"Yes . . . sometimes, a little."

I emphasize the "sometimes, a little," because her "really" made me think that telling her the truth might have been a bad idea.

"God, how I'd love to fuck you in one of those 'sometimes, a little' moments!"

I heave a mental sigh of relief and gaze at her in admiration as she goes back to stuffing the chicken. I know, I know—contained in her observation there's a deep significance to be assayed and appreciated, a subtle critique of society and standards, a penetrating psychological analysis of human behavior, but in spite of myself I focus on one thing only: the implicit acknowledgment of the distinct possibility that I may at some point be able to have sexual relations with Elisa.

72

After washing the last plate, I dry my hands and accompany Elisa out of the kitchen. It's nighttime, everyone's in their bedrooms except for Claudio, who's sleeping in front of the TV. They're showing his second favorite program, one of those broadcasts that features five minutes of soccer goals followed by two hours of yakking, commentary, and replay analysis of every play. He no longer demands the evening news shows, his porno fetish was a passing phase, and he's even starting to get tired of sports, maybe we've finally done it. Maybe we can finally turn the TV off entirely.

I take a look out the window, I open it partway, and the delicate notes of a piano concerto waft into the room. Elisa smiles at me and walks out into the garden. There's no moon, it's pitch dark outside. Before following her out, I pick up a large candle. We sit down on the grass. As soon as she sees the candle, she smiles ironically.

"Not tonight," I say.

"Okay, not tonight," she replies.

We watch as the flame gradually grows stronger, brighter, flickering occasionally.

"Too bad, there was something pretty good I wanted to say about men who use candles," she says.

"Go on, let's hear it," I egg her on with a snort.

I sit there waiting for the answer. Then I enjoy the truce. This isn't the kind of relationship I've always dreamed of, in fact, to be exact, this is a relationship that never even crossed my mind. In our fashion, I realize, we're embracing already. It's an apparently frigid relationship and yet it's so full of meaning that it manages to warm me up as if we were having sex already. We should still be full of life at our age, we should skip all the steps and be in bed every chance we get. We should have that magical night we'll always remember, the night in which we just gorge on sex, a night to keep us warm for every night yet to come, long after the passion has cooled. But maybe this is our magic night.

"In your opinion, are we actually making love right now?" I say.

Elisa turns and looks at me. Her gaze is tranquil and yet surprised. I'm surprised at myself.

"I knew it, you're not half as much of a turd as you seem." Ah, she took the words right out of my mouth.

73

Claudio's wife pulls up in a black hardtop sports car. Behind the wheel is a guy that the woman seems to have selected in accordance with a very specific criterion: he's as unlike her ex husband as it is possible for anyone to be. Tall, slim, and elegant with that added dollop of something that's just enough to betray his profound and intrinsic inelegance. He gets out of the car and the first thing he does is to check his suspension, the next thing he does is survey the surface of the road he'll have to jolt back down when it's time to leave, the third thing he does is take a hasty glance at the magnificent view. Antonia is a beautiful woman, blooming, handsome, without a touch of vulgarity, save for the possible exception of the man she's chosen. The ineluctable quality of her breakup with Claudio is unmistakable.

Claudio and Antonia exchange a hug, then there's a handshake and a friendly round of smiles with her man.

I was curious to see whether Antonia would notice any of the recent changes in her husband but, aside from a rapid glance at the hair that's growing back, for now she seems to have overlooked them entirely.

Her companion introduces himself with his first and last name, Gaetano something or other, shaking hands all around with a ridiculous overabundance of brash manliness. He's expansive, all hail-fellow-well-met, he asks lots of questions, he's interested in everything. All things considered, the one thing that's obvious is that he doesn't give a damn about a thing. He puts on the common touch, he toasts happily without noticing the fact that the glass isn't perfectly clean, he stretches out on a lounge chair in the garden saying how wonderful it all is, how he'd happily spend the rest of his life right in that spot. Or at least until his next appointment with his hairdresser, I find myself thinking.

Claudio shows his wife every corner of the farmhouse. She seems to be sincerely impressed and there are even fleeting moments of tenderness between them, right under Gaetano's eyes. But Gaetano pays no attention whatsoever, raptly engaged as he is in staring at the ass of a sixteen-year-old girl bending over to pick daisies on the lawn.

"Why don't you take a rest, and we'll serve lunch in a little while," Claudio tells the couple.

"Well, maybe a quick shower," Antonia says, and then she vanishes upstairs with her man.

I'm tempted to say something to Claudio. I'm tempted to tell him that he has a beautiful ex wife. But I decide against it. That it's not everyday that you see ex spouses on such genuinely cordial terms and that he must be proud of the civility with which they're handling their divorce. But what would be the point?

"Hot babe your ex wife," Fausto says.

"She was beautiful when she was young and she's even prettier now," Claudio replies in an untroubled voice.

"Plus congratulations, it's all very modern . . . you, her, the other guy . . . "

"Fausto!" Sergio shouts from the far end of the room.

"What's up?"

"Come on, let's get some firewood!"

"Firewood? What do we need firewood for?"

"Come on, damn it!"

Fausto stomps off snorting in annoyance and when Sergio turns his back to him pretends to kick him in the butt. This is no agritourism bed and breakfast, it's more like an elementary school playground.

"Well, is everything ready?" asks Claudio, who seems to have remained impervious to the awkward byplay.

"Is what ready?"

"Lunch. They must be starving, we can't make them wait until two o'clock to eat something!"

"Are you kidding? Of course not. You set the table. Elisa and I'll get lunch ready."

More than an hour later, Antonia and Gaetano are still in their room and I can't think of anything else to do to distract Claudio. There's a surreal silence, broken only by muffled thuds from the second floor. The noises could be anything, something falling on the floor, a heavy footstep, a slamming door. But they could also be the headboard of a bed slamming against a wall. I'm jumping out of my skin.

"Shall we go pick some flowers?" I ask loudly.

"Why not? We could put them in a centerpiece," Claudio replies.

Just as we're about to go outside, Gaetano comes downstairs, followed by Antonia. I do what Claudio really ought to be doing. I study them from head to foot, trying to figure out if they've been having sex. Gaetano looks impeccable, though there is a suspicious intensity to his gaze. She's adjusting her hair and looks a little rumpled. The slut.

"What a great bed!" Gaetano says loudly.

Holy crap, not that! What kind of manners does this guy have? There's going to be a shooting here today.

"I lay down for five minutes and bang! Fell sound asleep," he continues.

I catch my breath. But Antonia isn't saying a word and she seems unable to look her husband in the eye. They've definitely had sex, there's no mistaking the fact. And I can't be the only one to have that thought.

"Take a stroll in the garden while we get the food on the table," says Claudio.

Claudio is holding his breath the whole time, hoping for music, but there's not a sound from the Giulia. We take turns coming to his defense, saying that it happens sometimes, we go days without hearing the music, that it depends on the mood of Mario the symphony conductor. Antonia nods her head understandingly, like a mother deciding to make a show of believing a little boy's tall tales. Gaetano subscribes to the hypothesis of Mario's mood as the most likely explanation. He does it with a seriousness that would fool practically anyone, but not a professional con artist like me. I feel like breaking his nose for him. It's true, none of us have ever given this Gaetano half a chance, but who the hell cares? We're a group, and that frilly haired fop can't act supercilious with someone who's weaker than him.

To liven up the situation we've called Abu and his friends. They come out of the fields playing their bongo drums and immediately attract the interested gazes of our guests. Gaetano immediately removes the wallet from the inside pocket of his jacket that's draped over the back of his lounge chair and slips it into his trouser pocket for safekeeping. The drumming is infectious and everyone starts clapping along. I suddenly feel an urgent need to see Elisa and to find her very different from Antonia. There she is in the kitchen, going through recipes she's cut out of the newspaper and pasting them into an old elementary school notebook. She looks like a little girl pasting stickers into an album. She smiles at me, and I can't keep myself from sitting down beside her and offering to help. I take a page from the newspaper and with great focus and concentration, I carefully cut the panel out of the middle of the page, with a nice recipe for a French croque monsieur. Elisa waits serenely for me to finish the job and, when I present her with the perfectly clipped croque monsieur recipe, she picks up the newspaper that I've discarded, turns it over, and pastes the recipe for pasta flan into her notebook, with a neat croque monsieur recipe-sized hole in the middle.

The bongos have stopped playing and we turn to look out the window. Abu hushes the audience, raising both arms. With a theatrical gesture, like a symphony conductor, he quiets the residual hum of chatter. Followed by Alex, he begins brushing the drumskins rhythmically with his fingertips. His fingers touch the middle of the drumskin, brush against it, and lift away again. Samuel stands up, his eyes closed, and a rapturous expression on his face.

"Your arm in mine, I've descended a million stairs at least . . . " he says, with almost perfect pronunciation.

We stand open-mouthed. Just like the audience in the garden.

" . . . and now that you're not here, a void yawns at every step. Even so our long journey was brief."

"What, has he started writing poetry now?" I ask.

"It's Montale."

"He's my favorite," I shoot back, pointblank.

74

"A guy like you shouldn't have any trouble finding another woman," I tell Claudio.

"I already have a woman."

"This isn't good for you."

"What do you know about it? There are certain things that are just part of you, even if you don't materially possess them. Maybe there is something unhealthy about it, but I prefer to be alone and wait for her, rather than being with some other woman."

I don't know what to say to that. Gaetano and Antonia drove off with broad smiles on their faces, leaving a ten-foot skid mark on the gravel in the courtyard. Sitting next to my friend, I watch the car as it speeds away along the provincial road.

"It's just a phase," he tells me. "Right now, I understand perfectly that she wants to be with Gaetano instead of me. A guy like him makes her feel alive, desired. That's important to her at this age. But soon enough, Gaetano's time will end. The time will come when she'll need something more, an unconditional love, a partner she can count on, a foundation from which she can look out on the rest of her life with serenity . . . "

A caregiver, I think bitchily.

"When you plan to spend a life together with someone, then you can take into account the possibility that she might feel the need for someone else for a certain period. How many couples stay together even though they hate each other, they cheat on each other, and then suddenly they can't live without each other anymore? . . . See, that's how it is with us, except that we skipped the phase where we hate each other. It's just a short pause, just a parenthesis."

"But while you're waiting, don't you think you could make this parenthesis a little more enjoyable for yourself?" I say.

He doesn't seem to have heard me. His eyes are glistening and they're staring at something only they can see.

"I dream of taking care of her when she's old, massaging her legs when they're all swollen, telling her that she's beautiful when no one else would dream of doing it anymore, taking her places when she thinks that it's too late for that, making her laugh when all the other women are sitting alone at their windows with sad expressions. I'll know how to read the fear of death in her eyes and I'll be able to help her think of other, happier things . . . I want her to feel safe gripping my arm when she can no longer stand up without help, and when she's hard of hearing, I'll never get tired of repeating things to her for a second or third time."

He sits there in a momentary trance, then he turns to me with a smile.

"I'm sorry, did you ask me something?"

75

The arrival of the Carabiniere squad car is a new development that nobody's particularly happy about. We would have been much happier to see another carful of *camorristi* coming up the dirt road. After all, we know exactly what to expect from them. Thanks to the pocket binoculars we recently purchased, we have an extra couple of minutes, invaluable time in which to get properly organized. Sergio scrutinizes the car and relays information as he gathers it.

"Carabinieri. There's two of them. Assholes, to judge from their faces," he says in rapid sequence. Vito has enough time to vanish downstairs into the cellar, Sergio starts plaiting hemp ropes like an aging hippie, and Elisa hangs up perfectly dry laundry to give our little group the appearance of one big happy and harmless family.

From the old and faded Carabiniere squad car the two men emerge: a lance corporal in his very early twenties, pimply, and with a regulation goatee absolutely devoid of authority, and a Carabiniere inspector in his sixties, with a weary expression, a sizable gut, and white hair. As soon as they get out of the car, the minuet of chance appearances begins. Claudio emerges from the backyard with a bouquet of meadow flowers in one hand. Elisa sings happily. I walk toward the Carabinieri while Sergio greets them without ceasing his craft activity.

"*Buon giorno*," I say.

"*Buon giorno*," the inspector replies with a vague hint at a military salute.

"*Buon giorno*," Elisa says with a smile as she whips a broad white sheet over the clothesline.

"*Buon giorno*," says Claudio, waving the nosegay of flowers like a complete pansy.

"You've certainly fixed this place up nicely," the inspector says.

"It took a lot of work . . . "

"And you have a restaurant, too?"

"That's right, with a reservation you can come just to enjoy a nice meal."

"Then maybe one of these evenings I'll come have dinner with my wife . . . "

"By all means, we'd be delighted to have you."

Elisa starts to whistle nervously. The inspector wipes his forehead with a handkerchief.

"Would you like a glass of something cool, some wine, or some water?"

"No, thanks very much, we're not going to take up too much of your time . . . Basile!"

The lance corporal leans into the car and hands a sheet of paper to the inspector. It's a mugshot. Even before he shows it to me I've recognized Franco's face.

"Have you seen this man, by any chance?"

I take the photograph and look at it, jamming my elbows against my sides to limit the way my hands are shaking. I do my best not to seem overhasty, I look at it carefully, and when I sense that I can no longer look the two officers in the eye, I turn to show it to Sergio and Elisa.

"Have you ever seen him?" I ask. Sergio and Elisa walk over.

"I certainly don't remember seeing him," I tell the inspector. Elisa takes the mugshot.

"Has he ever been a guest here? . . . I don't know, I sure don't think so."

"I wouldn't think he'd have been a guest," says the inspector.

Sergio stands behind Elisa and stares at the photograph, shaking his head.

"Well, he definitely has never been here."

The inspector takes back the picture and adjusts his hat on his sweaty head.

"Well, all right, we won't keep you any longer . . . Basile!"

While the lance corporal gets back into the driver's seat, the inspector says goodbye with smiles and handshakes all around. Then he seems to remember something.

"How's business? Everything going nicely, is it?" he asks us.

"Yes, pretty well, we're starting to build a clientele, and word of mouth seems to be working for us . . . " I say.

I'm so evidently clueless that the inspector stares at me for a couple of seconds, without being able to make up his mind whether or not he should say anything more.

"I'm happy for you. Just remember, if you have problems of any kind, you can always turn to me," he says.

We all gather to wave goodbye as the policemen drive away. Plastered on our faces is the kind of smile you see in a commercial, with people who live in wonderful houses and wake up every morning happy and raring to go, cheerfully assembled around the dining room table enjoying breakfast.

Fausto joins us in the courtyard with a basket full of freshly picked greenbeans. The Carabinieri stayed for such a short time that his walk-on cameo was only cued after the squad car was already vanishing into the distance.

"He seems like a nice person," I say.

"Don't you even think about it," Sergio says.

None of says a thing, but clearly Sergio needs to convince himself even more than us, and he goes on.

"I imagine he's a perfectly nice person. But, even if we managed to explain away as legitimate defense the kidnapping and confinement of four, let me repeat, four *camorristi*, how on earth do you think they'd manage to protect us? Did you see their car?"

Claudio emerges whistling from behind the farmhouse with another nosegay of flowers.

"That's enough! Can't you see they've left?" Sergio shouts at him.

76

We're a pair of classic besotted sweethearts. We spend each day waiting for everyone else to go to bed and leave us alone. And when that finally happens, slight variant on the classic theme, we go out and sit on the grass and talk. It's two in the morning, even the toughest of our guests have given in to the siren song of sleep, and we stretch out exhausted on the same picnic blanket. An aura of stranding clouds scuds along before the moon, and the spectacle amply makes up for the lack of music.

"Why didn't you tell me that your father died?" she asks me.

"I don't know. I don't like talking about it."

"I don't think I'd do anything but talk about it. I'd be impossible to be around."

"Even without that, you manage to have that effect."

My cell phone beeps, lighting up my trouser pocket from within. I ignore it, because all day long I've been waiting for this moment to arrive, and an incoming text message wasn't part of the scenario.

"I'm not wondering in the slightest who would be sending you a text message at two in the morning," Elisa says.

"And it would never occur to me to tell you: 'That's not a text message, it's just the sound my phone makes when the battery's running low.'"

I pull the cell phone out of pocket and open the text message. There's only one person I know that sends text messages four pages long with all the commas and periods in the right places.

"It's from Alice," I say.

"It's a good thing I'm not the kind of person who would ask you if this Alice is one of your exes."

"Right, because I might even be the kind of person who'd respond that she's nothing but an ex-co-worker, and a homely one at that."

"Which is a good thing, because in that case I'd feel obligated to point out your use of the word 'homely' and ask: 'How so? If she were pretty, would that change things?'"

"Whereupon I'd feel dutybound to say: 'But you know I love only you.'"

"I'm starting to get angry."

"'Why no, darling, you know perfectly well that . . .'"

"No, not the imaginary me! The real me! The real me is getting angry, and for real!" Elisa says. I can't help laughing and she angrily turns her back on me.

"Alice is an ex-girlfriend," I tell her.

"Right," she says.

"I broke up with her a few months ago and this is the first time I've heard from her. She just wrote me to ask how I'm doing, but basically, I think she can't get over the breakup and she wants to see me again . . . "

"Right."

"And I can understand she's having a hard time getting over it . . . with all the lies I told her. She's a smart girl, if I'd just told her the truth she'd have dealt with it and moved on by now. It's all my fault, if only I'd just admitted to her that I'd fallen out of love with her, it would have spared her a lot of misery. But when you've been an asshole all your life, that never even occurs to you . . . "

"Right."

This last "right" came out slightly more languid, and she seems to be panting. So I continue, talking faster now.

"While I was lying to her, I told myself that I was doing the right thing, that at least this way I was sparing her some pain. Actually, though, all I wanted was to get out of the relationship without a lot of scenes, and maybe to keep my foot in the door in case I changed my mind. What an asshole I was . . . "

Elisa turns towards me. Her eyes are exhausted and have hidden depths. Then she closes those eyes and flings her arms behind her, onto the grass.

"An asshole, and as immature as any teenager," I add.

"Ri-i-ight," she moans.

77

In the morning I meet Elisa in the kitchen. Wordlessly, she makes me a cup of coffee. I sit next to her and sip. Through the window, I watch as Sergio sees off the last departing guests. A philosophy teacher from a high school in the leftist hotbed of Livorno, who expresses his parting farewell with a clenched raised fist, and his companion, a woman who owns an herbalist's shop, bustling out to the car with two large shopping bags stuffed with fresh greens.

The windowglass faintly reflects our image. Shifting focus, I observe our faces: they have the contented, satisfied look, accompanied by the dark circles under the eyes, that are usually typical signs of that special something that, in fact, however, we still haven't done.

"We're actually breaking even," says Fausto as he walks triumphantly into the kitchen.

"That's right, we've covered all our outlay and we may even have made a little money," Claudio confirms.

While Claudio's talking, Fausto queries me with a rapid pumping motion executed with the wrist bent back, a classic hand gesture with an unmistakable meaning.

"Sure . . . who'd have ever expected it!" I say, disguising my answer.

Right now, sincerity is a private matter between Elisa and me. I'd almost feel as if I were somehow betraying her if I started telling other people the truth.

Nonetheless, Fausto bursts into an attack of the giggles. The minute I see him laughing, I splutter on the coffee I'm drinking, and I drag Elisa and Claudio into our laughter with me. Sergio walks into the kitchen and laughs because we're all laughing. Who can say? Maybe we're just laughing at our faces, the faces of a bunch of former failures, at our lives, half of which we've wasted, laughing because the half we wasted was the better half, we laugh until our bellies ache.

"What the hell do you guys have to laugh about?" says Fausto, holding his belly.

"And to think that you used to sell shitty wristwatches at two in the morning," Sergio replies.

"It's true," Claudio says.

"What do you mean shitty? Those were Swiss timepieces!" Fausto says.

I don't think I've ever laughed so hard at the word "Swiss."

"You're one to talk," he says to Claudio, "since we've been drinking flat spumante for months now!"

"Stay right there, don't say another word," Claudio says, holding up one hand. "Let me go see if we still have a few bottles."

Sergio and Fausto go down to fetch Vito. We've decided to indulge in one last celebration and we can't do it without him. Elisa stretches the picnic blankets out on the lawn, I bring some firewood, and Claudio uncorks a bottle. When the cork pops anticlimactically with a morose *plop* we howl and twist with laughter. I fill a glass for Elisa, one for me, and one for Vito who reaches out for it with a smile.

"How's it going downstairs?" I ask him.

"No particular trouble, but the two youngsters are at the end of their rope," he says.

"I can imagine, they've been confined down there for quite some time . . . "

"No, no, it's that they can't stand being with Franco anymore. They told me that they were doing great until he showed up and started giving all the orders . . . "

"What, really?"

"What can I tell you, for the first time they didn't have anyone telling them what to do, they were free . . . Oh listen to that . . . " he says to me.

Mario, the ectoplasmic conductor, is sending us a treat.

"Mozart, *Concerto No. 21*, the Elvira Madigan concerto," Vito says.

"Nice," I say.

"It'll be nice the day we find out that he's just been making up all these concerto titles . . . " Fausto says.

But Vito doesn't bother to reply, he's too busy conducting the orchestra. I stretch out on my belly and lay the side of my head on the ground: I don't want to miss a note. Elisa follows suit. We find ourselves listening to the music with our gazes locked. Claudio, Fausto, and Sergio go on grinning and laughing and spraying each other with flat spumante.

An unpleasant sound begins to emerge deceptively in the midst of the swirling notes of the piano. It's a siren.

"Is it coming in this direction?" Sergio asks.

Vito hides under his oversized straw hat while we all track the progress of a police car's flashing lights as it sails past us along the provincial.

"No . . . it's going away," Claudio says.

"That's a good thing for them, at this point we have no more room downstairs," says Sergio, to a burst of laughter and applause.

The euphoria collapses when two ambulances and a squad car go racing by, lights flashing and sirens wailing.

"Is that normal?" Claudio asks.

"That's not even slightly normal," says Sergio.

"Something musta happened," says Vito.

The old man puts his hat back on his head and heads toward the farmhouse with Sergio. Claudio shoots me a glance and troops along after them.

"Where are you going? They're probably just cutting each other's throats, the way they always do!" Fausto shouts.

Another ambulance goes sailing past on the road and more sirens can be heard in the distance.

"Let's call Abu!" I say.

"I'm sick and tired of these bastards . . . they manage to spoil our party every damned time," Fausto says to me as I move off. "Maybe they're only wounded, like last time! But

304 · FABIO BARTOLOMEI

I'm going down there to finish the job! I'll show them how to do it, I'll kill them myself!"

78

We turn on the television and we surf through the channels, but nothing seems to be ruffling the equanimity of the home shopping emcees or the referees of culinary challenges. Vito tunes the radio to a local station. Our favorite DJ reads his song dedications with his usual unwarranted enthusiasm. The whole time, Sergio dials Abu's phone number.

"The phone is ringing but he's not answering," he says.

We take another tour of the channels and all the radio stations. Sergio, on pins and needles, turns on the computer and checks the website of ANSA, the national wire service. I stand behind him and read eagerly through the news items. The last flash is from half an hour ago and features a stabbing involving a father, a son, and some pointless disagreement. Someone playing music too loud may have triggered the tragedy.

"Could that be it?" I ask.

"It was in Turin, can't you see?" he says, jabbing a finger at the monitor.

"Come on, guys, we're getting worked up over nothing," says Fausto.

"There's no news here," adds Claudio after his last tour of the channels with the remote control.

"All we need to do is run into town . . . " says Vito.

"What are you talking about, run into town! We can't get worked up every time an ambulance goes by! Come on, guy, let's go get our glasses and fuck it!" says Fausto.

"They've murdered four people!" says Sergio.

I follow his finger and start reading with my eyes an inch from the screen.

"Shit, it was right here, right here in town . . . there were people wounded, too," I say. We cluster around the computer. We watch in silence as the reports are updated. All the dead are immigrants. African immigrants. One of the dead is a *camorrista*, the others are all Africans. There are five dead and three wounded. There are six dead and two of the wounded are in critical condition.

"Call Abu! Try again!" Fausto shouts.

Sergio makes one last attempt to reach Abu by phone, but it just rings without picking up. The quickest ones into the car are Sergio, Claudio, and Elisa. Fausto tries to grab the last seat, but Sergio tells him to stay behind, there should always be at least three people at the farmhouse. I can't seem to get to my feet. I'm weighed down by guilt. Somehow I feel responsible for an absurd enterprise, for having taken as acceptable the death of a *camorrista* and shrugged off the possibility of other innocent deaths.

"My God, what have we done . . . " I say.

I look at Vito, I'm eager for reassurance. He sits there, one hand on his forehead, staring at the table. He shakes his head.

79

After an hour, the wait becomes nerve-racking. There's no word from the three who went into town, and when we call them there's no answer.

"I can't take it any more, I've got to get out of here!" says Fausto.

A second later he's at the door. I take one look at his face and abandon any thought of trying to stop him.

"Abu!" says Fausto.

We go outside and we see the silhouette of Abu walking decisively toward us through the darkness. Fausto runs toward him, but when he gets within a few yards of him he skids to a sudden halt and slips to the ground.

"What are you doing?" he shouts.

I look at Vito uncomprehendingly, then I take a step forward to try to get a better idea of what's happening. Fausto frantically jumps up, awkwardly losing his footing on the wet grass. He walks backward, preceding Abu, both arms raised as he tries to calm him down. Only now do we realize that the African is gripping a hatchet in one hand.

"Fausto!" I shout.

"Maronna, this guy's going to kill us all . . . " says Vito. Pursued by Abu, Fausto comes galloping up the steps and runs into the house, slamming the door behind him.

"He wants to kill them!" he shouts.

The door starts shaking as Abu kicks at it furiously.

"Abu, calm down, this isn't right!" I say.

"This won't solve a thing, and you'll go straight to prison!" Fausto says.

The door stops shaking. I heave a sigh and shoot a frightened glance at Fausto, but he's shitting his pants even more than I am. A living room window shatters and we're forced to run for shelter in the kitchen. We barricade the door but the hatchet blows splinter the wood as if it were styrofoam.

"We've got to let them escape!" Fausto says.

The thought that by doing so, we'll decree the end of our adventure makes me hesitate for just a second too long.

"It's for Abu! Do you want to turn him into a murderer?" Fausto shouts at me.

We turn to look at Vito and he immediately rushes downstairs. Abu is chopping away at the hinges. It won't be long before he's able to tear the doors off their hinges and break through our barricade.

The three *camorristi* step out into the kitchen, Vito shows them the window, and they hasten to jump out to the ground below, encouraged by the glittering blade of Abu's hatchet emerging between the wooden planks. Franco is the first to jump, the two young men dive out in unison, and for a second they're wedged together in the window, legs waving in the air. Vito pushes them out, then he stands there motionless for a moment looking at us.

"Go!" we shout at him.

Abu sobs with his arms wrapped around Fausto. I got outside to get some air. After hearing the story of what happened, I smell blood everywhere and I feel like vomiting. They murdered Samuel and four other Africans; Alex may be wounded and still alive. But Abu says that when they loaded Alex onto the gurney, he heard a last strange rattle and then nothing more.

When someone you know has been shot, the scene you imagine isn't out of a movie by John Ford. Your friend doesn't collapse to the ground with a moan, clutching his chest. He doesn't lie stretched out in the dirt with a small, immaculate hole in his shirt. The scene that you conjure up in your head is out of a war movie by Spielberg. Your friend shouts and falls to the ground in a puddle of blood, his chest blown open by the bullet.

I sit on the veranda steps, holding my head in my hands. So many thoughts are spinning through my head that seizing on any one of them and understanding what I'm feeling is impossible. Did he die instantly? Did he see the blood gushing from his wound? Did the bullet hit his heart, a lung, or worse, his stomach? Did it penetrate his flesh, or did a shatter a few bones on the way in? A surge of gastric juices scorches my nostril, I clumsily spit it out, and I'm suddenly looking at something resembling a weird two-headed caterpillar on my knee.

A car's headlights first illuminate the provincial road and then turn up our dirt road.

"Turn off the lights!" I shout.

I run inside just in time to stop Abu, who has wriggled out of Fausto's grasp.

"Not now!" I say with a snarl.

We turn out all the lights. Fausto goes to open the rear door to give us a quick getaway into the fields. Hidden behind the window, we watch the car jerk as it hits a pothole and then lands with a dull metallic clank. It's Sergio's Renault. After its lurch, the car grinds to a halt in the courtyard. The three occupants emerge silently. Elisa is white as a sheet, but as soon as they see Abu they break into a run.

"Abu!" Elisa shouts.

Sergio throws his arms around him. Abu barely returns the bear hug.

"You have no idea how scared . . . " says Sergio.

"You wouldn't answer the phone, all those deaths . . . " says Claudio. Sergio realizes that Abu's embrace is listless, distracted.

"Samuel? Alex? Are they all right?" he asks.

It only takes him a quick glance at our faces to understand. Elisa hides her face against Claudio's shoulder; he staggers for a moment and then regains his strength, throws his arms around her.

I gesture for Sergio to come talk with me in private. Under the pergola I explain what happened. I tell him about Abu's fury, the decision that we were forced to make in the few seconds available, the liberation of the *camorristi*. Sergio nods as he listens to my account. And when I tell him that we may have to leave immediately, he nods; in fact, for a moment he almost seems to smile.

"You did the right thing," he says.

80

The massive presence of police and Carabinieri definitely affords us a few days of safety, but that's a calculation that we don't feel like relying on. We pack our bags with the intention of taking only the most important things. But in reality, we just stuff them with anything that comes to hand. We're doing everything mechanically, without a word and without making it clear even to ourselves just what we have in mind. When I get down to the kitchen Sergio is all set with his green rucksack on his back. Claudio, Fausto, and Elisa arrive shortly thereafter.

"We'll just have to come back to get the other things," Elisa whispers.

"Let's take what we can and forget the rest," says Sergio.

No one replies. We get in the car. It's not easy with five of us, and with our suitcases it's impossible. I toss my suitcase out the window.

"What the hell," I say.

Sergio does the same thing with his canvas rucksack, but when he does it, the Renault sways perilously. Then there's a loud crack and the car sags to one side.

"Fucking hell!" Sergio says.

We get out of the car to take a look. One of the rear wheels is visibly out of alignment.

"The suspension is shot," I say.

"Can't we fix it?" Elisa asks.

"Not here. We'd need a mechanic and some parts," I reply.

There's no time to wait, that much we know.

"Guys, on foot to the train station. We'll catch the first train coming through," says Sergio.

"That ain't such a good idea," says a voice behind us.

We whip around, first frightened and then relieved, all in the space of a couple of seconds. Standing in front of us is Vito.

"What are you doing here? Are you crazy?" I say.

"They scattered into the fields, no one'll be looking for you until tomorrow. But in any case, not the station. Too dangerous," he says.

"Damn it, we're stuck here!" says Fausto.

"There's the Giulia," says Vito. We exchange a glance.

"Do you have any idea how long it will take to dig it out? Believe me, burying it was child's play," says Sergio.

We look each other in the eye. We mentally calculate the work at hand and we reckon up our own strength. When we buried the car, we had Samuel and Alex here to help us, now we have Vito and Elisa. What about the time factor? How many hours did it take us to bury it the first time, and how long do we have now? A sharp, flat sound shakes us out of our despair. Abu has just driven the blade of his shovel into the lawn and with intense determination, he's started tossing clumps of earth the size of basketballs to one side.

"Come on, damn it!" Fausto says to us.

We run to the shed, Elisa leading the group, to grab the other shovels.

"It's incredible to think that Abu still wants to help us . . . " I say as I pick up my shovel.

"Yeah," Sergio says.

"You have nothing to do with it, Franco told me that they'd been planning this massacre for some time, a whole different matter, complicated politics . . . " says Vito.

"It's not our fault?" Fausto asks.

"We have nothing to do with it?" I ask.

"Not with the Africans, no . . . with the *camorrista* that they killed before, on the other hand . . . "

Vito hesitates, shakes his head, hems and haws.

"Well, okay, but who cares about a *camorrista* . . . " says Fausto. After what's happened to Samuel and Alex, actually, all things considered, being responsible for the death of a *camorrista* almost makes us happy.

"I mean, don't take this the wrong way, Vito, but fuck the *camorristi*," Sergio adds.

It's true, the work is much harder than the first time, but our hands have changed, and so has everything about us. We dig without talking, without complaint. We take turns resting and take over for our exhausted comrades when they ask us to. And to think that we were the same people who stopped, buffaloed, when presented with a clogged toilet, who put moistening lotion on our hands after using sandpaper, who had hysterical fits if the wind pushed the television antenna out of alignment.

Sergio's shovel hits something metallic.

"Sorry, Vito," he says, mortified.

Now we've reached the roof of the car and now, even if time is of the essence, we have to slow down and work more carefully to find the outline of the vehicle.

"You really did strap that tarp on good . . . " says Vito. We dig down the sides of the car and it's late night by the time we manage to free up enough space to open one of the doors. Sergio climbs into the cockpit to see if the car will start while we start digging the ramp. The car mutters weakly and then falls completely silent. All we hear is the click of the key in the ignition, while the starter motor gives absolutely no sign of life.

"Of course . . . now of all times!" says Fausto.

We have no jumper cable to connect the Giulia's battery to the live battery of the Renault. We waste precious time trying to detach the batteries in order to switch them, but without a socket wrench that's a hopeless task. Abu could get both a jumper cable and a socket wrench with a quick trip to town, but it would take at least an hour, and without him we'll never finish in time.

"It doesn't matter if it doesn't start, we can just pull it up ourselves," I say.

"It must weigh at least a metric ton . . . we could never do it," says Sergio.

"We can demand one last effort from the Renault . . . if she pulls and we push, we might be able to do it," Claudio suggests.

If we just shovel hard enough and manage to dig a ramp with a sufficiently gentle slope, then of course, we can do this. With that hope in mind, we go back to shoveling dirt, but the dirt keeps growing harder and denser.

When day begins to dawn, the ramp is still too steep. We've exhausted all our strength. Even Abu is worn out. He says that we're just going to have to make it work like this. We back the Renault into position at the top of the ramp and we hook it up to the Giulia with a steel cable. Elisa is behind the wheel. When we say go, the car begins pulling and we start pushing with all our might. Despite everything, the Giulia is like a block of lead, and it only moves an inch or two.

"Hold it, hold it . . . stop!" Sergio shouts.

We stand there panting while he pushes his way forward, climbs into the Giulia, and takes the hand brake off. He steps out with one arm raised apologetically and resumes his place, ready to push, indifferent to the array of astonished faces.

"Now go!" he shouts.

At last, the Giulia begins to inch backward, hauled by Sergio's car, whose tires slip on the wet grass as it swerves and sways from left to right, like a kite juddering in a rough wind. It slowly rises along the wooden planks that cover the ramp as we sink into the loose dirt up to our ankles. Sinister sounds come from the straining Renault, but they're nothing compared to our shouts of encouragement and the straining grunts we put out.

The last time that I bothered to look up, we weren't even halfway up the ramp, and I had definitely used up much more than half my strength. I forced myself from then on to keep pushing with my eyes closed. I can't even feel my arms anymore, so now I'm pushing by wedging my shoulder against the upright window frame. I've never felt such intense pain. Maybe I'm squeezing a nerve, because I feel a sharp electric stab run from the back of my neck to my thigh. I clench my teeth as I shout, but nobody pays me the slightest heed—my roaring moan just mingles with everyone else's. By now, I'm not even really pushing anymore; the car is inching up the ramp very slowly, and only because of Abu's rage, I have to guess. Now I pull out my own rage, and I strain every muscle in my body to make sure at least that the Giulia doesn't sink any lower between one push and the next. Then I can feel the car pulling away from me, my benumbed arms refuse to obey my will, I fall face first into the dirt.

"No . . . no-o-o," I gasp with what little breath remains to me.

My neck hurts so bad that I can't even turn my head. All I can hear is the other people's panting and the engine of the Renault coughing to a halt.

"No what? It's in perfect condition, the tires are just a little low," says Sergio.

With a tiny crack of my spine, I lift my face out of the dirt. The Giulia is motionless in front of me, beautiful and clean, on the lawn.

Abu immediately set out to walk into town. We told him to keep his eyes and ears open, to find out what he can about Alex, and to say in touch with Vito. We thanked him too, shamefaced at how little we had to offer him. After parking the Renault in the courtyard and doing our best to eliminate all the tire tracks in the grass, we stop to bid farewell to our farmhouse and to take one last proud loving look at the magnificent work we did.

"The farmhouse is focked. The minute Franco and his boys tell them what happened here, they'll burn the place down," says Vito.

"With all the police that will be stationed around here?" I say.

"You know how these things work, for a couple weeks that's all anyone talks about, then they get distracted, they start talking about something else, and then this place is ashes."

Sergio walks into the house and emerges a few minutes later carrying the wooden crate.

"Vito, the kids' cell phones and money are in here . . . it's up to you what to do, we'd be glad to come pick you up tonight if you say so," he says.

"For now, I'll stay heah. If I'm heah, there's a small chance we might be able to save the farmhouse."

I look at him hopefully, because that farmhouse is also the result of Samuel and Alex's hard work.

"It's just a question of honor, if word gets around that you kidnapped some *camorristi* they'd have to send a very strong signal. The fact is that the way I see it, they'd just as soon that word not get out. What would the family look like if four faggots managed to lock up four made men?"

"Faggots? Us? What are you talking about?" Fausto asks.

"What, you don't know? In town they call you the four pansies. Four men without women in a big old farmhouse . . . what else would you expect?"

"But what about Elisa?" asks Claudio.

"She showed up later, by then you already had the reputation."

We load our luggage into the car and we give it a push down the dirt road. The slight downward slope gets us going at a decent speed almost immediately and we climb aboard, squeezing into the seats. Sergio shifts into second and the Giulia jerks to life. The engine and a string section start in unison.

We drive cautiously, avoiding all the potholes. One after another, we turn to take a last look at the farmhouse. The violins are joined by a single flute. I remember this music, of course I recognize it. I quickly roll down the window and lean out, waving my finger in the air.

"Blavet! *Flute Concerto in A Minor*!" I shout at Vito.

The old man smiles at me and responds to my hand gestures as if he, too, could hear the music. Of course he hears it.

THE LIGHTS OF CLAUDIO

I've never lost a friend to violent death. One time I saw the photograph of a classmate of mine from junior high school in a newspaper. He was on the list of the victims of a plane crash.

But I was still young, I didn't understand, and I held out the paper to show my mother, saying, "Look, it's Federico!" I even think I smiled when I pointed out the article to her. It could have been us on that road, it could have been us lying motionless with white sheets covering our faces. And I know these may just sound like words, but I really do wish I could have been there myself, and that I'd had a chance to save them. I would have thrown myself on top of them, I would have shielded their bodies with my own without thinking twice. I don't know what good it would have done, but I would have shielded them. Maybe we'd have survived, maybe not, but it would have been worth the attempt, at least. Anyway, it doesn't end here, not like this. I'm going to let a little time go by, and then I'm going to give these guys a wake up call. We can't just give up this way. Perhaps it won't be easy to persuade Diego and Fausto, but I'm not going back to the life I was living before. Now I know how to do a few things: how to fix plumbing, how to lay hardware floors, how to stand up to organized crime. There is no way on earth I'm going back to collapsing in front of a television set or standing behind a refrigerator counter to swear that the mozzarella is fresh—very fresh! No one's going to say: "He's back, just as we thought," because I have a few surprises up my sleeves. I wasn't incompetent, I wasn't even a slacker. I was just a man living in a prison. I was trapped in the mentality of costs and benefits, and I had smeared the corporate ointment over my whole life, avoiding any and all risks, any personal investment that failed to generate an immediate return. With the costs and benefits mentality, I left college to work for the supermarket, I married Antonia when we were still too young, "before someone takes her away from me," I told myself. But now I know I was born to take risks, to invest all of myself, to chase after dreams even if it's too late now. We'll find another farmhouse, someplace nice and quiet, it'll be even better than the first one, and we won't let anyone take it away from us this time. Elisa will have a first-class contract, she'll be the queen of the bed and breakfast, official and aboveboard. We'll go back first thing and get Vito, Abu, and Alex, as soon as we've found the right place. We're a team of winners, if we all work together we'll be as invincible as the Spartans.

"Do you think Vito will be able to keep them from finding out about us?" I ask.

"That strikes me as a secondary problem. He's risking his life. If they have even the slightest suspicion, he's done for," says Sergio.

"And we're just going to leave him there?"

"If he left with us now it would be worse . . . he'd be a hunted man. Better if he waits for things to calm down."

"All right, but . . . "

"But what?"

"If you think about it for a second, do you realize?" I say and I look around at the others. "We had them fooled."

I've forced a half-smile to everyone's lips. Everyone but Fausto. He turns around in his seat and gives me a bitter look.

"You can never fool them. In the end, they'll even make you sorry you won," he says.

"Then we lost . . . " I say to him.

"We didn't lose . . . we fought them to a tie."

If you ask me, we played against the Camorra, in an away game, and we fought them to a tie. As if the local parish team scored 1-1 against Real Madrid at the Santiago Bernabéu stadium. Practically speaking, it's like we won. Listen to how this fucking radio newscaster reports the news:

"The number of victims of the massacre has risen to seven, another African died in the hospital today . . . " It's Alex, goddamnit, and all she can say is "another African," of course, because personal names suggest personal histories and that can trouble the listeners' consciences. I look to my friends to understand their reactions but no one speaks: their eyes say it all. And what would there be to say, anyhow? Poor Alex? Fucking country we live in? I'm not wasting anymore time getting mad, from now on I'm taking concrete action.

To start with, no matter what our friend the radio newscaster might think or say, I'm taking Alex and Samuel with me for all time, tattooed on my arm, nice and big, right under my Maori tribal tat. And then the vegetable patch: I'm turning that into a symbol, even if they decide to burn the house. Even if they blow it up with dynamite, the vegetable patch will still be there. I'm ready to come down here every other day, in the middle of the night if I have to, I'll wear my camo gear, I'll smear my face with black boot polish, and I'll care for the plants, they'll go on blooming and growing, day after day. It will be the new miracle of the farmhouse.

This fucking radio news report, I tell you, to hear them tell it, you'd think that the incidents between immigrants and the police were merely acts of vandalism—would you just give me a break? I can just see Abu now, he's probably in the front lines protesting. He's probably there where I ought to be, facing down the police with their riot clubs, shouting even louder than those demented sheep who shout at the Africans to just go back home. Listen to them, the Italian citizens, listen to how angry they get. They lived such happy lives in Camorropolis before these people washed up on their shores: they paid protection, they lowered their eyes when the boss came around, they scattered sawdust on the pools of blood in the middle of the street, and life went on. If you can understand it, you're smarter than I am: if you want this damn country to wake up you have to rely on the last ones to arrive, the most defenseless ones! It's not that this country needs strong arms to harvest our tomatoes: we need the balls that we seem to lack entirely. And Abu is a great man. A pair of balls as big as this. As soon as we have a chance to recover, we've got to make things clear immediately, we have to swear that they won't break our spirit, that we're going to get busy and find another place immediately. The minute we find it, the first thing we do is we go back and get Abu, and Vito too. We leave no one behind, we've got a rescue mission to undertake. I can't wait to introduce him to my friends. I can already see their faces. I'll just wait for the first wisecrack, the first phrase someone mutters under their breath, and I'll tell them. Where were you when I needed you? You were all my good friends when you wanted me to introduce you to some fashion model or get you some actor's autograph, but when it was me asking you for help, you all turned into a herd of shopkeepers, accounts in hand. But he was there, the negro, the illegal, the criminal until proven otherwise. He was there, he had nothing to call his own, but he knew how to lend a hand without asking for anything in return. Comrade Abu? Present!

Right now, it may still be too early. They're all still thinking about Alex, but tomorrow it could be too late. We need to talk about it while the adrenaline is still pumping. The minute we get off the highway, sure, when everyone feels safe. I don't know about you guys, but for me this is just a beginning! That's what I'll tell them. It'll take me just a second to convince Sergio, all I have to do is say it's a matter of the struggle of the proletariat against the exploitation of the oppressors and it's done. The others, I'm not sure—they might be discouraged by the lack of money.

"Boys, how much do we have in the till?" I ask.

"Now you want to know?" says Claudio in a small voice.

"Just enough," says Diego.

"And how much is that?" I ask.

"Us. And the Giulia," he tells me.

The Lights of Diego

Have they understood? For now, I'm not going to say a thing, I want them to think it over. But in no more than an hour from now, I'm going to look them in the eye, one by one, and let them know that I have no intention of giving up, that there is no group of people out there that can hold a candle to us, that deep inside we all have what it takes to start over.

I feel strong. I draw energy from everything, from Samuel and Alex, from Elisa's leg brushing against mine, from the memory of my father who stubbornly kept smiling at me, and for the first time, I even draw energy from myself. From my fear of turning back into who I was before.

A lot of things are going to change. Thousands of people will take to the streets, every year there'll be a torchlight parade in commemoration of the day the massacre took place, politicians, journalists, and writers will speak from the podium. And I'll be there. I form part of civil society by now, I'm one of those people who finally get mad, get up from the couch, and go out into the street to protest in the front lines, right behind the big banner that leads the march.

They'll erect an imposing monument, of course they will, and I'll be there for the inauguration. Let's hope it's not one of those chilly, modern, soulless sculptures with obelisks, spirals, and spheres. What's needed is a classical statue that can even speak to the most ignorant among us, a statue that depicts those bodies blessed by the Lord, those faces without hope but filled with dignity. I would like one of those figures to be clutching an anthology of Italian literature in one hand, and for the definition of the muscles to be realistic, so as to make it clear that Alex and the others could have kicked our asses if they'd chosen to, but instead they just came to this country to harvest our tomatoes.

I hope I can find a way of persuading them, I'll speak with honesty and I'll share what I now see clearly, even at the cost of seeming like a madman.

Look: it's not our fault that we're running away, believe me. That's what I'll say. We were raised to live in the fear of God, our creator, so we can't really blame ourselves if we're afraid of everything else too. We grew up with the myth of the good life, and we've done nothing but feed that myth with our devotion to a safe job, a career, and success, which is why we always feel poor and inadequate. We're running away because no one gave us the right weapons to fight back, and when we discover that the team we root for doesn't actually return the feeling, that our bank only remembers us when our checking account is in the red, that the job of a lifetime knows that that's exactly what it is, and therefore demands every minute of our lives, we feel defeated. It would have been enough for us simply to have followed models made up of thoughts and ideals, not just pixels, to have had dreams that were actually our dreams, dreams that sprang from our ambitions and not from a meeting room in the headquarters of some multinational corporation. In that case, we'd now be a group of perfectly normal human beings that are wetting our pants in fear, but still have the balls to turn the car around and go back. But who knows? Our story isn't finished. This day, after all, has only just begun.

ABOUT THE AUTHOR

Fabio Bartolomei works in advertising and lives in Rome. *Alfa Romeo 1300 and Other Miracles* is his first novel.

EUROPA EDITIONS BACKLIST
(alphabetical by author)

Fiction

Carmine Abate
Between Two Seas • 978-1-933372-40-2 • Territories: World
The Homecoming Party • 978-1-933372-83-9 • Territories: World

Milena Agus
From the Land of the Moon • 978-1-60945-001-4 • Ebook • Territories:
World (excl. ANZ)

Salwa Al Neimi
The Proof of the Honey • 978-1-933372-68-6 • Ebook • Territories: World
(excl UK)

Simonetta Agnello Hornby
The Nun • 978-1-60945-062-5 • Territories: World

Daniel Arsand
Lovers • 978-1-60945-071-7 • Ebook • Territories: World

Jenn Ashworth
A Kind of Intimacy • 978-1-933372-86-0 • Territories: US & Can

Beryl Bainbridge
The Girl in the Polka Dot Dress • 978-1-60945-056-4 • Ebook •
Territories: US

Muriel Barbery
The Elegance of the Hedgehog • 978-1-933372-60-0 • Ebook • Territories:
World (excl. UK & EU)
Gourmet Rhapsody • 978-1-933372-95-2 • Ebook • Territories: World
(excl. UK & EU)

Stefano Benni
Margherita Dolce Vita • 978-1-933372-20-4 • Territories: World
Timeskipper • 978-1-933372-44-0 • Territories: World

Romano Bilenchi
The Chill • 978-1-933372-90-7 • Territories: World

Kazimierz Brandys
Rondo • 978-1-60945-004-5 • Territories: World

Alina Bronsky
Broken Glass Park • 978-1-933372-96-9 • Ebook • Territories: World
The Hottest Dishes of the Tartar Cuisine • 978-1-60945-006-9 • Ebook •
Territories: World

Jesse Browner
Everything Happens Today • 978-1-60945-051-9 • Ebook • Territories:
World (excl. UK & EU)

Francisco Coloane
Tierra del Fuego • 978-1-933372-63-1 • Ebook • Territories: World

Rebecca Connell
The Art of Losing • 978-1-933372-78-5 • Territories: US

Laurence Cossé
A Novel Bookstore • 978-1-933372-82-2 • Ebook • Territories: World
An Accident in August • 978-1-60945-049-6 • Territories: World (excl. UK)

Diego De Silva
I Hadn't Understood • 978-1-60945-065-6 • Territories: World

Shashi Deshpande
The Dark Holds No Terrors • 978-1-933372-67-9 • Territories: US

Steve Erickson
Zeroville • 978-1-933372-39-6 • Territories: US & Can
These Dreams of You • 978-1-60945-063-2 • Territories: US & Can

Elena Ferrante
The Days of Abandonment • 978-1-933372-00-6 • Ebook • Territories: World
Troubling Love • 978-1-933372-16-7 • Territories: World
The Lost Daughter • 978-1-933372-42-6 • Territories: World

Linda Ferri
Cecilia • 978-1-933372-87-7 • Territories: World

Damon Galgut
In a Strange Room • 978-1-60945-011-3 • Ebook • Territories: USA

Santiago Gamboa
Necropolis • 978-1-60945-073-1 • Ebook • Territories: World

Jane Gardam
Old Filth • 978-1-933372-13-6 • Ebook • Territories: US
The Queen of the Tambourine • 978-1-933372-36-5 • Ebook • Territories: US
The People on Privilege Hill • 978-1-933372-56-3 • Ebook • Territories: US
The Man in the Wooden Hat • 978-1-933372-89-1 • Ebook • Territories: US
God on the Rocks • 978-1-933372-76-1 • Ebook • Territories: US
Crusoe's Daughter • 978-1-60945-069-4 • Ebook • Territories: US

Anna Gavalda
French Leave • 978-1-60945-005-2 • Ebook • Territories: US & Can

Seth Greenland
The Angry Buddhist • 978-1-60945-068-7 • Ebook • Territories: World

Katharina Hacker
The Have-Nots • 978-1-933372-41-9 • Territories: World (excl. India)

Patrick Hamilton
Hangover Square • 978-1-933372-06-8 • Territories: US & Can

James Hamilton-Paterson
Cooking with Fernet Branca • 978-1-933372-01-3 • Territories: US
Amazing Disgrace • 978-1-933372-19-8 • Territories: US
Rancid Pansies • 978-1-933372-62-4 • Territories: USA

Alfred Hayes
The Girl on the Via Flaminia • 978-1-933372-24-2 • Ebook •
Territories: World

Jean-Claude Izzo
The Lost Sailors • 978-1-933372-35-8 • Territories: World
A Sun for the Dying • 978-1-933372-59-4 • Territories: World

Gail Jones
Sorry • 978-1-933372-55-6 • Territories: US & Can

Ioanna Karystiani
The Jasmine Isle • 978-1-933372-10-5 • Territories: World
Swell • 978-1-933372-98-3 • Territories: World

Peter Kocan
Fresh Fields • 978-1-933372-29-7 • Territories: US, EU & Can
The Treatment and the Cure • 978-1-933372-45-7 • Territories: US, EU & Can

Helmut Krausser
Eros • 978-1-933372-58-7 • Territories: World

Amara Lakhous
Clash of Civilizations Over an Elevator in Piazza Vittorio •
978-1-933372-61-7 • Ebook • Territories: World
Divorce Islamic Style • 978-1-60945-066-3 • Ebook • Territories: World

www.europaeditions.com

Lia Levi
The Jewish Husband • 978-1-933372-93-8 • Territories: World

Valerio Massimo Manfredi
The Ides of March • 978-1-933372-99-0 • Territories: US

Leïla Marouane
The Sexual Life of an Islamist in Paris • 978-1-933372-85-3 •
Territories: World

Lorenzo Mediano
The Frost on His Shoulders • 978-1-60945-072-4 • Ebook •
Territories: World

Sélim Nassib
I Loved You for Your Voice • 978-1-933372-07-5 • Territories: World
The Palestinian Lover • 978-1-933372-23-5 • Territories: World

Amélie Nothomb
Tokyo Fiancée • 978-1-933372-64-8 • Territories: US & Can
Hygiene and the Assassin • 978-1-933372-77-8 • Ebook • Territories: US & Can

Valeria Parrella
For Grace Received • 978-1-933372-94-5 • Territories: World

Alessandro Piperno
The Worst Intentions • 978-1-933372-33-4 • Territories: World
Persecution • 978-1-60945-074-8 • Ebook • Territories: World

Lorcan Roche
The Companion • 978-1-933372-84-6 • Territories: World

Boualem Sansal
The German Mujahid • 978-1-933372-92-1 • Ebook • Territories: US & Can

Eric-Emmanuel Schmitt
The Most Beautiful Book in the World • 978-1-933372-74-7 • Ebook •
Territories: World
The Woman with the Bouquet • 978-1-933372-81-5 • Ebook • Territories:
US & Can

Angelika Schrobsdorff
You Are Not Like Other Mothers • 978-1-60945-075-5 • Ebook •
Territories: World

Audrey Schulman
Three Weeks in December • 978-1-60945-064-9 • Ebook • Territories: US
& Can

James Scudamore
Heliopolis • 978-1-933372-73-0 • Ebook • Territories: US

Luis Sepúlveda
The Shadow of What We Were • 978-1-60945-002-1 • Ebook • Territories:
World

Paolo Sorrentino
Everybody's Right • 978-1-60945-052-6 • Ebook • Territories: US & Can

Domenico Starnone
First Execution • 978-1-933372-66-2 • Territories: World

Henry Sutton
Get Me out of Here • 978-1-60945-007-6 • Ebook • Territories: US & Can

Chad Taylor
Departure Lounge • 978-1-933372-09-9 • Territories: US, EU & Can

Roma Tearne
Mosquito • 978-1-933372-57-0 • Territories: US & Can
Bone China • 978-1-933372-75-4 • Territories: US

André Carl van der Merwe
Moffie • 978-1-60945-050-2 • Ebook • Territories: World
(excl. S. Africa)

Fay Weldon
Chalcot Crescent • 978-1-933372-79-2 • Territories: US

Anne Wiazemsky
My Berlin Child • 978-1-60945-003-8 • Territories: US & Can

Jonathan Yardley
Second Reading • 978-1-60945-008-3 • Ebook • Territories: US & Can

Edwin M. Yoder Jr.
Lions at Lamb House • 978-1-933372-34-1 • Territories: World

Michele Zackheim
Broken Colors • 978-1-933372-37-2 • Territories: World

Alice Zeniter
Take This Man • 978-1-60945-053-3 • Territories: World

Tonga Books

Ian Holding
Of Beasts and Beings • 978-1-60945-054-0 • Ebook • Territories: US & Can

Sara Levine
Treasure Island!!! • 978-0-14043-768-3 • Ebook • Territories: World

www.europaeditions.com

Alexander Maksik
You Deserve Nothing • 978-1-60945-048-9 • Ebook • Territories: US, Can & EU (excl. UK)

Thad Ziolkowski
Wichita • 978-1-60945-070-0 • Ebook • Territories: World

Crime/Noir

Massimo Carlotto
The Goodbye Kiss • 978-1-933372-05-1 • Ebook • Territories: World
Death's Dark Abyss • 978-1-933372-18-1 • Ebook • Territories: World
The Fugitive • 978-1-933372-25-9 • Ebook • Territories: World
Bandit Love • 978-1-933372-80-8 • Ebook • Territories: World
Poisonville • 978-1-933372-91-4 • Ebook • Territories: World

Giancarlo De Cataldo
The Father and the Foreigner • 978-1-933372-72-3 • Territories: World

Caryl Férey
Zulu • 978-1-933372-88-4 • Ebook • Territories: World (excl. UK & EU)
Utu • 978-1-60945-055-7 • Ebook • Territories: World (excl. UK & EU)

Alicia Giménez-Bartlett
Dog Day • 978-1-933372-14-3 • Territories: US & Can
Prime Time Suspect • 978-1-933372-31-0 • Territories: US & Can
Death Rites • 978-1-933372-54-9 • Territories: US & Can

Jean-Claude Izzo
Total Chaos • 978-1-933372-04-4 • Territories: US & Can
Chourmo • 978-1-933372-17-4 • Territories: US & Can
Solea • 978-1-933372-30-3 • Territories: US & Can

www.europaeditions.com

Matthew F. Jones
Boot Tracks • 978-1-933372-11-2 • Territories: US & Can

Gene Kerrigan
The Midnight Choir • 978-1-933372-26-6 • Territories: US & Can
Little Criminals • 978-1-933372-43-3 • Territories: US & Can

Carlo Lucarelli
Carte Blanche • 978-1-933372-15-0 • Territories: World
The Damned Season • 978-1-933372-27-3 • Territories: World
Via delle Oche • 978-1-933372-53-2 • Territories: World

Edna Mazya
Love Burns • 978-1-933372-08-2 • Territories: World (excl. ANZ)

Yishai Sarid
Limassol • 978-1-60945-000-7 • Ebook • Territories: World (excl. UK,
AUS & India)

Joel Stone
The Jerusalem File • 978-1-933372-65-5 • Ebook • Territories: World

Benjamin Tammuz
Minotaur • 978-1-933372-02-0 • Ebook • Territories: World

Non-fiction

Alberto Angela
A Day in the Life of Ancient Rome • 978-1-933372-71-6 • Territories:
World • History

Helmut Dubiel
Deep In the Brain: Living with Parkinson's Disease • 978-1-933372-70-9 •
Ebook • Territories: World • Medicine/Memoir

James Hamilton-Paterson
Seven-Tenths: The Sea and Its Thresholds • 978-1-933372-69-3 • Territories:
USA • Nature/Essays

Daniele Mastrogiacomo
Days of Fear • 978-1-933372-97-6 • Ebook • Territories: World • Current
affairs/Memoir/Afghanistan/Journalism

Valery Panyushkin
Twelve Who Don't Agree • 978-1-60945-010-6 • Ebook • Territories:
World • Current affairs/Memoir/Russia/Journalism

Christa Wolf
One Day a Year: 1960-2000 • 978-1-933372-22-8 • Territories: World •
Memoir/History/20th Century

Children's Illustrated Fiction

Altan
Here Comes Timpa • 978-1-933372-28-0 • Territories: World (excl. Italy)
Timpa Goes to the Sea • 978-1-933372-32-7 • Territories: World (excl. Italy)
Fairy Tale Timpa • 978-1-933372-38-9 • Territories: World (excl. Italy)

Wolf Erlbruch
The Big Question • 978-1-933372-03-7 • Territories: US & Can
The Miracle of the Bears • 978-1-933372-21-1 • Territories: US & Can
(with **Gioconda Belli**) *The Butterfly Workshop* • 978-1-933372-12-9 •
Territories: US & Can